The
MAGNET
Book

Mike Weilbacher

Running Press • Philadelphia, Pennsylvania

Canadian representatives: General Publishing Co., Ltd., 30 Lesmill Road, Don
Mills, Ontario M3B 2T6.
International representatives: Worldwide Media Services, Inc.,
30 Montgomery Street, Jersey City, New Jersey 07302.

9 8 7 6 5 4 3 2 1
Digit on the right indicates the number of this printing.

Library of Congress Cataloging-in-Publication Number 92–50801
ISBN 1–56138–240–X

Edited by Steven Zorn
Cover design by Toby Schmidt
Cover illustrations and package artwork by Lili Schwartz
Interior design by Jacqueline Spadaro
Book interior illustrations by Nancy B. Schwamm
Picture research by Elizabeth Broadrup
Package back photographs: (top) © FPG International/Telegraph Colour Library;
(bottom) © Putsee Vannucci/FPG International
Book interior photographs: Courtesy of Argonne National Laboratory: p. 25. Courtesy of U.S. Department
of Defense (USAF Photo by David Nolan): p. 28. FPG International: p. 8 (© Peter Gridley), p. 9 (© Jeffrey
Sylvester), p. 18 (© Robin Smith), p. 19 (© Carolyn McKeone), p. 43 (© Dick Luria), p. 50 (© Putsee
Vannucci), p. 54 (© Nikolay Zurek), p. 58 (© Michael Tamborrino), p. 59 (© Ron Chapple). The Granger
Collection, New York: pp. 39, 40, 53, 62. © Grant Heilman/Grant Heilman Photography: p. 16 (detail).
Courtesy of Japan Railways Group: p. 61. © Dennis Kunkel: p. 24. Courtesy of NASA: pp. 5, 44, 63.
Nawrocki Stock Photo, Inc.: p. 13 (© Ken Graham), p. 14 (© Robert Lightfoot III), p. 57 (© Melanie Carr).
Photo Researchers: p. 10 (© Chester Higgins, Jr.), p. 11 (© Jeanne White), p. 12 (© Benelux Press). Courtesy
U.S. Department of Agriculture: p. 52. © Ken Yanoviak: p. 64.
Typography: Palatino with Insignia by Richard Conklin

Running Press Book Publishers
125 South Twenty-second Street
Philadelphia, Pennsylvania 19103

Contents

Welcome!

Imagine you're a knight living in the Middle Ages, hundreds of years ago. Tired from a long journey, you sit upon a boulder to rest, and your sword leans against the dark rock. You look down, and notice something very bizarre.

Small particles of rock are actually sticking to your sword. Surely this is magic! What else could cause rock to cling to iron?

You might know that the rock is magnetic, and you might even know that it's a magnetic mineral called lodestone. Today, the properties of that rock, and of the many magnets included in this kit, are much better understood. At least we know that magnets aren't supernatural.

Still, even though scientists have split atoms and walked on the moon, magnets remain pretty magical. Even the smartest scientist can't *fully* explain how they work. Though mysterious, magnetism is very important, and we use magnets every day to do all kinds of work. In fact, hundreds of magnets are hiding in your home right now. You'd be surprised to discover where!

This kit contains all the material and information you need to conduct a series of experiments to better understand magnetism. By the end of this book, you'll be a regular "magnetic magician."

And if you *were* that knight in the Middle Ages, your neighbors would soon consider you a sorcerer worthy of the company of Merlin himself.

Welcome to the extraordinary world of magnets. Shall we start exploring?

The Magnetic Challenge

What makes something magnetic? How does a magnet work? What's your "magnetic IQ"? Here are some questions about magnets that come to you with an invitation *and* a guarantee. The invitation: decide what you think the right answer to each question is. The guarantee: after doing the activities in the kit, you'll be able to answer *every* one of these questions. Easy. (If you get stumped, the answers are on page 63.)

1. True or false: All matter—this book, the chair you're sitting in, your house—is magnetic.
❑ a. true   ❑ b. false

2. True or false: Without magnets, electricity could not be delivered to your house.
❑ a. true   ❑ b. false

3. Which of the following uses magnets to operate?

❑ a. radio   ❑ d. VCR
❑ b. personal computer   ❑ e. none of these
❑ c. telephone   ❑ f. all of these

4. If you cut a magnet in half, which of these happens?

❑ a. the magnet's power is destroyed
❑ b. you get two magnets

5. Compasses point to the north because

❑ a. there's a giant magnetic mountain there
❑ b. the earth acts like a giant magnet
❑ c. no one's sure why

6. Who discovered magnetism?

❑ a. Ben Franklin   ❑ c. the ancient Egyptians
❑ b. the ancient Greeks   ❑ d. no one's sure who

7. True or false: Many animals have micro-magnets in their bodies.

❑ a. true   ❑ b. false

Magnets Everywhere

You probably never thought about it, but magnets are everywhere, used for many things. Magnets seal your refrigerator door tight, and a magnet in the refrigerator's motor makes it run. Magnets tucked inside loudspeakers let sound travel through your telephone, TV, and stereo.

Watch a movie on your VCR, and you're using magnets. The videocassette's tape is covered with millions of magnetic particles. As the VCR plays, the machine "reads" how the particles line up, and converts the information into images. Audiocassettes and computer floppy disks work the same way. All are magnetic.

Diskettes for computers are coated with tiny magnetic particles that store information.

Electricity is delivered to your home with the help of magnets.

When you flip a light switch, thank a magnet, too. Electricity is produced by a giant electromagnet inside a power plant. The current flows through wires to a transformer that converts high-voltage electricity in power lines to the smaller voltage used by your home's appliances. There's a transformer somewhere in your neighborhood. Guess what's inside. Of course: a magnet.

Magnetic compasses guide airplanes and ships. Your family's car can only operate when a magnet in the ignition helps start the car. The car's horn uses magnets, too.

Magnets can even be found in our language. People are said to have "magnetic" personalities, even "animal magnetism." At a wedding, guests might wonder how two very different people

Like seamen hundreds of years ago, today's captains depend on Earth's magnetic field in order to navigate.

might have fallen in love. "Well, opposites attract," they often say, not knowing they're quoting a law of magnetism.

Planets are magnetic, too, and the North Pole is one end of the giant magnet called Earth. The ends of magnets are always called poles.

Life as we know it would be impossible without magnetism—no TV, no video games, no cars. . . . Magnetism is one of the basic forces of the universe, along with energy and gravity, and understanding this force is essential for scientists in many fields, from medicine to geology.

Magnetic Moments

The lodestone is a form of the mineral iron that has naturally magnetic properties. Its formal scientific name is "magnetite."

We're not sure who discovered magnetism. Just like fire and the wheel, magnetism was discovered

Lodestone is a naturally magnetic form of iron.

long ago, before written history. For thousands of years, people knew that a certain dark rock had the power to attract metal.

Magnets are named for a town in western Turkey now called Manissa, but named Magnesia by the ancient Greeks. Rock surrounding the town was rich in lodestone, the naturally magnetic iron ore. In 550 B.C., a Greek named Thales of Miletus—widely thought to be the first scientist—first described lodestone's properties, and some think he coined the word "magnet."

The name lodestone comes from the Middle English word "lode," which means "course." Navigators at sea could use magnetic shards of lodestone to make compasses. Some ancient mariners, trying to explain this rock's amazing behavior, believed in Magnetic Mountain, a huge lodestone pinnacle to which all compasses pointed. It was said that if you sailed too close, Magnetic Mountain would pull every nail out of your ship!

Historians generally agree that the Chinese first invented the compass, and Chinese historians claim it happened way back in 2634 B.C. The compass came to Europe through Arabian traders, and Viking ships were using them by the 1100s. Columbus certainly had one on his famous voyages. The magnet made possible the Age of Exploration begun by Columbus. Without a compass, no one would have attempted to cross the ocean!

By the late 1500s, many scientists were carefully observing magnets, hoping to unlock their secrets. Francis Bacon, an English philosopher-scientist, considered the magnetic compass to be one of

Simple or ornate, a compass always points north.

The *Concorde* can fly faster than sound, but it uses a compass to find its way.

civilization's three most important inventions, the others being the printing press and gunpowder.

In 1600, Queen Elizabeth I's physician, William Gilbert, ground a lodestone into a sphere. As he moved his compass along his spherical lodestone, he observed where the needle pointed. Because the needle always pointed in the same direction, he determined there was no Magnetic Mountain, but that the Earth itself is a giant magnet, with a huge magnetic field that attracts compass needles.

In 1820, Denmark's Hans Christian Oersted discovered that magnetism and electricity were first cousins, and soon afterward the first electromagnet was built. With electromagnets, motors could generate electricity and machines could do work—and the Industrial Revolution was born, courtesy of the magnet.

Most historians agree that the Industrial Age has ended, and we now live in the Information Age, a time ruled by computers. Since computers use magnets to store data and run on current produced by magnets, we've actually never left the Magnetic Age.

From Columbus to Nintendo, magnets have made a huge impact on our lives. We hope this kit inspires you to become the next pioneer in understanding magnets.

As you focus your eyes on the front of the screen, a magnet focuses an electron beam on the back.

Magnetic Mystery Tour

To unlock the secrets of magnets, let's look at some of their basic properties. Find your magnetic wand, the magnet encased in plastic with a handle.

Your house is filled with things that attract magnets. Go on a Magnetic Mystery Tour of household objects provided on the list below. Which ones attract magnets? Which do not? Use a pencil to fill in the chart on the next page.

Wave your magnetic wand over these objects:

nail	plastic button	aluminum foil
dime	glass cup	paper clip
screwdriver	refrigerator door	newspaper or
soup can	fork or spoon	magazine
wooden tabletop	car door	ceramic mug

Think about what the magnet-attracting objects have in common. What makes them alike?

Take your wand on a walk through the house and predict whether you think an object will attract the magnet. Then test your prediction. How often are you right?

Caution: Never put a magnet near TVs, computers, computer disks, audiocassettes, videocassettes, automatic teller cards, or credit cards. You'll get yourself into *lots* of trouble.

Bird brains are more remarkable than you might think. Migrating birds have tiny magnets in their brains to keep them from getting lost.

Magnetic Mystery Chart

Which materials in your house attract magnets? Which do not?

Fill in these columns with names of objects that you discover to be either magnetic or non-magnetic.

Magnetic	Non-magnetic
--------------------------------	--------------------------------
--------------------------------	--------------------------------
--------------------------------	--------------------------------
--------------------------------	--------------------------------
--------------------------------	--------------------------------
--------------------------------	--------------------------------
--------------------------------	--------------------------------
--------------------------------	--------------------------------
--------------------------------	--------------------------------
--------------------------------	--------------------------------

The Case of the Fickle Nickel

During your Magnetic Mystery Tour, you might have noticed a pattern: everything your magnet sticks to is made of metal. But does *any* metal attract magnets?

Check your list. Nails do, but aluminum foil doesn't. Car doors do, but dimes don't. Only *some* metals are magnetic.

And that's part of magnetism's mystery: only *three* metals strongly attract magnets. Everything in the universe is made of a combination of 108 known elements, from argon to zinc. Only three are magnetic: iron, nickel, and cobalt. That's it.

Chances are pretty good that all the objects you listed in the left-hand column have one of

Nickel ore provides the metal for magnets and sometimes for nickels.

these metals in them. Usually it's iron, much more common in your house than the other two.

So let's test these magnetic metals. Find a nickel. Since nickel is one of the three magnetic metals, it must be attracted to your wand. Test it yourself. What happened?

If it's a United States nickel, the wand doesn't affect the coin. You've got two choices: either this book lied to you, or nickels aren't made of nickel. Which do you think it is?

In a foundry, iron ore is purified and made into a more usable form.

That's right. In the United States, five-cent pieces were once made of nickel, but no longer. However, the Canadian government still uses nickel in *its* five-cent coins. If you test a Canadian nickel, what do you predict will happen?

Though nickels aren't nickel, the magnets in your kit *are*. Most magnets are an alloy—a combination of metals—called alnico, short for their components: aluminum, nickel, and cobalt. Though they look like steel, these magnets have no iron in them.

Making Magnets

Your next feat as a magnetic magician is to transform an ordinary nail into a magnet. Here's how.

First, find a nail. It doesn't matter how big it is, as long as it sticks to a magnet.

Hold the magnetic wand horizontally in one hand. Place the end of the nail on the bottom of the wand, so it hangs straight down from underneath the wand, pointing toward the floor. Does it hang there?

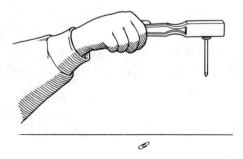

Now see if the free end of the nail will pick up a paper clip or a pin. Did the nail become magnetic?

Slowly and carefully remove the nail from the

magnetic wand without touching the paper clip. With the wand removed, the paper clip should stay attached to the nail. How long will this last?

Now drop the nail and paper clip onto a hard surface, such as a floor or desktop. Pick up the nail. Will it attract the paper clip? If it does, drop it again. By dropping the nail (or banging it on a desktop), you're destroying its magnetic abilities.

What's going on here? It's simple: Materials made from the magnetic metals can be turned into magnets themselves, just like you've done. But what changed *inside* the nail that allowed it to become a magnet itself, and then change back? Let's find out.

All matter is made of atoms, and all atoms are magnetic. You've read that only three materials strongly attract magnets. That's true. But one of the greatest mysteries of magnetism is this:

Everything is magnetic!

That's right, everything. You're magnetic. So is this book. So is your house, and your dog, and your shirt. Most things are incredibly weak magnets (like you!), but other materials show their magnetism more easily (like the nail).

In most materials, like you and this book, atoms are randomly arranged so that their "magnets" point in all possible directions, with magnetic attractions inside each atom cancelling each other. When you place a magnet against paper or wood, there is an attraction, but one so incredibly weak you just don't notice it.

Iron is different. Its atoms attract each other and arrange themselves into microscopic regions called **domains.** When a magnet comes near the iron, the domains line up in the same direction. The stronger the magnet, the more domains line up.

And as domains of atoms line up in the iron, it becomes a magnet, too.

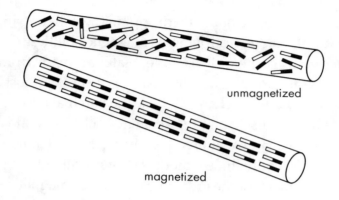

unmagnetized

magnetized

When its domains are random, a nail is just a nail. But when the domains line up, it becomes a magnet.

This is what you just did. When you touched your magnetic wand to the iron nail, your wand's permanent magnet lined up the domains inside the nail. The nail could then attract the paper clip, even after you removed the wand.

Dropping the nail shakes the domains. As the domains rattle, they begin to again face different directions and cancel each other out. The nail demagnetizes.

So you see that all atoms are magnetic, but some atoms are stronger magnets than others. Next time someone compliments your magnetic personality, make sure to remind that person that *everyone's* magnetic.

Chain Gangs

Using your magnetic wand and a bunch of paper clips you can make some magnetic chains.

Place one paper clip on the end of the wand. Use the bottom end of that clip to attract another clip. Attach a third to the second. Here's the challenge. How far can you go? Can you get five, six, seven clips lined up?

As this chain grows, you are pitting two forces against each other: gravity and magnetism. Magnetism holds the chain together; gravity pulls the chain apart. After how many paper clips does gravity win the tug of war?

Try again. Does gravity always win? Does gravity always win after the *same number* of clips?

Now make a chain of a variety of objects—nail, paper clips, safety pins, staples. Add a small magnet somewhere in the middle of the chain. Does that let you lengthen the chain? Why?

Use your imagination. Make chains of magnets and objects of different sizes and shapes. You're becoming a true scientist. Each time you play with these chains, you're testing the limits of magnets and learning more as you go. That's what a scientist does, too—even the best scientist has to play.

Instead of using light to illuminate objects, a scanning electron microscope uses electrons. The electrons are focused by magnets rather than lenses. This is an image of a common black ant.

Anti-Gravity Magnets I

In making chains of magnets, you made magnetism and gravity, two of the Earth's strongest forces, oppose each other. Eventually, when you tried putting just one more object on the chain, gravity won, and the whole chain collapsed.

But here's a trick that lets you conquer gravity!

Take one of the magnetic wheels—the circle magnets with a hole in the center, along with the wooden dowel.

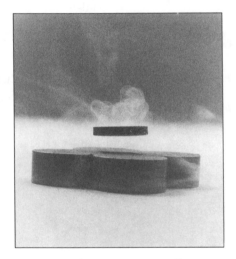

A superconducting ceramic pellet, cooled to -321 degrees F., resists the force of a strong magnet, causing the magnet to float.

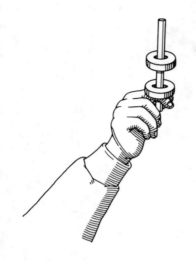

Place the dowel through one magnet, and rest the magnet on a table or desktop, nail standing straight up. Place the *second* circle magnet on the dowel as well.

If you're lucky, the second magnet floats above the first. They are **repelling** each other.

However, your second magnet might instead have **attracted** the first, and rather than float, it slammed onto the first. If that's the case, just

With your magnetic wheels and wooden dowel, you can defy gravity.

remove the second magnet, flip it over, and try again. Does it float now?

Congratulations! You've beaten gravity!

Loop the Loop

Use the circle magnets again. Hold one vertically between your thumb and forefinger, as shown in the picture.

Place a second circle magnet along the bottom edge of the first. (If the two magnets are repelling each other, simply flip one magnet over.)

Now rock your hand back and forth. The second magnet should slide around the edge of the one you're holding, in defiance of gravity.

Can you get the loose magnet to do a loop-the-loop, just like a roller coaster? Can you make the magnet travel

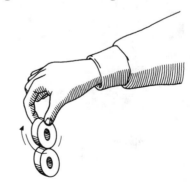

How many times can you loop-the-loop?

fully around the one you're holding?

Now let's make it even harder: can you do *two* loop-the-loops back-to-back, two revolutions of the second around the first? What happens if you try to spin the magnet too fast?

Once again, you're still pitting gravity against magnetism. If you can balance both forces, you're mastering magnetism.

Test the limits of this trick (three in a row?). Then defy gravity once more by turning this page.

Even the most high-tech aircraft depend on Earth's magnetic field for navigation.

EXPERIMENT!

Anti-Gravity Magnets II

You can make another magnet float. For this trick, you'll need the wand, one magnetic wheel, sewing thread, and some adhesive tape. Use a piece of tape to attach one end of the thread to the magnetic wheel.

Tape the other end of the thread to a flat surface, such as a tabletop. (Don't tape anything to a wooden table!) Now you're ready for more anti-gravity wizardry.

Hold your magnetic wand in one hand. With the other, hold the magnetic ball as high in the air as the thread allows. Slowly, very slowly, very, very slowly, bring the wand closer and closer to the wheel.

Can you get the wand *just close enough* for its magnetic attractions to make the wheel "float" in the air?

Now be creative. Can you rig something that holds the magnetic wand in just the right place, so you can have both

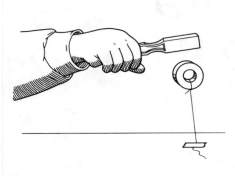

Make a floating magnet!

hands free? Perhaps a pile of books? Perhaps you can rest the wand on a glass or mug. Perhaps you can hang it from something. Arrange the wand so that it's just the right distance to float the magnet.

That accomplished, try an experiment. Can you break the attraction between the two magnets? Try placing a sheet of paper between them. Does it break the connection? How about plastic wrap? Aluminum foil? A tin can lid? (The tin can lid is difficult to try, because it will attract and stick to one of the magnets. It's tough, but not impossible.) Finally, does your finger break the attraction?

Amazingly, your magnets can exert a force on each other through many materials, but not all. Every magnet has a *field* of magnetism surrounding it, and the field attracts or repels objects inside it. The field is very strong close to the magnet, and weaker farther away.

The magnetic field might be invisible, but that doesn't mean you can't see it! You'll be able to "see" magnetic fields in the next experiment.

Magnetic Fields Forever

To see just what a magnet's field looks like, you'll need a sheet of white paper and four pencils. You'll also need your kit's bag of iron filings, plus three magnets: the wheel magnet, the bar magnet, and a disk magnet.

Lay the four pencils in a square. Place the bar magnet in the center of the square, and lay a sheet of white paper *over* the square, covering the magnet.

Carefully open the bag of iron filings. (Don't spill them!) Slowly sprinkle the filings over the paper. Start at the top and work your way down, making

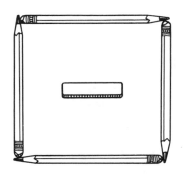

This simple setup will help you "see" invisible magnetic fields.

sure you don't use all the filings, just enough to do the job.

As you sprinkle, can you tell exactly where the magnet is underneath the paper? How can you tell?

When you've sprinkled the whole page, close the bag and place it somewhere safe.

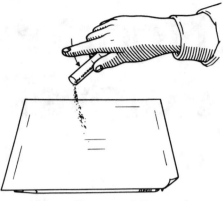

Sprinkle iron filings carefully.

With your forefinger, gently tap the sheet of paper, first at the top, then the sides, then the bottom. As you vibrate the paper, the filings will continue arranging themselves.

In addition to the magnet's outline, do you see curved lines of filings? Do you see how some curves start at one end of the magnet and flow toward its opposite end?

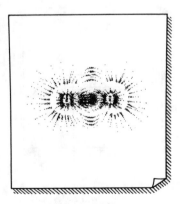

The magnetic field of a bar magnet

Look closely at the filings along both ends. Did some filings make chains that *go straight into the air?*

You're now seeing the bar magnet's field. It's strongest at the two ends. The magnetic force "flows" from one end of the magnet in a loop to the other. And the field is three-dimensional. The lines of force extend *above* and *below* the magnet, too.

After you've carefully examined this field, try another magnet. To change magnets, grasp the paper on each side. Lift it and move it away from the magnet.

You might need help here, but your goal is to fold the paper in half and pour the filings back into the vial. When this is done, close the bag and tap it 10 times on the table to de-magnetize your filings.

Replace the bar magnet with the wheel magnet, place the sheet of paper over it, and again sprinkle the filings. Is the wheel magnet's field the same shape as the bar magnet's? The lines of force flow from where to where?

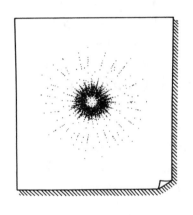

Then try the disk magnet. What does its field look like?

Look at the drawings of these magnetic fields. Do your observations of the filings match these drawings?

The magnetic field of a disk magnet

Now experiment a little more. Try different magnets in combination. Line up magnets alongside and on top of each other to make "field art." What's the most complex field you can make?

All magnets have fields around them, and the stronger the magnet, the larger its field. All magnetic fields flow from one side of a magnet to another.

Here's another magnetic mystery for you. Look at the picture of the bar magnet and its field on page 32. Let's say you could saw the bar magnet in half. (Don't try to do this; it's much easier just to imagine it.) What do you predict will happen to the magnetic field? Draw what you think the new fields will look like. If you cut a magnet in half, you will get two complete magnets, each with its own magnetic field.

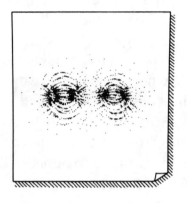

If you cut these into four, you'd get four magnets, and on and on.

Each magnet always has its own magnetic field, and every field always flows from one end of the magnet to another.

The magnetic field of one broken magnet is the same as the magnetic field of two magnets.

One Million Magnets

Now that you're an expert on magnetic fields, you can test your knowledge by making a **prediction**. Before any experiment, a scientist predicts what the outcome should be. After the experiment ends, the scientist decides if the conclusion matches the prediction. This is how scientists do science.

Here's the challenge: Based on what you've discovered so far, can you predict the shape of the magnetic field of the flexible vinyl magnet? Just like the previous experiment, use the pencils, paper, and filings to map a field.

Before you sprinkle the filings, try this. Place the magnet *on top of* the sheet of paper. Use a pencil to draw what you guess the pattern of the filings will be. Remember the three magnets you just mapped. Which one does this flexible magnet most closely resemble? What does its field look like?

After you've drawn your prediction for the magnet's field,

assemble your pencil square, lay the vinyl magnet down, and place the sheet of paper *over* the magnet. Try to line up your drawing with the magnet's position.

Now sprinkle the filings slowly on top.

Look at the pattern that emerges. Was your prediction right? Notice how the filings line up in neat rows. Each row includes small bars of arranged filings. One thing is clear: the vinyl magnet is *not* a bar magnet.

Vinyl is a plastic material, made from oil. It's not metallic, and not magnetic. To make this magnet, very small pieces of magnetized material are embedded in the vinyl. Look carefully at the pattern. Can you see how there are literally thousands of small bar magnets in the vinyl, each attracting a small pile of filings?

Your vinyl magnet is a thousand—maybe a million—magnets in one.

Surprise is an important part of science, for it's often that a prediction is just plain wrong. That's why it's called an experiment. You really don't know what will happen, and that's the most interesting part of science.

Now that you've seen magnetic fields of many kinds, you can find the North Pole.

Opposites Attract

"**I**t's a matter of fact," sings Paula Abdul in her hit song, "that opposites attract." It's true, and you can prove it.

Remember the magnetic field of your bar magnet? The lines of force flowed from one end of the magnet to the other. The ends of the bar magnet are **poles**—and *every* magnet has *two* poles: north and south.

The ends of your bar magnet are labeled N and S. Using this magnet, you can determine the poles of *any* other magnet.

Take the wand magnet. Move one end closer to the north pole of the bar magnet.

Does it repel or attract? Move that *same* end of the wand to the south pole of the bar magnet. Does it attract or repel?

Flip the bar magnet over, and repeat the above procedure with this end. A pattern emerges. The end of a bar magnet will *attract* one pole and *repel* the other.

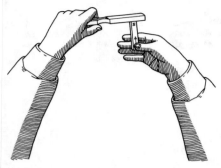

When you put the north pole of one magnet against the south pole of another, they attract one another.

In magnetism, like the song, the law is simple:

Opposites attract, and like repels.

The north pole of the bar magnet will repel the north pole of any other magnet in your kit. Two south poles repel each other, too. But any north will attract any south on any other magnet.

Find the poles of each magnet in your kit. Where are the poles of the disk magnet? The wheel?

Try the vinyl strip again. Notice that a bar magnet will weakly attract any point on the strip. There's *no* one north or south pole on the strip, because each of the tiny magnets in the strip has a north and a south pole.

Now that you know about poles, let's figure out why the magnetic poles are named north and south, not white and black, or Chris and Toby.

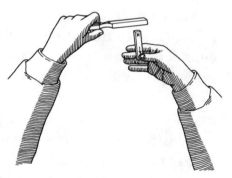

When you try to put like poles together, the magnets repel each other.

38

Polar Bearings

American Admiral Robert Peary led the first expedition to reach the North Pole, in 1909.

Let's say you decide to become a famous explorer, and it's time to hitch up the huskies and head north. But you've got one problem—which way's north?

Your kit has tools to help you find north. Use the bar magnet and the wand magnet. Use the bar's marked poles to determine the wand's north and south. (Remember: the horseshoe's north pole will repel the wand's north but attract its south.) Use a pencil or marker to label one side of your wand N.

Attach a length of string or thread to the center of the wand and dangle the wand freely in the air. When it settles down, something amazing will happen:

If you walk in the direction that the side labeled N is facing, you will be walking toward the north. Your magnet works just like a compass and points toward the planet's magnetic poles. The poles of magnets are named north and south because Earth is a giant polar magnet, too.

Matthew Henson was a key member of Admiral Peary's Arctic exploration team.

Twin Poles

As you read these words, the Earth is spinning dizzily at 1,000 miles per hour. Deep in the center of the Earth, 4,000 miles straight below you, molten iron and nickel swirl at the planet's core, baked at 5,000 degrees Fahrenheit.

Because it's a swiftly spinning ball with a core of molten metal, the Earth acts just as if it has a giant bar magnet inside, complete with a magnetic field and magnetic poles. Any freely-moving magnet on the Earth's surface will automatically point like a compass.

But the "bar magnet" inside the Earth isn't aligned perfectly with the geographical North and South Poles. No, it's tilted, so Earth has two sets of poles. The North and South Poles are the **geographic poles**, the axis around which the planet rotates. The north and south **magnetic poles** are the areas of greatest attraction and repulsion of the Earth's magnetic field. Check out the map here. See how far apart the geographic and magnetic poles are?

If you took your compass and walked straight north, would you reach the North Pole? No, you'd eventually come to an island in Canada's Hudson Bay, 1,000 miles from your destination. Luckily, explorers to the North Pole knew this fact and compensated when using their compasses.

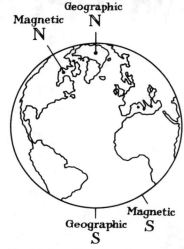

The Earth has two sets of poles—magnetic and geographic.

You may be wondering why the geographic poles and the magnetic poles have the same names even though they are different. That's a fair question. The truth is that unless you're traveling to the North or South Pole, the 1,000-mile difference between magnetic north and geographic north isn't enough to worry about. For navigating, north is north and south is south.

We've known about the Earth's magnetic field since 1600. But we're still not sure *how* it's made.

Our planet's core is mostly nickel and iron, two of the most strongly magnetic elements. You would think they would be responsible for Earth's magnetic field. Oddly enough, that's not it. Remember that iron becomes magnetic when numerous domains line up, with atomic magnets facing the same direction. In a swirling, liquid core, domains cannot line up, and neither iron nor nickel are magnetic at 5,000 degrees.

So what makes the magnetic field? Science's best guess is that as the planet spins, electrons in the molten metals are freed and create an electric current. It's the electric current inside the Earth that creates the magnetic field.

What happens to a compass needle when you're standing directly at magnetic north? Since the compass needles point along the lines of Earth's magnetic field, your needle will actually dip straight toward the ground.

There's another odd thing about the Earth's field: it changes. As the planet spins, the exact location of magnetic north moves just a little. Over thousands of years, it changes a lot.

Sometimes, for reasons we are very unsure of, the Earth switches poles—north becomes south, south becomes north. It's

happened nine times in the last four million years, and scientists are baffled as to why or when it'll happen again. Scientists discovered the switch when analyzing rock at the bottom of the Atlantic Ocean. As small particles of sediment settle to the ocean floor, some are weakly magnetic and, as they sink, point north. They form rock containing compass-like crystals, and the crystals have repeatedly changed the

This airplane cockpit is very sophisticated, but at its heart is an ordinary magnetic compass.

43

direction in which they point. This was a surprising discovery that led to a new area of science, paleomagnetism, the study of Earth's magnetic field in prehistoric times.

Magnets in Space

The Earth certainly isn't the only orbiting magnet. The sun is magnetic, so is the moon, and many planets have magnetic fields, too. Jupiter's was discovered in 1973, and Saturn's in 1979. Of all the planets, Jupiter's field is the strongest—five times stronger than Earth's.

Venus has a magnetic field, too, but it's one-thousandth the strength of the Earth's field. How Venus can have a magnetic field is a mystery because it appears that Venus spins too slowly for the electric current to become established.

Create-a-Compass

Here's your chance to build one of the most important navigational tools ever—a simple compass.

When Columbus set sail in 1492, he set the Santa Maria's compass due west—and stumbled upon the Americas. To return, he knew to sail east. You can imagine the importance of a compass to mariners like him, for how could you steer at night or in a storm without one?

Even today, compasses still mean the difference between life and death. Jet pilots know where to fly only by using the plane's compass, and air traffic controllers use compass directions to guide planes to safe landings.

To build your compass, you'll need to borrow a few things from around the house: a long metal needle, a small plastic button, some tape, and a bowl of water.

The needle will become the compass's arrow, but it first must be magnetized. Stroke the needle at least 50 times *in the same direction* with your kit's bar magnet. Your needle will become a weak magnet.

Rest the needle on top of the button, and fasten it with tape. The needle should be longer than the button so that both ends hang over the button. Carefully place the button in the center of the bowl of water, letting the button float freely. If it floats to the side, gently poke it back toward the middle.

Watch carefully. If you placed another compass alongside the bowl, it would tell you the direction your needle is pointing. Which way do you think it points? That's right—north and south.

Your homemade compass works just like an explorer's compass.

Here's another way to check the accuracy of your homemade compass. Face the direction the sun sets. That's west. Turn directly to your right. That's north. Is your needle pointing north?

Now bring one of your kit's magnets near the needle. What happens? So which magnetic field is stronger—the Earth's or your magnet's? As massive as the Earth is, its magnetic field is relatively weak.

You can use your floating magnet for the next activity.

Push and Pull

A magnet isn't the only thing that can affect the compass. Here's the material you will need to test this: your floating compass, bell wire, a nail, a rubber band, and a C or D battery. Wrap coils of wire around the nail, as the drawing shows.

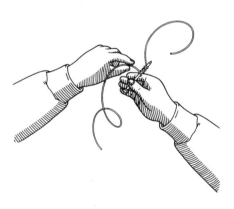

Use the rubber band to attach ends of the wire to the battery. Make sure the wire touches the battery.

You've now got a weak electric current flowing through the nail. Bring the end of the nail toward your floating compass's needle and watch the needle's behavior.

Can you attract the needle?

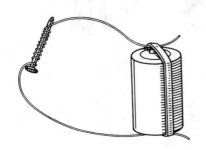

Use a rubber band to attach the wires to the battery.

Can you repel the needle? Can you explain why?

This is exactly what happened to Hans Christian Oersted in 1819. He accidentally brought his compass close to a live wire and watched the compass needle jump. He was the first to realize this fundamental fact: electric currents set up magnetic fields around themselves.

In fact, magnetic fields surround your refrigerator, TV, home computer, and so forth. This is **electromagnetism**, magnetism made by the flow of electric current.

Oersted wasn't looking for electromagnetism. He was actually lecturing to students about a phenomenon called the "toaster effect." You won't wonder what that is if you leave your battery connected to the wire too long—the wire will get very hot. Be careful and be sure to disconnect the battery as soon as you're done experimenting.

Wrap It Up

With the electromagnet you just made, you can perform scientific experiments to find out how to make it stronger or weaker.

You already know that an electromagnet can move a compass needle. First, find out whether your electromagnet has a north and south pole, too. How might you do that? Easy—take your bar magnet's north pole and bring it to one end of the nail. Does it attract? Does it repel? Remember: opposites attract and like repels.

Can you think of a way to reverse the poles of your electromagnet? Does winding the wire in the opposite direction have an effect? How about reversing the way the wire is attached to the battery?

Now see how many paper clips your electromagnet can pick up. How might you increase the magnet's strength? A larger nail? A bigger battery? How about this: Count the number of times your wire wraps around the nail. Then double it.

With more wraps, does the magnet pick up more clips? How many more?

With fewer wraps, what happens?

You might have seen those large magnets attached to cranes that pick up junked automobiles. They use powerful electromagnets with lots of iron and high voltage. When the current flows, the magnet picks up cars; when the current's turned off, what do you think happens?

See how long your nail stays charged after you detach it from the battery. Does the magnetic effect last?

Powerful electromagnets move heaps of scrap steel.

Make a Monster Magnet

If a battery and a wire wrapped around a nail can make a nail magnetic, what happens when you wrap a wire around something that's already magnetic?

Take the wand and find out how strong a magnet it is. First, count how many paper clips you can hang from the wand in a chain. Then, place a paper clip on a tabletop and slowly bring the wand toward the clip. How close to the clip does the wand first attract it? Can you measure the distance?

Now comes the experiment. You need the magnetic wand, rubber bands, wire, and a C or D battery. Wrap the wire around your wand's magnet, and attach the ends to the battery with a rubber band. Use another rubber band to fasten the battery onto the top of the wand. Your wand is now carrying its own powerpack!

Check out this magnet's strength. Will it hold more clips?

Magnetic fields? Magnets are sometimes fed to dairy cows to protect them from sharp pieces of metal they may swallow. The magnet holds the metal safely in the cow's first stomach.

What happens if you use more wire and wrap more coils around your magnet?

Try this with the bar magnet. Are the results the same?

An Introduction to Induction

In 1831, British scientist Michael Faraday performed a very simple experiment that single-handedly changed history.

He discovered **induction**, which is the creation of an electric current by moving a wire through a magnetic field. Here's what he did.

You've seen that electric currents set up magnetic fields. Faraday wondered if the reverse were true. Could magnetic fields set up electric currents? Could magnetism make electricity?

He attached a coil of wire to a galvanometer, a device that measures the flow of electricity.

Electrical pioneer Michael Faraday

He placed a magnet inside the coil and discovered that magnetism *does* create electricity—but only when the magnet moves back and forth through the coil.

This discovery led immediately to two dramatic advances: the invention of motors and the generation of electric power. A spinning coil of wire coupled with a magnet could make electricity flow and could do work.

More than 150 years later, that's still exactly how electricity flows into your house, and exactly how motors work.

How a Motor Works:

Coal and oil are burned in power plants to heat water; boiling water turns to steam and rises; steam turns a turbine; the spinning turbine turns a wire coil inside a giant electromagnet—and the electricity flows.

Even nuclear power uses magnetism. Splitting uranium atoms generate incredible amounts of heat to boil water, turn the turbine, and so forth.

Inside motors everywhere, there's a coil of wire spinning within an electromagnet, making your refrigerator hum and your car ignition start. The power of magnetism is simply everywhere.

A power-plant turbine converts steam into electricity.

Transformers!

As electricity travels from the power company to your room, it flows through several **transformers**. Some increase the current, some decrease it, so it arrives in your house many miles away at the right voltage for your appliances.

Michael Faraday, the same scientist who discovered induction, also invented the transformer, a hugely important device. Check out the diagrams on page 56.

On the left is an arrangement that resembles Faraday's experiment. Electricity flows from a power supply through wire, and the wire is wrapped around one side of an iron donut. There's another wire coiled on the donut's right side. Count the coils on each side. Which has more?

Here's what Faraday found: the current flowing out of the device had *doubled*. If you double the coils on the right, the current is doubly transformed. Triple the coils, triple the current.

And the reverse is true. The drawing on the right shows a transformer that produces what effect on the current?

Count the coils on the left, the coils on the right. What happens to the current?

It's cut in half.

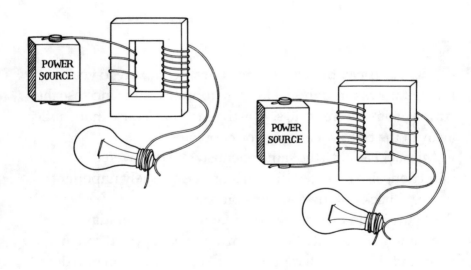

Transformers increase or decrease the amount of electricity flowing through a wire. The transformer on the left doubles the electric current. The transformer on the right cuts the current in half.

Even More Magnets

Every day, you rely on magnets in hundreds of ways.

Every credit card has a magnetic strip on the back that stores the owner's credit card number in bars of magnetic code. When the credit card is used, an electronic device scans the strip and identifies the number.

Automatic teller machines read the magnetic code on the back of ATM cards.

Magnetic fields are built into metal detectors used in airports and at the beach, coin-operated vending machines, and even traffic lights. Coils of wire inside metal detectors create a magnetic field, and when metal affects the field, an alarm sounds. The metal detector used for treasure-hunting sends a signal to headphones, and an airport metal detector beeps very loudly!

Vending machines are built so that a coin passes through a magnet in the slot—currents induced in the coin produce a magnetic field that slows the coin. The larger the coin, the less it slows. The magnetic test is one of several ways a vending machine makes sure a coin is not a slug or a forgery.

Some traffic lights can sense cars approaching. A loop of wire built into the road creates a magnetic field that the car interrupts to change the light.

Scanned by Magnets

One of the newest uses of magnets is a machine in hospitals that allows doctors to see deep inside your body. It's called the nuclear magnetic resonance (NMR) scanner, and it creates magnetic resonance imagery (MRI). This machine lets doctors examine a patient for tumors and growths while the patient feels nothing.

The patient slides into the round chamber that's surrounded by large curved panels containing hidden coils of wire. When switched on, the panels become electromagnets and surround the patient with a magnetic field.

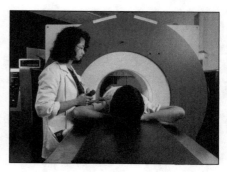

A patient prepares to enter a nuclear magnetic resonance (NMR) scanner.

Inside the strong field, the body's hydrogen atoms—of

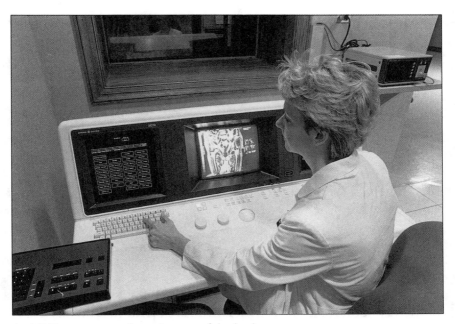

An NMR scanner produces images of the body on a computer screen.

which there are billions!—respond to the magnetic forces, re-aligning their own fields. The scanner sends a beam of radio waves into the patient, and these waves cause a weak electric current to flow within the body. The scanner uses the current to create pictures of the interior of the patient's body.

NMR can spot tumors, locate blocked blood vessels, spot areas of the brain affected by strokes, and can even let doctors measure the effects of drugs on the brain.

This is perhaps the most unusual invention using magnets.

Riding on Air

Magnets can detect metal and determine if you're well, and someday soon magnets may let you ride on air just inches above the ground.

Remember the levitating magnet trick? Remember that like poles repel each other? Scientists have long wondered if that force of magnetic repulsion could be put to work.

It has. The result: the magnetic-levitating train, otherwise known as the **maglev**.

The concept is simple. Imagine powerful magnets on the underside of a train repelling powerful magnets along the track. The train levitates along the track, needing no wheels!

But how do you produce motion? That's more complicated. Coils along the bottom of the train make a magnetic field that constantly shifts north and south poles. This field generates a response from magnets in the rail. Changing fields move the

The Maglev train carries passengers on a frictionless magnetic field. This one is in Japan.

train along as magnets are first attracted (pulled) and then repelled (pushed ahead to next magnet).

Perhaps one day you'll be traveling across the country at 300 miles per hour, levitating above the track on a maglev train!

And if you like the idea of riding on a maglev train, don't forget that these trains will need engineers, conductors, and magnetic repair-folk. Perhaps you'll be conducting the trains of the future!

Magnetic Magellans

In 1519, the Portuguese explorer Ferdinand Magellan set out on a three-year voyage around the entire world. He succeeded and became the first person to accomplish that goal. With him was, of course, his compass.

In 1989, 470 years later, NASA astronauts launched the *Magellan* spacecraft from the *Atlantis* Space Shuttle. This *Magellan* has a different world to discover—Venus. In October 1990, its sensors began sending the first pictures of the Venusian landscape back to

Magnetic explorer Ferdinand Magellan

Earth. On board the *Magellan*, computers operate using the power of electromagnetism.

It's still a magnetic world, and there are still discoveries left to be made. Continue experimenting with the magnets in your kit. Become a scientist, an inventor, a tinkerer, a Merlin who understands magnetism's magical abilities, or a Magellan who's unafraid to sail into the unknown.

Happy exploring!

Space explorer, the *Magellan* spacecraft

QUIZ ANSWERS (from page 6):
1. a; 2. a; 3. f; 4. b; 5. c; 6. d; 7. a

About the Author

Mike Weilbacher travels to schools throughout the country, performing his unique "science vaudeville shows" on topics such as dinosaurs, the environment, and marine life. He's a freelance writer and has written about Ben Franklin, outer space, futurism, and more. He hosts "Earth Talk," a public-radio environmental show in Philadelphia, and is Pennsylvania's 1991 Environmental Educator of the Year.

THE QUEST
FOR A CHILD

Offering Hope Through the Stress of Infertility

by

Anna-Marie Lockard

Published for the author
by **IMPACT BOOKS, INC.**
137 W. Jefferson, Kirkwood, Mo. 63122
Printed in the United States of America

Cover Design: S&CB Studios

Printed in the United States of America

ABOUT THE AUTHOR

Anna-Marie Lockard and her minister-husband Chuck, served churches in Ohio, South Africa, and Texas. She taught the History of Church Music and Hymnology course at a theological college in Port Elizabeth, South Africa.

She has been a women's speaker at retreats and seminars as well as a Bible Study teacher. She has served as Compassionate Ministries' Director for the World Mission Society of the West Texas District Church of the Nazarene.

Currently, she is co-director of Women's Ministries for the West Texas District, encompassing ninety churches. She is also a member of RESOLVE, a national infertility support group and resides in Homer City, Pennsylvania.

EDUCATION

Anna-Marie attended Nazarene Bible College in Colorado Springs, Colorado, majoring in speech communications and music. At Sinclair College in Dayton, Ohio, she majored in English and psychology. She furthered her bachelor studies at the University of South Africa and attended The Writing School in southern Africa.

PREVIOUSLY PUBLISHED WORKS

Her previously published works include articles in periodical magazines such as *World Mission magazine, The Herald of Holiness, The Preacher's Magazine*, and an international devotional magazine, *Come Ye Apart*. In 1988, she had an article published in the leading magazine for women, *Woman's Value*, in South Africa. She won an honorable mention in a writing contest in *The Christian Reader*, which was published in the July/August 1992 issue.

DEDICATION

To ...

my magnificent husband, Chuck,

For your constant love, devotion and unending

patience.

Thank you for "the gift."

THANKS

To Lillian Johnston and Marilyn Heavilin for taking time to review the manuscript and offer helpful suggestions.

To Dwane Matlock for your friendship and assistance in library research.

To my wonderful Lord for making my dreams live.

TABLE OF CONTENTS

INTRODUCTION

Every woman longs for fulfillment in some area of her life. This book identifies areas in which infertile women struggle for wholeness.

Disappointment is what infertility is all about. Several chapters show ways to refocus disappointment and channel passion to make the best of gifts and energies.

It is meant to be a helping hand reaching out to offer HOPE and encouragement along the painful path of childlessness. It is my hope that the message of the book will help to
                ... soothe the pain
                ... mend the wound
                ... restore to wholeness.

THE QUEST FOR A CHILD offers HOPE in the face of hopelessness.

HOPE

It is a word that has been worn so smooth that it has lost its bite. However, when I use the word 'HOPE' I am not referring to quick fixes. When I use the word 'HOPE' I am referring to a clear understanding that life is at best a risk - an uncharted voyage in which we know little about jutting shorelines and drifting debris. But, it is a voyage we want to take. [1]

And undaunted, we sail the journey with our hand in God's and discover ways to cushion the blows.

HOPE

It can be a quiet determination to rise above our circumstances; or a deliberate confidence in God. With hope we can reach a resolved attitude of complete trust.

Hope allows us to believe that even if our problem is not solved, we can still persevere; there is no mountain so tall God cannot remove it.

Hope is not setting our minds on getting our own way. Still, we may have to live out the consequences of an unwanted divorce, rebellious child or terminable health.

Yet, hope can continue to live! It offers us help for our hurt and pain. Hope provides us with the confidence to:

...walk through our circumstances

...learn ways to mend our brokenness

...gain confidence to cope.

Florence Littauer, in her remarkable book, *Hope For Hurting Women,* says, "Hope allows God to put a warm blanket of love over a suffering body. Hope gives us patience through our pain." [2]   That's the key, patient trust - in God - through our anguish.

FAITH

and

HOPE

...two inseparable companions on the quest for a child.

A SILENT CRY

Cries of the inner heart

Scream with silent tears

That never fall

Are never seen.

Masked anguish.

Mute, clamorous cries

Heard by God only,

He soothes the pain,

He mends the wound,

He restores to wholeness.

Anna-Marie Lockard

1990

CHAPTER 1

HOPE WHEN THINGS SEEM HOPELESS:

The Struggle For Fulfillment

"Why don't you have kids? Is it because you don't like kids, or you just don't want any?" intrusively remarked a pastor's wife. The insensitive comment seemed even more incredible in light of the fact that this was the first time I had ever met her.

Once again the query seared deeply into my already fragile emotions. However, having lived through seventeen years of infertility, one might think that I would have become immune to such remarks. But, that is simply not true. The potent sense of defectiveness may lessen, but it is ever before you.

The scorching hot afternoon sun penetrated our car windows. We searched the parking lot for a shade area to park, but our efforts were in vain. We were at the Ciskei's (in Southern Africa) government offices. A missionary friend, myself and my husband walked into the office of a fellow American missionary who was employed by the government. It was our first occasion to meet him. Perhaps ten minutes passed into the conversation when he flippantly probed the inevitable question that comes sooner or later,

"Do you have children?"
Chuck replied, "No we don't."

"What's the matter, do you watch too much TV?"

Being in the office with three men and no other women, I was quite embarrassed by the crude comment. I felt tears welling in my eyes but desperately fought against them. Later, walking to the car, Chuck took my hand gently in his.

We discussed the disturbing incident and tried to once again put it from our minds.

The pulsing neon light of infertility.

...non-productive

...fruitless

...inadequate

...barren

...devoid, lacking

Stark connotations, yet even the most precise dictionary meaning of the word cannot portray the disappointment, the anguish and grief of a childless marriage.

THE QUEST BEGINS

Sitting nervously in the gynecologist's posh Ohio office, I notice a photo of his wife and three children sitting proudly in a silver frame on top of his handsome oak desk. Behind the desk on the wall, hangs a poem that says, "M.D. Means My Daddy." I smile and think of a young child's love for his father, who sees beyond the professional degree to the tussle and play of a 'daddy.'

I, however, feel fortunate to be in the care of a renowned infertility specialist. I have been waiting twenty minutes for Dr. McLaughlin to come in and speak to me about my recent battery of infertility tests.

Abruptly, the office door swings open and the doctor briskly walks in. "Hello Ann, how are you today?" He smiles warmly. In a professional, yet compassionate manner, he continues, "Ann, we discovered three problems. You have polycystic ovaries. That is a condition whereby your ovaries are covered with multiple cysts and make it difficult for them to release an egg. The second problem is that you have a prolactic imbalance. This is a hormone produced by the pituitary gland that stimulates lactation. The third problem that we face is that you have endometriosis, which is the presence of uterine tissue in the lower abdomen. This is treatable with laser surgery and hormone therapy. We could also do a wedge resection of your ovaries," he concluded.

More surgery.

Hormone Therapy.

I'm only thirty years old.

I was beginning to feel a potent sense of defectiveness. Being a person who valued good health, it all sounded so debilitating and frightening.

Hesitatingly, I asked, "What are my chances of conceiving without further medical intervention?"

I watched as his expression changed from hopefulness to sadness as he said softly, "Without medical intervention you have a less then five percent chance of ever having a child."

Silence.

17

I sat in stunned disbelief.

Later, I learned that he was being polite. Instead of straightforwardly saying my chances were almost nil, he wisely offered a small ray of hope.

Forcing back hot burning tears, I courteously replied, "Thank you, I will have to discuss the situation with my husband."

He understood.

As I walked out of his office and into the crowded reception area, the many pregnant women reminded me of what I may never have. I felt a strong sense of despair. Where does a woman begin to tell her husband that it is nearly impossible to produce a child for him?

Where do you begin to pick up the pieces of a shattered dream? Will the dream ever be mended?

As I drove home, I began to reflect upon the twelve marvelous years of our married life. We lived a story book romance only in real life. What an adventure!

Early in our marriage, like others, we sloughed through financial hardship at Bible College in Colorado Springs. Now, three years later, we had our first pastoral assignment in Germantown, Ohio. We served a wonderful congregation of good people.

God gave me a magnificent gift when he sent Chuck into my life. I once told my father, "Daddy, in fifteen years of marriage Chuck has never even raised his voice to me."

"Never?" my father asked, surprised. "No, never Daddy."

It seemed incredulous to him. Although he did say he never knew a more patient man.

Chuck supported me and made me feel like the most special person in the world. We enjoyed an outstanding Christian marriage; communication, intimacy, friendship and respect with Christ at the center.

Yet, how we longed to let our love overflow into a child's life. A child to love and to teach God's ways to. A little one to offer back to God for His purposes; that was our longing.

But, God was not sending a child into our lives. We had hard questions without easy answers.

Today, I had to tell my splendid husband that our options were fertility drugs with more high-risk surgery. At best, medical science would increase my chances of conception by only fifty-percent. As Christians we had to face the moral implications of the "medical versus faith" dilemma. How far should a Christian go with invasive medical procedures?

That afternoon, I shared the doctor's report with him. Characteristically, he responded with such depth of love, "You are the most important person in my life. Let's put the whole matter in God's hands and leave it there. He knows what is best for us. He can work it out in His time."

'In His Time.' Patience was Chuck's strongest virtue, but not mine. Somehow his decision seemed too pat for me. My disposition is such that I cannot resist searching for answers - within myself, and from God. I discovered that God had lessons to teach us through years of tears and pain

Faith. Chuck had an unswerving confidence in

19

God. I, on the other hand, felt like Philip Yancey when he said, "I wanted a God who would roll up His sleeves and step into my life with power."[3] In His book, *Disappointment With God*, Yancey says, "God wanted faith, the Bible says, and that is the lesson Abraham finally learned. He learned to believe when there was no reason left to believe. Somehow that faith is what God valued."[4]

Intellectually, I believed God valued faith. I loved God and knew that he could intervene in any situation in life that we face. Yet, I yearned for understanding. That search would catapult me into one of the most despondent times of my life.

It began the next week. I found myself falling into a deep well of depression. It was a late October day. I looked out the living room window and noticed the dry, parched leaves dropping from the large maple tree. It seemed to symbolize loss and barrenness. 'However," I thought, 'at least the maple tree's loss will be restored next Spring. My loss may be permanent.'

Food and sleep had no appeal to me. I crawled into a cocoon of withdrawal from Chuck - the very one I loved and adored the most. My self-isolation included non-verbal communication. Chuck was troubled and concerned for me and lovingly tried to break the wall of silence, but I was unyielding. It seemed the emotional pain was too intense to voice to anyone. For the first time in my life I felt defective and inadequate.

Many times that week, the Lord tried to penetrate my solitary retreat, but I turned Him away, also. His question to me was, "If you never bear a child, can you still say God is good and continue to serve me? In essence God was saying, 'If I ask you to surrender something precious - are you willing to let go?'

20

For nearly one week that question haunted my thoughts night and day. I knew God was asking me to surrender all that was dearest to me - for His sake. I needed a little more time. I am grateful for the patience of God.

It was Saturday afternoon and I was resting in the guest bedroom of the parsonage, I craved privacy. So tenderly, God spoke. He seemed to say, 'You are at a crossroads in your life. You have a choice to make that no one else can make for you. You can decide to let Me walk through this dark ravine with you, or you can walk it alone and choose your own destination.'

God began to show me that if I chose my route, the self-pity would eventually consume me emotionally and I would be of little use to Chuck, God or the Church.

I knew what it was time to do. Tearfully, I slipped out of bed and knelt before a loving, all-knowing God. My aching heart was soothed in His presence. "Dear God," I wept, "it is going to be a painful path. I can't walk it alone. If you'll give me the strength I need to carry the load, I'll walk the road for You. I will tell others that God is good and worthy to be trusted."

The heavy emotional weight of that gloomy week was lifted and the sun shone brighter through the bedroom window. I determined then to rise above my circumstances and face an unknown future with a confidence in God's faithfulness. The uplifting words from Deuteronomy 33:25b came to my mind: "...as thy days so shall thy strength be." (KJV) I believed then, as I do today, that God provides strength when we need it most.

THAT RAY OF HOPE

Many are aware of the pain of a woman who loses a child through a stillbirth, Sudden Infant Death Syndrome, tragic accident, or a terminal illness. However, few are aware of the silent cries of an infertile woman. Often they suffer intensely and alone. I wrote the following poem during a time of great anguish. It describes the pain buried beneath the armor:

A SILENT CRY

Cries of the inner heart

Scream with silent tears

That never fall,

Are never seen.

Masked anguish.

Mute, clamorous cries

Heard by God only;

He soothes the pain,

Mends the wound,

Restores to wholeness.

The title of the poem is revealing; Infertile women often cry, but they are tears from within - no one sees them, but God. Beneath the armor is masked anguish. The cries are loud, but only God hears them. He is the only one who can assuage the pain and bring restoration and healing.

It is a cry that leads to an intense search for significance. I believe every woman longs for fulfillment in some area of her life;

...security

...recognition

...love

...intimacy

...success.

She yearns for some type of formula for success and satisfaction. That quest to feel complete may take many avenues. Walk with me on my journey. Along the way you will taste my tears and touch my pain. But, you will also discover ways that HOPE can live for you, too.

WHEN HOPE LIVES

April 25, 1990 was our twentieth wedding anniversary. My husband and I were celebrating twenty years of a magnificent marriage. We took a few days off and drove to a friend's condo in New Mexico. We reminisced with love and joy over the past years.

The Lord led us from a small coal mining town in western Pennsylvania to the beautiful Rocky Mountains in Colorado for three years, on to Ohio for six years. From there we accepted a pastoral assignment in the beautiful coastal city of Port Elizabeth, in the Republic of South Africa.

What an adventure! God gave us the opportunity to travel and meet people in five countries. We climbed mountains and forged rivers in Africa. There, we also fed the hungry and homeless and lived four years through culture shock of seeing abject poverty and social injustice.

From that setting God must have thought we needed some tranquility in our lives and sent us to Plainview, Texas, a small cotton-farming community in the state's Pan Handle between Amarillo and Lubbock.

With each move and each new ministry, God cemented our marriage together into a closer bond. To me, our marriage was the best thing this side of heaven.

Yet, there was an unmet longing in my life...an empty chasm...a void that no amount of adventure or activities could fill. For twenty years God had not chosen to send a child into our lives. A child's world was not part of our lives. There were no soft dolls or toy trucks to pick up at the end of the day. Our home was a quiet, peace-filled sanctuary that lacked the laughter of children at play.

We had no need to frequent playgrounds or PTAs. Often, during those quiet lonely hours I would dream of my home being filled with a child at play. How different it would be.

HOPE would soar and I would say, "Perhaps one day I will know the warmth and love of a newborn nestled at my breast. I'll know the joy of rocking my precious child gently in my arms...Yes, one day, I'll know!"

I clung to HOPE and would not let go.

Then five, ten, fifteen and finally twenty years passed and HOPE began to fade..."It's going to take a miracle, Lord," I said. God knew, too.

To have HOPE in the face of hopelessness takes courage and commitment. Courage to fearlessly face insensitive remarks by well-meaning people and deep commitment to a loving God who sometimes puts our prayers on hold; but who forever feels our hurt and pain.

THE QUEST FOR A CHILD is not only my story, but it could be your story, too. It is the tale of other women whose heartaches can be described in five words:

"And she had no child."

God offers HOPE and wholeness in every situation. There are lessons we can learn from others who have walked the painful path before us. Nine Hebrew women give offers of HOPE in the next chapter.

CHAPTER TWO

HOPE FOR THE BARREN

"Anna-Marie," wrote Stella, "you're not going to believe this! Remember the friend I told you about who had her first baby at age forty-two and her second one at forty four? This week, I just received a birth announcement from her. She delivered her third healthy baby at age forty-six. Some Sarah!"

Sarah and Abraham. Who doesn't think of these Old Testament figures when we talk about someone bearing a child in their old age? The account is familiar to most of us; Sarah was ninety years old when she first conceived. "Impossible!" some would scoff. However, the scriptures, give clear evidence to other accounts almost as surprising.

To Hebrew women, barrenness was looked upon as a gnawing grief and sometimes regarded as divine disfavor. Try to imagine the societal pressures they faced in their day. Their whole worth as a woman was woven into whether or not they could produce children.

Scriptures reveal three explanations for childlessness in biblical times: a reproach; a judgment, and an absence of God's blessing. Nine accounts are recorded in the Old and New Testaments. The following narratives are told of women from the scriptures who felt the intense sorrow and disappointment of a childless home. We can learn much from their unswerving faith and perseverance.

GOD CHIDES SARAH

The first recorded account of infertility is told in Genesis 16: 2. Sarai was the adored wife of the patriarch, Abram. Her name means 'princess' and she was known for the great beauty of her face and the grace of her stature.

The one great grief of Abraham and Sarah was that through their long life together, they had no children. Abraham's gentleness, kindness and forbearance off-set Sarah's expressive and possessive ways.

Sarai - beautiful, strong-willed and determined, the constant grief of barrenness caused her to make a great mistake. She rushed God's timetable. In the midst of her impatience, she said to her husband, "The Lord has prevented me from bearing children. Take my maid, perhaps I shall obtain children through her." Abram obliged and took Hagar, the Egyptian maid and she conceived.

It is important to remember that nowhere in scripture was this action sanctioned by God. Sarah's selfish decision would reap heartache and discord; the child that Hagar bore was a reproach and not the child of promise.

Years passed and Abraham was ninety-nine years old. The Lord appeared to him and promised that Sarah would bear a son. At this shocking news, Abraham fell on his face and laughed - Sarah was ninety...long past childbearing age.

When Abraham shared the remarkable revelation to her, Sarah scoffed. But the Lord's reply was, "Is anything too difficult for the Lord? This time next year Sarah shall have a son."

Genesis chapter twenty-one reveals the joyful

event:

> "Then the Lord took note of Sarah as
> He had said. And the Lord did for
> Sarah as He had promised. So Sarah
> conceived and bore a son to Abra-
> ham in his old age, at the appointed
> time of which God had spoken to
> him."

God remembered Sarah's pain.

God fulfilled His promise.

God accomplished it in His "appointed time."

GOD JUDGES MICHAL

II Samuel 6:23

Here, we are given the second example of a childless couple. Michal was the younger daughter of King
Saul. She was David's first wife. Let's discover the
reason why her barrenness was viewed as a judgment.

Michal loved David but did not love the Lord as
David did. A desire for prestige, an indifference to
holiness, and idolatry were marks of her flawed character.

When David became a fugitive from her father,
Saul, she had an adulterous affair with Phalti, a man on
his way to royalty. Later, she was reunited with David,
but her love for him waned.

One day David left with 30,000 men to bring the
Ark of the Covenant back to Jerusalem. David, in his
jubilation, was leaping and dancing before the Lord.

Michal saw this from her window. David was wearing a linen ephod and while leaping perhaps exposed parts of his body. This enraged Michal and she harshly rebuked him for it. This annoyed David and from then on she lived apart from him.[5]

The Bible says, "She had no child until the day of her death." Scripture views her childlessness as a judgment.

ABSENCE OF GOD'S BLESSING

The third narrative is seen as an absence of God's blessing recorded in Exodus 23:26. One of God's promises to Moses was that there would be no miscarrying or barrenness in his land.[6] Here for the first time, fertility is seen as a reward of God's blessing.

BEAUTIFUL BUT BARREN REBEKAH

Genesis 25:21

She was Sarah's daughter-in-law. "Her husband, Isaac prayed twenty years to the Lord on behalf of his wife, because she was barren; and the Lord answered him and Rebekah, his wife, conceived."

Motherhood came to Rebekah somewhat late in life when Isaac was an aging man. For twenty years she has been childless. The years of waiting on the part of Isaac and Rebekah show that God has His own timing for the fulfillment of His purposes. [7]

In an age of polygamy, Isaac took no handmaid, concubine or second wife. Rebekah and he were bound together by bonds of mutual affection. Isaac demonstrated a faith that did not falter.

GOD REMEMBERS RACHEL

Genesis 30:22

Lovely in form and face, Sarah's granddaughter and Rebekah's daughter-in-law developed a lasting love for Jacob. Jacob labored fourteen years to earn Rachel as his adored wife.

Once Rachel became Jacob's beloved wife, her continued barrenness created an unreasonable and impatient fretfulness within her soul. Rachel's whole being was bound up in the desire to become a mother, so she cried to Jacob, "Give me children or else I die." (Genesis 30:1) Rachel should have cried to God instead of Jacob. Grieving, childless Rachel was not forgotten by the Lord; He remembered her and opened her womb (Genesis 30:22-24).

She gave birth to a son and thereby took away her reproach. Of all the children of Jacob, Joseph became the greatest and godliest.[8]

Time spent in waiting and trusting always reaps dividends. Jacob's long labor to obtain Rachel for his wife, was worth the wait. Rachel's long awaited-for child proved to be the great joy of her life.

GOD RESTORES MANOAH'S WIFE

Judges 13:2,3,24

Her name is not recorded in scripture. We can guess it must have been a sweet and sensitive one for she was such a good woman. A God-fearing Israelite, her faith taught her that heaven knew about her maternal longing and of the vain waiting that saddened her life. Scripture does not record complaint or impatience over

31

her childless state. Calmly, she remained faithful, self-sacrificing, and holy.

At last the prayers of Manoah's wife were answered; she became a joyous mother. The angel appeared to her and said, "Behold, now you are barren and have borne no children, but you shall conceive and give birth to a son." In verse 24, "Then the woman gave birth to a son and named him Samson. And the child grew up; the Lord blessed him."

How grateful to God she must have been as the promised son was now a reality and nestling on her breast! Imagine for a moment the tender love she must have shown her precious little one. Her joy would know no bounds as she cared for him lovingly each day. A child receives a great gift to be born into a home filled with such love.[9]

HOPE FOR HANNAH

I Samuel 1:18-20

Hannah is an outstanding example of how the most unpleasant circumstances can produce a character that blesses the world. A character radiant with faith and HOPE; a woman unblemished...godly...devoted...trusting...patient and self-sacrificing.

Elkanah, her husband, loved her and recognized her deep longing for a child. Perhaps he sensed her feelings of inadequacy when he remarked, "Am I not better to thee than ten sons?" Why, he wondered, could Hannah not be satisfied with his love and devotion alone? Yet, only God and a woman can know the maternal yearning for a child from her own womb.

As the years passed Hannah's agony became more

intense; she cried day and night. Childless, Hannah was not prayerless. Barren, she still believed. Her pain found a refuge in prayer. She poured out her soul before God - vowing that if He would give her a son; she would give the child back to God for His exclusive use.

God granted her wish and the yearned-for child arrived. She named him Samuel, which means, "asked of the Lord."

Hannah prayed and promised. When her prayer was answered, she quietly redeemed her promise. More than anything in the world she had wanted a son. So, when God gave her one, she offered him back to the Lord as she had promised. After Samuel was weaned she took him to the temple, visiting him only yearly.[10]

We learn from Hannah that when sorrow sweeps over us like billowing waves at sea, God is a comforting retreat. Hannah carried her trial and yearning to God in prayer.

GOD REWARDS THE SHUNAMITE WOMAN

II Kings 4:14-17

A well-known female of high rank and riches, she is nameless in scripture; a great lady of social distinction, yet humble and a devout worshipper of Jehovah. This childless woman used her lovely home for the entertainment of God's people who passed that way.

Elisha experienced the delightful harmony in the home. It appeared she was much younger than her husband, "She hath not child and her husband is old." Elisha felt the Shunamite woman should have some reward for her kindnesses.

33

One day he sent his servant with a message that he wanted to reward her for her most gracious and frequent hospitality. Kindly and humbly, she declined any remuneration.

Elisha's servant reminded him of her childlessness. Elisha called for her and as she stood at the door, he pronounced the end of her misfortune and reproach. "Thou shalt embrace a son." She was overcome with emotion; an indication of the deep-seated feelings of barrenness.

Later that year, the miracle happened and the joyous day dawned when she nestled her promised baby to her bosom.

No greater reward could God have given this couple for their kind treatment of His servant!

GOD USES ELIZABETH

Luke 1:7, 13, 5:7

The adored wife of a priest, Elizabeth was a woman of unusual piety, strong faith, and spiritual gifts. However, scripture records five words that convey a life of heartache and disappointment:

"And they had no child."

For years they had both prayed and longed for a child of their own flesh. One they could nurture with seeds of God's love. A child to present to God for His service.

Time was passing swiftly, they were growing old. Would God remember their cries of anguish?

For this devout woman with a pious heart and cultivated intellect, God performed a miracle; "She conceived a son in her old age."[11] And John the Baptist
proved to be a godly son. Out in the lonely desert in
silence and solitude he found close fellowship with God.
God used Elizabeth to produce a godly son who would
prepare the way for the Son of God.

A BIBLICAL PERSPECTIVE

It is comforting to know that **GOD REMEMBERS**
the anguish cries of an aching heart. **GOD RESTORES**
to wholeness the one whose brokenness seems irrepara-
ble; He will mend the damaged pieces. And finally we
see through God's Word that **GOD REWARDS** the
faithful one who steadily trusts with patient HOPE. In
addition, there are six helpful lessons to be gleaned from
these narratives:

SIX LESSONS FROM THE
BEAUTIFUL, BUT BARREN:

1. **GOD HAS HIS OWN TIME FOR
    THE FULFILLMENT OF HIS PURPOSES:**

He knows exactly what we need and when we
need it. The difficulties we face are often a
result of our own vain efforts. An unknown
author wrote, "At all times there is within us a
degree of restlessness to be and to do, and yet
for weeks, or months or sometimes years we
are prevented from doing and being.

We feel impatient, we chafe, and become
discouraged. And yet one day God's perfect
time arrives; and we are fit, we are wiser, we
are ready to do what God wants to have done,
and He lets us do it."

From Isaac and Rebekah we learn to cling to a faith that will not falter. God can be trusted to fulfill His purposes - "In His Time."

2. **GOD'S TIMING MAY INCLUDE YEARS OF WAITING**

    Isaac prayed for Rebekah twenty years. Waiting requires patient trust and steadfast HOPE. In our fast-paced western society, we have come to expect immediate results; instant dinners, eyeglasses made in one hour, dry-cleaning done in one hour and instant credit. Waiting is just not conducive to our modern rapid-paced lifestyle. But, Scripture says that "God's ways are not our ways." There are lessons we can only learn from waiting on God.

3. **IMPATIENCE LEADS TO FRUSTRATION AND REMOVING THINGS FROM GOD'S CONTROL.**

    Someone wisely wrote, "Frustrations are a result of not seeing the opportunities." When we rush God's plan, we miss out on blessings God wants to give us. We must learn that God's way is far better than our way. The Psalmist wrote in Psalm 18:30 (NASB); "As for God, His way is perfect." Often, I have heard women say they "have placed things in God's hands." However, I see their lives as worry-filled and fretful. They hold back their trust from God and venture on their own pre-planned quest. In the midst of their fading faith, they lose patience and ask 'why?' Sarah's impatience led Abraham to father children by another woman. This was not

God's plan. God desires our undivided loyalty to His methods. He is omnipotent and doesn't require our assistance.

4. GOD HONORS FAITHFULNESS TO HIMSELF

In the midst of Hannah's heart-torn grief, she sought to live a devoted life for God and His purposes. The Lord honors a self-sacrificing spirit. We must ask, "Why do we want a child?" Is it just to relieve societal pressure from family and friends? Is it to have a child that will look, act and be like us? For the Christian woman the answer should be as Hannah's was; to offer that child in service to God and His purposes.

Hannah kept her vow to God and sacrificed young Samuel to temple life. God honored Hannah with additional sons. However, God's rewards are not always tangible. The spiritual strengths of peace of heart, steadfastness of faith and abiding joy cannot be measured materially. Yet, they are qualities of the Christian life that reap great dividends.

5. UNPLEASANT CIRCUMSTANCES CAN PRODUCE A BLESSING.

As we have learned through the scriptures, there was a social mark of disgrace upon barren women. God, in his great love, lifted that reproach; the result was unrestrained, joyful celebrations. The barren no longer had to endure stinging remarks from society. God has a way of turning disagreeable events into times of victory and HOPE.

6.   PATIENCE AND TRUST PRODUCE
    A GODLY CHARACTER.

Even through heartache and disappointment, a woman can cultivate a Christian character that allows God to shine through. Hannah's faith never faltered. But her's was not a benign faith of stoic resolution. She experienced intense agony and often wept before God in prayer day and night. Only through that experience could she rise up as a godly woman of immeasurable patience and trust. The products of her Christlike character stand as towers of examples to women who face continued sorrow and unfulfillment.

Finally, from these women, we learn that whatever our sorrow or loss, God is a comforting retreat. He will give us patience through our pain and trust through our turmoils.

CHAPTER 3

HOPE: THE SEARCH FOR A SOLUTION

For many couples, having a baby is not as easy as they thought it would be. Thousands of women are paying a high emotional and financial price to have a child.

"It's devastating. Money can't buy it for you." says Donna, who went through eight years of fertility treatments before adoption.

According to the American Fertility Society, infertility is the inability to achieve pregnancy after one year of regular, unprotected sexual relations, or the inability to carry a pregnancy to live birth.[12]

The incidence of infertility affects fifteen to twenty percent of married couples in the United States and rates are on the rise. More than 2.3 million American couples are infertile; and an estimated one in six couples between the ages of twenty-two and forty.

WHAT ARE THE CAUSES OF INFERTILITY?

Infertility affects men and women almost equally. Male infertility may be caused by insufficient or slow-moving sperm or defective live sperm, or a blocked sperm passage in the testicle.

There are four major causes of infertility in women:[13]

1. **OVULATION PROBLEMS:** A woman does not produce eggs at all or produces too little progesterone, preventing successful implantation of a fertilized egg.

2. **DAMAGE TO FALLOPIAN TUBES:** Can be caused by sexually transmitted diseases, endometriosis (presence of uterine tissue in the lower abdomen) or pelvic inflammatory disease (PID).

3. **CERVICAL PROBLEMS:** Infections or congenital abnormalities may block the cervical canal or affect production of cervical mucous.

4. **UTERINE DEFECTS:** Benign tumors or other malfunctions in the uterine lining may prevent embryo implantation.

WHAT TREATMENTS ARE AVAILABLE?

There are several conventional treatments. Depending on the type of infertility problem, a doctor may recommend one of the following:

1. **Fertility Drugs** are used for women with ovulating problems or for men with low sperm counts or for women with low hormone levels.

2. **Transcervical Balloon Tuboplasty** is a new technique for women with blocked or scarred Fallopian tubes. A woman is sedated and a tiny balloon is slipped into the Fallopian tube and inflated to clear any obstruction. This less invasive procedure may replace a surgical technique requiring general anesthesia, says Alan DeCherney, M.D., from Yale University medical school.

3. **Intrauterine Insemination** (also known as **artificial insemination**) is used for men with low sperm count, for women with cervical mucous problems, or for unexplained infertility. This procedure involves separating a man's sperm sample from the seminal fluid, and inserting the concentrated sperm directly into the women's uterine cavity.

If conventional treatments are ineffective, a doctor may suggest that a couple try **ART** (Assisted Reproductive Technology.) Although some infertility clinics claim success rates as high as 30%, the procedure works only 12% of the time according to the latest (1988) data of the American Fertility Society, a physician's group.

Dr. Francis Polansky, director of the Nova Fertility Clinic in San Mateo, California, recommends sticking to one treatment for no longer than six months. If it hasn't worked by then, stop wasting valuable time and switch to another approach.[14]

4. **In-Vitro Fertilization (IVF).** "Test tube" babies. A woman is given drugs to induce the ovaries to produce mature eggs, which are retrieved from the ovary and fertilized with a man's sperm in a petri dish. The resulting embryos are then transferred to the uterus (or they are frozen and used at a later date.) IVF has been used for women with blocked Fallopian tubes, endometriosis and for male infertility problems. It offers a last glimmer of hope for many.

Since the 1978 birth of the first "test tube baby" in Britain, IVF has moved into about 250 clinics in the USA. The field is strewn with disappointments: IVF is costly and success rates are frustratingly low.

Many women are wary of this procedure because of the ethical issue it raises; How far should a woman go in her quest for a child? Where is the line drawn from removing the situation from God's hands?

In my own life, I chose not to pursue many of the conventional treatments because I could not justify them in my own conscience. It is a choice that each woman must make between herself and God.

5. **Gamete Intrafallopian Transfer (GIFT)**: This treatment also involves retrieving a woman's eggs. But afterward the eggs are transferred into the Fallopian tube along with sperm so that fertilization can occur "naturally."

GIFT requires that a woman have healthy Fallopian tubes, but it is a good choice for women with mild endometriosis, cervical problems, or for men with low sperm counts or slow-moving sperm.

ON CHOOSING A CLINIC:

With prices ranging from $4-8,000 for a single IVF or GIFT treatment cycle, it is wise to select a clinic that has had success in treating your type of infertility.

PRECAUTIONS:

The American Fertility Society recommends that you ask:

1. What services are provided? Are conventional, less invasive and less expensive methods available as well as the more complicated ART?

2. How many doctors will participate in your case? Are one or more board certified in reproductive endocrinology? Is counseling provided?

3. What is the clinic's success rate for various ART procedures? Find out the "delivery rate" - the percentage of egg retrievals that have resulted in a delivery of a live baby. (A pregnancy rate alone is not a measure of success since pregnancy may result in miscarriage.)

If you would like additional information regarding infertility clinics across the nation, contact

The American Fertility Society.[15]
2140 11th Avenue, South Suite 200
Birmingham, AL 35205

Deborah, thirty-six and her husband, Kevin, thirty-nine, have spent nine years and $35,000 in infertility work-ups. But, they have no regrets, they say. They are only profoundly sorry medicine could not deliver them a child.[16]

On the other hand, thousands of women have been successfully treated. However, invasive infertility testing and surgery must be an individual decision. There are moral implications that must be faced; Is it morally right for a Christian woman to have artificial insemination from an anonymous donor? To what lengths are you willing to go to have a child?

Where is God? Are we leaving Him out completely in our search for a solution?

There is a point where you must weigh the emotional cost. Do you want a child at any cost? Do you simply want a child? Or do you long for your husband's child...a product of your love, devotion and faith? These are sobering questions that must be resolved.

I know because these same questions riddled my thoughts. They attacked my emotions with force once while we were on vacation in southern Africa.

The hot African sun scorched through the tall, dry grass. Inhaling the hot winds of the low mountain air, caused me to thirst. It had been a marvelous day at Mt. Zebra National Park. My in-laws were visiting from the states and we rented a chalet in this beautiful mountain resort area of southern Africa.

We spent the afternoon dipping in the cool waters of the resort pool. Later we enjoyed a safari through the park to view zebra in their natural habitat. A magnificent sight of black and white bodies standing boldly against a stark brown field. A gentle animal, they stood motionless when they spotted us at a distance.

That evening we enjoyed an Eland steak dinner at the chalet restaurant. We relaxed and basked in the scenic beauty from the deck. It was getting late and we were all tired from the events of the day, so we retired to bed.

Why was I feeling so restless since my in-laws arrived two weeks earlier? They were two of the best people anywhere. I had been anticipating their visit for months.

Finally, I realized. The emotional weight of my infertility began to weigh heavily on me. Chuck was the only son in his family of two sisters. I was not able to produce a grandchild for them. That night the emotional strain seemed more than I was able to bear.

With my face buried deep in my pillow, I wept softly until I could tolerate the aloneness no more.

Gently, I shook Chuck's arm. "Are you sleeping?" I cried.

"No," he replied.

"I need to talk to you." I sobbed.

He sat lovingly on the edge of the bed and held me in his arms...for quite some time...until all my tears seemed to flow out.

Finally, it gushed out. "I am feeling badly because we can't have children. With your mom and dad here, it has magnified the problem for me."

"It's all right. They aren't bothered about it. They have other grandchildren," he tried to console me.

This was one of the few times when my emotions were completely shattered. I was grasping for something that would stop the pain. "I would be willing to adopt if you want to."

It was the first time I had ever mentioned adoption. Once again Chuck's faith surfaced, "If God wants us to have a child, He will give us one."

Chuck continued to hold and comfort me - it brought great relief - it helped to release the floodgate on my fragile emotions.

God drew near and shared my pain; He soothed the wound. God gives HOPE to hurting couples. Trust Him.

CHAPTER FOUR

HOPE TOWARD WHOLENESS

Reaching For That Ray of Hope

Webster's dictionary meaning of the word 'whole' is "the entirety; a total; complete; entire; unbroken."[17]

The infertile woman has an insatiable desire to be made complete...unbroken...entire. The search for significance can dominate a woman's life; one's dreams for the future, one's relationship with others. Her quest for fulfillment becomes intensified as she seeks ways to repair the broken dreams.

Marilyn Heavilin, in her book, ***When Your Dreams Die***, describes the difference between destroyed dreams and damaged dreams:

> *Damaged dreams do not die; but they are altered severely. In some ways damaged dreams are even more difficult to deal with than dreams that have died because there is no permanent end to a damaged dream, no cut-off point where you can close the door on the old dream and start building a new dream. However, damaged dreams are usually salvageable to some extent. There is still hope.*[18]

Few crises are as challenging and overwhelming.

Yet, most of the attention is focused on the physical aspects of infertility. The emotional ones often go ignored or untreated. As a result, most people suffer intensely and alone. But, they don't have to; acknowledgement brings understanding and comfort.[19]

PHASES OF EMOTIONS

According to Serono Symposia, USA,[20] a couple will experience phases of emotions during extensive infertility treatments. Within these four stages there are eight steps through which individuals progress in their adjustment to infertility. There are some helpful coping methods for each stage.

STAGES OF ADJUSTMENT

1. **REALIZATION AND ACKNOWLEDG-MENT:** Numbness and shock are common emotions upon the initial diagnosis of infertility.

The "This-can't-be-happening-to-me" attitude forms the initial buffer for the later stages of emotional stress.

Jenny remembers her intense feelings during her infertility evaluation:

> *I remember feeling overwhelmed - the bottom of my stomach felt like it was falling out. I stayed in a state of shock for about a week. I was so threatened. I couldn't talk to anyone. Then I pulled myself together and set up a schedule for the procedures: The schedule made me feel more in control.*

HOW TO COPE: Work together as a couple; try to go to doctor's appointments together. Talk about your fears and frustrations with your husband.

Write down questions when visiting the doctor.

It is natural to experience emotions such as denial: guilt, blame, and self-pity.

2. EVALUATION AND DIAGNOSIS: During this phase, couples are searching for answers. The testing period can be grueling; anxiety-producing and expensive. There may be a lack of privacy due to invasive tests. A woman may experience shame and embarrassment over not functioning "normally." Sometimes there is an intense need for secrecy, which breeds isolation.

Gina remembers the anxiety she and her husband experienced:

> Richard was very self-conscious about our problem. He wouldn't let me tell anyone. I felt isolated from my family and friends. I had always been close to my mother, and I told her everything. Now I had to shut her out. I felt that her questions were intrusive and that she would never be able to understand our problems.

HOW TO COPE: At this point, often infertility dominates a person's life. It is the peak stress point. Some common feelings may be:

Anger At Infertility ruling your life without permission. *Frustration* over treatment that doesn't guarantee a baby, after spending so much time, money and emotional energy. *Anger* at passivity required to be injected, scanned, dosed, and operated on.

RESIST ISOLATION FROM OTHERS:

Because of pressure from family and friends, infertile couples take measures to change their social networks. Many couples alter their pattern of social interaction with family and friends. They purposely avoid situations which reinforce their failure in fertility. Events such as baby showers and family reunions are avoided. Friendships fade as the childless retreat in the face of a child-oriented world.[21]

I remember one example of this from my own life. Being a private person by nature, I had to strongly resist isolating myself from others by avoiding certain social settings.

It was October and we were approaching the summer season in South Africa. Chuck and I were attending a Pastors' and Wives' Retreat at a scenic resort area. White and black-roofed thatched rondowels sat surrounding a quiet man-made lake. A perfect place for refreshment and opportunity to absorb nature.

Chuck had decided to golf that afternoon with some other pastors. A black cloud of depression loomed over me. Thoughts of my infertility began to consume my thoughts and emotions. I knew that evening I would have to attend a social function that would necessitate new introductions. I did not want to face the inevitable question, "Do you have children?"

I withdrew in the hut - alone - and crawled into a cocoon of isolation. I tried praying, but God seemed to be absent. Depression deepened...feelings of great sadness and loneliness gripped me. Somehow, I was able to recognize them and realize where they were coming from. Then, God seemed to move in.

I knew I would need to make a conscious effort to resist withdrawing from others. I remember saying to God, "If only I had a friend, someone who could understand how I feel."

About a half hour later a knock came at the front door. I resisted the urge to ignore it, climbed off the bed, wiped the wetness from my eyes and walked to open the door.

There stood Sheryl; an American, the wife of a minister and herself an ordained minister. I admired and respected her very much. Smilingly she said, "Are you busy?" Why don't you come down with me for afternoon tea and fellowship with the other ladies?"

'Fellowship?' I sighed to myself. 'Just what I'm trying to avoid.' I felt, but resisted, a gentle nudging from the Lord.

"Oh, thanks very much, but I have slacks on and I don't feel like changing." I reasoned.

"That's no problem, be relaxed and come along with me," she offered.

Finally, I yielded, and we walked along the narrow path down to the recreation hall. She may never know how God used her that day to repair my splintered emotions. It seemed the moment I walked alongside her in that brilliant African sunlight, my gloom dissipated. She helped me to refocus my attention from self-pity.

That afternoon I enjoyed pleasant friendships with some remarkable women whom I will always hold special in my heart of meaningful memories.

3. **TREATMENT PHASE:** The treatment phase can cause considerable emotional stress. Jennifer is thirty-seven. She shares how she mourned every month:

> *Every time I get my period, I feel a*
> *lot of sadness and grief.*

A couple grieves the loss, even though it is something potential, not actual. And herein lies the difficulty, because there is no ritual to mourn something that is invisible month after month, year after year.[22]

HOW TO COPE: Consider restructuring your life if treatment becomes overwhelming. It may be necessary to stop treatment for a while. Try to keep your original closeness with your spouse; don't think of lovemaking only to produce a baby. It will become clinical and you will lose the romance. Seek emotional support from a counselor, pastor or support group such as RESOLVE.

4. **RESOLUTION:** Resolution can come through three avenues; adoption, pregnancy, or acceptance.

ADOPTION: For Gina and Richard, resolution came one and one-half years later when they adopted a healthy baby girl. Gina says, "I can't believe I failed to become pregnant. I thought surely I would be pregnant by now; I was totally frustrated. Although Richard and I were communicating and getting along, I knew we needed outside help. We just couldn't deal with our emotions."

RICHARD: "The support group enabled me to talk about my guilt. I hadn't even given adoption a thought until we met the adoptive parents in our group. Gina started pushing for adoption. It took me a long time to understand that I could truly love a child even if the baby didn't have my genes. After a lot of discussion with Gina and the group, I decided that I could happily adopt a child. For the first time, I grew hopeful."

PREGNANCY: Excitedly, Rachel shares, "We received incredible news; I was pregnant. The doctor had to tell me three times. I was numb, thrilled, and excited and afraid all at the same time. I was relieved that I wouldn't have to go through anymore infertility tests. But then I was deeply suspicious. I was frozen with fear that something would happen to the baby...a mis-carriage, a still birth. I couldn't believe after all I had gone through that I would really have a child."

(Nine months later, Rachel had a healthy baby boy.)

ACCEPTANCE: After a year of drug therapy, Susan was still not pregnant. Exhausted emotionally, physically and financially, the Smiths decided to stop treatment and considered the possibility of not having children. Susan recalls:

"I couldn't take it any longer...I was running on empty. It felt futile to continue. I needed to stop turning myself and my husband upside down for a child that might never be. Our infertility was a fact, but Chad and I still had each other. We loved each other in a deeper way after all we had been through...I still don't understand why I can't have children, but at least I can learn to accept the fact that there is no reason why. I decided to go back to school and get a degree in nursing. If I couldn't have a child, I still wanted to nurture and help others."[23]

Amy Carmichael, missionary to India wrote in her book, *Toward Jerusalem:*

> *He said, 'I will accept the breaking sorrow*
> *which God tomorrow*
> *Will to His Son explain.'*
> *Then did the turmoil deep within me cease.*
> *Not vain the word, not vain;*
> *For in acceptance lieth peace.*

Before reaching the final phase of resolution, many painful paths will be taken. The path to acceptance may take years. For Jane and her husband, it was nearly fifteen years before the emotional torment subsided.

HOW TO COPE: Talk to others who have successfully resolved their infertility. Stop trying to conceive before despondency and helplessness become uncontrollable. The point of acceptance is easier to live with than a life of despair...I know.

Focus on your spouse and get involved in meaningful activities together. This will cement your marital bond and love for one another. Outdoor activities from river rafting to mountain climbing in Africa (a first for me!) helped us to focus off our problem and marvel at God's handiwork in nature.

There is HOPE in resolving childlessness. Knowing that you are not alone in your struggle, that your feelings of grief, anger and guilt are shared by other women who struggle for wholeness, can do much to assuage your aloneness. Keep reaching for that ray of HOPE.

CHAPTER FIVE

HOPE FOR HURTING COUPLES

"It's a gnawing ache that never goes away," Karen shared, her brown eyes brimming with tears. I sat across the kitchen bar from her clinging tightly to the warmth of my tea cup. How well I remembered that pain.

"John and I are becoming distant. He doesn't seem to understand how much it hurts. It's affecting our marriage," she quietly confessed. I reached to refill her tea cup as she continued to release the floodgate on her carefully guarded emotions.

The on-going crisis of childlessness causes tremendous stress on individuals and couples. Infertility affects every part of a couple's relationship with self and others. It can produce a negative impact on the marital relationship as Karen was experiencing.[24]

It affects a woman's view of her self-worth, particularly as she perceives her role as a wife. Finally, infertility affects relationships with others. New friendships are not cultivated due to a tendency to isolationism.

As the stressors are identified, a woman can gain confidence to cope.

HOW INFERTILITY IMPACTS
THE MARITAL RELATIONSHIP

You become so serious. It can take on a life of its own. A woman can become so lost in her own sorrow -

so isolated in self-absorption that she cannot observe her spouse's level of grief. She must remember...he hurts, too.

Shapiro identifies the couple's response to infertility as both a crisis and a mourning process. He identifies two types of crises:

1. An expected crisis in the life cycle such as a first child leaving for school or a last child leaving home.
2. Unanticipated life crisis such as infertility. Since it is unexpected, most couples have not developed coping mechanisms to respond to the hurt that accompanies the inability to conceive or bear a child.[25]

HOW INFERTILITY AFFECTS
SELF ESTEEM

The stress of infertility has remarkable affects on a woman's self-worth. It hinders close relationships with others and clouds her concept of God. The question surfaces, "If God is so loving and caring, why doesn't he give us a child?"

Infertility affects the interpersonal need for a positive self-image. It is important to a woman to receive information and feedback that she is liked, valued, and respected. She needs to sense that she is loved and needed by others.

A close, warm relationship with a spouse can help to meet these important needs. Without that support, a woman will be prone to feelings of low self-worth and unfulfillment.

Chuck always remembered special days with thoughtful gifts. Also, there were many times when he would surprise me with a beautiful card in which he expressed his continued love and appreciation. Those times always made me feel very special, needed, and appreciated by the most valued person in my life...Childless women need to feel important to someone.

INFERTILITY AFFECTS SELF-EXPRESSION

There is often a strong desire to show self-expression. The infertile woman needs to be encouraged to do so.

I received a great sense of satisfaction and accomplishment when I would resort to a quilting project, do calligraphy, cross stitch or create music at the piano.

Another important interpersonal need is to receive encouragement and reinforcement to express positive and negative thoughts and feelings about self, current situations and plans for the future.

Again, it was my husband who met this important need in my life. Over the years we developed good communication. On long driving trips, I would often share my feelings with him. Always he was ready to listen and share suggestions. It helped tremendously to vocalize my needs and sad feelings. That communication created a strong bond between us.

INFERTILITY AFFECTS GUIDANCE NEEDS

Some women may need guidance and assistance in appraisal goal setting, problem definitions, problem solving, decision making and coping strategies. Particularly with long-term infertility when a woman has not reached resolution.

Often a woman feels there is no real direction in her life. Planning for a future without children seems pointless. She may be at a loss to identify a purpose for her life. Here is where a pastor, a friend in resolution, or a Christian psychologist will be able to offer direction and meaning to her life.

Barren women need to be encouraged to develop talents and gifts. This may mean enrolling in an adult education class at a local college, or pursuing art and music appreciation. It is vital that she be encouraged to develop new interests. She must keep involved in the church and the community.

INFERTILITY AFFECTS
RELATIONSHIPS WITH OTHERS

There is an increasing tendency to withdraw and isolate yourself from new social situations. The reason is, to avoid the inevitable question, "Do you have children?"

Holiday family gatherings are often uncomfortable. It is less painful to stay away.

God has given us wonderful churches to serve in Ohio, South Africa, and Texas. Folks have always been considerate of us being alone for the holidays. Always there is a family or two who invites us to share the holiday festivities with them. Often, we decline their generous invitations. To see families with their children and homes filled with laughter, makes us realize that we may never have that, and that we might grow old alone.

INFERTILITY GIVES A
CLOUDY CONCEPT OF GOD

The 'why me?' syndrome can rush over you in waves. It is especially difficult to see children born to parents who are not capable of adequately providing for their basic needs. Or worse yet, to see children born into abusive homes. I would endlessly see these situations and cry, "Why isn't God giving US a child?" It is easy to reason, "God must be angry with me." Disappointment with God must be guarded against because it can lead to spiritual decline. It is at this crucial point where absolute faith, trust and confidence in God's omniscience must be sought.

SOCIETAL PRESSURES

"You mean you don't have children, yet?"

"No children? So, you are foot-loose and fancy-free."

These are examples of the thoughtless and inaccurate comments by well-meaning friends and relatives. They emphasize the expectations that society places on having children. These pressures include, religious, cultural, and social values. They promote guilt and feelings of failure for infertile couples.

I remember three years ago sitting in an interview with a Church Board. They were in the process of calling a new pastor to their church. My husband was one candidate. One board member sat at the opposite end of the table. He questioned my husband, "Since you do not have children, how will you be able to counsel parents that may come to you for guidance with their wayward teenagers?"

I felt that old stab of pain, but sat silently beside Chuck. Wisely the district superintendent responded, "Sir, with that line of thinking you must feel that a man has to have served a prison term in order to minister effectively to prisoners." The board member clearly got the message.

Another man wondered, "Since you don't have children and there are only two of you, how do you feel about living in a big parsonage?"

My response to him was that their parsonage was smaller than the lovely twelve room manse we formerly lived in.

I give these examples only to emphasize the societal pressures on infertile couples. These good men showed hesitancy over our childlessness. Yet, not once did they express interest in my husband's ministerial experience and capabilities.

I have learned through these situations, to show courtesy and kindness in response to careless questioning. I have never allowed bitterness to take root. God can give you a gentle spirit.

THERE IS HOPE

The stress of infertility can disrupt virtually every aspect of a couple's life. "However, for a lot of couples the marriage gets better because the experience makes them assess their values and who they are and the meaning of their relationship," says Linda Applegarth, clinical instructor at Cornell University Medical College.

We have known few marriages with the depth of love and devotion that Chuck and I experience. We still walk hand in hand in the shopping malls. He reaches over and takes my hand while driving the car. We devote time to each other's needs and interests. He has walked through hundreds of dress shops with me...never a complaint! We enjoy unity and oneness that is inseparable and value our relationship as a priceless, rare treasure.

GAINING CONFIDENCE TO
COPE IN YOUR MARRIAGE

Remember, he has hurts, too. But God made men somewhat less emotional than women. They are masters at not wanting to reveal their soft side; they set a guard on their emotions and appear less vulnerable. Yet, their pain can be buried just as deep as ours.

Don't assume because your husband doesn't discuss your childlessness that he doesn't care or understand. Often their pain is too deep to voice. Ask God for patience and understanding and respect his privacy. Spend time together. Often. Togetherness creates a close lasting bond.

CHAPTER SIX

HOPE THROUGH ADOPTION

The National Committee for Adoption estimates that there are some 60,000 United States adoptions each year, including 10,000 from other countries.[26]

There is beauty to adoption, and symmetry as well. In an infant adoption, birth parents typically give their child better prospects than they can provide at a complicated time in their own lives; adoptive parents find, in the tiniest of packages, the answer to their desperate prayers.[27]

However, we will discover in this chapter that adoption is not for everyone. There are risks and consequences top be considered. It is important that both husband and wife fully agree that this is the direction God wants you to pursue.

For some, adoption is an avenue of HOPE.

This chapter is addressed to you who are pondering the question, "Is adoption right for me?"

All of us are aware that there are many children who desperately need homes and families to love them. However, numerous factors should be considered before a final decision is made. The ultimate question that must be answered is, "Will an adopted child fill the aching void in my life? Do I want a child, or do I want OUR child?"

To some of you, any adopted child will fill that great chasm of pain. To others, only a child produced by your own body will eliminate the brutal pain of infertility.

But, only *you* are able to make that decision. In Collette Dywasuk's book, ***Adoption, Is It For You?***, she writes,

> *Adoption has ancient roots. The Biblical account of the infant Moses' adoption by the Pharoah's daughter is probably the best known, earliest recorded adoption. Though adoption was provided for in early Roman law and carried on in European civil law, its prime purpose was to supply the adopter with an heir.*
>
> *It was not particularly for the benefit of homeless children. Only persons over twenty-one could be adopted and only those over fifty could adopt.*
>
> *Outraged by the cruel binding out of defenseless, often brutally abused, parentless children, public opinion demanded reform. Safeguards were first recorded in the USA in 1851, when Massachusetts passed a statute permitting legal adoption. By 1929 every state had passed the same kind of adoption legislation..." Since that time, enormous strides have been made regarding the adoption process.* [28]

WEIGHING THE RISKS OF ADOPTION

The American Academy of Pediatrics states in its manual on adoption that "the risks inherent in adoption are essentially the same as those inherent in family life generally."[29]

There may be defects as the child grows older, injury from accidents, illnesses, even possibly death. All of these things are unpredictable whether or not the child is adopted. Are you willing to become vulnerable to the heartbreak and distress that these problems will entail?

Some people show much concern about the child's unknown heredity as an added risk. Modern medical science has now identified more than 2,000 genetic diseases many of which don't appear until late in life. What part will a child's heredity play in his life--his personality--his future?

How will he grow up? To what extent will he be influenced by his background? Ann Perrot Rose, the author of *Room For One More*, writes, "Heredity gives you something and your environment makes you use it, misuse it, or throw it away." The most important influence on a child's future is not his heredity, but rather his home-life during his early formative years.

CONSIDER THE CONSEQUENCES:

Many couples wonder if the child will "fit" into their family? Will he look like, be like, seem like, feel like a part of the family? The decisions must be made whether or not you can accept and love him as part of your family.

Adoptive parents wonder what their children will think and feel about them in later years--will they want to be reunited with their birth parents?

Ann Kiemel Anderson, author and mother of two adopted sons, wrote in her book, *And With The Gift Came Laughter*, "Although I try to resolve my fears, I continually am afraid that when Taylor and Brock get older, they will somehow resent me...will they resent having me for a mother?"[30]

When they reach their teens, some adopted children do develop a consuming interest in their "secret" background. They feel intense yearnings to understand what adoption means to their lives. Even though children almost always feel loved, adoption doesn't free them from struggling with their past and present at each stage of development.

A generation ago, many parents tried to keep adoption a secret - often from the children themselves. Psychologists genuinely agree that it is a mistake to withhold information about their birth parents from children. Even though adoptive parents may spend tremendous effort in the initial explanation of adoption to their children, sometimes they fail to realize that they will continue to deal with the topic for years to come. Questions about relinquishment, "Why didn't they keep me?" "Did you have to pay for me?"- are common. Kids are also curious about their birth parents' appearance and whether they have siblings.[31]

However, the majority of adults who were adopted as children said they would not want to locate their natural parents. Others, who have made contact after many years, have regretted the reunion. One example is my friend, Marie.

Marie, is a first grade school teacher. At ten months of age she was placed in a foster home. In that Christian home, she felt loved. When I asked her when she first discovered she was a foster child, she smiled and replied, "I always knew it. But, because I felt loved, it didn't seem to matter."

She was never curious to find her birth mother. However in 1989, she and her husband were planning a trip to Syracuse, New York to visit relatives. They both knew that her birth mother lived in that area, as well.

When they arrived at a motel in Syracuse, her husband looked in the phone directory under Marie's maiden name. "Do you want me to call this number? I'm sure it is your mother," he questioned? "I don't know if I want to?" Marie hesitated. "I think we should," urged Dave.

The call was made and the question confirmed; it was Marie's birth mother; yes, they would meet the next evening at a restaurant.

Marie felt nervous and apprehensive about meeting her mother for the first time in over forty years. 'How would her mother react when meeting her? Should she show emotions and hug her?'

Marie's reunion was one of profound disappointment. The woman was late...'perhaps she decided not to come,' worried Marie. A glance at the doorway revealed a gray haired woman in her sixties, tall and heavily built. She was dressed simply in a cotton summer dress. The woman stood expressionless and when introduced to Marie showed no hint of emotion.

"Why did you give away four little girls?" questioned Marie's husband.

"My husband didn't want them. Everybody is different," she flatly replied.

Sadly, Marie was sorry that her mother gave no apologies or further explanation, other than her father is out of prison and living in Rochester, New York.

Today, Marie is grateful to God for entrusting her to the care of fine Christian foster parents. She is also the mother of two lovely teenagers.

There are risks in the adoption process that you must come to terms with. You must have faith in the child and enough confidence in yourself to believe that your adopted child can develop his full potential.

If the unknown factors of the child's heredity bother you, if you feel uneasy and unduly threatened by the responsibility, this is probably an indication that adoption is NOT for you. You may never feel comfortable adopting.

The readiness and ability to accept the risks involved are important factors in deciding whether or not to adopt.[32]

Attend seminars or courses on adoption. Group meetings discuss questions like:

"How do you feel about raising a child to whom someone else gave birth?"

"Would you be upset if your child wanted to seek out his or her birth mother?"

"When and how do you tell children they are adopted?"

"How do you deal with insensitive remarks like, 'Maybe now you'll be able to have one of your own.'?"

Adoption isn't for everyone. It's something you have to be happy with in the long run. You must ask, "Is having a child more important than having a biological one?"

Hope that the love you share, the security you afford your child will give him strength and self-assurance he will need to face the questions, "Who am I? Why am I here?"

You must believe and feel in your heart that you will be able to love that child as your own. If not, it may not be fair to seek relief from your pain of infertility through an adopted child. They need unconditional, unreserved love and acceptance. Remember that adoption is not always a pill for the pain.

IF YOU CHOOSE NOT TO ADOPT

The longer a couple remains childless, there will always be those individuals who will view them as self-absorbed. "After all," they reason, "why haven"t they adopted if they cannot have children of their own?"

In the course of our twenty childless years, I am certain there were good people who made such careless remarks.

If you decide against adoption, societal and family pressures will increase. People are shocked to discover that you have been married fifteen or more years without children (few people consider infertility as a reason). The social stigma is not nearly as great when you have only been married a few years.

You have to determine whether you have the courage to face these attitudes and pressures.

For childless women, the risks of adoption must be weighed against...aloneness...lack of fulfillment and purpose in life. The final question to resolve is, "Will adoption assuage the emotional pain and bring meaning to my life?" "Or, must I seek, with God, other avenues of wholeness?"

Each woman must discover her own path to resolution: prayerfully, the quest should be sought.

MYTH vs. FACT:

MYTH: "A couple without children is missing something; their lives are just not complete."

FACT: Children do not necessarily make a marriage happy. Happiness is a choice with or without children.

If adoption is for you, God will place the desire in your hearts to adopt. I believe God chooses specific couples to be in a position to adopt.

Ask HIM to always guide your path.

CHAPTER SEVEN

HOPE THROUGH FRIENDSHIPS

A Daisy

A daisy
Such a delicate object
A symbol of friendship.
Each petal signifies something to me;
The first petal is for honesty
The second for encouragement
The third for love
The fourth for Christian unity
And the fifth for integrity.
Today, I would not only like to give you
A handful of petals
But rather a whole daisy
As a symbol of our friendship.
Take it, it's yours.[33]

Michelle '88

WHAT IS FRIENDSHIP?

A friend is someone who is valuable in time of need:

> *Do not forsake your own friend or your*
> *father's friend, and do not go to your broth-*
> *er's house in the day of your calamity;*
> *Better is a neighbor who is near than a*
> *brother far away.*
> (Proverbs 27:10 NASB).

A friend is someone who is always faithful.

A friend Loves at all times.
(Proverbs 17:17a NASB).

The book of Proverbs emphasizes the whole area of relationships, but it pays close attention to the matter of friendships. Why are friendships so important? What role do they play in our times of distress and anguish?

THE FUSION OF FRIENDSHIP

Several years ago a Christian magazine offered a prize for the best definition of friendship. Thousands of answers were received but the one given first prize was this:

"A friend is the one who comes in when the world has gone out."

A friendship can be frightening, exciting, and at times exhausting. But it can also open up new possibilities, new trails, new adventures, new territories and new continents. We live deprived lives if we live without friends.

Selwyn Hughes says, "Because I have felt safe with them (friends), I have been able to reveal myself and in the revealing, I have come to know myself in a way that I could never have done with a mere acquaintance."[34]

ALLOW TIME FOR FRIENDSHIPS TO DEVELOP

Some relationships you have with people may never develop into close friendships. Don't be upset about that. If you are open and friendly, then God will guide you and show you where deep friendships are to be developed.

Remember that the opposite of friendship is isolation. We know that can result in damaged emotions. "The world is so empty," said Goethe; "if one thinks only of mountains, rivers, and cities, but to know someone here and there who thinks and feels with us and, though distant, is close to us in spirit, this makes earth an inhabited garden."

God made us for relationships and it is His will and purpose that we cultivate close friendships.

Robert Veninga says, "A close friend is one who opens the door a crack and lets light into the room."[35]

Let me share with you how God used friends in my life to smooth the rough places. Without those friends, the quest for a child would have been more wrenching and more lonely.

CALLED AND CAPABLE

She was my husband's college English professor; a warm people-person. A called and capable woman of God, she earned her Doctor of Ministry degree when she was beyond fifty years of age. A woman of exquisite tastes, her home reflects peace, serenity, and her love for beauty.

In the three years we lived in Colorado Springs, Colorado, I developed a cherished and respected friendship with her. Because I still hold her in such high esteem, today, sixteen years later, I can only refer to her as Mrs. Williams. Her students affectionately call her "Dr. J."

During my initial infertility workup in Ohio, she

phoned from Colorado to invite us to their home for a ski vacation. During our week's stay in their lovely mountain-view home, I shared with her my heartache and confusion. Her wise counsel reflects her godliness, "Anna-Marie, I don't know why God won't give you a child. Pray Hannah's prayer. Tell God how you are feeling. I will remember to pray for you every day."

I am grateful that she cared and was willing to carry a prayer-burden. Today, if I had an urgent need for prayer support, she would be one friend I would be sure to contact.

SHARING A COMMON BOND

It was a Friday afternoon and I promised to visit a friend's garage sale in West Carrollton, Ohio. As I climbed out of my car, I noticed a young woman of about thirty-five with full, shoulder length bobbed, brunette hair walking toward me. Alongside of her toddled the most adorable looking three-year-old little girl I had ever seen. Long brunette, natural curls bounced below her shoulders. "What a beautiful child!" I thought.

Cookie Kapsch introduced me to herself and her little girl, Sarah. She too, was visiting the garage sale as she was the new neighbor of my friend, Linda. Cookie and I had an instant rapport - a magnetism of personalities that was rare for me. That moment began our journey of a close, warm friendship. Soon, I would learn of Cookie's inability to carry a pregnancy to live birth. She had a history of four miscarriages before Sarah's birth. Here was a person who knew the pain of childlessness - the steps to recovery - the emotional scarring.

Several months later I stood and held her hand as we wept together. Shortly a nurse would come into her hospital room and wheel her into surgery to remove the tiny child who had died inside her womb. The next Sunday she had to leave church during the choir special because she was so overcome with painful memories of her recent loss. I saw her leave and went out to find her sitting alone in her car, weeping. I held her hand and we cried together.

Someone has said that our pain helps us to understand another's pain. Cookie was such a person to me; a great support during my infertility work-up. I knew she cared deeply and understood exactly where I was and what kinds of emotions I had to deal with. For she had traveled the same rocky path; we were in pursuit of the same quest.

WHAT IS A FRIEND

"How many friends do you think you will have in a lifetime?" asked my senior English teacher.

Hands raised all over the classroom.

"One hundred," quipped one handsome football player.

"Fifty"

"Six," said soft-spoken Kevin.

"You are closest, Kevin." replied Miss Balfour. "You will be most fortunate in your lifetime if you acquire three true friends."

'Three friends!' I exclaimed to myself. Her assumption seemed absurd to my seventeen-year-old mind.

However, more than twenty years later, her wise words are ringing true. In a lifetime, we will have met countless numbers of acquaintances. But, the treasure of a true and lasting friendship is a rare find.

A FOREVER FRIEND

A single, pretty brunette in her mid-twenties, my new South African friend had a maturity and spiritual sensitivity beyond her years. God sent her into my life to bring sunshine, fun and laughter. Although I never voiced my infertility with her, somehow I sensed her great empathy and gentleness. Not once did she offer insensitive remarks.

Michelle was a perceptive thinker who often wrote outstanding poetry which reflected her ability to absorb nature and display appreciation for God's beauty. Often, she would pop in and out of the manse. How I enjoyed her friendship of spontaneity and helpfulness. A caring, giving person, my home and office today is scattered with remembrances of her continued friendship.

She taught me a valuable lesson; that in order to have friends you must be a friend.

Sometimes her mood was quiet and reflective as we walked along white-sand beaches on the Indian Ocean in southern Africa. At other times her honesty surfaced: "You look like you were hit with a truck!" she gasped.

Chuck and I had just arrived from an eight hour car journey to Cape Town. On the way, I had a severe allergic reaction to a dust mite from a cottage we had stayed in the night before. Burning with fever, swollen sinuses and general lethargy, I was bedfast in a friend's guest house when Michelle arrived to welcome us to her home town. I must have looked as badly as I felt, considering her reaction.

Groggily, I opened my eyes. There she stood - hovering over me with a look of sheer shock on her face and a beautiful, fresh, red rose in her hand. Her sweet visit lifted my spirits. **A silent partner in my struggle.**

AN UNDERSTANDING FRIEND

Marise is a vivacious, single South African woman with whom God allowed me to develop a deep, lasting friendship. That God sent her my way is beyond doubt. Marise often sought my counsel and support as she tried to resolve the issue of singleness in her life. Issues of loneliness and isolation - insensitive remarks by well-meaning people at times engulfed her with despair. For example, one man walked up to her in church, brushed her shoulder with his hand then laughingly commented, "I'm just dusting you off because you have been sitting on the shelf so long."

At an ocean-side ladies' retreat, she asked if she could talk with me privately. I read pain and brokenness all over her face. Tears brimming her lovely brown eyes, she began to unburden the heaviness of her heart.

Listening to her anguish, I felt the Lord nudging me to share with her the similarities I faced in childlessness.

Stunned, I could not believe the Lord would want me to do this, yet I kept sensing His insistent urging. "Lord," I responded silently, "You know I don't share my problem with anyone; this is a personal, private issue. Besides Marise is a single young woman. How can the knowledge of my emotional pain bring comfort to her situation?" Still, I felt the Lord's nudging.

Following that time of mutual sharing, God forged a friendship between us and used her in my life as a tremendous tool of encouragement.

When she decided to take a job transfer to Johannesburg (a twelve hour drive by car), I grieved that distance would separate us. Yet, she kept in touch with caring letters and phone calls. Today, four years later and separated by oceans of water, our friendship is still vital and meaningful.

"A good friend is one who assures you that you can meet not only this challenge, but any challenge that life might put in your path."[36]

FRIENDSHIPS MATTER

Soldiers throughout history have learned one important lesson: Friendships matter. If you must enter any field of battle, have one good friend who will stick with you."[37]

Few of us are fortunate enough to be untouched by loss or pain. Yet, paradoxically, it is when we are suffering pain and grief that we feel most alive. With God we can discover ways to help assuage the pain. And one of those ways is by cultivating friendships. Reach out. Ask God to send a friend into your life, someone you can share openly with, someone who will empathize with your need to be under stood.

A listening, caring friend can be a healing and soothing balm.

A NEW-FOUND FRIEND

Briskly and confidently she walked into the adult Sunday School class a few minutes late. She was introduced as Gala; a young Russian woman of thirty-four. She spoke little English as she had just arrived in America one month earlier. Following class, I made my way over to welcome her. She reached for my extended hand warmly and I showed her into the sanctuary for the morning worship service.

Two weeks later on a Thursday evening, the door bell rang at the parsonage. I was surprised to see our new Russian friend standing with a white bag in her hand.

"Gala. How nice to see you. Welcome"

"Thank you," she smiled. "A present for you," she said as she handed me the bag she had been holding. In it were six lovely, hand-painted wooden dolls from Russia.

"How beautiful! Thank you very much, Gala."

"You are welcome."

Our conversation was slow and concentrated. Often she had to refer to her Russian/English dictionary.

Slowly, I ventured, "Gala, in Russia, did you go to church?"

"In Russia, no Nazarene Church, no Baptist Church, no Methodist Church. House church. Every Sunday, every Tuesday with my mother and brother," she proceeded with slow, faltering English.

We spoke of her father who died two years earlier, of her city of one million people along the Volga river.

After about an hour of visiting, she looked at me and shyly asked, "Maria (the name by which she referred to me) twenty years, you, no children?" Apparently she had been asking someone in the church whether or not we had children. They told her of our inability to have a child after twenty years of marriage.

"Problem, Maria?" she inquired.

"Yes, several problems."

She offered, "I married twelve years, no babies. Very difficult. Cry, cry, cry every day."

"Have you seen a doctor in Russia?" I asked.

"Yes, many doctors, many hospitals. They say, 'no babies, no babies, no babies.'

Here was a young woman from another country and another culture, experiencing the same hurt and hopelessness of any other barren women. I encouraged her to see a doctor here in America and to keep HOPING.

During the course of the next month we began to forge a lovely friendship...she asked me to teach her how to make pizza and she taught me how to make Russian perog...a magnificent savory tart.

Yesterday, she had to return to Russia; some technical problem with her visa in Moscow. I saw her off at the airport in Lubbock. We embraced with tears brimming in each of our eyes. I watched her walk alone down that long narrow corridor onto the American Airline Boeing 747. She does not have a return ticket to America, but longs to come back to be with her husband who remained. There is a strong possibility that I may never see her again.

I pray that God was able to use me to offer her hope and trust on her quest for a child.

Friends. They are special people God sends into our lives - for a time - for memories - for comfort. They HOPE with us, and for us.

CHAPTER EIGHT

HOPE THROUGH THE WORD

"There is no substitute remedy for the pains of life; we must saturate ourselves in the Scripture," says Florence Littauer in her book, ***Hope For Hurting Women.***[38]

IMMERSE YOURSELF IN GOD'S WORD

Hope for me came through scriptural inspiration, not religious answers; "Trust God, He knows best," Or, "All things work together for good." Even though these statements are true, they offer little hope.

Instead, God soothed my emotional anguish through reading His Word. For instance, in Psalm 16, the Lord reminded me of the need to constantly keep my focus on Him. His Word promises me that when I do this, my life will exude joy and gladness.

PSALM 16:7-9 (NASB)

I will bless the Lord who counseled me;
Indeed my mind instructs me in the night.
I have set the Lord continually before me;
Because He is at my right hand, I will not be
shaken.
Therefore my heart is glad, and my glory
rejoices;
My flesh also will dwell securely.

In the still, quiet hours of late night when we wrestle with anguish and hard questions, the words of the Psalmist brings comfort: (God) "instructs me in the night," because we know God is ever with us, we deliberately choose not to allow circumstances to rock our faith. The result is a glad heart!

A RESCUE

Living in the scenic coastal city of Port Elizabeth, South Africa, we had close access to the magnificent emerald blue beaches of the Indian Ocean. It was low tide early one morning and I was wading out to knee-deep warm waters with my back to the sea. Reveling in the quietness of the morning, I saw the hot African sun reflecting off the white sand dunes. Suddenly, I felt a jolt as a crashing wave rushed over my head thrusting me face down on the floor of the sea. Several seconds later, I surfaced...dazed...without sunglasses or beach hat. The tidal wave swept with great force. Suddenly...Unexpectedly...Without warning.

Often the emotional pain of childlessness surfaces itself just like that giant wave at sea - catching me off guard and leaving me shaken and bewildered. God's Word always provides the needed rescue.

JEREMIAH 29:11 (NASB)

For I know the plans I have for you, declares the Lord. Plans for welfare and not calamity to give you a future and a hope.

Following five, ten then fifteen years of the fading hope of having a child, one day I felt particularly discouraged when the Lord led me to a promise which provided great encouragement and lasting hope. In Psalm 13, David was crying for help in the face of hopelessness:

PSALM 13:1-6 (NASB)

How long, O Lord? Wilt thou forget me forever?
How long wilt thou hide thy face from me?
How long shall I take counsel in my soul,
Having sorrow in my heart all the day?
How long will my enemy be exalted over me?
Consider and answer me, O Lord my God;
Enlighten my eyes lest I sleep the sleep of death,
Lest my enemy say, "I have overcome him,"
Lest my adversaries rejoice when I am shaken.
But I have trusted in thy lovingkindness;
My heart shall rejoice in thy salvation.
I will sing to the Lord,
Because He has dealt bountifully with me.

David felt his enemies were scoffing at him. Have you ever asked God, "How long? How long? How long? Victory and hope were restored to David when he TRUSTED (verse 5) in God's lovingkindness. He discovered that God saw his state of hopelessness; joy once again filled his heart.

It was July 1986, a cool winter's day in southern Africa. The day was characterized by great political unrest throughout the country. I was feeling somewhat lonely and isolated from family more than 10,000 miles away. Racial tension was so thick you could cut it with a knife. That day I discovered a scripture of strength in I Samuel 12:24 (NASB):

Only fear the Lord and serve Him in truth, with
all your heart, for consider what great things He
has done for you.

It was Samuel Rutherford who said, "Grace grows best in winter."

83

In Hebrew the term "Psalms" means praises. The poetic book of Psalms inspired me in four areas of my life;

1. *To realize God's presence;* to sense and know that God is always with me, through the storms and through the joys.

2. *To realize my need for thanksgiving.* Psalm 9 says, "I will give thanks to the Lord with all my heart; I will tell of all thy wonders. I will be glad and exalt in thee; I will sing praises to thy name, O most High."

   My need for thanksgiving should be voiced not only during the good times, but in the difficult times, as well.

3. *To realize my need for personal communion with God.* There is no substitute for an intimate relationship with a loving heavenly Father. He knows our anguish before we even voice it to Him. He is always ready to open His loving arms to our wounded spirits. Psalm 8 aided me in my personal approach to God in worship.

   O Lord, our Lord how majestic is Thy name in all the earth. When I consider Thy heavens, the word of Thy fingers, The moon and the stars, which Thou has ordained; What is man that Thou dost take thought of him?

   Only when we reflect upon the greatness of God, can we truly give adoration and praise to his wonderful name.

4. *To realize my need for a refuge and a defense...* A place to turn to for protection when emotional stresses weigh too heavily.

PSALM 11:1a (NASB)

In the Lord I take refuge.

When we think of the meaning of the word "refuge" as being "a place of shelter from harm," we can grasp the full impact of Psalm 16:

> *Preserve me, O God, for I take refuge in Thee.*
> *I said to the Lord, Thou art my Lord;*
> *I have no good besides Thee.*
> *I have set the Lord continually before me;*
> *Because He is at my right hand, I will not be shaken.*
> *Therefore my heart is glad, and my glory rejoices.*

PSALM 18:1-3a (NASB)

> *I love Thee; O Lord; my strength.*
> *The Lord is my rock and my fortress*
> *and my deliverer, My God; my rock, in*
> *whom I take refuge; My shield and the*
> *horn of my salvation, my stronghold,*
> *I call upon the Lord who is worthy to*
> *be praised.*

Psalm 18:30 has become one of my most treasured promises:

> *As for God, His way is blameless,*
> *The word of the Lord is tried;*
> *He is a shield to all who take refuge in Him.*

Choosing God's way does not guarantee problem-free living. However, He does promise strength and courage to face the difficulties. The word of God becomes a buffer against life's stresses.

HOPE THROUGH THE WORD

In the summer of 1982 I sat on the platform as recording secretary at a large missionary convention. A missionary from the Caribbean region rose to speak. His text for the message that afternoon was taken from John 9:3;

"This happened so that the work of God might be displayed in Your life."

Those words suddenly spoke meaning to my heart. The Lord seemed to say through them, "This is a promise I want you to cling to and remember." At that moment, my mind began to relive the many unanswered questions of my childlessness. God was whispering softly to me, "Trust me, I will be glorified through your endurance."

At that time, it was a puzzling thought. I could not see how God was being glorified through my barrenness. Because the emotional pain was severe, I closed communication on the subject with anyone. I felt there was just no one who could understand my pain. Yet, God was now saying that His work would be displayed in my life. It would be nearly eight years later before God would unveil this mystery to me.

THE REAL BLESSING

So often we seek to accumulate material goods in this life. Desiring...obtaining...desiring...obtaining. We run the endless cycle seeking satisfaction and happiness. God's Word contains a promise in Proverbs 10:22 that discourages self-seeking:

"The Lord's blessing is our greatest wealth."

It's wealth beyond measure. When we pause to evaluate our riches in Christ, we soon discover how truly affluent we are. Reflecting upon spiritual wealth and blessings today, I remember:

....friends I have influenced for God now serve Him in South Africa, England, New Zealand, Canada, Swaziland, and USA.

....a marvelous Christian husband who keeps getting better; by far, he is my greatest earthly blessing.

....a great church to serve God in.

....my greatest wealth is to be a child of the King. I became rich in God's blessings the day I became a Christian in August 1972 - the most pivotal point of my life

When I evaluate my happiness, my petty gripes seem to pale in the sunlight of God's infinite goodness. It helps to view clearly the important things in life.

The searching truth and profoundness of the scriptures have never failed to...

....buffer the emotional pain

....soothe weariness in well-doing

....and offer HOPE in times of hopelessness.

HOPE OFFERS:

Comfort

Expectation

Confidence

Trust

This hope we have as an anchor of the soul, a hope both sure and steadfast.
(Hebrews 6:19 NASB).

CHAPTER NINE

HOPE OFFERS HELP

"What helped me through those difficult years of self-doubt was the confidence that God would be with me through it all. I had something that many others do not have - hope."[39]

That quote is from Doris Van Stone's book, *No Place To Cry*. It is the remarkable story of her struggle and victory. In it she conveys the tragic events of her childhood sexual abuse.

"The first step toward recovery is to begin to hope," Doris says.

HOPE THROUGH ACCEPTANCE

There are several ways in which God enabled me to reach a point of acceptance during twenty years of childlessness. I share these with you in great HOPE that they, too, will be a source of strength and encouragement on your quest.

1. **A PERSONAL RELATIONSHIP WITH GOD IS VITAL**: One of the best loved hymns is, "What A Friend We Have In Jesus." That friendship begins when we acknowledge Him as our Lord and Saviour. We come to Christ in our moment of need realizing that He is our sole source of power. When He becomes our Friend, we will want to spend time communing with Him

in prayer. Our friendship with Him will grow as we attend a Bible-believing church. Our relationship will be further enhanced as we try to get into a weekly Women's Bible Study. There, we can grow and mature as a Christian.

2. **SATURATE YOURSELF WITH GOD'S WORD:** When we immerse ourselves in the study of the *Bible,* God will make himself known and relevant to us. The Lord will bring its message to mind when we need it most.

You may want to begin by reading systematically the *Daily Devotional Bible.* A portion of Scripture is given from the Old and New Testaments for each day of the year. As you read, keep a journal notebook beside you. As a particular passage speaks encouragement to you, jot it down. During emotionally low times, dip into your journal to discover nuggets of profound truths that will meet your need. Romans 8:6b (NASB) says, *But the mind set on the spirit is life and peace.*

3. **MINIMIZE SELF-PITY:** Joni Erickson Tada, in her book, *A Step Further*, explains that we have a tendency to want to evaluate ourselves on the scale of human suffering. There are always those who suffer more than we do and those who suffer less. We have a natural tendency to want to believe that the pain of our problem is greater than the pain of any other. But when we face reality and stand beside those who suffer more, we find our purple heart medals don't shine so brightly.

We must make a conscious effort to resist self-pity which leads to anger, resentment and bitterness. Self-pity can be minimized when we direct focus away from our problems. Find someone whose day can be brightened by a visit; a card of encouragement or a welcomed phone call. You will gain a sense of purpose and peace as your own load is lightened.

4.   **RESIST IMPATIENCE:** It's natural to wonder why God is taking His time in answering our prayers. It is helpful to remember that God doesn't operate on our timetable. Remember David's cry in Psalm 13:1, "How long, O Lord? How long?" How long? How long? Victory came for David when he stopped questioning and simply started trusting. Someone has said, "Sometimes God asks us to wait when we want to forge ahead. God sometimes purposely keeps us in the dark when we ask for light. And there are times when God is silent."

But, one day, we look back and discover that He was there all the time.

We resist impatience when we pray and fully trust God. There will be times when we will be tempted to believe that God has forgotten us. We will fret...We will doubt...During these times we must hold steady and not lose HOPE.

5.   **RELEASE ANGER AND GUILT:** It helps to release all questions to the Lord. Often I prayed, "Lord, I don't understand but I believe you must have a very good reason for not giving me a child."

By releasing anger, we become free to trust. Guilt is caused by believing myths such as, barrenness is a "curse from God." God does not cause infertility; yet according to Scripture, He sometimes does allow it. It is important that we see the difference or we will become guilt-ridden.

We must walk beyond our anger and guilt. By releasing these two emotions we proceed closer to a life of peace and purpose. HOPE can dispel anger and guilt.

6. **SEEK A REFUGE THROUGH PRAYER:** Andrew Murray, in his classic book, ***The Believer's Secret Of Waiting On God***, explains that when we pray we express our sense of need to God; we express our faith in His help; and we wait quietly before God until the deep, restful assurance fills us. When we practice waiting on God, we will walk all day in the enjoyment of God's light and leading. We have the living assurance that waiting on God through prayer can never be in vain. [40]

Begin to see prayer as a powerful privilege rather than an obligation.

The word "refuge" means protection or shelter away from harm and pain. Solace will come, not from your husband, not from a counselor or best friend; solace will come from God. Turn to Him in prayer often; depend on Him to assuage your anguish. He alone will understand our deepest hurts when no one else can.

7. **ACCEPTANCE:** Coming to terms with our childlessness may mean that we accept those things that we cannot change - by the grace of God. Reaching the point of acceptance may take many years. Then, one day when you think you have really come to terms with it...the emotional pain strikes with full force all over again. You will know you have reached the point of resolution when...

a. Insensitive remarks from well-meaning people lose their sting.

b. Mother's Day and family gatherings are anticipated without dread or excused absences.

For me, it took nearly fifteen years for emotional healing. At that time I did reach the point where I believed that this was the life God planned for me and by His grace I would make the most of it.

Peace comes through acceptance.

8. **HOPE IN GOD:** In Jesus Christ there is HOPE. Always! HOPE is realizing that it's never too late to begin again...to love...to give...to serve. There may be new beginnings, new directions or new purposes. God may re-direct original goals, but He will always give you a new HOPE. Read prayerfully again, Jeremiah 29:11. Dare to believe that God will do great and mighty things in your life.

9. **ASK GOD FOR JOY:** ...a deep well of joy that doesn't depend upon our circumstances...joy in the midst of sorrow and loss. Ask God to let people see Him in your life instead of your pain and problems.

Her name was Virginia. She was a lovely young Chinese woman. One day while at home with her three-month-old baby and two-year-old child, three cruel men forced their way into her South African home. They brutally beat her, gang-raped her and left her for dead. A short time later, her six-year-old son arrived home and discovered her blood-stained body. She was barely alive when he ran to the neighbors for help.

Three months later she was still recovering in a local hospital. I will never forget the first time I visited her in the hospital ward. I was prepared to see a very embittered, angry woman. Who could have blamed her for feeling that way? Instead, I saw a young woman whose face was aglow with the love of Christ. "Hello, Virginia, you don't know me, but I have come to let you know that our church has been praying for you and your family." I offered, while standing at the foot of her bed.

She motioned with her hands to come to her side. As I did she reached out in trust and grasped my hand in hers. "Thank you," she smiled. "I have forgiven the men who harmed me. I am so glad they did not hurt my children. Rather me than my children," she responded with the depth of Christian love that only Christ can give.

I handed her a scripture verse I had written in calligraphy on a stone from the beach. It was from I Samuel and said, "God is my strength and my power."

Tears began to stream down her cheeks as she smiled and said, trembling, "That's it! God is my strength and my power!"

Virginia is the greatest example I know of a person to whom God gave joy in the midst of her suffering and deep anguish.

WAITING ON GOD

When we see God as our Friend...meditate on His Word...commune with Him in prayer, our self-pity, anger, guilt and impatience will pale in the sunlight of His love. HOPE and joy will be restored. He will then fashion us into strong vessels for His use.

"My soul, wait only upon God."
Psalm 62:5

94

CHAPTER TEN

HOPE FOR BROKENNESS:

How To Comfort and Counsel Infertile Women

Disappointment is what infertility is all about. Imagine trying to conceive for five, ten, fifteen years and always having it futile. Anguish and frustration intensifies and couples find themselves on an emotional rollercoaster of incredible intensity. Infertility leads couples into a unique, secret universe - one that is incomprehensible to outsiders.[41]

As increasing numbers of couples enter treatment for their infertility, pastors and counselors must increase their knowledge of, and sensitivity to, the unique needs of the couples.

Only through the knowledge of the multiple complex factors affecting infertile couples, can counselors provide the sensitive, effective assistance that infertile couples need to adjust successfully to their situational crisis.

There are ten ways in which pastors/counselors can help women cope and deal with their feelings and behavior:

1.   **COUNSELORS MUST FIRST ACKNOWLEDGE THE CRISIS:** They must be aware that lack of social support, anger, sadness, and feelings of helplessness are very realistic responses. The woman may feel a great sense of loss of

control over her life due to intrusive medical tests and procedures in which she is involved.

2. **ACKNOWLEDGE THE COUPLE'S FEELINGS OF LOSS OF CONTROL:** "The worst thing for couples is the total loss of control," says Alan H. Decherney, M.D., director of Reproductive Endocrinology and Infertility at Yale University School of Medicine. "These are people who have had complete control over their destiny and now they have lost control of that destiny," he adds.

3. **ASSIST HER IN REFOCUSING GOALS:** Counselors may help a woman refocus her control in several ways. For example, a woman can be shown her importance as a homemaker and her worth to and influence upon her husband as God intended her to be. Help her to see the amount of control she does have over other major life events.

4. **IT IS IMPORTANT THAT COUNSELORS HELP WOMEN TO REDUCE THE IMPORTANCE OF UNATTAINABLE GOALS.** For many women, fertility will be an unattainable goal; it is out of their control. However, that can attain other goals such as a college degree, job promotion, a trip overseas or other accomplishments. Sometimes in life we experience irreversible losses. Help women focus on the fact that they can put their energies on those goals over which they have some control.[42]

5. **HELP HER TO ASSESS HER SOCIAL SUPPORT SYSTEM.** She should be encouraged to seek regular support either from a close friend or RESOLVE.[43] Studies regarding the emotional effects of infertility on women have

shown that women who have a strong support
system have higher self-worth and lower rates of
depression.[44]

Remember, however, that not every woman will
feel comfortable in a support group. Personally, I
was able to find strength through one or two close
friends.

6. **THE COUNSELOR NEEDS TO UNDER-
STAND THE WOMAN'S IMPORTANCE
HIERARCHY.** What holds first priority in her
life? If it is the ability to bear a child, then this
loss will have an effect on other goals. It will
cloud her social network of family and friends.

7. **THE COUNSELOR SHOULD ASSIST THE
WOMAN IN ASSESSING HER GOALS.** Help
her to see clearly the control she does have over
many of her goals.

8. **THE COUNSELOR, FROM THE BEGIN-
NING SHOULD DISPEL THE MYTH THAT
HER INFERTILITY IS A SIGN OF GOD'S
DISFAVOR.** God does not cause infertility
because of some past sin. However, he some-
times permits it and that reason is unknown.

9. **AVOID SPIRITUAL CLICHE'S SUCH AS:**
"Trust God, He knows best." While this is true, it
is sometimes seen as a pat answer and offers little
consolation. Often, she seeks a caring, listening
ear who will offer HOPE and understanding.

10. **COUNSELORS MUST REALIZE THAT
THE CRISIS OF INFERTILITY IS NOT A
ONE-TIME EVENT.** Emotions fluctuate from
low to high. Seasonal events such as Christmas,
Mother's Day, Father's Day, will be low points.

Pastors should be considerate of the way in which they present a Mother's Day message. Remember the hurts of infertile women especially on that day.

Finally, in a barren woman's search for significance, she seeks that RAY OF HOPE from a listening ear, someone who is simply willing to hear her hurt, to understand and to care.

CHAPTER ELEVEN:

WHEN HOPE LIVES

It was April 1988 and my husband had made the decision to leave South Africa following four marvelous years of fruitful ministry at a church in Port Elizabeth. This was followed by a great emotional upheaval in both our lives. We had grown to love the South African people and their beautiful country. Leaving them would be very difficult.

Since I had not had a gynecological check-up for four years, I thought perhaps it would be wise to get one before returning to the States. A friend recommended a gynecologist and I phoned to make an appointment for the following Monday afternoon.

The next week when I arrived for my appointment with Dr. Gooysen, I was sitting calmly in his reception area when the nurse called my name and showed me to the exam room.

I had no reason to feel anxious because it was a routine pap and pelvic examination; I was not experiencing any problems. I felt pleased that his office was modern, clean and professional. Dr. Gooysen walked in and introduced himself in a strong British accent. A large, imposing man, I noticed immediately how enormous his hands were as he shook my right hand.

He took several minutes to review my health history. I patiently answered the questions I had so often answered in the past. Looking very concerned he reasoned that my health history was not compatible with endometriosis, polycystic ovaries and a low prolactin. "Were you ever treated with medication for your endometriosis?" he asked.

"No, I was never told it should be treated," I said, surprised.

"Well, if it is not treated, you are heading for a hysterectomy," were his shocking words to me.

At that moment, I began to feel very anxious. I was there for a routine exam; I was unprepared emotionally to deal with these questions and new developments.

"The only way we can be certain whether or not you have endometriosis is by doing a laparoscopy." I knew the surgery he was talking about because I had had one in Ohio.

He concluded the exam and advised that I talk to my husband and schedule the surgery as soon as possible.

As I drove home from his office, I was physically shaken at the thought of a possible hysterectomy. To an infertile woman, that is the last word she ever wants to hear. I was still clinging to that small ray of HOPE.

Arriving home, I discussed the traumatic visit with Chuck and we both agreed that the surgery should be done. The next day I phoned Dr. Gooysen's office and made an appointment for surgery that Thursday afternoon. I was unprepared for what that day would reveal.

Thursday morning came and I entered the hospital. After all the preliminaries, I was administered a short-acting anesthetic. Shortly after surgery, I was fully awake and a nurse was at my side offering me a cup of hot tea. At the same time, Dr. Gooysen walked into my room. He looked at Chuck and said, "She does not have endometriosis. She does not have polycystic ovaries and her hormone levels are normal. She is a very healthy young woman."

Completely baffled, I asked, "To what then do you attribute my infertility problem?"

He simply shook his head. The medical profession terms it a "spontaneous cure." Medically, it cannot be explained.

GOD'S PERFECT TIMING

But God knew.

Within a few weeks we flew out of South Africa from Johannesburg. It would be three days before we would arrive in Pennsylvania to be reunited with our families. Due to leaving South Africa, re-entry shock back into American culture and reunion with our loved ones, our infertility problems were placed on hold.

Nearly two years later on April 25, 1990, we celebrated our twentieth wedding anniversary. It was a reminder that time had ticked off another childless year. However, I was beginning to come to terms with my barrenness. I felt peace more often than pressure.

To celebrate the occasion, we spent four days at a friend's condo in Ruidoso, New Mexico. We reveled in the scenic beauty and mountain majesty, hiked through fresh pine forests in a secluded wooded area. As we absorbed nature, we marveled at the great handiwork of God.

That afternoon while Chuck enjoyed playing a game of golf, I did some writing in the condo. Later in the evening we enjoyed a romantic candlelight seafood dinner at the country club. Adventure and romance had been a major part of our magnificent marriage for twenty years. Over dinner that evening we reminisced about past anniversary celebrations; our fifteenth was celebrated in Graff Reinet, South Africa...the home of that great Dutch Reformed minister, Andrew Murray. We talked about God's goodness in our lives and thanked Him for one another.

During our stay at Ruidoso, I felt more tired than usual, but attributed it to many possible causes:
...the cold rainstorm I was caught in the week before
...the hectic schedule
...emotional stress
...high altitude

Pregnancy was not on my list of reasons and I did not give it the remotest possibility. With solid faith in God I had resolved my infertility in 1987.

Several days following our trip, the thought of pregnancy began to re-surface...that flicker of HOPE. However, I quickly squelched the thought. It was years since I had allowed those feelings to take hold. I wasn't prepared to unearth the emotional distress of past heart-wrenching disappointments. I had, at last, reached the point of accepting my childlessness and the pain lessened. I was just beginning to face Mother's Day and Christmas without the gamut of unrestrained emotional anguish...emptiness...loneliness.

I could not risk disappointment again. Yet, two weeks later, I was not able to ignore the physical symptoms I was experiencing; swollen, tender breasts, nausea, missed menstrual period.

HOPE began to slowly soar.

'Can it be?' I wondered.

Protecting my private nature, I reasoned to myself, 'I'll do a home pregnancy test. That way if it is negative, I won't have to tell anyone, especially Chuck. Only I, alone, will have to bear the crushing load of disappointment.'

The next morning after Chuck had left for the office, I anxiously drove to the pharmacy. 'This is ridiculous,' I thought. 'Nothing is going to come out of this.'

I felt extremely nervous and apprehensive when I entered the pharmacy. I had never had a pregnancy test; I had never been pregnant! I was hoping a sales clerk would not ask me what I needed. "Ma'am, may I help you find something," a bright, cheery clerk asked.

"Where are your pregnancy test kits," I whispered. "Back in the corner on your far left."

I purchased the cheapest one, hoping no one was watching. I don't know why I felt as though I was doing something terribly wrong. Quickly, I paid the cashier and made a fast exit to my car.

Arriving back home my hands visibly shook as I unfolded the package directions. I locked the bathroom door behind me, although I was home alone. I felt an intense need for secrecy.

The directions said, "Wait twenty minutes, if the paper is still white, the results are negative. If the paper is blue, results are a positive pregnancy."

Nervously, I set the timer on my kitchen stove and paced and prayed.

It was an unending twenty minutes. The sudden,

shrill buzzing of the timer jolted my thoughts. I stopped pacing, but stood frozen for a few moments.

'What if it's negative? What if it's POSITIVE?!' It took a long while before I could muster enough courage to walk back into the bathroom. Emotions of elated joy to sadness whirled in my head. Old HOPES that laid buried began to re-surface:

> How will I tell Chuck?
> Will it be a boy or a girl?
> How will I decorate the nursery?
> How will we select names?

Cowardly, I walked slowly into the bathroom not fully prepared for the surprising discovery. From the corner of my eye, I looked down at the paper lying there undisturbed, unaffected, resolutely.

There was no question about it.

The paper was as blue as a west Texas sky. I stood in shocked disbelief; 'I must have done something wrong,' I reasoned, 'I better re-read the instructions.'

The years of intense emotional pain now created a pool of denial. Pregnancy simply did not seem possible to me.
...I was thirty-nine years old
...Chuck was forty-seven
...we had been childless for twenty years
...there had been no medical intervention to cause pregnancy

As I read the percentage of accuracy of the test (99%), for the first time, HOPE soared like an eagle. Never had I been given such high hopes of fertility.

I knew Chuck would have to "see it to believe it,"

so I left the test results out until he arrived home for lunch. About twenty minutes later, calmly, unsuspectingly, he walked in the front door. We greeted each other, as usual, with a warm hug.

"Come, I want to show you something," I said as we walked to the bathroom where he saw an array of vials, papers and other paraphernalia. With a puzzled look on his face, I'm sure he must have wondered what on earth I was up to.

I began to explain my suspicions and findings. In his characteristic, unruffled way, he smiled and hugged me tightly. With a sense of urgency, I said, "What do we do now?"

Wisely he offered, "Let's make a doctor's appointment." We were fortunate to get an appointment that afternoon with Dr. Joe Horn, a fine Christian doctor.

When he asked the reason for the visit, I told him. "How many children will this make for you?" he asked.

"This will be our first child after twenty years of marriage," I announced.

Quickly, his eyes darted to Chuck sitting on a stool. "Well, this is a surprise, isn't it? You will have to wait twenty minutes for the blood test results, I will be back in then." he offered. Another waiting period.

The office door opened and Dr. Horn walked in with his eyes looking down at the test results. He glanced up and said, "Well praise God, it's positive." I felt my heart take a leap as tears of joy welled up in my eyes.

Because of my unique situation, he wanted to refer me to a high-risk specialist in Lubbock. I wasn't able to get in to see him for three months. When the appointment date arrived, I was extremely nervous and worried. One nagging fear kept plaguing me, "What if he says, 'You are not pregnant, I'm sorry but the tests are false.'"

That morning as I sat on Dr. Owen's examining table, Chuck was sitting in a chair across the room. I was extremely apprehensive. Just then Dr. Owen walked in, tall, slender and probably in his early forties; with an easy, relaxed manner. He smiled and introduced himself. "The first thing I want you to know is that I don't do abortions under any circumstances."

I knew then we had chosen the right doctor. As he intently listened to the baby's heart beat (11 weeks) he smiled and said, "There sure is a baby in there." It was impossible to constrain my emotions any longer. At that moment, I released a floodgate of tears, but for the first time, they were tears of inexpressible joy!

HOPE.

Anticipation.

Chuck quickly made his way to my side and hugged me.

Dr. Owen patted my leg.

HOPE began to live.

Someone has said, "There is within the human heart a hope which knows no defeat."

HOPE ALLOWS US TO

... walk through our circumstances

... learn ways to mend our brokenness

... gain comfort and courage

HOPE GIVES US

... patience through our pain

... growth in spirit, mind and health

... strength in weakness

WHEN HOPE LIVES

... hearts are mended

... dreams resurrected

... lives affected

In the presence of the King!

THE GIFT

A new love
Before unknown.
Deep, expressible JOY!
Abounding Laughter
Fills our home,
Our hearts,
Our lives.
A child is born,
To us.

Anna-Marie Lockard
24 April 1991

On December 26, 1990, God presented a priceless, rare treasure to us; a cherished, pink-faced, chubby, baby girl weighing seven pounds, seven ounces and twenty inches long.

Annique (rhymes with Monica) Marise Lockard.

Words are inadequate to describe our gratitude to God and the depth of love for our child.

Some of you who will be reading this chapter are experiencing intense emotional agony; 'Why can't it be me? It isn't fair. Why isn't God giving ME a child?'

Dear friend, I know your anguish. It was a long time before I could pick up Ann Kiemel Anderson's book, ***And With The Gift Came Laughter***, whose front cover portrayed her, Will, and their two bouncing boys. Her success seemed to minimize my suffering.

I realized how selfish I was being and got a copy of her book and read it. Characteristically, Ann's life and messages display sensitivity to others who may be hurting. Let me share with you her words that soothed my hurting heart.

> *there is a private place in my heart*
> *that is very tender, very sensitive to*
> *some of you who will read this*
> *book. some of you, as yet, have no*
> *children. you may be today where I*
> *have been - wrenched and grieved*
> *and aching for a child. please*
> *know that though God has blessed*
> *me with two little sons whom Will*
> *and I love beyond description, I*
> *have not forgotten where you are. i*
> *have been through too much pain*
> *to forget your place. it once was*
> *my place. remember, i believe for*
> *you.* [45]

In closing, I have a prayer for you as you pursue your quest for a child. It is a plea to God that you will always continue to TRUST and HOPE in God; Jehovah Rapha (the God who heals). I believe HOPE can live for you, too.

NOTES

(1) Veninga, Robert, A GIFT OF HOPE,
(Boston, MA: Little, Brown & Co., 1985) page 276.

(2) Littauer, Florence, HOPE FOR HURTING WOMEN,
(Dallas, TX; Word Publishing, 1985)

(3) Yancey, Philip, **DISAPPOINTMENT WITH GOD**,
(Grand Rapids, MI: Zondervan Publishing House, 1988)
pages 66-67.

(4) Ibid.

(5) Lockyer, Herbert, **ALL THE WOMEN OF THE BIBLE**,
(Grand Rapids, MI: Zondervan Publishing House, 1967)
pages 109-110. (Used by permission).

(6) Ibid, pages 138-140

(7) Ibid, pages 128-129

(8) Ibid, pages 185-187

(9) Ibid, page 65

(10) Ibid, pages 66-67

(11) Ibid, pages 203-207

(12) American Fertility Society, 2131 Magnolia Ave., Suite 201,
Birmingham, AL 35256, is the world's largest sub-specialty devoted
to problems of infertility.

(13) In addition to physical causes for infertility, in certain cases there
may be spiritual roots. These are explored in the book, *Deliverance
From Childlessness*. (Bill Banks, Impact Books, Inc., 1990)

(14) Amy Dunkin, "IN VITRO FERTILIZATION: DELIVERING THAT RAY OF HOPE," *Business Week* magazine, Sept. 3, 1990. pages 112-113

(15) Halpern, Sue, "INFERTILITY: A SEARCH FOR SOLUTIONS" Reader's Digest, July 1989, pages 129-136.

(16) Holland, Lisa, "HOPE FOR INFERTILE COUPLES," Good Housekeeping Magazine, March 1991, page 219.

(17) Webster's **NEW HANDY POCKET DICTIONARY**, NY, NY (Universal Publishing and Distributing Corp., 1970) page 326.

(18) Heavilin, Marilyn, **WHEN YOUR DREAMS DIE**, (San Bernardino, CA; Here's Life Publishers, 1990) page 36.

(19) Cook, Sally Streeter, Ruth and Serono Symposia, USA, "INFERTILITY: THE EMOTIONAL ROLLER COASTER," pamphlet

(20) Serono Symposia, USA is a division of Serono Labs, Inc. It has a long term commitment to physicians, health care professionals and patient education.

(21) Costigan, Kelly; "THE PAIN OF BABY CRAVING," HEALTH, Jan. 1989

(22) Ibid.

(23) Serono Symposia, USA, pamphlet, "Insights into Infertility."

(24) Nadya A. Fouad and Kristin Kons Fahje, "An Exploratory Study of the Psychological Correlated of Infertility on Women," *Journal of Counseling and Development,* Sept/Oct 1989.

(25) C. Shipiro, *"The Impact of Infertility on the Marital Relationship,"* Social Casework: *The Journal of Contemporary Social Work, 1982*, pages 387-393.

(26) John McCormick and Pat Wingert, *Newsweek,* summer 1991, page 60.

111

(27) Ibid, page 58.

(28) Collette Dywasuk, **ADOPTION, IS IT FOR YOU?** (Wheaton, IL: Harper and Row, 1973)

(29) Ibid, page 81

(30) Ann Kiemel Anderson, **AND WITH THE GIFT CAME LAUGHTER**, (Wheaton, IL: Tyndale House, 1987) pages 123-124.

(31) Collette Dywasuk, **ADOPTION, IS IT FOR YOU?** (Wheaton, IL: Harper and Row, 1973) pages 90-91.

(32) Philip Goodwin, "OVERCOMING INFERTILITY," *Better Homes and Gardens,* May 1989, pages 44-49.

(33) Michelle, Macgillicuddy, unpublished poem; used by permission.

(34) Selwyn Hughes, *Everyday with Jesus*, booklet (Aug. 17-23, 1991.) July-August 1991 devotional booklet. (Waverley Abbey House, Waverly Lane, Farnham, Surrey, England GU9 8EP).

(35) Robert Veninga, **A GIFT OF HOPE**, (Boston, MA: Little, Brown and Company, 1985).

(36) Ibid.

(37) Ibid.

(38) Florence Littauer, **HOPE FOR HURTING WOMEN**, (Dallas, TX: Word Publishing, 1985) page 57.

(39) Dorie Van Stone and Erwin W. Lutzer, **NO PLACE TO CRY**, Chicago, IL: Moody Press, 1990) page 45.

(40) Andrew Murray, **THE BELIEVER'S SECRET OF WAITING ON GOD**, (Bethany House Publishers, 1986).

(41) Sally Cook and Ruth Streeter and Seronoymposia, USA, *"Infertility: The Emotional Roller Coaster,"* pamphlet.

112

(no copyright date indicated)

(42) Nadya A. Fouad and Kristin Kons Fahje, "An Exploratory Study of the Psychological Correlated of Infertility on Women," *Journal of Counseling and Development,* Sept/Oct 1989.

(43) **RESOLVE** is a non-profit organization established in 1973 that provides referrals, support and medical information to infertile individuals.

(44) T. E. Pearson, "The Definition and Measurement of Social Support," **THE JOURNAL OF COUNSELING AND DEVELOPMENT**, 1964, pages 390-395.

(45) Ann Kiemel Anderson, **AND WITH THE GIFT CAME LAUGHTER**, (Wheaton, IL: Tyndale House, 1987) page 14.

Anna-Marie Lockard

Is available to speak to your church, ladies group or organization. You may contact her in care of the following address:

Mrs. Anna-Marie Lockard
P.O. Box 34,
Homer City, PA 15748

The Variety of Poetry

AN ANTHOLOGY

THE VARIETY OF
Poetry

AN ANTHOLOGY

EDWARD A. BLOOM
CHARLES H. PHILBRICK
ELMER M. BLISTEIN
Brown University

New York . THE ODYSSEY PRESS . INC.

Acknowledgments

CURTIS BROWN, LTD.

for "The Private Dining Room" from *Verses from 1929 on*, copyright © 1951 by Ogden Nash, reprinted by permission of the author.

CRITERION BOOKS, INC.

for "Sonnet to My Mother," copyright 1957 by Criterion Books, Inc., from George Barker's *Collected Poems, 1930–1955*, published in New York in 1958, reprinted by permission of Criterion Books, Inc.

THE JOHN DAY COMPANY, INC.

for "The Sirens," copyright © 1946 by The John Day Company, from *Selected Verse* by John Manifold, reprinted by permission of The John Day Company, Inc., publisher.

DOUBLEDAY & COMPANY, INC.

for "Danny Deever" by Rudyard Kipling, reprinted by permission of Mrs. George Bambridge and published by Doubleday & Company, Inc.

HARCOURT, BRACE & WORLD, INC.

for "All in Green Went My Love Riding," copyright 1923, 1951 by E. E. Cummings, and "My Father Moved Through Dooms of Love," copyright 1940 by E. E. Cummings, from *Poems 1923–1954* by E. E. Cummings. For "As a Plane Tree by the Water" from *Lord Weary's Castle*, copyright 1944, 1946 by Robert Lowell. For "The Death of a Toad" from *Ceremony and Other Poems*, copyright 1948, 1949, 1950 by Richard Wilbur. For "Fall in Corrales," © 1956 by Richard Wilbur, from *Advice to a Prophet and Other Poems*. All of these poems reprinted by permission of Harcourt, Brace & World, Inc.

HARVARD UNIVERSITY PRESS

for "A Narrow Fellow in the Grass" from *The Poems of Emily Dickinson*, reprinted by permission of the Publishers and the Trustees of Amherst College from Thomas H. Johnson, Editor, *The Poems of Emily Dickinson*, Cambridge, Mass., The Belknap Press of Harvard University Press, copyright 1951, 1955, by The President and Fellows of Harvard College.

HOLT, RINEHART AND WINSTON, INC.

for "The Carpenter's Son" and "To an Athlete Dying Young" from "A Shropshire Lad," Authorized Edition, from *Complete Poems by A. E. Housman*, copyright © 1959 by Holt, Rinehart and Winston, Inc. For "The Oven Bird" and "The Wood-Pile" from *Complete Poems of Robert Frost*, copyright 1916, 1921, 1930, 1939 by Holt, Rinehart and Winston, Inc., copyright renewed 1944 by Robert Frost. All of these poems reprinted by permission of Holt, Rinehart and Winston, Inc.

HOUGHTON MIFFLIN COMPANY

for "Ars Poetica," "Vicissitudes of the Creator," and "You, Andrew Marvell" by Archibald MacLeish, reprinted by permission of Houghton Mifflin Company.

ALFRED A. KNOPF, INC.

for "Bells for John Whiteside's Daughter," copyright 1924 by Alfred A. Knopf, Inc., copyright renewed 1952 by John Crowe Ransom, and "Here Lies a Lady," copyright 1924 by Alfred A. Knopf, Inc., copyright renewed 1952 by John Crowe Ransom, from *Selected Poems* by John Crowe Ransom. For "Anecdote of the Jar," copyright 1923, 1951 by Wallace Stevens, and "Peter Quince at the Clavier," copyright 1923, 1951 by Wallace Stevens, from *The Collected Poems of Wallace Stevens*. All of these poems reprinted by permission of Alfred A. Knopf, Inc.

LIVERIGHT PUBLISHING CORPORATION

for "The Broken Tower" and "Voyages: II" from *The Collected Poems of Hart Crane*, copyright ⓡ R, 1961 by Liveright Publishing Corporation, reprinted by permission of Liveright Publishing Corporation.

THE MACMILLAN COMPANY

for "New England" from *Dionysus in Doubt*, by Edwin Arlington Robinson, copyright 1925 by Edwin Arlington Robinson, renewed 1952 by Ruth Nivison and Barbara R. Holt. For "Byzantium," copyright 1933 by The Macmillan Company, renewed 1961 by Bertha Georgie Yeats; "Leda and the Swan," copyright 1928 by The Macmillan Company, renewed 1956 by Georgie Yeats; "Prayer for My Daughter," copyright 1924 by The Macmillan Company, renewed 1952 by Bertha Georgie Yeats, all from *Collected Poems* by William Butler Yeats. For "At the Draper's," "At Tea," "By Her Aunt's Grave," and "In Church" from *Collected Poems* by Thomas Hardy, copyright 1925 by The Macmillan Company. All of these poems reprinted by permission of The Macmillan Company.

WILLIAM MORRIS AGENCY, INC.

for "Bearded Oaks" from *Selected Poems 1923-1943*, published by Harcourt, Brace and Company, copyright ⓒ 1944 by Robert Penn Warren, reprinted by permission of William Morris Agency, Inc.

NEW DIRECTIONS

for "In a Station of the Metro" and "The River Merchant's Wife: A Letter" from *Personae: The Collected Poems of Ezra Pound*, copyright 1926, 1954 by Ezra Pound. For "The Yachts," "The Contagious Hospital," and "The Red Wheelbarrow" from *The Collected Earlier Poems of William Carlos Williams*, copyright 1938, 1951 by William Carlos Williams. For "Over Sir John's Hill" and "A Refusal to Mourn the Death by Fire of a Child in London" from *The Collected Poems of Dylan Thomas*, ⓒ 1957 by New Directions. All of these poems reprinted by permission of New Directions, Publishers.

OXFORD UNIVERSITY PRESS

for "Snow" and "The Sunlight on the Garden" from *Eighty-Five Poems* by Louis MacNeice, copyright 1959 by Louis MacNeice. For "Poem 28" from *Collected Poems* by Conrad Aiken, copyright 1953 by Conrad Aiken. For "Carrion Comfort," "Thou Art Indeed Just, Lord," and "The Windhover" from *Poems of Gerard Manley Hopkins*, Third Edition, edited by W. H. Gardner, copyright 1948 by Oxford University Press, Inc. All of these poems reprinted by permission of Oxford University Press, Inc.

PRINCETON UNIVERSITY PRESS

for "Meditation Seven" from *The Poetical Works of Edward Taylor*, edited with an Introduction and Notes by Thomas H. Johnson, copyright 1939 by Rockland Editions and 1943 by Princeton University Press, reprinted by permission of Princeton University Press.

RANDOM HOUSE, INC.

for "Lay Your Sleeping Head, My Love," copyright 1940 by W. H. Auden, and "O Where Are You Going?" copyright 1934 and renewed 1961 by W. H. Auden, from *The Collected Poetry of W. H. Auden*. For "The Bloody Sire" from *Be Angry at the Sun and Other Poems* by Robinson Jeffers, copyright 1941 by Robinson Jeffers. For "Cassandra," copyright 1948 by Robinson Jeffers, from *The Double Axe and Other Poems* by Robinson Jeffers. For "To the Stone-Cutters," copyright 1924 and renewed 1951 by Robinson Jeffers, from *The Selected Poetry of Robinson Jeffers*. For "The Express," copyright 1934 and renewed 1961 by Stephen Spender, from *Collected Poems 1928–1953*. For "Autumnal Equinox on Mediterranean Beach" from *You, Emperors, and Others: Poems 1957–1960* by Robert Penn Warren, © copyright 1958, 1959, 1960 by Robert Penn Warren. All of these poems reprinted by permission of Random House, Inc.

CHARLES SCRIBNER'S SONS

for "The Mediterranean" from *Poems*, by Allen Tate. For "Miniver Cheevy," copyright 1907 by Charles Scribner's Sons and renewed 1935, and "For a Dead Lady," copyright 1910 by Charles Scribner's Sons and renewed 1938 by Ruth Nivison, from *The Town Down the River* by Edwin Arlington Robinson. All of these poems reprinted by permission of Charles Scribner's Sons.

THE VIKING PRESS, INC.

for "Piano" and "Snake" from *Collected Poems*, by D. H. Lawrence, copyright 1929 by Jonathan Cape and Harrison Smith, Inc. and renewed © 1957 by Frieda Lawrence Ravagli, reprinted by permission of The Viking Press, Inc.

To the Reader

ANYONE who sets about compiling a new anthology of poetry, no matter how generously the publisher has allocated space to him, quickly faces the melancholy truth that he simply cannot include everything he once thought he could nor even select verses that will satisfy all of his readers. The selecting of poems written in English over a period of five-hundred years thus becomes a frustrating experience. But it is one which also has its gratifications, for the compiler undertakes a sharply critical review of the best—and the worst—that has been written.

His task, in this sense, is a pleasantly selfish one. Works he has not read for years come back to him as fresh delights. Works he has perhaps long forgotten are reconsidered, and he must reproach himself for neglecting them. A few which are perhaps completely unfamiliar become valuable additions to his store. The editors of this volume thus fully appreciate the opportunity they have been given to reappraise what they have known or to discover what hitherto they have not known.

First of all, therefore, we acknowledge the inescapable subjectivity that has gone into this book. Insofar as the contents must largely represent the editors' individual and collective tastes, this basis of selection is vulnerable and yet, we are confident, defensible. At the same time, however, we have never thought of this anthology as a kind of private scrapbook. We can justify it only on the assumption that the book is between the reader and the editors, that the editors have an obligation to share their pleasure and judgment with the reader.

We have spoken of our reintroduction to, or even discovery of, new poems which are now a part of this volume. We are not so brash as to imply, however, that our poems have been suggested to us by nostalgic reflection or casual reading. We

have, in fact, employed a largely experiential, objective basis of
selection to support our personal tastes. Most of the poems
have already been tested in the classroom. Subjecting them to
rigorous critical standards, whose reliability we hope you are
about to try for yourself, we have found that these poems "teach"
well. We are convinced that the majority of them are good
poems in themselves; and we know that discussion of them with
students raises important questions about the poetic process and
poetic values. As for those poems which we have not yet tested
for ourselves, we are equally convinced that they deserve your
earnest critical attention.

Finally, our selections have been made to illustrate and sup-
plement our text in *The Order of Poetry: An Introduction*. You will
observe, consequently, that the poems have been arranged according to the five chapters in that book: (1) "The Language
of Poetry," (2) "Symbol, Myth, and Allegory," (3) "Narrative
and Dramatic Structure," (4) "Theme, Mood, Tone, and Intention," (5) "Versification." The logic of this manner of pro-
ceeding in the analysis and appreciation of poetry has been one
of the outcomes of our classroom experience and, obviously, we
recommend it to you. Since (if your training in poetic studies
is to parallel our suggestions) *The Order of Poetry: An Introduction*
is readily available, we have seen no need to repeat what we
have said there.

On the other hand, we do not insist that there is no other
satisfactory way of studying poetry. Whatever approach to this
rewarding discipline happens to be dictated by your instruction,
we hope that our anthology has merit independent of the *Introduction*. Our aim has been to make the anthology flexible enough
to accompany any text designed to teach the close reading of
poems, as well as to promote a general understanding of the
principles of poetic art and of the poetic mode of making statements.

Our distribution of poems according to rather formalized
poetic aspects or elements may seem arbitrary. Obviously, no
poem worth studying can be fully understood and appreciated
if one sees it only as an example of, say, metaphor, or symbol,
or tone, or rhythm. Any given poem contains most of the poetic

elements, but they do not function in isolation and they must therefore be understood in relation to the whole. If the reader is to understand the poet's intent, he must read the complete poem (for this reason we have not reproduced any fragments of poems but have included songs from plays because they can be treated as organizationally complete) and must consider it in the totality of its effect, in the cumulative power of its analyzable elements.

Still, because of instructional expedience, we feel that the student must proceed by taking a step at a time, gradually acquiring confidence in his capacity for discernment and in his sense of esthetic balance and so progressing steadily through the entire poetic process. At the beginning, he cannot look, listen, and think in every direction at once. Moreover, granting that a poem must ultimately be understood as a whole, different poems contain the various poetic elements in differing proportions and so lend themselves temporarily to different approaches and emphases. Each poem has therefore been assigned to a category, which is to say a chapter, consistent with its dominant elements. The arrangement of poems is thus designed for progressive study; but with time, experience, and an enterprising spirit, the student can easily double back for further exploration and fresh insights.

Our approach is essentially critical rather than historical. Nevertheless, we wish to make clear our high regard for technical progression and cultural continuity. We have therefore tried to be responsible to the course and variety of verse in English by arranging our poems chronologically within the divisions to which we have assigned them. Similarly, although we have tried to enliven our book with a number of selections which are less well known, we have reproduced a sizable number of familiar, traditional pieces.

In most instances, we have dated and placed poems according to their first publication in book form but have amended this practice under special circumstances. For example, we have used two dates for Shakespeare's songs, the first to indicate when each appeared in a play, the second to indicate the date of initial publication. Authors like Thomas Traherne and Edward

Taylor died long before their verses were published. In these and other instances, the date of composition has seemed to us the one to dictate chronological position. We have also, in our chronology, acknowledged revisions made by poets in their collected works after separate publication of single poems.

Textually, we have tried to be conservative in several directions. We perpetuate eccentricities of spelling and punctuation only when they seem to reflect intended pronunciation or to preserve the "flavor" of a period's style. This principle applies, for example, to certain Renaissance archaisms or the persistent contractions employed by neoclassical poets. We have, however, normalized or modernized punctuation and spelling which appear to owe their original form to mere scribal or typographical idiosyncrasy, without visible poetic purpose. The beginning reader of poetry will be deviled by enough other problems without having to be concerned with specialized textual and typographical problems.

Our general aim in headnotes and footnotes has been to throw essential light—and nothing else—on the poems. Statements by authors, thus, are frequently useful clues to the original intention of a work of art. Our own footnotes are confined to matters of specialized knowledge—historic events, specific individuals, dialect words, and the like—which are relevant to interpretation. Commonplaces of history and biography, dated words, and so forth, whose explanation would have no immediate bearing, are not annotated. The curious student will find references in his library. In the main, any word or any reference to myth which the reader can find in the customary sources, we have studiously not glossed. Above all, we hope that each poem will speak for itself.

We offer this anthology as a book to use and enjoy, not primarily as a program to follow. We hope that the poems we have chosen, and the arrangement in which we have set them, will help the student of English literature to see some order in its poetic variety.

E. A. B.

C. H. P.

E. M. B.

Contents

CHAPTER 1

The Language of
Poetry

Care-Charmer Sleep

SAMUEL DANIEL (1562?–1619)

Care-charmer sleep, son of the sable night,
    Brother to death, in silent darkness born,
    Relieve my languish and restore the light;
    With dark forgetting of my care, return.
And let the day be time enough to mourn
    The shipwreck of my ill-adventured youth;
    Let waking eyes suffice to wail their scorn
    Without the torment of the night's untruth.
Cease, dreams, th' images of day-desires,
    To model forth the passions of the morrow;
    Never let rising sun approve you liars,
    To add more grief to aggravate my sorrow.
Still let me sleep, embracing clouds in vain,
And never wake to feel the day's disdain.   1592

Sonnet 55

WILLIAM SHAKESPEARE (1564–1616)

Not marble, nor the gilded monuments
Of princes, shall outlive this powerful rime;
But you shall shine more bright in these contents
Than unswept stone, besmear'd with sluttish time.
When wasteful war shall statues overturn,
And broils root out the work of masonry,
Nor Mars his sword nor war's quick fire shall burn
The living record of your memory.
'Gainst death and all-oblivious enmity
Shall you pace forth; your praise shall still find room
Even in the eyes of all posterity
That wear this world out to the ending doom.
 So, till the judgment that yourself arise,
 You live in this, and dwell in lovers' eyes.   1609

Sonnet 73

WILLIAM SHAKESPEARE (1564–1616)

That time of year thou mayst in me behold
When yellow leaves, or none, or few, do hang
Upon those boughs which shake against the cold,
Bare ruin'd choirs, where late the sweet birds sang.
In me thou see'st the twilight of such day
As after sunset fadeth in the west;
Which by and by black night doth take away,
Death's second self, that seals up all in rest.
In me thou see'st the glowing of such fire,
That on the ashes of his youth doth lie,
As the death-bed whereon it must expire,
Consum'd with that which it was nourish'd by.
 This thou perceiv'st, which makes thy love more strong,
 To love that well which thou must leave ere long.   1609

2

Sonnet 97

WILLIAM SHAKESPEARE (1564–1616)

How like a winter hath my absence been
From thee, the pleasure of the fleeting year!
What freezings have I felt, what dark days seen!
What old December's bareness everywhere!
And yet this time remov'd was summer's time,
The teeming autumn, big with rich increase,
Bearing the wanton burden of the prime,
Like widow'd wombs after their lords' decease:
Yet this abundant issue seem'd to me
But hope of orphans and unfather'd fruit;
For summer and his pleasures wait on thee,
And, thou away, the very birds are mute:
    Or, if they sing, 'tis with so dull a cheer,
    That leaves look pale, dreading the winter's near.   1609

Sonnet 129

WILLIAM SHAKESPEARE (1564–1616)

Th' expense of spirit in a waste of shame
Is lust in action; and till action, lust
Is perjur'd, murderous, bloody, full of blame,
Savage, extreme, rude, cruel, not to trust;
Enjoy'd no sooner but despised straight;
Past reason hunted, and no sooner had,
Past reason hated, as a swallow'd bait
On purpose laid to make the taker mad:
Mad in pursuit, and in possession so;
Had, having, and in quest to have, extreme;
A bliss in proof—and prov'd a very woe;
Before, a joy propos'd; behind, a dream.
    All this the world well knows; yet none knows well
    To shun the heaven that leads men to this hell.   1609

3

A Valediction: Forbidding Mourning

As virtuous men pass mildly away,
  And whisper to their souls to go,
Whilst some of their sad friends do say,
  "The breath goes now," and some say, "No,"

So let us melt and make no noise,
  No tear-floods nor sigh-tempests move;
'Twere profanation of our joys
  To tell the laity our love.

Moving of th' earth brings harms and fears;
  Men reckon what it did and meant;   10
But trepidation of the spheres,
  Though greater far, is innocent.

Dull sublunary lovers' love,
  Whose soul is sense, cannot admit
Absence, because it doth remove
  Those things which elemented it.

But we by a love so much refin'd
  That ourselves know not what it is,
Interassurèd of the mind,
  Care less eyes, lips, and hands to miss.   20

Our two souls, therefore, which are one,
  Though I must go, endure not yet
A breach, but an expansion,
  Like gold to airy thinness beat.

If they be two, they are two so
  As stiff twin compasses are two;
Thy soul, the fix'd foot, makes no show
  To move, but doth if th' other do.

And though it in the center sit,
  Yet when the other far doth roam,   30
It leans and hearkens after it,
  And grows erect as that comes home.

Such wilt thou be to me, who must,
  Like th' other foot, obliquely run;
Thy firmness makes my circle just,
  And makes me end where I begun.   1633

4

Jordan [1]

GEORGE HERBERT (1593–1633)

Who says that fictions only and false hair
Become a verse? Is there in truth no beauty?
Is all good structure in a winding stair?
May no lines pass except they do their duty
    Not to a true, but painted chair?

Is it no verse except enchanted groves
And sudden arbors shadow coarse-spun lines?
Must purling streams refresh a lover's loves?
Must all be veiled, while he that reads, divines,
    Catching the sense at two removes?

Shepherds are honest people; let them sing.
Riddle who list for me, and pull for prime;
I envy no man's nightingale or spring,
Nor let them punish me with loss of rhyme,
    Who plainly say, My God, my King.   1633

Jordan [2]

GEORGE HERBERT (1593–1633)

When first my lines of heav'nly joys made mention,
Such was their luster, they did so excel,
That I sought out quaint words and trim invention;
My thoughts began to burnish, sprout, and swell,
Curling with metaphors a plain intention,
Decking the sense as if it were to sell.

Thousands of notions in my brain did run,
Off'ring their service, if I were not sped.
I often blotted what I had begun:
This was not quick enough, and that was dead.
Nothing could seem too rich to clothe the sun,
Much less those joys which trample on his head.

As flames do work and wind when they ascend,
So did I weave myself into the sense.
But while I bustled, I might hear a friend
Whisper, How wide is all this long pretense!
There is in love a sweetness ready penned,
Copy out only that, and save expense.   1633

5

Mediocrity in Love Rejected

THOMAS CAREW (1594?–1639?)

Give me more love or more disdain:
  The torrid or the frozen zone
Bring equal ease unto my pain,
  The temperate affords me none;
Either extreme of love or hate
Is sweeter than a calm estate.

Give me a storm; if it be love,
  Like Danaë in that golden shower,
I swim in pleasure; if it prove
  Disdain, that torrent will devour
My vulture-hopes; and he's possessed
Of heaven, that's but from hell released.
    Then crown my joys or cure my pain;
    Give me more love or more disdain.   1640

The Night Piece, to Julia

ROBERT HERRICK (1591–1674)

Her eyes the glow-worm lend thee,
The shooting stars attend thee;
    And the elves also,
    Whose little eyes glow
Like the sparks of fire, befriend thee.

No will-o'-th'-wisp mis-light thee,
Nor snake, or slow-worm bite thee;
    But on, on thy way
    Not making a stay,
Since ghost there's none to affright thee.

Let not the dark thee cumber;
What though the moon does slumber?
    The stars of the night
    Will lend thee their light,
Like tapers clear without number.

Then, Julia, let me woo thee,
Thus, thus to come unto me;
    And when I shall meet
    Thy silv'ry feet,
My soul I'll pour into thee.   1648

6

Delight in Disorder

ROBERT HERRICK (1591–1674)

A sweet disorder in the dress
Kindles in clothes a wantonness;
A lawn about the shoulders thrown
Into a fine distraction,
An erring lace, which here and there
Enthralls the crimson stomacher,
A cuff neglectful, and thereby
Ribands to flow confusedly,
A winning wave, deserving note,
In the tempestuous petticoat,
A careless shoe-string, in whose tie
I see a wild civility,
Do more bewitch me than when art
Is too precise in every part.   1648

Upon the Body of Our Blessed Lord, Naked and Bloody

RICHARD CRASHAW (1612–1649)

They have left thee naked, Lord; O that they had!
This garment too I would they had denied.

Thee with thyself they have too richly clad,
Opening the purple wardrobe in thy side.

O never could there be garment too good
For thee to wear, but this, of thine own blood.   1652

Sonnet

JOHN MILTON (1608–1674)

When I consider how my light is spent
   Ere half my days in this dark world and wide,
   And that one talent which is death to hide
   Lodged with me useless, though my soul more bent
To serve therewith my Maker, and present
   My true account, lest he returning chide,
   "Doth God exact day-labour, light denied?"
   I fondly ask. But Patience, to prevent
That murmur, soon replies, "God doth not need
   Either man's work or his own gifts. Who best
   Bear his mild yoke, they serve him best. His state
Is kingly: thousands at his bidding speed,
   And post o'er land and ocean without rest;
   They also serve who only stand and wait."

                             (1653? 1673)

2. *half my days:* Milton was about 43 years old when he became totally blind.

Sonnet

JOHN MILTON (1608–1674)

Methought I saw my late espousèd saint
   Brought to me like Alcestis from the grave
   Whom Jove's great son to her glad husband gave,
   Rescued from Death by force, though pale and faint.
Mine, as whom washed from spot of child-bed taint
   Purification in the Old Law did save,
   And such as yet once more I trust to have
   Full sight of her in Heaven without restraint,
Came vested all in white, pure as her mind.
   Her face was veiled; yet to my fancied sight
   Love, sweetness, goodness, in her person shined
So clear, as in no face with more delight.
   But, oh! as to embrace me she inclined,
   I waked, she fled, and day brought back my night.

                            (1658; 1673)

1–5. *Methought . . . taint:* Milton's second wife, Catherine Woodcock, died in childbirth in February, 1658.

The Definition of Love

ANDREW MARVELL (1621–1678)

My love is of a birth as rare
As 'tis for object strange and high;
It was begotten by despair
Upon impossibility.

Magnanimous despair alone
Could show me so divine a thing,
Where feeble hope could ne'er have flown,
But vainly flapped its tinsel wing.

And yet I quickly might arrive
Where my extended soul is fixed,   10
But fate does iron wedges drive,
And always crowds itself betwixt.

For fate with jealous eye does see
Two perfect loves, nor lets them close;
Their union would her ruin be,
And her tyrannic power depose.

And therefore her decrees of steel
Us as the distant poles have placed,
Though love's whole world on us doth wheel,
Not by themselves to be embraced;   20

Unless the giddy heaven fall,
And earth some new convulsion tear,
And, us to join, the world should all
Be cramped into a planisphere.

As lines, so loves, oblique may well
Themselves in every angle greet;
But ours so truly parallel,
Though infinite, can never meet.

Therefore the love which us doth bind,
But fate so enviously debars,   30
Is the conjunction of the mind,
And opposition of the stars.   1681

9

Meditation Seven

EDWARD TAYLOR (1645?–1729)

Psalms 45:2.   Grace is poured into thy lips.

Thy humane frame, my glorious Lord, I spy,
  A golden still with heavenly choice drugs fill'd:
Thy holy love, the glowing heat whereby
    The spirit of grace is graciously distill'd.
    Thy mouth the neck through which these spirits still,
    My soul thy vial make, and therewith fill.

Thy speech the liquor in thy vessel stands,
  Well ting'd with grace, a blessed tincture, loe,
Thy words distill'd grace in thy lips pour'd, and
    Give grace's tincture in them where they go.
    Thy words in grace's tincture still'd, Lord, may
    The tincture of thy grace in me convey.

That golden mint of words thy mouth divine
  Doth tip these words, which by my fall were spoil'd;
And dub with gold dug out of grace's mine,
    That they thine image might have in them foil'd.
    Grace in thy lips pour'd out's as liquid gold:
    Thy bottle make my soul, Lord, it to hold.   1684

To a Child of Quality Five Years Old

MATTHEW PRIOR (1664–1721)

Lords, knights, and squires, the numerous band
    That wear the fair Miss Mary's fetters,
Were summoned by her high command,
    To show their passions by their letters.

My pen amongst the rest I took,
    Lest those bright eyes that cannot read
Should dart their kindling fires, and look
    The power they have to be obeyed.

Nor quality nor reputation
    Forbid me yet my flame to tell;   10
Dear five years old befriends my passion,
    And I may write till she can spell.

For while she makes her silk-worms beds
    With all the tender things I swear,
Whilst all the house my passion reads,
    In papers round her baby's hair,

She may receive and own my flame,
    For though the strictest prudes should know it,
She'll pass for a most virtuous dame,
    And I for an unhappy poet.   20

Then too, alas! when she shall tear
    The lines some younger rival sends,
She'll give me leave to write, I fear,
    And we shall still continue friends;

For, as our different ages move,
    'Tis so ordained, would fate but mend it!
That I shall be past making love
    When she begins to comprehend it.   1704

2. *Miss Mary:* Lady Mary Villiers (1690?–1735), a daughter of the first
Earl of Jersey.
16. *baby's:* doll's.

A Description of a City Shower

JONATHAN SWIFT (1667–1745)

Careful observers may foretell the hour
(By sure prognostics) when to dread a shower.
While rain depends, the pensive cat gives o'er
Her frolics and pursues her tail no more.
Returning home at night, you'll find the sink
Strike your offended sense with double stink.
If you be wise, then go not far to dine;
You'll spend in coach-hire more than save in wine.
A coming shower your shooting corns presage,
Old aches throb, your hollow tooth will rage: 10
Saunt'ring in coffee-house is Dulman seen;
He damns the climate and complains of spleen.

Meanwhile the South, rising with dabbled wings,
A sable cloud athwart the welkin flings,
That swilled more liquor than it could contain,
And, like a drunkard, gives it up again.
Brisk Susan whips her linen from the rope,
While the first drizzling shower is borne aslope:
Such is that sprinkling which some careless quean
Flirts on you from her mop, but not so clean: 20
You fly, invoke the gods; then turning, stop
To rail; she singing, still whirls on her mop,
Not yet the dust had shunned th' unequal strife,
But, aided by the wind, fought still for life,
And wafted with its foe by violent gust,
'Twas doubtful which was rain and which was dust.
Ah! where must needy poet seek for aid,
When dust and rain at once his coat invade?
Sole coat, where dust cemented by the rain,
Erects the nap, and leaves a mingled stain.   30

Now in contiguous drops the flood comes down,
Threat'ning with deluge this devoted town,
To shops in crowds the daggled females fly,
Pretend to cheapen goods, but nothing buy.
The Templar spruce, while ev'ry spout's abroach,
Stays till 'tis fair, yet seems to call a coach.
The tucked-up sempstress walks with hasty strides,

35. *Templar:* a barrister or student of law who had chambers in the Temple in London; the original buildings belonged to the Knights Templars.

12

While streams run down her oiled umbrella's sides.
Here various kinds, by various fortunes led,
Commence acquaintance underneath a shed.   40
Triumphant Tories and desponding Whigs
Forget their feuds and join to save their wigs.
Boxed in a chair the beau impatient sits,
While spouts run clatt'ring o'er the roof by fits;
And ever and anon with frightful din
The leather sounds, he trembles from within.
So when Troy chairmen bore the wooden steed,
Pregnant with Greeks impatient to be freed
(Those bully Greeks, who, as the moderns do,
Instead of paying chairmen run them thro'),   50
Laocoön struck the outside with his spear,
And each imprisoned hero quaked for fear.
   Now from all parts the swelling kennels flow,
And bear their trophies with them as they go:
Filth of all hues and odours seem to tell
What street they sailed from, by their sight and smell.
They, as each torrent drives with rapid force,
From Smithfield or St. Pulchre's shape their
      course,
And in huge confluence join at Snow Hill Ridge,
Fall from the conduit prone to Holborn Bridge.   60
Sweepings from butchers' stalls, dung, guts, and
      blood,
Drowned puppies, stinking sprats, all drenched
      in mud,
Dead cats, and turnip-tops come tumbling down
      the flood.   1710

On a Lady Throwing Snowballs at Her Lover

CHRISTOPHER SMART (1722–1771)

When, wanton fair, the snowy orb you throw,
I feel a fire before unknown in snow,
E'en coldest snow I find has pow'r to warm
My breast, when flung by Julia's lovely arm.
T'elude love's powerful arts I strive in vain,
If ice and snow can latent fires contain.
These frolicks leave; the force of beauty prove;
With equal passion cool my ardent love.   1754

Lines

PERCY BYSSHE SHELLEY (1792–1822)

When the lamp is shattered,
The light in the dust lies dead—
When the cloud is scattered,
The rainbow's glory is shed.
When the lute is broken,
Sweet tones are remembered not;
When the lips have spoken,
Loved accents are soon forgot.

As music and splendor
Survive not the lamp and the lute,   10
The heart's echoes render
No song when the spirit is mute—
No song but sad dirges,
Like the wind through a ruined cell,
Or the mournful surges
That ring the dead seaman's knell.

When hearts have once mingled
Love first leaves the well-built nest;
The weak one is singled
To endure what it once possessed.   20
O Love! who bewailest
The frailty of all things here,
Why choose you the frailest
For your cradle, your home, and your bier?

Its passions will rock thee
As the storms rock the ravens on high;
Bright reason will mock thee,
Like the sun from a wintry sky.
From thy nest every rafter
Will rot, and thine eagle home   30
Leave thee naked to laughter,
When leaves fall and cold winds come.   1824

The Snow-Storm

RALPH WALDO EMERSON (1803–1882)

Journal, *November 27, 1832: "Instead of lectures on Architecture, I will make
a lecture on God's architecture, one of his beautiful works, a Day. I will draw a
sketch of a winter's day. I will trace as I can a rude outline of the far-assembled
influences, the contribution of the universe wherein this magical structure rises
like an exhalation, the wonder and charm of the immeasurable deep."*

Announced by all the trumpets of the sky,
Arrives the snow, and, driving o'er the fields,
Seems nowhere to alight: the whited air
Hides hills and woods, the river, and the heaven,
And veils the farm-house at the garden's end.
The sled and traveller stopped, the courier's feet
Delayed, all friends shut out, the housemates sit
Around the fireplace, enclosed
In a tumultuous privacy of storm.

Come see the north wind's masonry.   10
Out of an unseen quarry evermore
Furnished with tile, the fierce artificer
Curves his white bastions with projected roof
Round every windward stake, or tree, or door.
Speeding, the myriad-handed, his wild work
So fanciful, so savage, nought cares he
For number or proportion. Mockingly,
On coop or kennel he hangs Parian wreaths;
A swan-like form invests the hidden thorn;
Fills up the farmer's lane from wall to wall,   20
Maugre the farmer's sighs; and at the gate
A tapering turret overtops the work.
And when his hours are numbered, and the world
Is all his own, retiring, as he were not,
Leaves, when the sun appears, astonished Art
To mimic in slow structures, stone by stone,
Built in an age, the mad wind's night-work,
The frolic architecture of the snow.   1841

15

Smoke

HENRY DAVID THOREAU (1817–1862)

Light-winged smoke, Icarian bird,
Melting thy pinions in thy upward flight,
Lark without song, and messenger of dawn,
Circling above the hamlets as thy nest;
Or else, departing dream, and shadowy form
Of midnight vision, gathering up thy skirts;
By night star-veiling, and by day
Darkening the light and blotting out the sun;
Go thou my incense upward from this hearth,
And ask the Gods to pardon this clear flame.   1843

The Eagle

FRAGMENT

ALFRED, LORD TENNYSON (1809–1892)

He clasps the crag with crooked hands;
Close to the sun in lonely lands,
Ringed with the azure world, he stands.

The wrinkled sea beneath him crawls;
He watches from his mountain walls,
And like a thunderbolt he falls.   1851

Dover Beach

MATTHEW ARNOLD (1822–1888)

The sea is calm tonight,
The tide is full, the moon lies fair
Upon the straits;—on the French coast the light
Gleams and is gone; the cliffs of England stand,
Glimmering and vast, out in the tranquil bay.
Come to the window, sweet is the night-air!

Only, from the long line of spray
Where the sea meets the moon-blanched land,
Listen! you hear the grating roar
Of pebbles which the waves draw back, and fling,   10
At their return, up the high strand,
Begin, and cease, and then again begin,
With tremulous cadence slow, and bring
The eternal note of sadness in.

Sophocles long ago
Heard it on the Aegean, and it brought
Into his mind the turbid ebb and flow
Of human misery; we
Find also in the sound a thought,
Hearing it by this distant northern sea.   20

The Sea of Faith
Was once, too, at the full, and round earth's shore
Lay like the folds of a bright girdle furled.
But now I only hear
Its melancholy, long, withdrawing roar,
Retreating, to the breath
Of the night-wind, down the vast edges drear
And naked shingles of the world.

Ah, love, let us be true
To one another! for the world, which seems   30
To lie before us like a land of dreams,
So various, so beautiful, so new,
Hath really neither joy, nor love, nor light,
Nor certitude, nor peace, nor help for pain;
And we are here as on a darkling plain
Swept with confused alarms of struggle and flight,
Where ignorant armies clash by night.   1867

Barren Spring

DANTE GABRIEL ROSSETTI (1828–1882)

Sonnet 83 *from* THE HOUSE OF LIFE (1881)

Once more the changed year's turning wheel returns:
And as a girl sails balanced in the wind
And now before and now again behind
Stoops as it swoops, with cheek that laughs and burns,—
So Spring comes merry towards me here, but earns
No answering smile from me, whose life is twin'd
With the dead boughs that winter still must bind,
And whom to-day the Spring no more concerns.
Behold, this crocus is a withering flame;
This snowdrop, snow; this apple-blossom's part
To breed the fruit that breeds the serpent's art.
Nay, for these Spring-flowers, turn thy face from them,
Nor stay till on the year's last lily-stem
The white cup shrivels round the golden heart.   1870

Jabberwocky

CHARLES LUTWIDGE DODGSON "LEWIS CARROLL" (1832–1898)

'Twas brillig and the slithy toves
    Did gyre and gimble in the wabe;
All mimsy were the borogoves,
    And the mome raths outgrabe.

"Beware the Jabberwock, my son!
    The jaws that bite, the claws that catch!
Beware the Jubjub bird, and shun
    The frumious Bandersnatch!"

1. *brillig:* this word as well as most of the other invented and "portmanteau" words in *Jabberwocky* are defined by Humpty Dumpty in Lewis Carroll's *Through the Looking Glass.*

He took his vorpal sword in hand:
  Long time the manxome foe he sought—   10
So rested he by the Tumtum tree.
  And stood awhile in thought.

And as in uffish thought he stood,
  The Jabberwock, with eyes of flame,
Came whiffling through the tulgey wood,
  And burbled as it came!

One, two! One, two! And through and through
  The vorpal blade went snicker-snack!
He left it dead, and with its head
  He went galumphing back.   20

"And hast thou slain the Jabberwock?
  Come to my arms, my beamish boy!
O frabjous day! Callooh! Callay!"
  He chortled in his joy.

'Twas brillig and the slithy toves
  Did gyre and gimble in the wabe;
All mimsy were the borogoves,
  And the mome raths outgrabe.   1872

A Slant of Sun

STEPHEN CRANE (1871–1900)

A slant of sun on dull brown walls,
A forgotten sky of bashful blue.

Toward God a mighty hymn,
A song of collisions and cries,
Rumbling wheels, hoof-beats, bells,
Welcomes, farewells, love-calls, final moans,
Voices of joy, idiocy, warning, despair,
The unknown appeals of brutes,
The chanting of flowers,
The screams of cut trees,
The senseless babble of hens and wise men—
A cluttered incoherency that says at the stars:
"O God, save us!"   1899

The Trees in the Garden

STEPHEN CRANE (1871–1900)

The trees in the garden rained flowers.
Children ran there joyously.
They gathered the flowers
Each to himself.
Now there were some
Who gathered great heaps—
Having opportunity and skill—
Until, behold, only chance blossoms
Remained for the feeble.
Then a little spindling tutor   10
Ran importantly to the father, crying:
"Pray, come hither!
See this unjust thing in your garden!"
But when the father had surveyed,
He admonished the tutor:
"Not so, small sage!
This thing is just.
For, look you,
Are not they who possess the flowers
Stronger, bolder, shrewder   20
Than they who have none?
Why should the strong—
The beautiful strong—
Why should they not have the flowers?"
Upon reflection, the tutor bowed to the ground.
"My lord," he said,
"The stars are displaced
By this towering wisdom."   1899

In a Station of the Metro

EZRA POUND (1885–   )

The apparition of these faces in the crowd:
Petals on a wet, black bough.   1913

The Contagious Hospital

WILLIAM CARLOS WILLIAMS (1883–1963)

Poem 1 *from* SPRING AND ALL

By the road to the contagious hospital
under the surge of the blue
mottled clouds driven from the
northeast—a cold wind. Beyond, the
waste of broad, muddy fields
brown with dried weeds, standing and fallen

patches of standing water
the scattering of tall trees

All along the road the reddish
purplish, forked, upstanding, twiggy   10
stuff of bushes and small trees
with dead, brown leaves under them
leafless vines—

Lifeless in appearance, sluggish
dazed spring approaches—

They enter the new world naked,
cold, uncertain of all
save that they enter. All about them
the cold, familiar wind—

Now the grass, tomorrow   20
the stiff curl of wildcarrot leaf

One by one objects are defined—
It quickens: clarity, outline of leaf

But now the stark dignity of
entrance—Still, the profound change
has come upon them: rooted, they
grip down and begin to awaken.   1923

21

The Red Wheelbarrow

WILLIAM CARLOS WILLIAMS (1883–1963)

Poem 21 *from* SPRING AND ALL

  so much depends
  upon

  a red wheel
  barrow

  glazed with rain
  water

  beside the white
  chickens   1923

New England

EDWIN ARLINGTON ROBINSON (1869–1935)

Here where the wind is always north-north-east
And children learn to walk on frozen toes,
Wonder begets an envy of all those
Who boil elsewhere with such a lyric yeast
Of love that you will hear them at a feast
Where demons would appeal for some repose,
Still clamouring where the chalice overflows
And crying wildest who have drunk the least.

Passion is here a soilure of the wits,
We're told, and Love a cross for them to bear;
Joy shivers in the corner where she knits
And Conscience always has the rocking-chair,
Cheerful as when she tortured into fits
The first cat that was ever killed by Care. 1925

Ars Poetica

ARCHIBALD MAC LEISH (1892–   )

A poem should be palpable and mute
As a globed fruit

Dumb
As old medallions to the thumb

Silent as the sleeve-worn stone
Of casement ledges where the moss has grown—

A poem should be wordless
As the flight of birds

*

A poem should be motionless in time
As the moon climbs   10

Leaving, as the moon releases
Twig by twig the night-entangled trees,

Leaving, as the moon behind the winter leaves,
Memory by memory the mind—

A poem should be motionless in time
As the moon climbs

*

A poem should be equal to:
Not true

For all the history of grief
An empty doorway and a maple leaf   20

For love
The leaning grasses and two lights above the sea—

A poem should not mean
But be   1926

Voyages: II

HART CRANE (1899–1932)

—And yet this great wink of eternity,
Of rimless floods, unfettered leewardings,
Samite sheeted and processioned where
Her undinal vast belly moonward bends,
Laughing the wrapt inflections of our love;

Take this Sea, whose diapason knells
On scrolls of silver snowy sentences,
The sceptered terror of whose sessions rends
As her demeanors motion well or ill,
All but the pieties of lovers' hands.   10

And onward, as bells off San Salvador
Salute the crocus lusters of the stars,
In these poinsettia meadows of her tides,—
Adagios of islands, O my Prodigal,
Complete the dark confessions her veins spell.

Mark how her turning shoulders wind the hours,
And hasten while her penniless rich palms
Pass superscription of bent foam and wave,—
Hasten, while they are true,—sleep, death, desire,
Close round one instant in one floating flower.   20

Bind us in time, O Seasons clear, and awe.
O minstrel galleons of Carib fire,
Bequeath us to no earthly shore until
Is answered in the vortex of our grave
The seal's wide spindrift gaze toward paradise.   1926

The Broken Tower

HART CRANE (1899–1932)

The bell-rope that gathers God at dawn
Dispatches me as though I dropped down the knell
Of a spent day—to wander the cathedral lawn
From pit to crucifix, feet chill on steps from hell.

Have you not heard, have you not seen that corps
Of shadows in the tower, whose shoulders sway
Antiphonal carillons launched before
The stars are caught and hived in the sun's ray?

The bells, I say, the bells break down their tower;
And swing I know not where. Their tongues engrave   10
Membrane through marrow, my long-scattered score
Of broken intervals. . . . And I, their sexton slave!

Oval encyclicals in canyons heaping
The impasse high with choir. Banked voices slain!
Pagodas, campaniles with reveilles outleaping—
O terraced echoes prostrate on the plain! . . .

And so it was I entered the broken world
To trace the visionary company of love, its voice
An instant in the wind (I know not whither hurled)
But not for long to hold each desperate choice.   20

My word I poured. But was it cognate, scored
Of that tribunal monarch of the air
Whose thigh embronzes earth, strikes crystal Word
In wounds pledged once to hope—cleft to despair?

The steep encroachments of my blood left me
No answer (could blood hold such a lofty tower
As flings the question true?)—or is it she
Whose sweet mortality stirs latent power?—

And through whose pulse I hear, counting the strokes
My veins recall and add, revived and sure   30
The angelus of wars my chest evokes:
What I hold healed, original now, and pure . . .

And builds, within, a tower that is not stone
(Not stone can jacket heaven)—but slip
Of pebbles—visible wings of silence sown
In azure circles, widening as they dip

The matrix of the heart, lift down the eye
That shrines the quiet lake and swells a tower . . .
The commodious, tall decorum of that sky
Unseals her earth, and lifts love in its shower.   1933   40

A Refusal to Mourn the Death, by Fire, of a Child in London

DYLAN THOMAS (1914–1953)

Never until the mankind making
Bird beast and flower
Fathering and all humbling darkness
Tells with silence the last light breaking
And the still hour
Is come of the sea tumbling in harness

And I must enter again the round
Zion of the water bead
And the synagogue of the ear of corn
Shall I let pray the shadow of a sound   10
Or sow my salt seed
In the least valley of sackcloth to mourn

The majesty and burning of the child's death.
I shall not murder
The mankind of her going with a grave truth
Nor blaspheme down the stations of the breath
With any further
Elegy of innocence and youth.

Deep with the first dead lies London's daughter,
Robed in the long friends,   20
The grains beyond age, the dark veins of her mother,
Secret by the unmourning water
Of the riding Thames.
After the first death, there is no other.   1945

Vicissitudes of the Creator

ARCHIBALD MACLEISH (1892–   )

Fish has laid her succulent eggs
Safe in Saragossa weed
So wound and bound that crabbed legs
Nor clattering claws can find and feed.

Thus fish commits unto the sea
Her infinite future and the Trade
Blows westward toward eternity
The universe her love has made.

But when, upon this leeward beach,
The measureless sea journey ends
And ball breaks open, from the breach
A deft, gold, glossy crab extends

In ring-side ritual of self-applause
The small ironic silence of his claws.   1954

CHAPTER 2

Symbol, Myth, and Allegory

Song

WILLIAM SHAKESPEARE (1564–1616)

From LOVE'S LABOUR'S LOST

SPRING

When daisies pied and violets blue
  And lady smocks all silver-white
And cuckoo buds of yellow hue
  Do paint the meadows with delight,
The cuckoo then, on every tree,
Mocks married men; for thus sings he—"Cuckoo,
Cuckoo, cuckoo!" Oh, word of fear,
Unpleasing to a married ear!

When shepherds pipe on oaten straws,
  And merry larks are plowmen's clocks,   10
When turtles tread, and rooks, and daws,
  And maidens bleach their summer smocks,
The cuckoo then, on every tree,
Mocks married men; for thus sings he—"Cuckoo,
Cuckoo, cuckoo!" Oh, word of fear,
Unpleasing to a married ear!

WINTER

When icicles hang by the wall,
   And Dick the shepherd blows his nail,
And Tom bears logs into the hall,
   And milk comes frozen home in pail,   20
When blood is nipped and ways be foul,
Then nightly sings the staring owl—"Tu-whit,
Tu-who," a merry note,
While greasy Joan doth keel the pot.

When all aloud the wind doth blow,
   And coughing drowns the parson's saw,
And birds sit brooding in the snow,
   And Marian's nose looks red and raw,
When roasted crabs hiss in the bowl,
Then nightly sings the staring owl—"Tu-whit,   30
Tu-who," a merry note,
While greasy Joan doth keel the pot.   1594;1598

Holy Sonnet 7

JOHN DONNE (1572–1631)

At the round earth's imagin'd corners, blow
Your trumpets, angels; and arise, arise
From death, you numberless infinities
Of souls, and to your scatter'd bodies go;
All whom the flood did, and fire shall o'erthrow,
All whom war, dearth, age, agues, tyrannies,
Despair, law, chance, hath slain, and you whose eyes
Shall behold God, and never taste death's woe.
But let them sleep, Lord, and me mourn a space,
For if, above all these, my sins abound,
'Tis late to ask abundance of Thy grace
When we are there; here on this lowly ground,
Teach me how to repent; for that's as good
As if Thou'dst sealed my pardon with Thy blood.   1633

Holy Sonnet 14

JOHN DONNE (1572–1631)

Batter my heart, three-person'd God, for you
As yet but knock, breathe, shine, and seek to mend;
That I may rise and stand, o'erthrow me and bend
Your force to break, blow, burn, and make me new.
I, like an usurp'd town t' another due,
Labor t' admit you, but O, to no end!
Reason, your viceroy in me, me should defend,
But is captiv'd, and proves weak or untrue.
Yet dearly I love you and would be loved fain,
But am betroth'd unto your enemy.
Divorce me, untie, or break that knot again,
Take me to you, imprison me, for I,
Except y' enthrall me, never shall be free,
Nor ever chaste except you ravish me.   1633

The Night

HENRY VAUGHAN (1622–1695)
John 3:2

Through that pure virgin-shrine,
That sacred veil drawn o'er thy glorious noon,
That men might look and live, as glow-worms shine,
      And face the moon,
      Wise Nicodemus saw such light
      As made him know his God by night.

Most blest believer he!
Who in that land of darkness and blind eyes
Thy long-expected healing wings could see
      When thou didst rise,   10
      And what can never more be done,
      Did at midnight speak with the Sun!

Oh, who will tell me where
He found thee at that dead and silent hour?
What hallowed solitary ground did bear
      So rare a flower;
      Within whose sacred leaves did lie
      The fullness of the Deity?

No mercy-seat of gold,
No dead and dusty cherub, nor carved stone,   20
But his own living works did my Lord hold
    And lodge alone;
  Where trees and herbs did watch and peep
  And wonder, while the Jews did sleep.

Dear night! this world's defeat;
The stop to busy fools; care's check and curb;
The day of spirits; my soul's calm retreat
    Which none disturb;
  Christ's progress, and his prayer time;
  The hours to which high heaven doth chime.   30

God's silent, searching flight;
When my Lord's head is filled with dew, and all
His locks are wet with the clear drops of night;
    His still, soft call;
  His knocking time; the soul's dumb watch,
  When spirits their fair kindred catch.

Were all my loud, evil days
Calm and unhaunted as is thy dark tent,
Whose peace but by some angel's wing or voice
    Is seldom rent,   40
  Then I in heaven all the long year
  Would keep, and never wander here.

But living where the Sun
Doth all things wake, and where all mix and tire
Themselves and others, I consent and run
    To ev'ry mire,
  And by this world's ill-guiding light,
  Err more than I can do by night.

There is in God (some say)
A deep, but dazzling darkness; as men here   50
Say it is late and dusky, because they
    See not all clear.
  O for that night! where I in him
  Might live invisible and dim.   1655

The Rape of the Lock

An Heroic-Comical Poem

ALEXANDER POPE (1688–1744)

Nolueram, Belinda, tuos violare capillos;
Sed juvat, hoc precibus me tribuisse tuis.
MART., *Epigr.* XII, 84.

TO MRS. ARABELLA FERMOR

Madam,

It will be in vain to deny that I have some Regard for this Piece, since I Dedicate it to You. Yet You may bear me Witness, it was intended only to divert a few young Ladies, who have good Sense and good Humour enough, to laugh not only at their Sex's little unguarded Follies, but at their own. But as it was communicated with the Air of a Secret, it soon found its Way into the World. An imperfect Copy having been offer'd to a Bookseller, You had the Good-Nature for my Sake to consent to the Publication of one more correct: This I was forc'd to before I had executed half my Design, for the Machinery *was entirely wanting to compleat it.*

The Machinery, *Madam, is a Term invented by the Criticks, to signify that Part which the Deities, Angels, or Daemons, are made to act in a Poem: For the ancient Poets are in one respect like many modern Ladies; Let an Action be never so trivial in itself, they always make it appear of the utmost Importance. These Machines I determin'd to raise on a very new and odd Foundation, the* Rosicrucian *Doctrine of Spirits.*

I know how disagreeable it is to make use of hard Words before a Lady; but 'tis so much the Concern of a Poet to have his Works understood, and particularly by your Sex, that You must give me leave to explain two or three difficult Terms.

The Rosicrucians are a People I must bring You acquainted with. The best Account I know of them is in a French Book call'd Le Comte de Gabalis, *which both in its Title and Size is so like a* Novel, *that many of the Fair Sex*

Nolueram . . . tuis: "I did not wish, Belinda, to profane thy locks; but I am glad to have granted this much to thy prayers." The poem originated from an incident that occurred among several of Pope's friends. Robert, Lord Petre (the Baron), snipped a lock of hair from the head of Arabella Fermor (Belinda). Pope was asked by a mutual friend, John Caryll, to write a poem to heal the estrangement that followed between the two families.

have read it for one by Mistake. According to these Gentlemen, the four Elements are inhabited by Spirits, which they call Sylphs, Gnomes, Nymphs, *and* Salamanders. *The* Gnomes, *or Daemons of Earth, delight in Mischief; but the* Sylphs, *whose Habitation is in the Air, are the best-condition'd Creatures imaginable. For they say, any Mortals may enjoy the most intimate Familiarities with these gentle Spirits, upon a Condition very easie to all true* Adepts, *an inviolate Preservation of Chastity.*

As to the following Canto's, all the Passages of them are as Fabulous, as the Vision at the Beginning, or the Transformation at the End; (except the Loss of your Hair, which I always mention with Reverence.) The Human Persons are as Fictitious as the Airy ones; and the character of Belinda, *as it is now manag'd, resembles You in nothing but in Beauty.*

If this Poem had as many Graces as there are in Your Person, or in Your Mind, yet I could never hope it should pass thro' the World half so Uncensured as You have done. But let its Fortune be what it will, mine is happy enough, to have given me this Occasion of assuring You that I am, with the truest Esteem,

Madam,
Your Most Obedient,
Humble Servant.
A. Pope.

CANTO I

What dire offence from am'rous causes springs,
What mighty contests rise from trivial things,
I sing—This verse to Caryll, Muse! is due;
This, ev'n Belinda may vouchsafe to view:
Slight is the subject, but not so the praise,
If she inspire, and he approve my lays.
   Say what strange motive, Goddess! cou'd compel
A well-bred lord t'assault a gentle belle?
Oh say what stranger cause, yet unexplor'd,
Cou'd make a gentle belle reject a lord?   10
In tasks so bold, can little men engage,
And in soft bosoms dwells such mighty rage?
   Sol through white curtains shot a tim'rous ray,
And op'd those eyes that must eclipse the day;
Now lap-dogs give themselves the rousing shake,
And sleepless lovers, just at twelve, awake:

Thrice rung the bell, the slipper knock'd the ground,
And the press'd watch return'd a silver sound.
Belinda still her downy pillow prest,
Her guardian Sylph prolong'd the balmy rest.   20
'Twas he had summon'd to her silent bed
The morning-dream that hover'd o'er her head.
A youth more glitt'ring than a birth-night beau,
(That ev'n in slumber caus'd her cheek to glow)
Seem'd to her ear his winning lips to lay,
And thus in whispers said, or seem'd to say:
    "Fairest of mortals, thou distinguish'd care
Of thousand bright inhabitants of air!
If e'er one vision touch'd thy infant thought,
Of all the nurse and all the priest have taught,   30
Of airy elves by moonlight shadows seen,
The silver token, and the circled green,
Or virgins visited by angel-pow'rs,
With golden crowns and wreaths of heav'nly flow'rs;
Hear and believe! thy own importance know,
Nor bound thy narrow views to things below.
Some secret truths, from learned pride conceal'd,
To maids alone and children are reveal'd:
What though no credit doubting wits may give?
The fair and innocent shall still believe.   40
Know then, unnumber'd spirits round thee fly,
The light militia of the lower sky;
These, tho' unseen, are ever on the wing,
Hang o'er the box, and hover round the Ring.
Think what an equipage thou hast in air,
And view with scorn two pages and a chair.
As now your own, our beings were of old,
And once inclos'd in woman's beauteous mold;
Thence, by a soft transition, we repair
From earthly vehicles to these of air.   50
Think not, when woman's transient breath is fled,

    18. *press'd watch:* a watch for night use, which, when pressed, sounded
the hour and quarter hour just past.
    23. *birth-night:* dressed elegantly for a royal birthday.
    32. *silver token:* the sixpence that fairies leave in the shoes of maids that
please them.
    44. *box:* theater-box.
    44. *Ring:* a circular road in London's Hyde Park where fashionable
ladies rode in their carriages.

That all her vanities at once are dead:
Succeeding vanities she still regards,
And though she plays no more, o'erlooks the cards.
Her joy in gilded chariots, when alive,
And love of ombre, after death survive.
For when the fair in all their pride expire,
To their first elements their souls retire:
The sprites of fiery termagants in flame
Mount up, and take a salamander's name.   60
Soft yielding minds to water glide away,
And sip, with nymphs, their elemental tea.
The graver prude sinks downward to a gnome,
In search of mischief still on earth to roam.
The light coquettes in sylphs aloft repair,
And sport and flutter in the fields of air.
    "Know farther yet; whoever fair and chaste
Rejects mankind, is by some sylph embrac'd:
For spirits, freed from mortal laws, with ease
Assume what sexes and what shapes they please.   70
What guards the purity of melting maids,
In courtly balls, and midnight masquerades,
Safe from the treach'rous friend, the daring spark,
The glance by day, the whisper in the dark;
When kind occasion prompts their warm desires,
When music softens, and when dancing fires?
'Tis but their sylph, the wise celestials know,
Though honour is the word with men below.
    "Some nymphs there are, too conscious of their face,
For life predestin'd to the gnomes' embrace.   80
These swell their prospects and exalt their pride,
When offers are disdain'd, and love denied.
Then gay ideas crowd the vacant brain,
While peers, and dukes, and all their sweeping train,
And garters, stars, and coronets appear,
And in soft sounds, Your Grace salutes their ear.
'Tis these that early taint the female soul,
Instruct the eyes of young coquettes to roll,
Teach infant-cheeks a bidden blush to know,
And little hearts to flutter at a beau.   90

56. *ombre:* a game of cards imported from Spain. Pope's detailed de-
scription of the game in Canto III parodies the hand-to-hand combat
between knights in epic poetry.

"Oft, when the world imagine women stray,
The sylphs through mystic mazes guide their way,
Through all the giddy circle they pursue,
And old impertinence expel by new.
What tender maid but must a victim fall
To one man's treat, but for another's ball?
When Florio speaks, what virgin could withstand,
If gentle Damon did not squeeze her hand?
With varying vanities, from ev'ry part,
They shift the moving toyshop of their heart;   100
Where wigs with wigs, with sword-knots sword-knots strive,
Beaux banish beaux, and coaches coaches drive.
This erring mortals levity may call,
Oh blind to truth! the sylphs contrive it all.
   "Of these am I, who thy protection claim,
A watchful sprite, and Ariel is my name.
Late, as I rang'd the crystal wilds of air,
In the clear mirror of thy ruling star
I saw, alas! some dread event impend,
Ere to the main this morning sun descend.   110
But Heav'n reveals not what, or how, or where:
Warn'd by thy sylph, O pious maid, beware!
This to disclose is all thy guardian can.
Beware of all, but most beware of man!"
   He said; when Shock, who thought she slept too long,
Leapt up, and wak'd his mistress with his tongue.
'Twas then, Belinda, if report say true,
Thy eyes first open'd on a billet-doux;
Wounds, charms, and ardours were no sooner read,
But all the vision vanish'd from thy head.   120
   And now, unveil'd, the toilet stands display'd,
Each silver vase in mystic order laid.
First, rob'd in white, the nymph intent adores,
With head uncover'd, the cosmetic pow'rs.
A heav'nly image in the glass appears,
To that she bends, to that her eyes she rears;
Th' inferior priestess, at her altar's side,
Trembling begins the sacred rites of Pride.
Unnumber'd treasures ope at once, and here
The various off'rings of the world appear;   130
From each she nicely culls with curious toil,
And decks the goddess with the glitt'ring spoil.
This casket India's glowing gems unlocks,

And all Arabia breathes from yonder box.
The tortoise here and elephant unite,
Transform'd to combs, the speckled, and the white.
Here files of pins extend their shining rows,
Puffs, powders, patches, bibles, billet-doux.
Now awful beauty puts on all its arms;
The fair each moment rises in her charms,   140
Repairs her smiles, awakens ev'ry grace,
And calls forth all the wonders of her face;
Sees by degrees a purer blush arise,
And keener lightnings quicken in her eyes.
The busy sylphs surround their darling care;
These set the head, and those divide the hair,
Some fold the sleeve, whilst others plait the gown;
And Betty's prais'd for labours not her own.

CANTO II

Not with more glories, in th' ethereal plain,
The sun first rises o'er the purpled main,
Than issuing forth, the rival of his beams
Launch'd on the bosom of the silver Thames.
Fair nymphs, and well-drest youths around her shone,
But ev'ry eye was fix'd on her alone.
On her white breast a sparkling cross she wore,
Which Jews might kiss, and infidels adore.
Her lively looks a sprightly mind disclose,
Quick as her eyes, and as unfix'd as those: 10
Favours to none, to all she smiles extends;
Oft she rejects, but never once offends.
Bright as the sun, her eyes the gazers strike,
And, like the sun, they shine on all alike.
Yet graceful ease, and sweetness void of pride,
Might hide her faults, if belles had faults to hide:
If to her share some female errors fall,
Look on her face, and you'll forget 'em all.
    This nymph, to the destruction of mankind,
Nourish'd two locks, which graceful hung behind   20
In equal curls, and well conspir'd to deck
With shining ringlets her smooth iv'ry neck.
Love in these labyrinths his slaves detains,
And mighty hearts are held in slender chains.
With hairy springes we the birds betray,
Slight lines of hair surprise the finny prey,
Fair tresses man's imperial race insnare,

And beauty draws us with a single hair.
　　Th' advent'rous baron the bright locks admir'd;
He saw, he wish'd, and to the prize aspir'd.   30
Resolv'd to win, he meditates the way,
By force to ravish, or by fraud betray;
For when success a lover's toil attends,
Few ask, if fraud or force attain'd his ends.
　　For this, ere Phœbus rose, he had implor'd
Propitious Heav'n, and ev'ry pow'r ador'd,
But chiefly Love—to Love an altar built
Of twelve vast French romances, neatly 'gilt.
There lay three garters, half a pair of gloves;
And all the trophies of his former loves;   40
With tender billet-doux he lights the pyre,
And breathes three am'rous sighs to raise the fire.
Then prostrate falls, and begs with ardent eyes
Soon to obtain, and long possess the prize:
The pow'rs gave ear, and granted half his pray'r,
The rest, the winds dispers'd in empty air.
　　But now secure the painted vessel glides,
The sunbeams trembling on the floating tides:
While melting music steals upon the sky,
And soften'd sounds along the waters die.   50
Smooth flow the waves, the zephyrs gently play,
Belinda smil'd, and all the world was gay.
All but the sylph—with careful thoughts opprest,
Th' impending woe sat heavy on his breast.
He summons straight his denizens of air;
The lucid squadrons round the sails repair:
Soft o'er the shrouds aerial whispers breathe,
That seem'd but zephyrs to the train beneath.
Some to the sun their insect-wings unfold,
Waft on the breeze, or sink in clouds of gold;   60
Transparent forms, too fine for mortal sight,
Their fluid bodies half dissolv'd in light.
Loose to the wind their airy garments flew,
Thin glitt'ring textures of the filmy dew;
Dipt in the richest tincture of the skies,
Where light disports in ever-mingling dyes,
While ev'ry beam new transient colours flings,
Colours that change whene'er they wave their wings.
Amid the circle, on the gilded mast,
Superior by the head, was Ariel plac'd;   70
His purple pinions op'ning to the sun,

He rais'd his azure wand, and thus begun:
   "Ye sylphs and sylphids, to your chief give ear!
Fays, fairies, genii, elves, and demons, hear!
Ye know the spheres, and various tasks assign'd
By laws eternal to th' aerial kind.
Some in the fields of purest ether play,
And bask and whiten in the blaze of day.
Some guide the course of wand'ring orbs on high,
Or roll the planets through the boundless sky.   80
Some less refin'd, beneath the moon's pale light
Pursue the stars that shoot athwart the night,
Or suck the mists in grosser air below,
Or dip their pinions in the painted bow,
Or brew fierce tempests on the wintry main,
Or o'er the glebe distill the kindly rain.
Others on earth o'er human race preside,
Watch all their ways, and all their actions guide:
Of these the chief the care of nations own,
And guard with arms divine the British throne.   90
   "Our humbler province is to tend the fair,
Not a less pleasing, though less glorious care;
To save the powder from too rude a gale,
Nor let th' imprison'd essences exhale,
To draw fresh colours from the vernal flow'rs;
To steal from rainbows ere they drop in show'rs
A brighter wash; to curl their waving hairs,
Assist their blushes, and inspire their airs;
Nay oft, in dreams, invention we bestow,
To change a flounce, or add a furbelow.   100
   "This day, black omens threat the brightest fair,
That e'er deserv'd a watchful spirit's care;
Some dire disaster, or by force, or slight;
But what, or where, the Fates have wrapp'd in night.
Whether the nymph shall break Diana's law,
Or some frail china jar receive a flaw;
Or stain her honour, or her new brocade;
Forget her pray'rs, or miss a masquerade;
Or lose her heart, or necklace, at a ball;
Or whether Heav'n has doom'd that Shock must fall.   110
Haste then, ye spirits! to your charge repair;
The flutt'ring fan be Zephyretta's care;
The drops to thee, Brillante, we consign;
And, Momentilla, let the watch be thine;
Do thou, Crispissa, tend her fav'rite lock;

Ariel himself shall be the guard of Shock.
"To fifty chosen sylphs, of special note,
We trust th' important charge, the petticoat:
Oft have we known that sev'nfold fence to fail,
Tho' stiff with hoops, and arm'd with ribs of whale.   120
Form a strong line about the silver bound,
And guard the wide circumference around.
    "Whatever spirit, careless of his charge,
His post neglects, or leaves the fair at large,
Shall feel sharp vengeance soon o'ertake his sins,
Be stopp'd in vials, or transfix'd with pins;
Or plung'd in lakes of bitter washes lie,
Or wedg'd whole ages in a bodkin's eye:
Gums and pomatums shall his flight restrain,
While clogg'd he beats his silken wings in vain;   130
Or alum-styptics with contracting power
Shrink his thin essence like a rivell'd flower:
Or, as Ixion fix'd, the wretch shall feel
The giddy motion of the whirling mill,
In fumes of burning chocolate shall glow,
And tremble at the sea that froths below!"
    He spoke; the spirits from the sails descend;
Some, orb in orb, around the nymph extend,
Some thrid the mazy ringlets of her hair,
Some hang upon the pendants of her ear;   140
With beating hearts the dire event they wait,
Anxious, and trembling for the birth of Fate.

CANTO III

Close by those meads, forever crown'd with flow'rs,
Where Thames with pride surveys his rising tow'rs,
There stands a structure of majestic frame,
Which from the neighb'ring Hampton takes its name.
Here Britain's statesmen oft the fall foredoom
Of foreign tyrants, and of nymphs at home;
Here thou, great Anna! whom three realms obey,
Dost sometimes counsel take—and sometimes tea.
    Hither the heroes and the nymphs resort,
To taste a while the pleasures of a court;   10
In various talk th' instructive hours they past,
Who gave the ball, or paid the visit last;
One speaks the glory of the British Queen,

4. *Hampton Court:* one of the royal palaces near London.
7. *Anna:* Queen Anne, last of the Stuart monarchs. She reigned from
1702 until 1714.

And one describes a charming Indian screen;
A third interprets motions, looks, and eyes;
At ev'ry word a reputation dies.
Snuff, or the fan, supply each pause of chat,
With singing, laughing, ogling, and all that.
    Meanwhile, declining from the noon of day,
The sun obliquely shoots his burning ray;   20
The hungry judges soon the sentence sign,
And wretches hang that jury-men may dine;
The merchant from th' Exchange returns in peace,
And the long labours of the toilette cease—
Belinda now, whom thirst of fame invites,
Burns to encounter two advent'rous knights,
At ombre singly to decide their doom;
And swells her breast with conquests yet to come.
Straight the three bands prepare in arms to join,
Each band the number of the sacred Nine.   30
Soon as she spreads her hand, th' aerial guard
Descend, and sit on each important card:
First Ariel perch'd upon a Matadore,
Then each, according to the rank they bore;
For sylphs, yet mindful of their ancient race,
Are, as when women, wondrous fond of place.
    Behold, four kings in majesty rever'd,
With hoary whiskers and a forky beard;
And four fair queens, whose hands sustain a flow'r,
Th' expressive emblem of their softer pow'r;   40
Four knaves in garbs succinct, a trusty band,
Caps on their heads, and halberts in their hand;
And parti-colour'd troops, a shining train,
Draw forth to combat on the velvet plain.
    The skilful nymph reviews her force with care;
"Let spades be trumps!" she said, and trumps they were.
    Now move to war her sable Matadores,
In show like leaders of the swarthy Moors.
Spadillio first, unconquerable lord!
Led off two captive trumps, and swept the board.   50
As many more Manillio forc'd to yield,
And march'd a victor from the verdant field.
Him Basto follow'd, but his fate more hard
Gain'd but one trump and one plebeian card.
With his broad sabre next, a chief in years,
The hoary Majesty of Spades appears;
Puts forth one manly leg, to sight reveal'd;

29. *bands:* hands of cards.   41. *succinct:* tucked up.

The rest, his many-colour'd robe conceal'd.
The rebel-Knave, who dares his prince engage,
Proves the just victim of his royal rage.   60
Even mighty Pam, that kings and queens o'erthrew
And mow'd down armies in the fights of loo,
Sad chance of war! now, destitute of aid,
Falls undistinguish'd by the victor spade!
  Thus far both armies to Belinda yield;
Now to the baron fate inclines the field.
His warlike Amazon her host invades,
Th' imperial consort of the crown of spades.
The club's black tyrant first her victim died,
Spite of his haughty mien, and barb'rous pride: 70
What boots the regal circle on his head,
His giant limbs in state unwieldy spread?
That long behind he trails his pompous robe,
And, of all monarchs, only grasps the globe?
  The baron now his diamonds pours apace;
Th' embroider'd King who shows but half his face,
And his refulgent Queen, with pow'rs combin'd,
Of broken troops an easy conquest find.
Clubs, diamonds, hearts, in wild disorder seen,
With throngs promiscuous strow the level green.   80
Thus when dispers'd a routed army runs,
Of Asia's troops, and Afric's sable sons,
With like confusion diff'rent nations fly,
Of various habit, and of various dye,
The pierc'd battalions disunited fall,
In heaps on heaps; one fate o'erwhelms them all.
  The Knave of Diamonds tries his wily arts,
And wins (oh shameful chance!) the Queen of Hearts.
At this, the blood the virgin's cheek forsook,
A livid paleness spreads o'er all her look;   90
She sees, and trembles at th' approaching ill,
Just in the jaws of ruin, and codille.
And now (as oft in some distemper'd state)
On one nice trick depends the gen'ral fate.
An Ace of Hearts steps forth: the King unseen
Lurk'd in her hand, and mourn'd his captive Queen.
He springs to vengeance with an eager pace,
And falls like thunder on the prostrate Ace.
The nymph exulting fills with shouts the sky,
The walls, the woods, and long canals reply.   100
  Oh thoughtless mortals! ever blind to fate,

Too soon dejected, and too soon elate!
Sudden, these honours shall be snatch'd away,
And curs'd forever this victorious day.
　For lo! the board with cups and spoons is crown'd,
The berries crackle, and the mill turns round;
On shining altars of japan they raise
The silver lamp; the fiery spirits blaze.
From silver spouts the grateful liquors glide,
While China's earth receives the smoking tide.　　　　110
At once they gratify their scent and taste,
And frequent cups prolong the rich repast.
Straight hover round the fair her airy band;
Some, as she sipp'd, the fuming liquor fann'd,
Some o'er her lap their careful plumes display'd,
Trembling, and conscious of the rich brocade.
Coffee (which makes the politician wise,
And see through all things with his half-shut eyes)
Sent up in vapours to the baron's brain
New stratagems, the radiant lock to gain.　　　　120
Ah cease, rash youth! desist ere 'tis too late,
Fear the just gods, and think of Scylla's fate!
Chang'd to a bird, and sent to flit in air,
She dearly pays for Nisus' injur'd hair!
　But when to mischief mortals bend their will,
How soon they find fit instruments of ill!
Just then, Clarissa drew with tempting grace
A two-edg'd weapon from her shining case;
So ladies in romance assist their knight,
Present the spear, and arm him for the fight.　　　　130
He takes the gift with rev'rence, and extends
The little engine on his fingers' ends,
This just behind Belinda's neck he spread,
As o'er the fragrant steams she bends her head:
Swift to the lock a thousand sprites repair,
A thousand wings, by turns, blow back the hair,
And thrice they twitch'd the diamond in her ear,
Thrice she look'd back, and thrice the foe drew near.
Just in that instant, anxious Ariel sought
The close recesses of the virgin's thought;　　　　140
As on the nosegay in her breast reclin'd,
He watch'd th' ideas rising in her mind,
Sudden he view'd, in spite of all her art,
An earthly lover lurking at her heart.
Amaz'd, confus'd, he found his pow'r expir'd,
Resign'd to fate, and with a sigh retir'd.

The peer now spreads the glitt'ring forfex wide,
T' enclose the lock; now joins it, to divide.
Ev'n then, before the fatal engine clos'd,
A wretched sylph too fondly interpos'd;   150
Fate urg'd the shears, and cut the sylph in twain,
(But airy substance soon unites again)
The meeting points the sacred hair dissever
From the fair head, for ever, and for ever!
  Then flash'd the living lightning from her eyes,
And screams of horror rend th' affrighted skies.
Not louder shrieks to pitying Heav'n are cast,
When husbands, or when lap-dogs breathe their last;
Or when rich china vessels fall'n from high,
In glitt'ring dust and painted fragments lie!   160
  "Let wreaths of triumph now my temples twine,"
The victor cried, "the glorious prize is mine!
While fish in streams, or birds delight in air,
Or in a coach and six the British fair,
As long as *Atalantis* shall be read,
Or the small pillow grace a lady's bed,
While visits shall be paid on solemn days,
When num'rous wax-lights in bright order blaze,
While nymphs take treats, or assignations give,
So long my honour, name, and praise shall live!   170
What time wou'd spare, from steel receives its date,
And monuments, like men, submit to fate!
Steel cou'd the labour of the gods destroy,
And strike to dust th' imperial tow'rs of Troy;
Steel cou'd the works of mortal pride confound,
And hew triumphal arches to the ground.
What wonder then, fair nymph! thy hairs shou'd feel
The conqu'ring force of unresisted steel?"

CANTO IV

But anxious cares the pensive nymph opprest,
And secret passions labour'd in her breast.
Not youthful kings in battle seiz'd alive,
Not scornful virgins who their charms survive,
Not ardent lovers robb'd of all their bliss,
Not ancient ladies when refus'd a kiss,
Not tyrants fierce that unrepenting die,
Not Cynthia when her manteau's pinn'd awry,
E'er felt such rage, resentment, and despair,

165. *Atalantis:* a slanderous novel of the day.

As thou, sad virgin! for thy ravish'd hair.   10
   For, that sad moment, when the sylphs withdrew,
And Ariel weeping from Belinda flew,
Umbriel, a dusky, melancholy sprite,
As ever sullied the fair face of light,
Down to the central earth, his proper scene,
Repair'd to search the gloomy cave of Spleen.
   Swift on his sooty pinions flits the gnome,
And in a vapour reach'd the dismal dome.
No cheerful breeze this sullen region knows,
The dreaded east is all the wind that blows.   20
Here in a grotto, shelter'd close from air,
And screen'd in shades from day's detested glare,
She sighs for ever on her pensive bed,
Pain at her side, and Megrim at her head.
Two handmaids wait the throne: alike in place,
But diff'ring far in figure and in face.
Here stood Ill-nature like an ancient maid,
Her wrinkled form in black and white array'd;
With store of pray'rs, for mornings, nights, and noons,
Her hand is fill'd; her bosom with lampoons.   30
   There Affectation, with a sickly mien,
Shows in her cheek the roses of eighteen,
Practis'd to lisp, and hang the head aside,
Faints into airs, and languishes with pride,
On the rich quilt sinks with becoming woe,
Wrapp'd in a gown, for sickness, and for show.
The fair ones feel such maladies as these,
When each new night-dress gives a new disease.
   A constant vapour o'er the palace flies;
Strange phantoms rising as the mists arise;   40
Dreadful as hermits' dreams in haunted shades,
Or bright, as visions of expiring maids.
Now glaring fiends, and snakes on rolling spires,
Pale spectres, gaping tombs, and purple fires:
Now lakes of liquid gold, Elysian scenes,
And crystal domes, and angels in machines.
   Unnumber'd throngs on ev'ry side are seen,
Of bodies chang'd to various forms by Spleen.
Here living teapots stand, one arm held out,
One bent; the handle this, and that the spout: 50

20. *east:* this wind was supposed to cause the spleen.
24. *Megrim:* migraine, a severe headache.

A pipkin there, like Homer's tripod walks;
Here sighs a jar, and there a goose-pie talks;
Men prove with child, as pow'rful fancy works,
And maids turn'd bottles, call aloud for corks.
  Safe pass'd the gnome through this fantastic band,
A branch of healing spleenwort in his hand.
Then thus addrest the pow'r—"Hail, wayward Queen!
Who rule the sex to fifty from fifteen:
Parent of vapours and of female wit,
Who give th' hysteric, or poetic fit,   60
On various tempers act by various ways,
Make some take physic, others scribble plays;
Who cause the proud their visits to delay,
And send the godly in a pet, to pray.
A nymph there is, that all thy pow'r disdains,
And thousands more in equal mirth maintains.
But oh! if e'er thy gnome could spoil a grace,
Or raise a pimple on a beauteous face,
Like citron-waters matrons' cheeks inflame,
Or change complexions at a losing game;   70
If e'er with airy horns I planted heads,
Or rumpled petticoats, or tumbled beds,
Or caus'd suspicion when no soul was rude,
Or discompos'd the head-dress of a prude,
Or e'er to costive lap-dog gave disease,
Which not the tears of brightest eyes could ease:
Hear me, and touch Belinda with chagrin,
That single act gives half the world the spleen."
  The goddess with a discontented air
Seems to reject him, tho' she grants his pray'r.   80
A wondrous bag with both her hands she binds,
Like that where once Ulysses held the winds;
There she collects the force of female lungs,
Sighs, sobs, and passions, and the war of tongues.
A vial next she fills with fainting fears,
Soft sorrows, melting griefs, and flowing tears.
The gnome rejoicing bears her gifts away,
Spreads his black wings, and slowly mounts to day.
  Sunk in Thalestris' arms the nymph he found,
Her eyes dejected, and her hair unbound.   90
Full o'er their heads the swelling bag he rent,
And all the Furies issu'd at the vent.
Belinda burns with more than mortal ire,

56. *spleenwort:* a popular remedy for the spleen.
  89. *Thalestris:* Mrs. Morley, sister of Sir George Brown (Sir Plume, IV,
121 ff.).

And fierce Thalestris fans the rising fire.
"Oh wretched maid!" she spread her hands, and cried
(While Hampton's echoes, "Wretched maid!" replied)
"Was it for this you took such constant care
The bodkin, comb, and essence to prepare;
For this your locks in paper durance bound,
For this with tort'ring irons wreath'd around?   100
For this with fillets strain'd your tender head,
And bravely bore the double loads of lead?
Gods! shall the ravisher display your hair,
While the fops envy, and the ladies stare!
Honour forbid! at whose unrivall'd shrine
Ease, pleasure, virtue, all our sex resign.
Methinks already I your tears survey,
Already hear the horrid things they say,
Already see you a degraded toast,
And all your honour in a whisper lost!   110
How shall I, then, your helpless fame defend?
'Twill then be infamy to seem your friend!
And shall this prize, th' inestimable prize,
Expos'd through crystal to the gazing eyes,
And heighten'd by the diamond's circling rays,
On that rapacious hand forever blaze?
Sooner shall grass in Hyde Park Circus grow,
And wits take lodgings in the sound of Bow;
Sooner let earth, air, sea, to chaos fall,
Men, monkeys, lap-dogs, parrots, perish all!"   120
    She said; then raging to Sir Plume repairs,
And bids her beau demand the precious hairs
(Sir Plume, of amber snuff-box justly vain,
And the nice conduct of a clouded cane);
With earnest eyes, and round unthinking face,
He first the snuff-box open'd, then the case,
And thus broke out—"My Lord, why, what the devil?
Z—ds! damn the lock! 'fore Gad, you must be civil!
Plague on't! 'tis past a jest—nay prithee, pox!
Give her the hair"—he spoke, and rapp'd his box.   130
    "It grieves me much," replied the peer again,
"Who speaks so well should ever speak in vain.
But by this lock, this sacred lock, I swear
(Which never more shall join its parted hair;
Which never more its honours shall renew,
Clipp'd from the lovely head where late it grew),

118. *in . . . Bow:* within sound of the bells of St. Mary-le-Bow—i.e., in
the unfashionable business section of London.

That while my nostrils draw the vital air,
This hand, which won it, shall forever wear."
He spoke, and speaking, in proud triumph spread
The long-contended honours of her head.   140
    But Umbriel, hateful gnome! forbears not so;
He breaks the vial whence the sorrows flow.
Then see! the nymph in beauteous grief appears,
Her eyes half-languishing, half-drown'd in tears;
On her heav'd bosom hung her drooping head,
Which, with a sigh, she rais'd; and thus she said:
    "Forever curs'd be this detested day,
Which snatch'd my best, my fav'rite curl away!
Happy! ah ten times happy had I been,
If Hampton Court these eyes had never seen!   150
Yet am not I the first mistaken maid,
By love of courts to num'rous ills betray'd.
Oh had I rather unadmir'd remain'd
In some lone isle, or distant northern land;
Where the gilt chariot never marks the way,
Where none learn ombre, none e'er taste bohea!
There kept my charms conceal'd from mortal eye,
Like roses that in deserts bloom and die.
What mov'd my mind with youthful lords to roam?
Oh had I stay'd, and said my pray'rs at home!   160
'Twas this, the morning omens seem'd to tell,
Thrice from my trembling hand the patch-box fell;
The tott'ring china shook without a wind,
Nay, Poll sat mute, and Shock was most unkind!
A sylph too warn'd me of the threats of fate,
In mystic visions, now believ'd too late!
See the poor remnants of these slighted hairs!
My hands shall rend what ev'n thy rapine spares:
These, in two sable ringlets taught to break,
Once gave new beauties to the snowy neck.   170
The sister-lock now sits uncouth, alone,
And in its fellow's fate foresees its own;
Uncurl'd it hangs, the fatal shears demands,
And tempts, once more, thy sacrilegious hands.
Oh hadst thou, cruel! been content to seize
Hairs less in sight, or any hairs but these!''

CANTO V

She said: the pitying audience melt in tears,
But Fate and Jove had stopp'd the baron's ears.
In vain Thalestris with reproach assails,
For who can move when fair Belinda fails?

Not half so fix'd the Trojan could remain,
While Anna begg'd and Dido rag'd in vain.
Then grave Clarissa graceful wav'd her fan;
Silence ensu'd, and thus the nymph began:
  "Say, why are beauties prais'd and honour'd most,
The wise man's passion, and the vain man's toast?   10
Why deck'd with all that land and sea afford,
Why angels call'd, and angel-like ador'd?
Why round our coaches crowd the white-glov'd beaux,
Why bows the side-box from its inmost rows?
How vain are all these glories, all our pains,
Unless good sense preserve what beauty gains:
That men may say, when we the front-box grace,
'Behold the first in virtue, as in face!'
Oh! if to dance all night, and dress all day,
Charm'd the smallpox, or chas'd old age away;   20
Who would not scorn what housewife's cares produce,
Or who would learn one earthly thing of use?
To patch, nay ogle, might become a saint,
Nor could it sure be such a sin to paint.
But since, alas! frail beauty must decay,
Curl'd or uncurl'd, since locks will turn to grey;
Since painted, or not painted, all shall fade,
And she who scorns a man, must die a maid;
What then remains, but well our pow'r to use,
And keep good humour still whate'er we lose?   30
And trust me, dear! good humour can prevail,
When airs, and flights, and screams, and scolding fail.
Beauties in vain their pretty eyes may roll;
Charms strike the sight, but merit wins the soul."
  So spoke the dame, but no applause ensu'd;
Belinda frown'd, Thalestris call'd her prude.
"To arms, to arms!" the fierce virago cries,
And swift as lightning to the combat flies.
All side in parties, and begin th' attack;
Fans clap, silks rustle, and tough whalebones crack;   40
Heroes' and heroines' shouts confus'dly rise,
And bass and treble voices strike the skies.
No common weapons in their hands are found,

---

   7. *Clarissa:* a new character introduced in the subsequent editions, to
open more clearly the moral of the poem, in a parody of the speech of
Sarpedon to Glaucus in Homer. [Pope.] The parody was added when the
poem was included in the 1717 quarto.
   14. *side-box:* The ladies at this time always sat in the front, the gentlemen
in the side-boxes. [Nichols.]

Like gods they fight, nor dread a mortal wound.
So when bold Homer makes the gods engage,
And heav'nly breasts with human passions rage;
'Gainst Pallas, Mars; Latona, Hermes arms;
And all Olympus rings with loud alarms:
Jove's thunder roars, Heav'n trembles all around,
Blue Neptune storms, the bellowing deeps resound;   50
Earth shakes her nodding tow'rs, the ground gives way;
And the pale ghosts start at the flash of day!
  Triumphant Umbriel on a sconce's height,
Clapt his glad wings, and sate to view the fight:
Propt on their bodkin spears, the sprites survey
The growing combat, or assist the fray.
  While through the press enrag'd Thalestris flies,
And scatters death around from both her eyes,
A beau and witling perish'd in the throng,
One died in metaphor, and one in song.   60
"O cruel nymph! a living death I bear,"
Cried Dapperwit, and sunk beside his chair.
A mournful glance Sir Fopling upwards cast,
"Those eyes are made so killing"—was his last.
Thus on Meander's flow'ry margin lies
Th' expiring swan, and as he sings he dies.
  When bold Sir Plume had drawn Clarissa down,
Chloe stept in, and kill'd him with a frown;
She smil'd to see the doughty hero slain,
But at her smile, the beau reviv'd again.   70
  Now Jove suspends his golden scales in air,
Weighs the men's wits against the lady's hair;
The doubtful beam long nods from side to side;
At length the wits mount up, the hairs subside.
  See fierce Belinda on the baron flies,
With more than usual lightning in her eyes;
Nor fear'd the chief th' unequal fight to try,
Who sought no more than on his foe to die.
But this bold lord with manly strength indu'd,
She with one finger and a thumb subdu'd: 80
Just where the breath of life his nostrils drew,
A charge of snuff the wily virgin threw;
The gnomes direct, to ev'ry atom just,
The pungent grains of titillating dust.

---

62. *Dapperwit . . . Sir Fopling: Dapperwit* is the name of a ludicrous character in *Love in a Wood,* a comedy by William Wycherley; *Sir Fopling* is a
nervous character in *The Man of Mode,* a comedy by Sir George Etherege.

Sudden, with starting tears each eye o'erflows,
And the high dome re-echoes to his nose.
  "Now meet thy fate," incens'd Belinda cried,
And drew a deadly bodkin from her side.
(The same, his ancient personage to deck,
Her great great grandsire wore about his neck   90
In three seal-rings; which after, melted down,
Form'd a vast buckle for his widow's gown:
Her infant grandame's whistle next it grew,
The bells she jingled, and the whistle blew;
Then in a bodkin grac'd her mother's hairs,
Which long she wore, and now Belinda wears.)
  "Boast not my fall," he cried, "insulting foe!
Thou by some other shalt be laid as low.
Nor think, to die dejects my lofty mind;
All that I dread is leaving you behind!   100
Rather than so, ah let me still survive,
And burn in Cupid's flames—but burn alive."
  "Restore the lock!" she cries; and all around
"Restore the lock!" the vaulted roofs rebound.
Not fierce Othello in so loud a strain
Roar'd for the handkerchief that caus'd his pain.
But see how oft ambitious aims are cross'd,
And chiefs contend 'till all the prize is lost!
The lock, obtain'd with guilt, and kept with pain,
In ev'ry place is sought, but sought in vain: 110
With such a prize no mortal must be blest,
So Heav'n decrees! with Heav'n who can contest?
  Some thought it mounted to the lunar sphere,
Since all things lost on earth are treasur'd there.
There heroes' wits are kept in pond'rous vases,
And beaux' in snuff-boxes and tweezer-cases.
There broken vows, and death-bed alms are found,
And lovers' hearts with ends of ribbon bound,
The courtier's promises, and sick man's pray'rs,
The smiles of harlots, and the tears of heirs,   120
Cages for gnats, and chains to yoke a flea,
Dried butterflies, and tomes of casuistry.
  But trust the Muse—she saw it upward rise,
Tho' mark'd by none but quick, poetic eyes:
(So Rome's great founder to the heav'ns withdrew,
To Proculus alone confess'd in view.)
A sudden star, it shot thro' liquid air,
And drew behind a radiant trail of hair.

Not Berenice's locks first rose so bright,
The heav'ns bespangling with dishevel'd light.   130
The sylphs behold it kindling as it flies,
And pleas'd pursue its progress through the skies.
    This the beau-monde shall from the Mall survey,
And hail with musick its propitious ray.
This the blest lover shall for Venus take,
And send up vows from Rosamonda's lake.
This Partridge soon shall view in cloudless skies,
When next he looks through Galileo's eyes;
And hence th' egregious wizard shall foredoom
The fate of Louis, and the fall of Rome.   140
    Then cease, bright nymph! to mourn thy ravish'd hair,
Which adds new glory to the shining sphere!
Not all the tresses that fair head can boast
Shall draw such envy as the lock you lost.
For, after all the murders of your eye,
When, after millions slain, yourself shall die;
When those fair suns shall set, as set they must,
And all those tresses shall be laid in dust;
This lock, the Muse shall consecrate to fame,
And 'midst the stars inscribe Belinda's name!   150

                                              1712; 1714

The Lamb

WILLIAM BLAKE (1757–1827)

Little Lamb, who made thee?
    Dost thou know who made thee?
Gave thee life, and bid thee feed
By the stream and o'er the mead;
Gave thee clothing of delight,
Softest clothing, woolly, bright;
Gave thee such a tender voice,
Making all the vales rejoice?
    Little Lamb, who made thee?
    Dost thou know who made thee?   10

129. *Berenice's . . . bright:* Berenice was an Egyptian queen who dedi-
cated her beautiful hair to Venus for the safe return of her husband from
war. The hair was changed into a comet.
    133. *Mall:* a fashionable promenade in St. James's Park, often the
scene of impromptu music and dancing.
    136. *Rosamonda's lake:* an oblong pond near the southwest corner of St.
James's Park and associated with disastrous love and elegiac poetry.
    137. *Partridge:* a fraudulent stargazer, whose almanacs pretended to
foretell the future.   140. *Louis:* Louis XIV of France.

Little Lamb, I'll tell thee,
Little Lamb, I'll tell thee:
He is callèd by thy name,
For he calls himself a Lamb,
He is meek, and he is mild;
He became a little child.
I a child, and thou a lamb,
We are callèd by his name.
    Little Lamb, God bless thee!
    Little Lamb, God bless thee!   1789   20

The Tiger

WILLIAM BLAKE (1757–1827)

Tiger! Tiger! burning bright
In the forests of the night,
What immortal hand or eye
Could frame thy fearful symmetry?

In what distant deeps or skies
Burnt the fire of thine eyes?
On what wings dare he aspire?
What the hand dare seize the fire?

And what shoulder and what art,
Could twist the sinews of thy heart?   10
And when thy heart began to beat,
What dread hand? and what dread feet?

What the hammer? what the chain?
In what furnace was thy brain?
What the anvil? what dread grasp
Dare its deadly terrors clasp?

When the stars threw down their spears,
And watered heaven with their tears,
Did he smile his work to see?
Did he who made the Lamb make thee?   20

Tiger! Tiger! burning bright
In the forests of the night,
What immortal hand or eye
Dare frame thy fearful symmetry?   1794

The Garden of Love

WILLIAM BLAKE (1757–1827)

I went to the Garden of Love,
And saw what I never had seen;
A chapel was built in the midst,
Where I used to play on the green.

And the gates of this chapel were shut,
And "Thou shalt not" writ over the door;
So I turn'd to the Garden of Love
That so many sweet flowers bore;

And I saw it was fillèd with graves,
And tomb-stones where flowers should be;
And priests in black gowns were walking their rounds,
And binding with briars my joys and desires.   1794

A Poison Tree

WILLIAM BLAKE (1757–1827)

I was angry with my friend:
I told my wrath, my wrath did end.
I was angry with my foe:
I told it not, my wrath did grow.

And I watered it in fears
Night and morning with my tears,
And I sunnèd it with smiles
And with soft deceitful wiles.

And it grew both day and night,
Till it bore an apple bright,
And my foe beheld it shine,
And he knew that it was mine—

And into my garden stole
When the night had veiled the pole;
In the morning, glad, I see
My foe outstretched beneath the tree.   1794

Frost at Midnight

SAMUEL TAYLOR COLERIDGE (1772–1834)

The frost performs its secret ministry,
Unhelped by any wind. The owlet's cry
Came loud—and hark, again! loud as before.
The inmates of my cottage, all at rest,
Have left me to that solitude, which suits
Abstruser musings: save that at my side
My cradled infant slumbers peacefully.
'Tis calm indeed! so calm, that it disturbs
And vexes meditation with its strange
And extreme silentness. Sea, hill, and wood,   10
This populous village! Sea, and hill, and wood,
With all the numberless goings-on of life,
Inaudible as dreams! the thin blue flame
Lies on my low-burnt fire, and quivers not;
Only that film, which fluttered on the grate,
Still flutters there, the sole unquiet thing.
Methinks, its motion in this hush of nature
Gives it dim sympathies with me who live,
Making it a companionable form,
Whose puny flaps and freaks the idling spirit   20
By its own moods interprets, everywhere
Echo or mirror seeking of itself,
And makes a toy of thought.

                     But O! how oft,
How oft, at school, with most believing mind,
Presageful, have I gazed upon the bars,
To watch that fluttering stranger! and as oft
With unclosed lids, already had I dreamt
Of my sweet birth-place, and the old church-tower,
Whose bells, the poor man's only music, rang
From morn to evening, all the hot Fair-day,   30
So sweetly, that they stirred and haunted me
With a wild pleasure, falling on mine ear
Most like articulate sounds of things to come!
So gazed I, till the soothing things, I dreamt,
Lulled me to sleep, and sleep prolonged my dreams!
And so I brooded all the following morn,
Awed by the stern preceptor's face, mine eye
Fixed with mock study on my swimming book:

Save if the door half opened, and I snatched
A hasty glance, and still my heart leaped up,   40
For still I hoped to see the stranger's face,
Townsman, or aunt, or sister more beloved,
My playmate when we both were clothed alike!

Dear Babe, that sleepest cradled by my side,
Whose gentle breathings, heard in this deep calm,
Fill up the interspersèd vacancies
And momentary pauses of the thought!
My babe so beautiful! it thrills my heart
With tender gladness, thus to look at thee,
And think that thou shalt learn far other lore,   50
And in far other scenes! For I was reared
In the great city, pent 'mid cloisters dim,
And saw nought lovely but the sky and stars.
But thou, my babe! shalt wander like a breeze
By lakes and sandy shores, beneath the crags
Of ancient mountain, and beneath the clouds,
Which image in their bulk both lakes and shores
And mountain crags: so shalt thou see and hear
The lovely shapes and sounds intelligible
Of that eternal language, which thy God   60
Utters, who from eternity doth teach
Himself in all, and all things in himself.
Great universal Teacher! he shall mold
Thy spirit, and by giving make it ask.

Therefore all seasons shall be sweet to thee,
Whether the summer clothe the general earth
With greenness, or the redbreast sit and sing
Betwixt the tufts of snow on the bare branch
Of mossy apple-tree, while the nigh thatch
Smokes in the sun-thaw; whether the eavedrops fall   70
Heard only in the trances of the blast,
Or if the secret ministry of frost
Shall hang them up in silent icicles,
Quietly shining to the quiet moon.   1798

Prometheus

GEORGE NOEL GORDON, LORD BYRON (1788–1824)

Titan! to whose immortal eyes
  The sufferings of mortality,
  Seen in their sad reality,
Were not as things that gods despise;
What was thy pity's recompense?
A silent suffering, and intense;
The rock, the vulture, and the chain,
All that the proud can feel of pain,
The agony they do not show,
The suffocating sense of woe,   10
Which speaks but in its loneliness,
And then is jealous lest the sky
Should have a listener, nor will sigh
  Until its voice is echoless.

Titan! to thee the strife was given
  Between the suffering and the will,
  Which torture where they cannot kill;
And the inexorable Heaven,
And the deaf tyranny of Fate,
The ruling principle of Hate,   20
Which for its pleasure doth create
The things it may annihilate,
Refused thee even the boon to die:
The wretched gift Eternity
Was thine—and thou hast borne it well.
All that the thunderer wrung from thee
Was but the menace which flung back
On him the torments of thy rack;
The fate thou didst so well foresee,
But would not to appease him tell;   30
And in thy silence was his sentence,
And in his soul a vain repentance,
And evil dread so ill dissembled,
That in his hand the lightnings trembled.

Thy Godlike crime was to be kind,
  To render with thy precepts less
  The sum of human wretchedness,
And strengthen man with his own mind;
But baffled as thou wert from high,

57

Still in thy patient energy,   40
In the endurance, and repulse
    Of thine impenetrable spirit,
Which Earth and Heaven could not convulse,
    A mighty lesson we inherit:
Thou art a symbol and a sign
    To mortals of their fate and force;
Like thee, man is in part divine,
    A troubled stream from a pure source;
And man in portions can foresee
His own funereal destiny;   50

His wretchedness, and his resistance,
And his sad unallied existence:
To which his spirit may oppose
Itself—an equal to all woes,
    And a firm will, and a deep sense,
Which even in torture can descry
    Its own concentered recompense,
Triumphant where it dares defy,
And making Death a Victory.   1816

Ode to a Nightingale

JOHN KEATS (1795–1821)

My heart aches, and a drowsy numbness pains
    My sense, as though of hemlock I had drunk,
Or emptied some dull opiate to the drains
    One minute past, and Lethe-wards had sunk:
'Tis not through envy of thy happy lot,
    But being too happy in thine happiness—
        That thou, light-wingéd Dryad of the trees,
            In some melodious plot
Of beechen green, and shadows numberless,
    Singest of summer in full-throated ease.   10

O, for a draught of vintage! that hath been
    Cooled a long age in the deep-delvéd earth,
Tasting of Flora and the country green,
    Dance, and Provençal song, and sunburnt mirth!
O for a beaker full of the warm South,
    Full of the true, the blushful Hippocrene,
        With beaded bubbles winking at the brim,
            And purple-stainéd mouth;

That I might drink, and leave the world unseen,
    And with thee fade away into the forest dim: 20

Fade far away, dissolve, and quite forget
    What thou among the leaves hast never known,
The weariness, the fever, and the fret
    Here, where men sit and hear each other groan;
Where palsy shakes a few, sad, last gray hairs,
    Where youth grows pale, and specter-thin, and dies;
        Where but to think is to be full of sorrow
            And leaden-eyed despairs,
    Where Beauty cannot keep her lustrous eyes,
        Or new Love pine at them beyond tomorrow.   30

Away! away! for I will fly to thee,
    Not charioted by Bacchus and his pards,
But on the viewless wings of Poesy,
    Though the dull brain perplexes and retards:
Already with thee! tender is the night,
    And haply the Queen-Moon is on her throne,
        Clustered around by all her starry Fays;
            But here there is no light,
    Save what from heaven is with the breezes blown
        Through verdurous glooms and winding mossy ways.   40

I cannot see what flowers are at my feet,
    Nor what soft incense hangs upon the boughs,
But, in embalmèd darkness, guess each sweet
    Wherewith the seasonable month endows
The grass, the thicket, and the fruit-tree wild;
    White hawthorn, and the pastoral eglantine;
        Fast fading violets covered up in leaves;
            And mid-May's eldest child,
The coming musk-rose, full of dewy wine,
    The murmurous haunt of flies on summer eves.   50

Darkling I listen; and, for many a time,
    I have been half in love with easeful Death,
Called him soft names in many a musèd rime,
    To take into the air my quiet breath;
Now more than ever seems it rich to die,
    To cease upon the midnight with no pain,
        While thou art pouring forth thy soul abroad
            In such an ecstasy!
Still wouldst thou sing, and I have ears in vain—
    To thy high requiem become a sod.   60

32. *pards:* leopards which drew the chariot in which rode Bacchus, the god of wine.   33. *viewless:* invisible.

Thou wast not born for death, immortal Bird!
No hungry generations tread thee down;
The voice I hear this passing night was heard
In ancient days by emperor and clown:
Perhaps the self-same song that found a path
Through the sad heart of Ruth, when, sick for home,
She stood in tears amid the alien corn;
The same that oft-times hath
Charmed magic casements, opening on the foam
Of perilous seas, in faery lands forlorn.

Forlorn! the very word is like a bell
To toll me back from thee to my sole self,
Adieu! the fancy cannot cheat so well
As she is famed to do, deceiving elf.
Adieu! adieu! thy plaintive anthem fades
Past the near meadows, over the still stream,
Up the hillside; and now 'tis buried deep
In the next valley glades:
Was it a vision, or a waking dream?
Fled is that music—Do I wake or sleep?   1819   80

To Autumn

JOHN KEATS (1795–1821)

Season of mists and mellow fruitfulness,
Close bosom-friend of the maturing sun;
Conspiring with him how to load and bless
With fruit the vines that round the thatch-eaves run;
To bend with apples the mossed cottage-trees,
And fill all fruit with ripeness to the core;
To swell the gourd, and plump the hazel shells
With a sweet kernel; to set budding more,
And still more, later flowers for the bees,
Until they think warm days will never cease,   10
For Summer has o'er-brimmed their clammy cells.

Who hath not seen thee oft amid thy store?
Sometimes whoever seeks abroad may find
Thee sitting careless on a granary floor,
Thy hair soft-lifted by the winnowing wind;
Or on a half-reaped furrow sound asleep,
Drowsed with the fume of poppies, while thy hook
Spares the next swath and all its twinéd flowers:

And sometimes like a gleaner thou dost keep
   Steady thy laden head across a brook;   20
   Or by a cider-press, with patient look,
     Thou watchest the last oozings, hours by hours.

Where are the songs of Spring? Ay, where are they?
   Think not of them, thou hast thy music too—
While barréd clouds bloom the soft-dying day,
   And touch the stubble-plains with rosy hue;
Then in a wailful choir the small gnats mourn
   Among the river sallows, borne aloft
     Or sinking as the light wind lives or dies;
And full-grown lambs loud bleat from hilly bourn;   30
   Hedge-crickets sing; and now with treble soft
   The redbreast whistles from a garden-croft,
     And gathering swallows twitter in the skies.   1820

Ode to the West Wind

PERCY BYSSHE SHELLEY (1792–1822)

1

O wild West Wind, thou breath of Autumn's being,
Thou, from whose unseen presence the leaves dead
Are driven, like ghosts from an enchanter fleeing,

Yellow, and black, and pale, and hectic red,
Pestilence-stricken multitudes: O thou,
Who chariotest to their dark wintry bed

The wingéd seeds, where they lie cold and low,
Each like a corpse within its grave, until
Thine azure sister of the Spring shall blow

Her clarion o'er the dreaming earth, and fill   10
(Driving sweet buds like flocks to feed in air)
With living hues and odors plain and hill:

Wild Spirit, which art moving everywhere;
Destroyer and preserver; hear, oh, hear!

2

Thou on whose stream, mid the steep sky's commotion,
Loose clouds like earth's decaying leaves are shed,
Shook from the tangled boughs of Heaven and Ocean,

9. *sister of the Spring:* the south wind.

Angels of rain and lightning: there are spread
On the blue surface of thine aery surge,
Like the bright hair uplifted from the head   20

Of some fierce Maenad, even from the dim verge
Of the horizon to the zenith's height,
The locks of the approaching storm. Thou dirge

Of the dying year, to which this closing night
Will be the dome of a vast sepulcher,
Vaulted with all thy congregated might

Of vapors, from whose solid atmosphere
Black rain, and fire, and hail will burst: oh, hear!

3

Thou who didst waken from his summer dreams
The blue Mediterranean, where he lay,   30
Lulled by the coil of his crystalline streams,

Beside a pumice isle in Baiae's bay,
And saw in sleep old palaces and towers
Quivering within the wave's intenser day,

All overgrown with azure moss and flowers
So sweet, the sense faints picturing them! Thou
For whose path the Atlantic's level powers

Cleave themselves into chasms, while far below
The sea-blooms and the oozy woods which wear
The sapless foliage of the ocean, know   40

Thy voice, and suddenly grow gray with fear,
And tremble and despoil themselves: oh, hear!

4

If I were a dead leaf thou mightest bear,
If I were a swift cloud to fly with thee;
A wave to pant beneath thy power, and share

The impulse of thy strength, only less free
Than thou, O uncontrollable! If even
I were as in my boyhood, and could be
                                                                   s
32. *Baiae* (Baia): a seaport village in southern Italy, west of Naples. A.
an ancient village it was a Roman resort, noted for luxury and immorality
39–42. *sea-blooms . . . hear:* of these lines Shelley says that "the vegetation
at the bottom of the sea, of rivers, and of lakes, sympathizes with that of
the land in the change of seasons, and is consequently influenced by the
winds which announce it."

The comrade of thy wanderings over Heaven,
As then, when to outstrip thy skyey speed   50
Scarce seemed a vision; I would ne'er have striven

As thus with thee in prayer in my sore need.
Oh, lift me as a wave, a leaf, a cloud!
I fall upon the thorns of life! I bleed!

A heavy weight of hours has chained and bowed
One too like thee: tameless, and swift, and proud.

5

Make me thy lyre, even as the forest is:
What if my leaves are falling like its own!
The tumult of thy mighty harmonies

Will take from both a deep, autumnal tone,   60
Sweet though in sadness.   Be thou, Spirit fierce,
My spirit! Be thou me, impetuous one!

Drive my dead thoughts over the universe
Like withered leaves to quicken a new birth!
And, by the incantation of this verse,

Scatter, as from an unextinguished hearth
Ashes and sparks, my words among mankind!
Be through my lips to unawakened earth

The trumpet of a prophecy! O Wind,
If Winter comes, can Spring be far behind?   1820   70

To a Skylark

PERCY BYSSHE SHELLEY (1792–1822)

Hail to thee, blithe Spirit!
    Bird thou never wert,
That from Heaven, or near it,
    Pourest thy full heart
In profuse strains of unpremeditated art.

Higher still and higher
    From the earth thou springest
Like a cloud of fire;
    The blue deep thou wingest,
And singing still dost soar, and soaring ever singest.   10

In the golden lightning
  Of the sunken sun,
O'er which clouds are bright'ning,
  Thou dost float and run;
Like an unbodied joy whose race is just begun.

The pale purple even
  Melts around thy flight;
Like a star of Heaven,
  In the broad daylight
Thou art unseen, but yet I hear thy shrill delight,   20

Keen as are the arrows
  Of that silver sphere,
Whose intense lamp narrows
  In the white dawn clear
Until we hardly see—we feel that it is there.

All the earth and air
  With thy voice is loud,
As, when night is bare,
  From one lonely cloud
The moon rains out her beams, and Heaven is overflowed.   30

What thou art we know not;
  What is most like thee?
From rainbow clouds there flow not
  Drops so bright to see
As from thy presence showers a rain of melody.

Like a Poet hidden
  In the light of thought,
Singing hymns unbidden,
  Till the world is wrought
To sympathy with hopes and fears it heeded not: 40

Like a high-born maiden
  In a palace-tower,
Soothing her love-laden
  Soul in secret hour
With music sweet as love, which overflows her bower:

Like a glowworm golden
  In a dell of dew,
Scattering unbeholden
  Its aereal hue
Among the flowers and grass, which screen it from the view! 50

Like a rose embowered
   In its own green leaves,
By warm winds deflowered,
   Till the scent it gives
Makes faint with too much sweet those heavy-wingéd thieves:

Sound of vernal showers
   On the twinkling grass,
Rain-awakened flowers,
   All that ever was
Joyous, and clear, and fresh, thy music doth surpass: 60

Teach us, Sprite or Bird,
   What sweet thoughts are thine:
I have never heard
   Praise of love or wine
That panted forth a flood of rapture so divine.

Chorus Hymeneal,
   Or triumphal chant,
Matched with thine would be all
   But an empty vaunt,
A thing wherein we feel there is some hidden want.   70

What objects are the fountains
   Of thy happy strain?
What fields, or waves, or mountains?
   What shapes of sky or plain?
What love of thine own kind? what ignorance of pain?

With thy clear keen joyance
   Languor cannot be:
Shadow of annoyance
   Never came near thee:
Thou lovest—but ne'er knew love's sad satiety.   80

Waking or asleep,
   Thou of death must deem
Things more true and deep
   Than we mortals dream,
Or how could thy notes flow in such a crystal stream?

We look before and after,
   And pine for what is not:
Our sincerest laughter
   With some pain is fraught;
Our sweetest songs are those that tell of saddest thought.   90

Yet if we could scorn
  Hate, and pride, and fear;
If we were things born
  Not to shed a tear,
I know not how thy joy we ever should come near.

Better than all measures
  Of delightful sound,
Better than all treasures
  That in books are found,
Thy skill to poet were, thou scorner of the ground!   100

Teach me half the gladness
  That thy brain must know,
Such harmonious madness
  From my lips would flow
The world should listen then—as I am listening now.   1820

The Kraken

ALFRED, LORD TENNYSON (1809–1892)

Below the thunders of the upper deep,
Far, far beneath in the absymal sea,
His ancient, dreamless, uninvaded sleep
The Kraken sleepeth: faintest sunlights flee
About his shadowy sides; above him swell
Huge sponges of millennial growth and height;
And far away into the sickly light,
From many a wondrous grot and secret cell
Unnumber'd and enormous polypi
Winnow with giant arms the slumbering green.
There hath he lain for ages, and will lie
Battening upon huge sea-worms in his sleep,
Until the latter fire shall heat the deep;
Then once by man and angels to be seen,
In roaring he shall rise and on the surface die.   1830

When Lilacs Last in the Dooryard Bloom'd

WALT WHITMAN (1819–1892)

Lincoln was shot by an assassin on the night of April 14, 1865, while attending the theater. He died the following day. His body lay in state in Washington until April 21. On that day started the procession through Philadelphia, New York, Chicago and other cities to the place of interment in Springfield, Illinois. The burial took place there on May 4.

In Specimen Days, *Whitman wrote: "Of all the days of the war, there are two especially I can never forget. These were the day following the news, in New York and Brooklyn, of that first Bull Run defeat, and the day of Abraham Lincoln's death. I was home in Brooklyn on both occasions. The day of the murder we heard the news very early in the morning. Mother prepared breakfast—and other meals afterward—as usual; but not a mouthful was eaten all day by either of us. We each drank half a cup of coffee; that was all. Little was said. We got every newspaper morning and evening, and the frequent extras of that period, and pass'd them silently to each other."*

1

When lilacs last in the dooryard bloom'd,
And the great star early droop'd in the western sky in the night,
I mourn'd, and yet shall mourn with ever-returning spring.

Ever-returning spring, trinity sure to me you bring,
Lilac blooming perennial and drooping star in the west,
And thought of him I love.

2

O powerful western fallen star!
O shades of night—O moody, tearful night!
O great star disappear'd—O the black murk that hides the star!
O cruel hands that hold me powerless—O helpless soul of me!   10
O harsh surrounding cloud that will not free my soul.

3

In the dooryard fronting an old farm-house near the white-wash'd
          palings,
Stands the lilac-bush tall-growing with heart-shaped leaves of rich green,
With many a pointed blossom rising delicate, with the perfume strong
          I love,
With every leaf a miracle—and from this bush in the dooryard,
With delicate-color'd blossoms and heart-shaped leaves of rich green,
A sprig with its flower I break.

4

In the swamp in secluded recesses,
A shy and hidden bird is warbling a song.

Solitary the thrush,   20
The hermit withdrawn to himself, avoiding the settlements,
Sings by himself a song.

Song of the bleeding throat,
Death's outlet song of life, (for well dear brother I know,
If thou wast not granted to sing thou would'st surely die.)

5

Over the breast of the spring, the land, amid cities,
Amid lanes and through old woods, where lately the violets peep'd from
      the ground, spotting the gray debris,
Amid the grass in the fields each side of the lanes, passing the endless
      grass,
Passing the yellow-spear'd wheat, every grain from its shroud in the
      dark-brown fields uprisen,
Passing the apple-tree blows of white and pink in the orchards,   30
Carrying a corpse to where it shall rest in the grave,
Night and day journeys a coffin.

6

Coffin that passes through lanes and streets,
Through day and night with the great cloud darkening the land,
With the pomp of the inloop'd flags with the cities draped in black,
With the show of the states themselves as of crape-veil'd women
      standing,
With processions long and winding and the flambeaus of the night,
With the countless torches lit, with the silent sea of faces and the
      unbared heads,
With the waiting depot, the arriving coffin, and the sombre faces,
With dirges through the night, with the thousand voices rising strong
      and solemn,   40
With all the mournful voices of the dirges pour'd around the coffin,
The dim-lit churches and the shuddering organs — where amid these
      you journey,
With the tolling tolling bells' perpetual clang,
Here, coffin that slowly passes,
I give you my sprig of lilac.

7

(Nor for you, for one alone,
Blossoms and branches green to coffins all I bring,
For fresh as the morning, thus would I chant a song for you O sane
    and sacred death.

All over bouquets of roses,
O death, I cover you over with roses and early lilies,   50
But mostly and now the lilac that blooms the first,
Copious I break, I break the sprigs from the bushes,
With loaded arms I come, pouring for you,
For you and the coffins all of you O death.)

8

O western orb sailing the heaven,
Now I know what you must have meant as a month since I walk'd,
As I walk'd in silence the transparent shadowy night,
As I saw you had something to tell as you bent to me night after night,
As you droop'd from the sky low down as if to my side, (while the
    other stars all look'd on,)
As we wander'd together the solemn night, (for something I know not
    what kept me from sleep,)   60
As the night advanced, and I saw on the rim of the west how full you
    were of woe,
As I stood on the rising ground in the breeze in the cool transparent
    night,
As I watch'd where you pass'd and was lost in the netherward black of
    the night,
As my soul in its trouble dissatisfied sank, as where you sad orb,
Concluded, dropt in the night, and was gone.

9

Sing on there in the swamp,
O singer bashful and tender, I hear your notes, I hear your call,
I hear, I come presently, I understand you,
But a moment I linger, for the lustrous star has detain'd me,
The star my departing comrade holds and detains me.   70

10

O how shall I warble myself for the dead one there I loved?
And how shall I deck my song for the large sweet soul that has gone?
And what shall my perfume be for the grave of him I love?

Sea-winds blown from east and west,
Blown from the Eastern sea and blown from the Western sea, till there
  on the prairies meeting,
These and with these and the breath of my chant,
I'll perfume the grave of him I love.

11

O what shall I hang on the chamber walls?
And what shall the pictures be that I hang on the walls,
To adorn the burial-house of him I love?   80

Pictures of growing spring and farms and homes,
With Fourth-month eve at sundown, and the gray smoke lucid and
  bright,
With floods of the yellow gold of the gorgeous, indolent, sinking sun,
  burning, expanding the air,
With the fresh sweet herbage under foot, and the pale green leaves of
  the trees prolific,
In the distance the flowing glaze, the breast of the river, with a wind-
  dapple here and there,
With ranging hills on the banks, with many a line against the sky, and
  shadows,
And the city at hand with dwellings so dense, and stacks of chimneys,
And all the scenes of life and the workshops, and the workmen homeward returning.

12

Lo, body and soul—this land,
My own Manhattan with spires, and the sparkling and hurrying tides,
  and the ships,   90
The varied and ample land, the South and the North in the light,
  Ohio's shores and flashing Missouri,
And ever the far-spreading prairies cover'd with grass and corn.

Lo, the most excellent sun so calm and haughty,
The violet and purple morn with just-felt breezes,
The gentle soft-born measureless light,
The miracle spreading bathing all, the fulfill'd noon,
The coming eve delicious, the welcome night and the stars,
Over my cities shining all, enveloping man and land.

13

Sing on, sing on you gray-brown bird,
Sing from the swamps, the recesses, pour your chant from the bushes, 100
Limitless out of the dusk, out of the cedars and pines.

Sing on dearest brother, warble your reedy song,
Loud human song, with voice of uttermost woe.

O liquid and free and tender!
O wild and loose to my soul — O wondrous singer!
You only I hear — yet the star holds me, (but will soon depart,)
Yet the lilac with mastering odor holds me.

14

Now while I sat in the day and look'd forth,
In the close of the day with its light and the fields of spring, and the
    farmers preparing their crops,
In the large unconscious scenery of my land with its lakes and forests, 110
In the heavenly aerial beauty, (after the perturb'd winds and the
    storms,)
Under the arching heavens of the afternoon swift passing, and the
    voices of children and women,
The many-moving sea-tides, and I saw the ships how they sail'd,
And the summer approaching with richness, and the fields all busy
    with labor,
And the infinite separate houses, how they all went on, each with its
    meals and minutia of daily usages,
And the streets how their throbbings throbb'd, and the cities pent — lo,
    then and there,
Falling upon them all and among them all, enveloping me with the rest,
Appear'd the cloud, appear'd the long black trail,
And I knew death, its thought, and the sacred knowledge of death.

Then with the knowledge of death as walking one side of me,   120
And the thought of death close-walking the other side of me,
And I in the middle as with companions, and as holding the hands of
    companions,
I fled forth to the hiding receiving night that talks not,
Down to the shores of the water, the path by the swamp in the dimness,
To the solemn shadowy cedars and ghostly pines so still.

And the singer so shy to the rest receiv'd me.
The gray-brown bird I know receiv'd us comrades three,
And he sang the carol of death, and a verse for him I love.

From deep secluded recesses,
From the fragrant cedars and the ghostly pines so still,   130
Came the carol of the bird.

And the charm of the carol rapt me,
As I held as if by their hands my comrades in the night,
And the voice of my spirit tallied the song of the bird.

Come lovely and soothing death,
Undulate round the world, serenely arriving, arriving,
In the day, in the night, to all, to each,
Sooner or later delicate death.

Prais'd be the fathomless universe,
For life and joy, and for objects and knowledge curious,   140
And for love, sweet love—but praise! praise! praise!
For the sure-enwinding arms of cool-enfolding death.

Dark mother always gliding near with soft feet,
Have none chanted for thee a chant of fullest welcome?
Then I chant it for thee, I glorify thee above all,
I bring thee a song that when thou must indeed come, come unfalteringly.

Approach strong deliveress,
When it is so, when thou hast taken them, I joyously sing the dead,
Lost in the loving floating ocean of thee,
Laved in the flood of thy bliss O death.   150

From me to thee glad serenades,
Dances for thee I propose saluting thee, adornments and feastings for thee,
And the sights of the open landscape and the highspread sky are fitting,
And life and the fields, and the huge and thoughtful night.

The night in silence under many a star,
The ocean shore and the husky whispering wave whose voice I know,
And the soul turning to thee O vast and well-veil'd death,
And the body gratefully nestling close to thee.

Over the tree-tops I float thee a song,
Over the rising and sinking waves, over the myriad fields and the prairies wide,
Over the dense-pack'd cities all and the teeming wharves and ways,   161
I float this carol with joy, with joy to thee O death.

15

To the tally of my soul,
Loud and strong kept up the gray-brown bird,
With pure deliberate notes spreading filling the night.
Loud in the pines and cedars dim,
Clear in the freshness moist and the swamp-perfume,
And I with my comrades there in the night.

While my sight that was bound in my eyes unclosed,
As to long panoramas of visions. 170

And I saw askant the armies,
I saw as in noiseless dreams hundreds of battle-flags,
Borne through the smoke of the battles and pierc'd with missiles I saw
them,
And carried hither and yon through the smoke, and torn and bloody,
And at last but a few shreds left on the staffs, (and all in silence,)
And the staffs all splinter'd and broken.

I saw battle-corpses, myriads of them,
And the white skeletons of young men, I saw them,
I saw the debris and debris of all the slain soldiers of the war,
But I saw they were not as was thought, 180
They themselves were fully at rest, they suffer'd not,
The living remain'd and suffer'd, the mother suffer'd,
And the wife and the child and the musing comrade suffer'd,
And the armies that remain'd suffer'd.

16

Passing the visions, passing the night,
Passing, unloosing the hold of my comrades' hands,
Passing the song of the hermit bird and the tallying song of my soul,
Victorious song, death's outlet song, yet varying ever-altering song,
As low and wailing, yet clear the notes, rising and falling, flooding the
night,
Sadly sinking and fainting, as warning and warning, and yet again
bursting with joy, 190
Covering the earth and filling the spread of the heaven,
As that powerful psalm in the night I heard from recesses,
Passing, I leave thee lilac with heart-shaped leaves,
I leave thee there in the door-yard, blooming, returning with spring.

I cease from my song for thee,
From my gaze on thee in the west, fronting the west, communing with
thee,
O comrade lustrous with silver face in the night.

Yet each to keep and all, retrievements out of the night,
The song, the wondrous chant of the gray-brown bird,
And the tallying chant, the echo arous'd in my soul, 200
With the lustrous and drooping star with the countenance full of woe,
With the holders holding my hand nearing the call of the bird,

Comrades mine and I in the midst, and their memory ever to keep, for
the dead I loved so well,
For the sweetest, wisest soul of all my days and lands — and this for his
dear sake,
Lilac and star and bird twined with the chant of my soul,
There in the fragrant pines and the cedars dusk and dim.

1865–1866; 1881

The Snake

EMILY DICKINSON (1830–1886)

A narrow fellow in the grass
Occasionally rides;
You may have met him — did you not?
His notice sudden is.

The grass divides as with a comb,
A spotted shaft is seen;
And then it closes at your feet
And opens further on.

He likes a boggy acre,
A floor too cool for corn.   10
Yet when a child, and barefoot,
I more than once, at morn,

Have passed, I thought, a whip-lash
Unbraiding in the sun —
When, stooping to secure it,
It wrinkled, and was gone.

Several of nature's people
I know, and they know me;
I feel for them a transport
Of cordiality;   20

But never met this fellow,
Attended or alone,
Without a tighter breathing,
And zero at the bone.   1890

The Carpenter's Son

A. E. HOUSMAN (1859–1936)

"Here the hangman stops his cart:
Now the best of friends must part.
Fare you well, for ill fare I:
Live, lads, and I will die.

"Oh, at home had I but stayed
'Prenticed to my father's trade,
Had I stuck to plane and adze,
I had not been lost, my lads.

"Then I might have built perhaps
Gallows-trees for other chaps,   10
Never dangled on my own,
Had I left but ill alone.

"Now, you see, they hang me high,
And the people passing by
Stop to shake their fists and curse;
So 'tis come from ill to worse.

"Here hang I, and right and left
Two poor fellows hang for theft:
All the same's the luck we prove,
Though the midmost hangs for love.   20

"Comrades all, that stand and gaze,
Walk henceforth in other ways;
See my neck and save your own:
Comrades all, leave ill alone.

"Make some day a decent end,
Shrewder fellows than your friend.
Fare you well, for ill fare I:
Live, lads, and I will die."   1896

The Wood-Pile

ROBERT FROST (1874–1963)

Out walking in the frozen swamp one grey day,
I paused and said, "I will turn back from here.
No, I will go on farther — and we shall see."
The hard snow held me, save where now and then
One foot went through. The view was all in lines
Straight up and down of tall slim trees
Too much alike to mark or name a place by
So as to say for certain I was here
Or somewhere else: I was just far from home.
A small bird flew before me. He was careful   10
To put a tree between us when he lighted,
And say no word to tell me who he was
Who was so foolish as to think what *he* thought.
He thought that I was after him for a feather —
The white one in his tail; like one who takes
Everything said as personal to himself.
One flight out sideways would have undeceived him.
And then there was a pile of wood for which
I forgot him and let his little fear
Carry him off the way I might have gone,   20
Without so much as wishing him good-night.
He went behind it to make his last stand.
It was a cord of maple, cut and split
And piled — and measured, four by four by eight.
And not another like it could I see.
No runner tracks in this year's snow looped near it.
And it was older sure than this year's cutting,
Or even last year's or the year's before.
The wood was grey and the bark warping off it
And the pile somewhat sunken. Clematis   30
Had wound strings round and round it like a bundle.
What held it though on one side was a tree
Still growing, and on one a stake and prop,
These latter about to fall. I thought that only
Someone who lived in turning to fresh tasks
Could so forget his handiwork on which
He spent himself, the labour of his axe,
And leave it there far from a useful fireplace
To warm the frozen swamp as best it could
With the slow smokeless burning of decay.   1914   40

Snake

D. H. LAWRENCE (1885–1930)

A snake came to my water-trough
On a hot, hot day, and I in pyjamas for the heat,
To drink there.

In the deep, strange-scented shade of the great dark carob-tree
I came down the steps with my pitcher
And must wait, must stand and wait, for there he was at the trough
    before me.

He reached down from a fissure in the earth-wall in the gloom
And trailed his yellow-brown slackness soft-bellied down, over the edge
    of the stone trough
And rested his throat upon the stone bottom,
And where the water had dripped from the tap, in a small clearness, 10
He sipped with his straight mouth,
Softly drank through his straight gums, into his slack long body,
Silently.

Someone was before me at my water-trough,
And I, like a second comer, waiting.

He lifted his head from his drinking, as cattle do,
And looked at me vaguely, as drinking cattle do,
And flickered his two-forked tongue from his lips, and mused a moment,
And stooped and drank a little more,
Being earth brown, earth golden from the burning burning bowels of
    the earth   20
On the day of Sicilian July, with Etna smoking.

The voice of my education said to me
He must be killed,
For in Sicily the black, black snakes are innocent, the gold are ven-
    omous.

And voices in me said, If you were a man
You would take a stick and break him now, and finish him off.

But must I confess how I liked him,
How glad I was he had come like a guest in quiet, to drink at my
    water-trough
And depart peaceful, pacified, and thankless,
Into the burning bowels of this earth?   30

Was it cowardice, that I dared not kill him?
Was it perversity, that I longed to talk to him?
Was it humility, to feel so honoured?
I felt so honoured.

And yet those voices:
If you were not afraid, you would kill him!

And truly I was afraid, I was most afraid,
But even so, honoured still more
That he should seek my hospitality
From out the dark door of the secret earth.   40

He drank enough
And lifted his head, dreamily, as one who has drunken,
And flickered his tongue like a forked night on the air, so black,
Seeming to lick his lips,
And looked around like a god, unseeing, into the air,
And slowly turned his head,
And slowly, very slowly, as if thrice adream,
Proceeded to draw his slow length curving round
And climb again the broken bank of my wall-face.

And as he put his head into that dreadful hole,   50
And as he slowly drew up, snake-easing his shoulders, and entered
        farther,
A sort of horror, a sort of protest against his withdrawing into that
        horrid black hole,
Deliberately going into the blackness, and slowly drawing himself after,
Overcame me now his back was turned.

I looked round, I put down my pitcher,
I picked up a clumsy log
And threw it at the water-trough with a clatter.

I think it did not hit him,
But suddenly that part of him that was left behind convulsed in un-
        dignified haste,
Writhed like lightning, and was gone   60
Into the black hole, the earth-lipped fissure in the wall-front,
At which, in the intense still noon, I stared with fascination.

And immediately I regretted it.
I thought how paltry, how vulgar, what a mean act!
I despised myself and the voices of my accursed human education.

And I thought of the albatross,
And I wished he would come back, my snake.

For he seemed to me again like a king,
Like a king in exile, uncrowned in the underworld,
Now due to be crowned again.   **70**

And so, I missed my chance with one of the lords
Of life.
And I have something to expiate:
A pettiness.   1923

Peter Quince at the Clavier

WALLACE STEVENS (1879–1955)

I

Just as my fingers on these keys
Make music, so the self-same sounds
On my spirit make a music, too.

Music is feeling, then, not sound;
And thus it is that what I feel,
Here in this room, desiring you,

Thinking of your blue-shadowed silk,
Is music. It is like the strain
Waked in the elders by Susanna.

Of a green evening, clear and warm,   **10**
She bathed in her still garden, while
The red-eyed elders watching, felt

The basses of their beings throb
In witching chords, and their thin blood
Pulse pizzicati of Hosanna.

Title. Peter Quince is the carpenter who directs "the most lamentable
comedy" in Shakespeare's *A Midsummer Night's Dream*.

II

In the green water, clear and warm,
Susanna lay.
She searched
The touch of springs,
And found   20
Concealed imaginings.
She sighed,
For so much melody.

Upon the bank, she stood
In the cool
Of spent emotions.
She felt, among the leaves,
The dew
Of old devotions.

She walked upon the grass,   30
Still quavering.
The winds were like her maids,
On timid feet,
Fetching her woven scarves,
Yet wavering.

A breath upon her hand
Muted the night.
She turned —
A cymbal crashed,
And roaring horns.   40

III

Soon, with a noise like tambourines,
Came her attendant Byzantines.

They wondered why Susanna cried
Against the elders by her side;

And as they whispered, the refrain
Was like a willow swept by rain.

Anon, their lamps' uplifted flame
Revealed Susanna and her shame.

And then, the simpering Byzantines
Fled, with a noise like tambourines.   50

IV

Beauty is momentary in the mind —
The fitful tracing of a portal;
But in the flesh it is immortal.

The body dies; the body's beauty lives.
So evenings die, in their green going,
A wave, interminably flowing.
So gardens die, their meek breath scenting
The cowl of winter, done repenting.
So maidens die, to the auroral
Celebration of a maiden's choral.   60
Susanna's music touched the bawdy strings
Of those white elders; but, escaping,
Left only Death's ironic scraping.
Now, in its immortality, it plays
On the clear viol of her memory,
And makes a constant sacrament of praise.   1923

Leda and the Swan

WILLIAM BUTLER YEATS (1865–1939)

A sudden blow: the great wings beating still
Above the staggering girl, her thighs caressed
By the dark webs, her nape caught in his bill,
He holds her helpless breast upon his breast.

How can those terrified vague fingers push
The feathered glory from her loosening thighs?
And how can body, laid in that white rush,
But feel the strange heart beating where it lies?

A shudder in the loins engenders there
The broken wall, the burning roof and tower
And Agamemnon dead.
                         Being so caught up,
So mastered by the brute blood of the air,
Did she put on his knowledge with his power
Before the indifferent beak could let her drop?   1928

Byzantium

WILLIAM BUTLER YEATS (1865–1939)

The unpurged images of day recede;
The Emperor's drunken soldiery are abed;
Night resonance recedes, night-walkers' song
After great cathedral gong;
A starlit or a moonlit dome disdains
All that man is,
All mere complexities,
The fury and the mire of human veins.

Before me floats an image, man or shade,
Shade more than man, more image than a shade;   10
For Hades' bobbin bound in mummy-cloth
May unwind the winding path;
A mouth that has no moisture and no breath
Breathless mouths may summon;
I hail the superhuman;
I call it death-in-life and life-in-death.

Miracle, bird or golden handiwork,
More miracle than bird or handiwork,
Planted on the star-lit golden bough,
Can like the cocks of Hades crow,   20
Or, by the moon embittered, scorn aloud
In glory of changeless metal
Common bird or petal
And all complexities of mire or blood.

At midnight on the Emperor's pavement flit
Flames that no faggot feeds, nor steel has lit,
Nor storm disturbs, flames begotten of flame,
Where blood-begotten spirits come
And all complexities of fury leave,
Dying into a dance,   30
An agony of trance,
An agony of flame that cannot singe a sleeve.

Astraddle on the dolphin's mire and blood,
Spirit after spirit! The smithies break the flood,
The golden smithies of the Emperor!
Marbles of the dancing floor
Break bitter furies of complexity,
Those images that yet
Fresh images beget,
That dolphin-torn, that gong-tormented sea.   1933   40

The Yachts

WILLIAM CARLOS WILLIAMS (1883–1963)

contend in a sea which the land partly encloses
shielding them from the too heavy blows
of an ungoverned ocean which when it chooses

tortures the biggest hulls, the best man knows
to pit against its beatings, and sinks them pitilessly.
Mothlike in mists, scintillant in the minute

brilliance of cloudless days, with broad bellying sails
they glide to the wind tossing green water
from their sharp prows while over them the crew crawls

ant-like, solicitously grooming them, releasing,   **10**
making fast as they turn, lean far over and having
caught the wind again, side by side, head for the mark.

In a well guarded arena of open water surrounded by
lesser and greater craft which, sycophant, lumbering
and flittering follow them, they appear youthful, rare

as the light of a happy eye, live with the grace
of all that in the mind is feckless, free and
naturally to be desired. Now the sea which holds them

is moody, lapping their glossy sides, as if feeling
for some slightest flaw but fails completely.   **20**
Today no race. Then the wind comes again. The yachts

move, jockeying for a start, the signal is set and they
are off. Now the waves strike at them but they are too
well made, they slip through, though they take in canvas.

Arms with hands grasping seek to clutch at the prows.
Bodies thrown recklessly in the way are cut aside.
It is a sea of faces about them in agony, in despair

until the horror of the race dawns staggering the mind,
the whole sea become an entanglement of watery bodies
lost to the world bearing what they cannot hold. Broken,   **30**

beaten, desolate, reaching from the dead to be taken up
they cry out, failing, failing! their cries rising
in waves still as the skillful yachts pass over.   1935

Snow

LOUIS MAC NEICE (1907–1963)

The room was suddenly rich and the great bay-window was
Spawning snow and pink roses against it
Soundlessly collateral and incompatible:
World is suddener than we fancy it.

World is crazier and more of it than we think,
Incorrigibly plural. I peel and portion
A tangerine and spit the pips and feel
The drunkenness of things being various.

And the fire flames with a bubbling sound for world
Is more spiteful and gay than one supposes —
On the tongue on the eyes on the ears in the palms of one's hands —
There is more than glass between the snow and the huge roses.   1935

The Sirens

JOHN MANIFOLD (1915–   )

Odysseus heard the sirens; they were singing
Music by Wolf and Weinberger and Morley
About a region where the swans go winging,
Vines are in colour, girls are growing surely

Into nubility, and pylons bringing
Leisure and power to farms that live securely
Without a landlord. Still, his eyes were stinging
With salt and seablink, and the ropes hurt sorely.

Odysseus saw the sirens; they were charming,
Blonde, with snub breasts and little neat posteriors,
But could not take his mind off the alarming

Weather report, his mutineers in irons,
The radio failing; it was bloody serious.
In twenty minutes he forgot the sirens.   1946

2. Hugo *Wolf:* a nineteenth-century Austrian composer, chiefly of songs.
Jaromir *Weinberger:* a twentieth-century Czech-born composer of theater-
music and operas. Thomas *Morley:* a sixteenth-century English composer,
chiefly of madrigals.

As a Plane Tree by the Water

ROBERT LOWELL (1917–   )

Darkness has called to darkness, and disgrace
Elbows about our windows in this planned
Babel of Boston where our money talks
And multiplies the darkness of a land
Of preparation where the Virgin walks
And roses spiral her enamelled face
Or fall to splinters on unwatered streets.
Our Lady of Babylon, go by, go by,
I was once the apple of your eye;
Flies, flies are on the plane tree, on the streets.   10

The flies, the flies, the flies of Babylon
Buzz in my ear-drums while the devil's long
Dirge of the people detonates the hour
For floating cities where his golden tongue
Enchants the masons of the Babel Tower
To raise tomorrow's city to the sun
That never sets upon these hell-fire streets
Of Boston, where the sunlight is a sword
Striking at the withholder of the Lord:
Flies, flies are on the plane tree, on the streets.   20

Flies strike the miraculous waters of the iced
Atlantic and the eyes of Bernadette
Who saw Our Lady standing in the cave
At Massabielle, saw her so squarely that
Her vision put out reason's eyes. The grave
Is open-mouthed and swallowed up in Christ.
O walls of Jericho! And all the streets
To our Atlantic wall are singing: "Sing,
Sing for the resurrection of the King."
Flies, flies are on the plane tree, on the streets.   1946   30

CHAPTER 3

Narrative and Dramatic Structure

Johnie Armstrong

ANONYMOUS

There dwelt a man in faire Westmerland,
    Jonnë Armestrong men did him call,
He had nither lands nor rents coming in,
    Yet he kept eight score men in his hall.

He had horse and harness for them all,
    Goodly steeds were all milke-white;
O the golden bands an about their necks,
    And their weapons, they were all alike.

Newes then was brought unto the king
    That there was a sicke a won as hee,   10
That livëd lyke a bold out-law,
    And robbëd all the north country.

The king he writt an a letter then,
    A letter which was large and long;
He signëd it with his owne hand,
    And he promised to doe him no wrong.

When this letter came Jonnë untill,
    His heart it was as blythe as birds on the tree:
"Never was I sent for before any king,
    My father, my grandfather, nor none but mee.   20

86

"And if wee goe the king before,
  I would we went most orderly;
Every man of you shall have his scarlet cloak,
  Laced with silver laces three.

"Every won of you shall have his velvett coat,
  Laced with silver lace so white;
O the golden bands an about your necks,
  Black hatts, white feathers, all alyke."

By the morrow morninge at ten of the clock,
  Towards Edenburough gon was hee,   30
And with him all his eight score men;
  Good lord, it was a goodly sight for to see!

When Jonnë came befower the king,
  He fell downe on his knee;
"O pardon, my soveraine leige," he said,
  "O pardon my eight score men and mee!"

"Thou shalt have no pardon, thou traytor strong,
  For thy eight score men nor thee;
For to-morrow morning by ten of the clock,
  Both thou and them shall hang on the gallow-tree."   40

But Jonnë looke'd over his left shoulder,
  Good Lord, what a grevious look looked hee!
Saying, "Asking grace of a graceless face —
  Why there is none for you nor me."

But Jonnë had a bright sword by his side,
  And it was made of the mettle so free,
That had not the king stept his foot aside,
  He had smitten his head from his faire boddë.

Saying, "Fight on, my merry men all,
  And see that none of you be ta'en;   50
For rather then men shall say we were hange'd,
  Let them report how we were slaine."

Then, God wott, faire Eddenburrough rose,
  And so besett poore Jonnë rounde,
That fowerscore and tenn of Jonnës best men
  Lay gasping all upon the ground.

Then like a mad man Jonně laide about,
   And like a mad man then fought hee,
Untill a falce Scot came Jonně behinde,
   And runn him through the faire boddee.   60

Saying, "Fight on, my merry men all,
   And see that none of you be taine;
For I will stand by and bleed but awhile,
   And then will I come and fight againe."

Newes then was brought to young Jonně Armestrong,
   As he stood by his nurses knee,
Who vowed if ere he live'd for to be a man,
   O the treacherous Scots revengd hee'd be.   *Before* 1600

Get Up and Bar the Door

ANONYMOUS

It fell about the Martinmas time,
   And a gay time it was then,
When our goodwife got puddings to make,
   And she's boild them in the pan.

The wind sae cauld blew south and north,
   And blew into the floor;
Quoth our goodman to our goodwife,
   "Gae out and bar the door."

"My hand is in my hussyfskap,
   Goodman, as ye may see;   10
An it should nae be barrd this hundred **year**,
   It's no be barrd for me."

They made a paction tween them twa,
   They made it firm and sure,
That the first word whaeer shoud speak,
   Shoud rise and bar the door.

Then by there came two gentlemen,
   At twelve o'clock at night,
And they could neither see house nor **hall**,
   Nor coal nor candle-light.   20

9. *hussyfskap:* household chores.

"Now whether is this a rich man's house,
  Or whether is it a poor?"
But neer a word wad ane o them speak,
  For barring of the door.

And first they ate the white puddings,
  And then they ate the black;
Tho muckle thought the goodwife to hersel,
  Yet neer a word she spake.

Then said the one unto the other,
  "Here, man, tak ye my knife;   30
Do ye tak aff the auld man's beard.
  And I'll kiss the goodwife."

"But there's nae water in the house,
  And what shall we do than?"
"What ails ye at the pudding-broo,
  That boils into the pan?"

O up then started our goodman,
  An angry man was he:
"Will ye kiss my wife before my een,
  And scad me wi pudding-bree?"   40

Then up and started our goodwife,
  Gied three skips on the floor:
"Goodman, you've spoken the foremost word,
  Get up and bar the door!"   *Before* 1600

Holy Willie's Prayer

ROBERT BURNS (1759–1796)

"Holy Willie," according to the poet, "was a rather oldish bachelor elder, in the parish of Mauchline, and much and justly famed for that polemical chattering which ends in tipply orthodoxy, and for that spiritualized bawdry which refines to liquorish devotion. In a sessional process with a gentleman in Mauchline— a Mr. Gavin Hamilton—Holy Willie and his priest, Father Auld, after full hearing in the Presbytery of Ayr, came off but second best, owing partly to the oratorical powers of Mr. Robert Aiken, Mr. Hamilton's counsel; but chiefly to Mr. Hamilton's being one of the most irreproachable and truly respected characters in the country. On losing his process, the muse overheard him at his devotions as follows—"

O Thou, wha in the Heavens dost dwell,
Wha, as it pleases best Thysel',
Sends ane to heaven an' ten to hell
    A' for Thy glory,
And no for onie guid or ill
    They've done bafore Thee!

I bless and praise Thy matchless might,
Whan thousands Thou hast left in night,
That I am here before Thy sight,
    For gifts an' grace,   10
A burning an' a shining light,
    To a' this place.

What was I, or my generation,
That I should get sic exaltation?
I, wha deserv'd sic just damnation
    For broken laws,
Five thousand years 'fore my creation,
    Thro' Adam's cause!

When frae my mither's womb I fell,
Thou might hae plung'd me deep in hell,   20
To gnash my gums, to weep and wail,
    In burnin' lake,
Where damnéd devils roar and yell,
    Chain'd to a stake.

Yet I am here, a chosen sample,
To show Thy grace is great and ample;
I'm here a pillar in Thy temple,
    Strong as a rock,

A guide, a buckler, an example
      To a' Thy flock.   30

O Lord, Thou kens what zeal I bear,
When drinkers drink, and swearers swear,
And singin there and dancin here,
      Wi' great an' sma':
For I am keepit by Thy fear,
      Free frae them a'.

But yet, O Lord! confess I must:
At times I'm fash'd wi' fleshly lust;
An' sometimes, too, wi' warldly trust,
      Vile self gets in;   40
But Thou remembers we are dust,
      Defil'd in sin.

O Lord! yestreen, Thou kens, wi' Meg —
Thy pardon I sincerely beg,
O! may it ne'er be livin plague
      To my dishonor!
An' I'll ne'er lift a lawless leg
      Again upon her.

Besides, I farther maun allow,
Wi' Lizzie's lass, three times, I trow;   50
But, Lord, that Friday I was fou,
      When I came near her,
Or else, Thou kens, Thy servant true
      Wad ne'er hae steered her.

May be Thou lets this fleshly thorn
Beset Thy servant e'en and morn,
Lest he owre high and proud should turn,
      'Cause he's sae gifted;
If sae, Thy hand maun e'en be borne,
      Until Thou lift it.   60

Lord, bless Thy chosen in this place,
For here Thou hast a chosen race;
But God confound their stubborn face,
      And blast their name,
Wha bring Thy elders to disgrace,
      An' public shame!

38. *fash'd:* beset.   39. *warldly:* worldly.   49. *maun:* must.
51. *fou:* full, drunk.   54. *steered:* meddled with.

Lord, mind Gau'n Hamilton's deserts:
He drinks, an' swears, an' plays at cartes,
Yet has sae monie takin arts
    Wi' grit and sma',   70
Frae God's ain Priest the people's hearts
    He steals awa'.

An' whan we chasten'd him therefore,
Thou kens how he bred sic a splore,
As set the warld in a roar
    O' laughin at us;
Curse Thou his basket and his store,
    Kail and potatoes!

Lord, hear my earnest cry an' pray'r
Against that Presbyt'ry o' Ayr!   80
Thy strong right hand, Lord, make it bare
    Upo' their heads;
Lord, weigh it down, an' dinna spare,
    For their misdeeds!

O Lord my God! that glib-tongu'd Aiken,
My very heart and flesh are quakin,
To think how we stood sweatin, shakin,
    An' pish'd wi' dread,
While he, wi' hingin lip an' snakin,
    Held up his head.   90

Lord, in the day of vengeance try him;
Lord, visit him wha did employ him,
And pass not in Thy mercy by 'em,
    Nor hear their pray'r:
But, for Thy people's sake, destroy 'em,
    An' dinna spare.

But, Lord, remember me and mine
Wi' mercies temp'ral and divine,
That I for gear and grace may shine,
    Excelled by nane;   100
And a' the glory shall be Thine,
    Amen, Amen.   1785;1808

67. *Gau'n Hamilton:* Gavin Hamilton. See headnote.
68. *cartes:* cards. Card playing was against the rule of the church.
74. *sic a splore:* such a fuss.   89. *snakin:* sneering.
99. *gear:* wealth.   100. *nane:* none.

The Rime of the Ancient Mariner

SAMUEL TAYLOR COLERIDGE (1772–1834)

In Seven Parts

How a Ship having passed the Line was driven by storms to the cold Country towards the South Pole; and how from thence she made her course to the tropical Latitude of the Great Pacific Ocean; and of the strange things that befell; and in what manner the Ancyent Marinere came back to his own Country.

PART I

An ancient Mariner meeteth three Gallants bidden to a wedding-feast, and detaineth one.

It is an ancient Mariner
And he stoppeth one of three.
"By thy long grey beard and glittering eye,
Now wherefore stopp'st thou me?

"The Bridegroom's doors are opened wide,
And I am next of kin,
The guests are met, the feast is set:
May'st hear the merry din."

He holds him with his skinny hand,
"There was a ship," quoth he.   10
"Hold off! unhand me, grey-beard loon!"
Eftsoons his hand dropt he.

The Wedding-Guest is spellbound by the eye of the old seafaring man, and constrained to hear his tale.

He holds him with his glittering eye—
The Wedding-Guest stood still,
And listens like a three years' child:
The Mariner hath his will.

The Wedding-Guest sat on a stone:
He cannot choose but hear;
And thus spake on that ancient man,
The bright-eyed Mariner.   20

"The ship was cheered, the harbor cleared,
Merrily did we drop
Below the kirk, below the hill,
Below the light-house top.

The Mariner tells how the ship sailed southward with a good wind and fair weather till it reached the Line.

"The sun came up upon the left,
Out of the sea came he!
And he shone bright, and on the right
Went down into the sea.

93

"Higher and higher every day,
Till over the mast at noon—"   30
The Wedding-Guest here beat his breast,
For he heard the loud bassoon.

The Wedding-Guest heareth the bridal music; but the Mariner continueth his tale.

The bride hath paced into the hall,
Red as a rose is she;
Nodding their heads before her goes
The merry minstrelsy.

The Wedding-Guest he beat his breast,
Yet he cannot choose but hear;
And thus spake on that ancient man,
The bright-eyed Mariner.   40

The ship driven by a storm toward the south pole.

"And now the storm-blast came, and he
Was tyrannous and strong:
He struck with his o'ertaking wings,
And chased us south along.

"With sloping masts and dipping prow,
As who pursued with yell and blow
Still treads the shadow of his foe,
And forward bends his head,
The ship drove fast, loud roared the blast,
And southward aye we fled.   50

"And now there came both mist and snow,
And it grew wondrous cold:
And ice, mast-high, came floating by,
As green as emerald.

The land of ice, and of fearful sounds where no living thing was to be seen.

"And through the drifts the snowy clifts
Did send a dismal sheen:
Nor shapes of men nor beasts we ken—
The ice was all between.

"The ice was here, the ice was there,
The ice was all around: 60
It cracked and growled, and roared and howled,
Like noises in a swound!

Till a great sea-bird, called the Albatross, came through the snow-fog, and was received with great joy and hospitality.

"At length did cross an Albatross,
Thorough the fog it came;
As if it had been a Christian soul,
We hailed it in God's name.

64. *Thorough:* through.

"It ate the food it ne'er had eat,
And round and round it flew.
The ice did split with a thunder-fit;
The helmsman steered us through!   70

*And lo! the Albatross
proveth a bird of good
omen, and followeth
the ship as it returned
northward through fog
and floating ice.*

"And a good south wind sprung up behind;
The Albatross did follow,
And every day, for food or play,
Came to the mariners' hollo!

"In mist or cloud, on mast or shroud,
It perched for vespers nine;
Whiles all the night, through fog-smoke white,
Glimmered the white moon-shine."

*The ancient Mariner
inhospitably killeth the
pious bird of good omen.*

"God save thee, ancient Mariner!
From the fiends, that plague thee thus!—   80
Why look'st thou so?"—"With my cross-bow
I shot the Albatross!"

PART II

"The Sun now rose upon the right:
Out of the sea came he,
Still hid in mist, and on the left
Went down into the sea.

"And the good south wind still blew behind,
But no sweet bird did follow,
Nor any day for food or play
Came to the mariners' hollo!   90

*His shipmates cry out
against the ancient
Mariner, for killing the
bird of good luck.*

"And I had done a hellish thing,
And it would work 'em woe:
For all averred, I had killed the bird
That made the breeze to blow.
'Ah wretch!' said they, 'the bird to slay,
That made the breeze to blow!'

75. *shroud:* a rope running from the masthead to the side of the ship.
83. *Sun now rose:* the ship has sailed around Cape Horn and is making
its way north into the Pacific Ocean.

*But when the fog
cleared off they justify
the same, and thus
make themselves
accomplices in the crime.*

"Nor dim nor red, like God's own head,
The glorious Sun uprist:
Then all averred, I had killed the bird
That brought the fog and mist.   100
' 'Twas right,' said they, 'such birds to slay,
That bring the fog and mist.'

*The fair breeze con-
tinues; the ship enters
the Pacific Ocean, and
sails northward, even
till it reaches the Line.*

"The fair breeze blew, the white foam flew,
The furrow followed free;
We were the first that ever burst
Into that silent sea.

*The ship hath been
suddenly becalmed.*

"Down dropped the breeze, the sails dropped
    down,
'Twas sad as sad could be;
And we did speak only to break
The silence of the sea!   110

"All in a hot and copper sky,
The bloody Sun, at noon,
Right up above the mast did stand,
No bigger than the Moon.

"Day after day, day after day,
We stuck, nor breath nor motion;
As idle as a painted ship
Upon a painted ocean.

*And the Albatross begins
to be avenged.*

"Water, water, every where,
And all the boards did shrink;   120
Water, water, every where,
Nor any drop to drink.

"The very deep did rot: O Christ!
That ever this should be!
Yea, slimy things did crawl with legs
Upon the slimy sea.

"About, about, in reel and rout
The death-fires danced at night;
The water, like a witch's oils,
Burned green, and blue and white.   130

---

128. *death-fires:* possibly the phenomenon known as St. Elmo's fires, or un-
named phosphorescent lights thought to be presages of disaster.

"And some in dreams assured were
Of the Spirit that plagued us so;
Nine fathom deep he had followed us
From the land of mist and snow.

"And every tongue, through utter drought,
Was withered at the root;
We could not speak, no more than if
We had been choked with soot.

"Ah! well-a-day! what evil looks
Had I from old and young!   140
Instead of the cross, the Albatross
About my neck was hung."

PART III

"There passed a weary time. Each throat
Was parched, and glazed each eye.
A weary time! a weary time!
How glazed each weary eye,
When looking westward, I beheld
A something in the sky.

"At first it seemed a little speck,
And then it seemed a mist;   150
It moved and moved, and took at last
A certain shape, I wist.

"A speck, a mist, a shape, I wist!
And still it neared and neared:
As if it dodged a water-sprite,
It plunged and tacked and veered.

"With throats unslaked, with black lips baked,
We could nor laugh nor wail;
Through utter drought all dumb we stood!
I bit my arm, I sucked the blood,   160
And cried, 'A sail! a sail!'

"With throats unslaked, with black lips baked,
Agape they heard me call:
Gramercy! they for joy did grin,
And all at once their breath drew in,
As they were drinking all.

*And horror follows.
For can it be a ship
that comes onward
without wind or tide?*

" 'See! see!' (I cried) 'she tacks no more!
Hither to work us weal—
Without a breeze, without a tide,
She steadies with upright keel!'   170

"The western wave was all aflame,
The day was well nigh done!
Almost upon the western wave
Rested the broad bright Sun;
When that strange shape drove suddenly
Betwixt us and the Sun.

*It seemeth him but the
skeleton of a ship.*

"And straight the Sun was flecked with bars,
(Heaven's Mother send us grace!)
As if through a dungeon-grate he peered
With broad and burning face.   180

"Alas! (thought I, and my heart beat loud)
How fast she nears and nears!
Are those her sails that glance in the Sun,
Like restless gossameres?

*And its ribs are seen
as bars on the face of
the setting Sun.
The Specter-Woman and
her Death-mate, and no
other on board the
skeleton-ship. Like
vessel, like crew!*

"Are those her ribs through which the Sun
Did peer, as through a grate?
And is that Woman all her crew?
Is that a Death? and are there two?
Is Death that woman's mate?

"Her lips were red, her looks were free,   190
Her locks were yellow as gold:
Her skin was as white as leprosy,
The Night-mare Life-in-Death was she,
Who thicks man's blood with cold.

*Death and Life-in-
Death have diced for
the ship's crew, and
she (the latter)
winneth the ancient
Mariner.*

"The naked hulk alongside came,
And the twain were casting dice;
'The game is done! I've won, I've won!'
Quoth she, and whistles thrice.

*No twilight within the
courts of the Sun.*

"The Sun's rim dips; the stars rush out:
At one stride comes the dark;   200
With far-heard whisper, o'er the sea,
Off shot the specter-bark.

*At the rising of the
Moon,*

"We listened and looked sideways up!
Fear at my heart, as at a cup,
My life-blood seemed to sip!

The stars were dim, and thick the night,
The steersman's face by his lamp gleamed white;
From the sails the dew did drip—
Till clomb above the eastern bar
The hornéd Moon with one bright star   210
Within the nether tip.

One after another,

"One after one, by the star-dogged Moon,
Too quick for groan or sigh,
Each turned his face with a ghastly pang,
And cursed me with his eye.

*His shipmates drop
down dead.*

"Four times fifty living men
(And I heard nor sigh nor groan),
With heavy thump, a lifeless lump,
They dropped down one by one.

*But Life-in-Death
begins her work on the
ancient Mariner.*

"The souls did from their bodies fly—   220
They fled to bliss or woe!
And every soul, it passed me by
Like the whizz of my cross-bow!"

PART IV

*The Wedding-Guest
feareth that a Spirit
is talking to him;*

"I fear thee, ancient Mariner!
I fear thy skinny hand!
And thou art long, and lank, and brown,
As is the ribbed sea-sand.

*But the ancient
Mariner assureth him
of his bodily life, and
proceedeth to relate
his horrible penance.*

"I fear thee and thy glittering eye,
And thy skinny hand, so brown."—
"Fear not, fear not, thou Wedding-Guest!   230
This body dropt not down.

"Alone, alone, all, all alone,
Alone on a wide, wide sea!
And never a saint took pity on
My soul in agony.

*He despiseth the
creatures of the calm.*

"The many men, so beautiful!
And they all dead did lie:
And a thousand thousand slimy things
Lived on; and so did I.

210. *Moon . . . tip:* according to Coleridge, "it is a common superstition among sailors that something evil is about to happen whenever a star dogs the moon."

*And envieth that they
should live, and so
many lie dead.*

"I looked upon the rotting sea,   240
And drew my eyes away;
I looked upon the rotting deck,
And there the dead men lay.

"I looked to heaven, and tried to pray;
But or ever a prayer had gusht,
A wicked whisper came, and made
My heart as dry as dust.

"I closed my lids, and kept them close,
And the balls like pulses beat;
For the sky and the sea, and the sea and the sky
Lay like a load on my weary eye,   251
And the dead were at my feet.

*But the curse liveth
for him in the eye of
the dead men.*

"The cold sweat melted from their limbs,
Nor rot nor reek did they:
The look with which they looked on me
Had never passed away.

"An orphan's curse would drag to hell
A spirit from on high;
But oh! more horrible than that
Is the curse in a dead man's eye!   260
Seven days, seven nights, I saw that curse,
And yet I could not die.

*In his loneliness and
fixedness he yearneth
towards the journeying
Moon, and the stars
that still sojourn, yet
still move onward; and
everywhere the blue sky
belongs to them, and is
their appointed rest, and
their native country and
their own natural homes,
which they enter
unannounced, as lords
that are certainly ex-
pected, and yet there is a
silent joy at their arrival.*

*By the light of the
Moon he beholdeth
God's creatures of the
great calm.*

"The moving Moon went up the sky,
And no where did abide:
Softly she was going up,
And a star or two beside—

"Her beams bemocked the sultry main,
Like April hoar-frost spread;
But where the ship's huge shadow lay,
The charmèd water burned alway   270
A still and awful red.

"Beyond the shadow of the ship,
I watched the water-snakes:
They moved in tracks of shining white,
And when they reared, the elfish light
Fell off in hoary flakes.

"Within the shadow of the ship
I watched their rich attire:
Blue, glossy green, and velvet black,
They coiled and swam; and every track   280
Was a flash of golden fire.

*Their beauty and
their happiness.*

"O happy living things! no tongue
Their beauty might declare:
A spring of love gushed from my heart,

*He blesseth them in
his heart.*

And I blessed them unaware:
Sure my kind saint took pity on me,
And I blessed them unaware.

*The spell begins to
break.*

"The self-same moment I could pray;
And from my neck so free
The Albatross fell off, and sank   290
Like lead into the sea."

PART V

"Oh sleep! it is a gentle thing,
Beloved from pole to pole!
To Mary Queen the praise be given!
She sent the gentle sleep from Heaven,
That slid into my soul.

*By grace of the holy
Mother, the ancient
Mariner is refreshed
with rain.*

"The silly buckets on the deck,
That had so long remained,
I dreamt that they were filled with dew;
And when I awoke, it rained.   300

"My lips were wet, my throat was cold,
My garments all were dank;
Sure I had drunken in my dreams,
And still my body drank.

"I moved, and could not feel my limbs:
I was so light—almost
I thought that I had died in sleep,
And was a blessed ghost.

*He heareth sounds
and seeth strange
sights and commotions
in the sky and the
elements.*

"And soon I heard a roaring wind:
It did not come anear;   310
But with its sound it shook the sails,
That were so thin and sere.

297. *silly:* literally happy, good (from Anglo-Saxon *saelig*) or innocent; by
extension, unused, empty.

"The upper air burst into life!
And a hundred fire-flags sheen,
To and fro they were hurried about!
And to and fro, and in and out,
The wan stars danced between.

"And the coming wind did roar more loud,
And the sails did sigh like sedge;
And the rain poured down from one black cloud;
The Moon was at its edge.   321

"The thick black cloud was cleft, and still
The Moon was at its side:
Like waters shot from some high crag,
The lightning fell with never a jag,
A river steep and wide.

The bodies of the
ship's crew are inspired,
and the ship moves on;

"The loud wind never reached the ship,
Yet now the ship moved on!
Beneath the lightning and the Moon
The dead men gave a groan.   330

"They groaned, they stirred, they all uprose,
Nor spake, nor moved their eyes;
It had been strange, even in a dream,
To have seen those dead men rise.

"The helmsman steered, the ship moved on;
Yet never a breeze up-blew;
The mariners all 'gan work the ropes,
Where they were wont to do;
They raised their limbs like lifeless tools—
We were a ghastly crew.   340

"The body of my brother's son
Stood by me, knee to knee:
The body and I pulled at one rope,
But he said nought to me."

But not by the souls of
the men, nor by demons
of earth or middle air,
but by a blessed troop
of angelic spirits, sent
down by the invocation
of the guardian saint.

"I fear thee, ancient Mariner!"
"Be calm, thou Wedding-Guest!
'Twas not those souls that fled in pain,
Which to their corses came again,
But a troop of spirits blest:

314. *fire-flags:* perhaps the Northern Lights.

"For when it dawned—they dropped their arms,
And clustered 'round the mast;　　　　351
Sweet sounds rose slowly through their mouths,
And from their bodies passed.

"Around, around, flew each sweet sound,
Then darted to the Sun;
Slowly the sounds came back again,
Now mixed, now one by one.

"Sometimes a-dropping from the sky
I heard the skylark sing;
Sometimes all little birds that are,　　360
How they seemed to fill the sea and air
With their sweet jargoning!

"And now 'twas like all instruments,
Now like a lonely flute;
And now it is an angel's song,
That makes the heavens be mute.

"It ceased; yet still the sails made on
A pleasant noise till noon,
A noise like of a hidden brook
In the leafy month of June,　　　　370
That to the sleeping woods all night
Singeth a quiet tune.

"Till noon we quietly sailed on,
Yet never a breeze did breathe:
Slowly and smoothly went the ship,
Moved onward from beneath.

*The lonesome Spirit
from the South Pole
carries on the ship
as far as the Line, in
obedience to the angelic
troop, but still requireth
vengeance.*

"Under the keel nine fathom deep,
From the land of mist and snow,
The Spirit slid: and it was he
That made the ship to go.　　　　380
The sails at noon left off their tune,
And the ship stood still also.

"The Sun, right up above the mast,
Had fixed her to the ocean:
But in a minute she 'gan stir,
With a short uneasy motion—
Backwards and forwards half her length,
With a short uneasy motion.

"Then like a pawing horse let go,
She made a sudden bound: 390
It flung the blood into my head,
And I fell down in a swound.

"How long in that same fit I lay,
I have not to declare;
But ere my living life returned,
I heard, and in my soul discerned
Two voices in the air.

" 'Is it he?' quoth one, 'Is this the man?
By him who died on cross,
With his cruel bow he laid full low   400
The harmless Albatross.

" 'The Spirit who bideth by himself
In the land of mist and snow,
He loved the bird that loved the man
Who shot him with his bow.'

"The other was a softer voice,
As soft as honey-dew:
Quoth he, 'The man hath penance done,
And penance more will do.' "

The Polar Spirit's fellow-demons, the invisible inhabitants of the element, take part in his wrong; and two of them relate, one to the other, that penance long and heavy for the ancient Mariner hath been accorded to the Polar Spirit, who returneth southward.

PART VI

First Voice

" 'But tell me, tell me! speak again,   410
Thy soft reponse renewing—
What makes that ship drive on so fast?
What is the ocean doing?'

Second Voice

" 'Still as a slave before his lord,
The ocean hath no blast;
His great bright eye most silently
Up to the Moon is cast—

" 'If he may know which way to go;
For she guides him, smooth or grim.
See, brother, see! how graciously   420
She looketh down on him.'

FIRST VOICE

" 'But why drives on that ship so fast,
Without or wave or wind?'

SECOND VOICE

" 'The air is cut away before,
And closes from behind.

" 'Fly, brother, fly! more high, more high!
Or we shall be belated:
For slow and slow that ship will go,
When the Mariner's trance is abated.'

"I woke, and we were sailing on   430
As in a gentle weather:
'Twas night, calm night, the moon was high;
The dead men stood together.

"All stood together on the deck,
For a charnel-dungeon fitter:
All fixed on me their stony eyes,
That in the Moon did glitter.

"The pang, the curse, with which they died,
Had never passed away:
I could not draw my eyes from theirs,   440
Nor turn them up to pray.

"And now this spell was snapt: once more
I viewed the ocean green,
And looked far forth, yet little saw
Of what had else been seen—

"Like one, that on a lonesome road
Doth walk in fear and dread,
And having once turned round, walks on,
And turns no more his head;
Because he knows, a frightful fiend   450
Doth close behind him tread.

"But soon there breathed a wind on me,
Nor sound nor motion made:
Its path was not upon the sea,
In ripple or in shade.

"It raised my hair, it fanned my cheek
Like a meadow-gale of spring—
It mingled strangely with my fears,
Yet it felt like a welcoming.

"Swiftly, swiftly flew the ship,   460
Yet she sailed softly too:
Sweetly, sweetly blew the breeze—
On me alone it blew.

*And the ancient
Mariner beholdeth his
native country.*

"Oh! dream of joy! is this indeed
The light-house top I see?
Is this the hill? is this the kirk?
Is this mine own countree?

"We drifted o'er the harbor-bar,
And I with sobs did pray—
O let me be awake, my God!   470
Or let me sleep alway.

"The harbor-bay was clear as glass,
So smoothly it was strewn!
And on the bay the moonlight lay,
And the shadow of the Moon.

"The rock shone bright, the kirk no less,
That stands above the rock:
The moonlight steeped in silentness
The steady weathercock.

"And the bay was white with silent light,   480
Till, rising from the same,
Full many shapes, that shadows were,
In crimson colors came.

*The angelic spirits
leave the dead bodies,*

*And appear in their
own forms of light.*

"A little distance from the prow
Those crimson shadows were:
I turned my eyes upon the deck—
Oh, Christ! what saw I there!

"Each corse lay flat, lifeless and flat,
And, by the holy rood!
A man all light, a seraph-man,   490
On every corse there stood.

"This seraph-band, each waved his hand:
It was a heavenly sight!
They stood as signals to the land,
Each one a lovely light;

"This seraph-band, each waved his hand,
No voice did they impart—
No voice; but oh! the silence sank
Like music on my heart.

"But soon I heard the dash of oars,   500
I heard the Pilot's cheer;
My head was turned perforce away,
And I saw a boat appear.

"The Pilot, and the Pilot's boy,
I heard them coming fast:
Dear Lord in Heaven! it was a joy
The dead men could not blast.

"I saw a third—I heard his voice:
It is the Hermit good!
He singeth loud his godly hymns   510
That he makes in the wood.
He'll shrieve my soul, he'll wash away
The Albatross's blood."

PART VII

"This Hermit good lives in that wood
Which slopes down to the sea.
How loudly his sweet voice he rears!
He loves to talk with marineres
That come from a far countree.

"He kneels at morn, and noon, and eve—
He hath a cushion plump: 520
It is the moss that wholly hides
The rotted old oak-stump.

"The skiff-boat neared: I heard them talk,
'Why, this is strange, I trow!
Where are those lights so many and fair,
That signal made but now?'

" 'Strange, by my faith!' the Hermit said—
'And they answered not our cheer!
The planks look warped! and see those sails,
How thin they are and sere!   530
I never saw aught like to them,
Unless perchance it were

" 'Brown skeletons of leaves that lag
My forest-brook along;
When the ivy-tod is heavy with snow,
And the owlet whoops to the wolf below,
That eats the she-wolf's young.'

" 'Dear Lord! it hath a fiendish look—
(The Pilot made reply)
I am a-feared'—'Push on, push on!'   540
Said the Hermit cheerily.

"The boat came closer to the ship,
But I nor spake nor stirred;
The boat came close beneath the ship,
And straight a sound was heard.

The ship suddenly sinketh.

"Under the water it rumbled on,
Still louder and more dread:
It reached the ship, it split the bay;
The ship went down like lead.

The ancient Mariner is saved in the Pilot's boat.

"Stunned by that loud and dreadful sound,   550
Which sky and ocean smote,
Like one that hath been seven days drowned,
My body lay afloat;
But swift as dreams, myself I found
Within the Pilot's boat.

"Upon the whirl, where sank the ship,
The boat spun round and round;
And all was still, save that the hill
Was telling of the sound.

"I moved my lips—the Pilot shrieked,   560
And fell down in a fit;
The holy Hermit raised his eyes,
And prayed where he did sit.

"I took the oars: the Pilot's boy,
Who now doth crazy go,
Laughed loud and long, and all the while
His eyes went to and fro.
'Ha! ha!' quoth he, 'full plain I see,
The Devil knows how to row.'

"And now, all in my own countree,   570
I stood on the firm land!

The Hermit stepped forth from the boat,
And scarcely he could stand.

" 'O shrieve me, shrieve me, holy man!'
The Hermit crossed his brow,
'Say quick,' quoth he, 'I bid thee say—
What manner of man art thou?'

"Forthwith this frame of mine was wrenched
With a woeful agony,
Which forced me to begin my tale;   580
And then it left me free.

"Since then, at an uncertain hour,
That agony returns;
And till my ghastly tale is told,
This heart within me burns.

"I pass, like night, from land to land;
I have strange power of speech;
That moment that his face I see,
I know the man that must hear me:
To him my tale I teach.   590

"What loud uproar bursts from that door!
The wedding-guests are there:
But in the garden-bower the bride
And bride-maids singing are:
And hark the little vesper bell,
Which biddeth me to prayer!

"O Wedding-Guest! this soul hath been
Alone on a wide, wide sea:
So lonely 'twas, that God himself
Scarce seemèd there to be.   600

"O sweeter than the marriage-feast,
'Tis sweeter far to me,
To walk together to the kirk
With a goodly company!—

"To walk together to the kirk,
And all together pray,
While each to his great Father bends,
Old men, and babes, and loving friends,
And youths and maidens gay!

"Farewell, farewell! but this I tell   610
To thee, thou Wedding-Guest!
He prayeth well, who loveth well
Both man and bird and beast.

"He prayeth best, who loveth best
All things both great and small;
For the dear God who loveth us,
He made and loveth all."

The Mariner, whose eye is bright,
Whose beard with age is hoar,
Is gone: and now the Wedding-Guest   620
Turned from the bridegroom's door.

He went like one that hath been stunned,
And is of sense forlorn:
A sadder and a wiser man,
He rose the morrow morn.   1798

La Belle Dame sans Merci

JOHN KEATS (1795–1821)

O what can ail thee, knight-at-arms,
Alone and palely loitering?
The sedge has wither'd from the lake,
And no birds sing.

O what can ail thee, knight-at-arms,
So haggard and so woe-begone?
The squirrel's granary is full,
And the harvest's done.

I see a lily on thy brow   10
With anguish moist and fever dew,
And on thy cheeks a fading rose
Fast withereth too.

I met a lady in the meads,
Full beautiful — a faery's child,
Her hair was long, her foot was light,
And her eyes were wild.

I made a garland for her head,
   And bracelets too, and fragrant zone;
She look'd at me as she did love,
   And made sweet moan.   20

I set her on my pacing steed,
   And nothing else saw all day long,
For sidelong would she bend, and sing
   A faery's song.

She found me roots of relish sweet,
   And honey wild, and manna dew,
And sure in language strange she said,
   "I love thee true."

She took me to her elfin grot,
   And there she wept, and sigh'd full sore,   30
And there I shut her wild, wild eyes
   With kisses four.

And there she lullèd me asleep
   And there I dream'd — ah! woe betide! —
The latest dream I ever dream'd
   On the cold hill side.

I saw pale kings, and princes too,
   Pale warriors, death-pale were they all;
They cried — "La belle dame sans merci
   Hath thee in thrall!"   40

I saw their starvèd lips in the gloam
   With horrid warning gapèd wide,
And I awoke and found me here
   On the cold hill side.

And this is why I sojourn here
   Alone and palely loitering
Though the sedge is wither'd from the lake,
   And no birds sing.   1820

Ulysses

ALFRED, LORD TENNYSON (1809–1892)

It little profits that an idle king,
By this still hearth, among these barren crags,
Matched with an aged wife, I mete and dole

Unequal laws unto a savage race,
That hoard, and sleep, and feed, and know not me.
I cannot rest from travel; I will drink
Life to the lees. All times I have enjoyed
Greatly, have suffered greatly, both with those
That loved me, and alone; on shore, and when
Through scudding drifts the rainy Hyades   10
Vexed the dim sea. I am become a name;
For always roaming with a hungry heart
Much have I seen and known—cities of men
And manners, climates, councils, governments,
Myself not least, but honored of them all—
And drunk delight of battle with my peers,
Far on the ringing plains of windy Troy.
I am a part of all that I have met;
Yet all experience is an arch wherethrough
Gleams that untraveled world whose margin fades   20
Forever and forever when I move.
How dull it is to pause, to make an end,
To rust unburnished, not to shine in use!
As though to breathe were life! Life piled on life
Were all too little, and of one to me
Little remains; but every hour is saved
From that eternal silence, something more,
A bringer of new things; and vile it were
For some three suns to store and hoard myself,
And this gray spirit yearning in desire   30
To follow knowledge like a sinking star,
Beyond the utmost bound of human thought.
    This is my son, mine own Telemachus,
To whom I leave the scepter and the isle—
Well-loved of me, discerning to fulfill
This labor, by slow prudence to make mild
A rugged people, and through soft degrees
Subdue them to the useful and the good.
Most blameless is he, centered in the sphere
Of common duties, decent not to fail   40
In offices of tenderness, and pay
Meet adoration to my household gods,
When I am gone. He works his work, I mine.
    There lies the port; the vessel puffs her sail;
There gloom the dark, broad seas. My mariners,
Souls that have toiled, and wrought, and thought with me—
That ever with a frolic welcome took

The thunder and the sunshine, and opposed
Free hearts, free foreheads—you and I are old;
Old age hath yet his honor and his toil.   50
Death closes all; but something ere the end,
Some work of noble note, may yet be done,
Not unbecoming men that strove with gods.
The lights begin to twinkle from the rocks;
The long day wanes; the slow moon climbs; the deep
Moans round with many voices. Come, my friends.
'Tis not too late to seek a newer world.
Push off, and sitting well in order smite
The sounding furrows; for my purpose holds
To sail beyond the sunset, and the baths   60
Of all the western stars, until I die.
It may be that the gulfs will wash us down;
It may be we shall touch the Happy Isles,
And see the great Achilles, whom we knew.
Though much is taken, much abides; and though
We are not now that strength which in old days
Moved earth and heaven, that which we are, we are—
One equal temper of heroic hearts,
Made weak by time and fate, but strong in will
To strive, to seek, to find, and not to yield.   1842   70

My Last Duchess

Ferrara

ROBERT BROWNING (1812–1889)

That's my last Duchess painted on the wall,
Looking as if she were alive. I call
That piece a wonder, now: Frà Pandolf's hands
Worked busily a day, and there she stands.
Will't please you sit and look at her? I said
"Frà Pandolf" by design, for never read
Strangers like you that pictured countenance,
The depth and passion of its earnest glance,
But to myself they turned (since none puts by
The curtain I have drawn for you, but I)   10
And seemed as they would ask me, if they durst,
How such a glance came there; so, not the first

Are you to turn and ask thus. Sir, 'twas not
Her husband's presence only, called that spot
Of joy into the Duchess' cheek: perhaps
Frà Pandolf chanced to say "Her mantle laps
Over my Lady's wrist too much," or "Paint
Must never hope to reproduce the faint
Half-flush that dies along her throat": such stuff
Was courtesy, she thought, and cause enough   20
For calling up that spot of joy. She had
A heart — how shall I say? — too soon made glad,
Too easily impressed; she liked whate'er
She looked on, and her looks went everywhere.
Sir, 'twas all one! My favour at her breast,
The dropping of the daylight in the West,
The bough of cherries some officious fool
Broke in the orchard for her, the white mule
She rode with round the terrace—all and each
Would draw from her alike the approving speech,   30
Or blush, at least. She thanked men, — good! but thanked
Somehow—I know not how—as if she ranked
My gift of a nine-hundred-years-old name
With anybody's gift. Who'd stoop to blame
This sort of trifling? Even had you skill
In speech—(which I have not)—to make your will
Quite clear to such an one, and say "Just this
Or that in you disgusts me; here you miss,
Or there exceed the mark"—and if she let
Herself be lessoned so, nor plainly set   40
Her wits to yours, forsooth, and made excuse,
—E'en then would be some stooping, and I choose
Never to stoop. Oh, Sir, she smiled, no doubt
Whene'er I passed her; but who passed without
Much the same smile? This grew; I gave commands;
Then all smiles stopped together. There she stands
As if alive. Will't please you rise? We'll meet
The company below, then. I repeat,
The Count your master's known munificence
Is ample warrant that no just pretence   50
Of mine for dowry will be disallowed;
Though his fair daughter's self, as I avowed
At starting, is my object. Nay, we'll go
Together down, Sir! Notice Neptune, tho',
Taming a sea-horse, thought a rarity,
Which Claus of Innsbruck cast in bronze for me!   1842

The Bishop Orders His Tomb at Saint Praxed's Church

Rome, 15—

ROBERT BROWNING (1812–1889)

Vanity, saith the preacher, vanity!
Draw round my bed: is Anselm keeping back?
Nephews—sons mine . . . ah God, I know not! Well—
She, men would have to be your mother once,
Old Gandolf envied me, so fair she was!
What's done is done, and she is dead beside,
Dead long ago, and I am Bishop since,
And as she died so must we die ourselves,
And thence ye may perceive the world's a dream.
Life, how and what is it? As here I lie 10
In this state-chamber, dying by degrees,
Hours and long hours in the dead night, I ask
"Do I live, am I dead?" Peace, peace seems all.
Saint Praxed's ever was the church for peace;
And so, about this tomb of mine, I fought
With tooth and nail to save my niche, ye know:
—Old Gandolf cozened me, despite my care;
Shrewd was that snatch from out the corner South
He graced his carrion with, God curse the same!
Yet still my niche is not so cramped but thence 20
One sees the pulpit o' the epistle-side
And somewhat of the choir, those silent seats,
And up into the aery dome where live
The angels, and a sunbeam's sure to lurk:
And I shall fill my slab of basalt there,
And 'neath my tabernacle take my rest,
With those nine columns round me, two and two,
The odd one at my feet where Anselm stands:
Peach-blossom marble all, the rare, the ripe
As fresh-poured red wine of a mighty pulse. 30
—Old Gandolf with his paltry onion-stone,
Put me where I may look at him! True peach,
Rosy and flawless: how I earned the prize!
Draw close: that conflagration of my church
—What then? So much was saved if aught were missed!
My sons, ye would not be my death? Go dig
The white-grape vineyard where the oil-press stood,

Drop water gently till the surface sink,
And if ye find . . . Ah God, I know not, I! . . .
Bedded in store of rotten fig-leaves soft,   40
And corded up in a tight olive-frail,
Some lump, ah God, of *lapis lazuli*,
Big as a Jew's head cut off at the nape,
Blue as a vein o'er the Madonna's breast . . .
Sons, all have I bequeathed you, villas, all,
That brave Frascati villa with its bath,
So, let the blue lump poise between my knees,
Like God the Father's globe on both his hands
Ye worship in the Jesu Church so gay,
For Gandolf shall not choose but see and burst!   50
Swift as a weaver's shuttle fleet our years:
Man goeth to the grave, and where is he?
Did I say basalt for my slab, sons? Black—
'T was ever antique-black I meant! How else
Shall ye contrast my frieze to come beneath?
The bas-relief in bronze ye promised me,
Those Pans and Nymphs ye wot of, and perchance
Some tripod, thyrsus, with a vase or so,
The Saviour at his sermon on the mount,
Saint Praxed in a glory, and one Pan   60
Ready to twitch the Nymph's last garment off,
And Moses with the tables . . . but I know
Ye mark me not! What do they whisper thee,
Child of my bowels, Anselm? Ah, ye hope
To revel down my villas while I gasp
Bricked o'er with beggar's mouldy travertine
Which Gandolf from his tomb-top chuckles at!
Nay, boys, ye love me—all of jasper, then!
'T is jasper ye stand pledged to, lest I grieve.
My bath must needs be left behind, alas!   70
One block, pure green as a pistachio-nut,
There's plenty jasper somewhere in the world—
And have I not Saint Praxed's ear to pray
Horses for ye, and brown Greek manuscripts,
And mistresses with great smooth marbly limbs?
—That's if ye carve my epitaph aright,
Choice Latin, picked phrase, Tully's every word,
No gaudy ware like Gandolf's second line—
Tully, my masters? Ulpian serves his need!
And then how I shall lie through centuries,   80
And hear the blessed mutter of the mass,

And see God made and eaten all day long,
And feel the steady candle-flame, and taste
Good strong thick stupefying incense-smoke!
For as I lie here, hours of the dead night,
Dying in state and by such slow degrees,
I fold my arms as if they clasped a crook,
And stretch my feet forth straight as stone can point,
And let the bedclothes, for a mortcloth, drop
Into great laps and folds of sculptor's-work: 90
And as yon tapers dwindle, and strange thoughts
Grow, with a certain humming in my ears,
About the life before I lived this life,
And this life too, popes, cardinals and priests,
Saint Praxed at his sermon on the mount,
Your tall pale mother with her talking eyes,
And new-found agate urns as fresh as day,
And marble's language, Latin pure, discreet,
—Aha, ELUCESCEBAT quoth our friend?
No Tully, said I, Ulpian at the best!   100
Evil and brief hath been my pilgrimage.
All *lapis*, all, sons! Else I give the Pope
My villas! Will ye ever eat my heart?
Ever your eyes were as a lizard's quick,
They glitter like your mother's for my soul,
Or ye would heighten my impoverished frieze,
Piece out its starved design, and fill my vase
With grapes, and add a visor and a Term,
And to the tripod ye would tie a lynx
That in his struggle throws the thyrsus down,   110
To comfort me on my entablature
Whereon I am to lie till I must ask
"Do I live, am I dead?" There, leave me, there!
For ye have stabbed me with ingratitude
To death—ye wish it—God, ye wish it! Stone—
Gritstone, a-crumble! Clammy squares which sweat
As if the corpse they keep were oozing through—
And no more *lapis* to delight the world!
Well, go! I bless ye. Fewer tapers there,
But in a row: and, going, turn your backs   120.
—Ay, like departing altar-ministrants,
And leave me in my church, the church for peace,
That I may watch at leisure if he leers—
Old Gandolf, at me, from his onion-stone,
As still he envied me, so fair she was!   1845

Fable

RALPH WALDO EMERSON (1803–1882)

The mountain and the squirrel
Had a quarrel,
And the former called the latter "Little Prig";
Bun replied,
"You are doubtless very big;
But all sorts of things and weather
Must be taken in together,
To make up a year
And a sphere.
And I think it no disgrace
To occupy my place.
If I'm not so large as you,
You are not so small as I,
And not half so spry.
I'll not deny you make
A very pretty squirrel track;
Talents differ; all is well and wisely put;
If I cannot carry forests on my back,
Neither can you crack a nut."   *About* 1845

Love in the Valley

GEORGE MEREDITH (1828–1909)

Under yonder beech-tree single on the greensward,
  Couched with her arms behind her golden head,
Knees and tresses folded to slip and ripple idly,
  Lies my young love sleeping in the shade.
Had I the heart to slide an arm beneath her,
  Press her parting lips as her waist I gather slow,
Waking in amazement she could not but embrace me:
  Then would she hold me and never let me go?

Shy as the squirrel and wayward as the swallow,
  Swift as the swallow along the river's light   10
Circleting the surface to meet his mirrored winglets,
  Fleeter she seems in her stay than in her flight.
Shy as the squirrel that leaps among the pinetops,
  Wayward as the swallow overhead at set of sun,
She whom I love is hard to catch and conquer,
  Hard, but O the glory of the winning were she won!

118

When her mother tends her before the laughing mirror,
  Tying up her laces, looping up her hair,
Often she thinks, were this wild thing wedded,
  More love should I have, and much less care.   20
When her mother tends her before the lighted mirror,
  Loosening her laces, combing down her curls,
Often she thinks, were this wild thing wedded,
  I should miss but one for many boys and girls.

Heartless she is as the shadow in the meadows
  Flying to the hills on a blue and breezy noon.
No, she is athirst and drinking up her wonder:
  Earth to her is young as the slip of the new moon.
Deals she an unkindness, 'tis but her rapid measure,
  Even as in a dance; and her smile can heal no less: 30
Like the swinging May-cloud that pelts the flowers with hailstones
  Off a sunny border, she was made to bruise and bless.

Lovely are the curves of the white owl sweeping
  Wavy in the dusk lit by one large star.
Lone on the fir-branch, his rattle-note unvaried,
  Brooding o'er the gloom, spins the brown eve-jar.
Darker grows the valley, more and more forgetting:
  So were it with me if forgetting could be willed.
Tell the grassy hollow that holds the bubbling wellspring,
  Tell it to forget the source that keeps it filled.   40

Stepping down the hill with her fair companions,
  Arm in arm, all against the raying West,
Boldly she sings, to the merry tune she marches,
  Brave is her shape, and sweeter unpossessed.
Sweeter, for she is what my heart first awaking
  Whispered the world was; morning light is she.
Love that so desires would fain keep her changeless;
  Fain would fling the net, and fain have her free.

Happy happy time, when the white star hovers
  Low over dim fields fresh with bloomy dew,   50
Near the face of dawn, that draws athwart the darkness,
  Threading it with color, like yewberries the yew.
Thicker crowd the shades as the grave East deepens
  Glowing, and with crimson a long cloud swells.
Maiden still the morn is; and strange she is, and secret;
  Strange her eyes; her cheeks are cold as cold seashells.

Sunrays, leaning on our southern hills and lighting
  Wild cloud-mountains that drag the hills along,
Oft ends the day of your shifting brilliant laughter
  Chill as a dull face frowning on a song.   60
Ay, but shows the South-West a ripple-feathered bosom
  Blown to silver while the clouds are shaken and ascend
Scaling the mid-heavens as they stream, there comes a sunset
  Rich, deep like love in beauty without end.

When at dawn she sighs, and like an infant to the window
  Turns grave eyes craving light, released from dreams,
Beautiful she looks, like a white water-lily
  Bursting out of bud in havens of the streams.
When from bed she rises clothed from neck to ankle
  In her long nightgown sweet as boughs of May,   70
Beautiful she looks, like a tall garden lily
  Pure from the night, and splendid for the day.

Mother of the dews, dark eye-lashed twilight,
  Low-lidded twilight, o'er the valley's brim,
Rounding on thy breast sings the dew-delighted skylark,
  Clear as though the dewdrops had their voice in him.
Hidden where the rose-flush drinks the rayless planet,
  Fountain-full he pours the spraying fountain-showers.
Let me hear her laughter, I would have her ever
  Cool as dew in twilight, the lark above the flowers.   80

All the girls are out with their baskets for the primrose;
  Up lanes, woods through, they troop in joyful bands.
My sweet leads: she knows not why, but now she loiters,
  Eyes the bent anemones, and hangs her hands.
Such a look will tell that the violets are peeping,
  Coming the rose: and unaware a cry
Springs in her bosom for odors and for color,
  Covert and the nightingale; she knows not why.

Kerchiefed head and chin she darts between her tulips,
  Streaming like a willow gray in arrowy rain: 90
Some bend beaten cheek to gravel, and their angel
  She will be; she lifts them, and on she speeds again.
Black the driving raincloud breasts the iron gateway:
  She is forth to cheer a neighbor lacking mirth.
So when sky and grass met rolling dumb for thunder
  Saw I once a white dove, sole light of earth.

Prim little scholars are the flowers of her garden,
   Trained to stand in rows, and asking if they please.
I might love them well but for loving more the wild ones:
   O my wild ones! they tell me more than these.   100
You, my wild one, you tell of honeyed fieldrose,
   Violet, blushing eglantine in life; and even as they,
They by the wayside are earnest of your goodness,
   You are of life's, on the banks that line the way.

Peering at her chamber the white crowns the red rose,
   Jasmine winds the porch with stars two and three.
Parted is the window; she sleeps; the starry jasmine
   Breathes a falling breath that carries thoughts of me.
Sweeter unpossessed, have I said of her my sweetest?
   Not while she sleeps: while she sleeps the jasmine **breathes,**   110
Luring her to love; she sleeps; the starry jasmine
   Bears me to her pillow under white rose-wreaths.

Yellow with birdfoot-trefoil are the grass-glades;
   Yellow with cinquefoil of the dew-gray leaf;
Yellow with stonecrop; the moss-mounds are yellow;
   Blue-necked the wheat sways, yellowing to the sheaf.
Green-yellow bursts from the copse the laughing yaffle;
   Sharp as a sickle is the edge of shade and shine:
Earth in her heart laughs looking at the heavens,
   Thinking of the harvest: I look and think of mine.   120

This I may know: her dressing and undressing
   Such a change of light shows as when the skies in sport
Shift from cloud to moonlight; or edging over thunder
   Slips a ray of sun; or sweeping into port
White sails furl; or on the ocean borders
   White sails lean along the waves leaping green.
Visions of her shower before me, but from eyesight
   Guarded she would be like the sun were she seen.

Front door and back of the mossed old farmhouse
   Open with the morn, and in a breezy link   130
Freshly sparkles garden to stripe-shadowed orchard,
   Green across a rill where on sand the minnows wink.
Busy in the grass the early sun of summer
   Swarms, and the blackbird's mellow fluting notes
Call my darling up with round and roguish challenge:
   Quaintest, richest carol of all the singing throats!

Cool was the woodside; cool as her white dairy
  Keeping sweet the cream-pan; and there the boys from school,
Cricketing below, rushed brown and red with sunshine;
  O the dark translucence of the deep-eyed cool!   140
Spying from the farm, herself she fetched a pitcher
  Full of milk, and tilted for each in turn the beak.
Then a little fellow, mouth up and on tiptoe,
  Said, "I will kiss you": she laughed and leaned her cheek.

Doves of the fir-wood walling high our red roof
  Through the long noon coo, crooning through the coo.
Loose droop the leaves, and down the sleepy roadway
  Sometimes pipes a chaffinch; loose droops the blue.
Cows flap a slow tail knee-deep in the river,
  Breathless, given up to sun and gnat and fly.   150
Nowhere is she seen; and if I see her nowhere,
  Lightning may come, straight rains and tiger sky.

O the golden sheaf, the rustling treasure-armful!
  O the nutbrown tresses nodding interlaced!
O the treasure-tresses one another over
  Nodding! O the girdle slack about the waist!
Slain are the poppies that shot their random scarlet
  Quick amid the wheatears: wound about the waist,
Gathered, see these brides of Earth one blush of ripeness!
  O the nutbrown tresses nodding interlaced!   160

Large and smoky red the sun's cold disk drops,
  Clipped by naked hills, on violet shaded snow:
Eastward large and still lights up a bower of moonrise,
  Whence at her leisure steps the moon aglow.
Nightlong on black print-branches our beech-tree
  Gazes in this whiteness: nightlong could I.
Here may life on death or death on life be painted.
  Let me clasp her soul to know she cannot die!

Gossips count her faults; they scour a narrow chamber
  Where there is no window, read not heaven or her.   170
"When she was a tiny," one aged woman quavers,
  Plucks at my heart and leads me by the ear.
Faults she had once as she learned to run and tumbled:
  Faults of feature some see, beauty not complete.
Yet, good gossips, beauty that makes holy
  Earth and air, may have faults from head to feet.

Hither she comes; she comes to me; she lingers,
    Deepens her brown eyebrows, while in new surprise
High rise the lashes in wonder of a stranger;
    Yet am I the light and living of her eyes.   180
Something friends have told her fills her heart to brimming,
    Nets her in her blushes, and wounds her, and tames.—
Sure of her haven, O like a dove alighting,
    Arms up, she dropped: our souls were in our names.

Soon will she lie like a white-frost sunrise.
    Yellow oats and brown wheat, barley pale as rye,
Long since your sheaves have yielded to the thresher,
    Felt the girdle loosened, seen the tresses fly.
Soon will she lie like a blood-red sunset.
    Swift with the to-morrow, green-winged Spring!   190
Sing from the South-West, bring her back the truants,
    Nightingale and swallow, song and dipping wing.

Soft new beech-leaves, up to beamy April
    Spreading bough on bough a primrose mountain, you,
Lucid in the moon, raise lilies to the skyfields,
    Youngest green transfused in silver shining through:
Fairer than the lily, than the wild white cherry:
    Fair as in image my seraph love appears
Borne to me by dreams when dawn is at my eyelids:
    Fair as in the flesh she swims to me on tears.   200

Could I find a place to be alone with heaven,
    I would speak my heart out: heaven is my need.
Every woodland tree is flushing like the dogwood,
    Flashing like the whitebeam, swaying like the reed.
Flushing like the dogwood crimson in October;
    Streaming like the flag-reed South-West blown;
Flashing as in gusts the sudden-lighted whitebeam:
    All seem to know what is for heaven alone.   1878

Danny Deever

RUDYARD KIPLING (1865–1936)

"What are the bugles blowin' for?" said Files-on-Parade.
"To turn you out, to turn you out," the Colour-Sergeant said.
"What makes you look so white, so white?" said Files-on-Parade.
"I'm dreadin' what I've got to watch," the Colour-Sergeant said.
 For they're hangin' Danny Deever, you can hear the Dead March play,
  The regiment's in 'ollow square—they're hangin' him today;
  They've taken of his buttons off an' cut his stripes away,
  An' they're hangin' Danny Deever in the mornin'.

"What makes the rear-rank breathe so 'ard?" said Files-on-Parade.
"It's bitter cold, it's bitter cold," the Colour-Sergeant said.   10
"What makes that front-rank man fall down?" said Files-on-Parade.
"A touch o' sun, a touch o' sun," the Colour-Sergeant said.
 They are hangin' Danny Deever, they are marchin' of 'im round,
  They 'ave 'alted Danny Deever by 'is coffin on the ground;
  An' 'e'll swing in 'arf a minute for a sneakin' shootin' hound—
  O they're hangin' Danny Deever in the mornin'!

"'Is cot was right-'and cot to mine," said Files-on-Parade.
"E's sleepin' out an' far to-night," the Colour-Sergeant said.
"I've drunk 'is beer a score o' times," said Files-on-Parade.
"E's drinkin' bitter beer alone," the Colour-Sergeant said.   20
 They are hangin' Danny Deever, you must mark 'im to 'is place,
  For 'e shot a comrade sleepin'—you must look 'im in the face;
  Nine 'undred of 'is county an' the regiment's disgrace,
  While they're hangin' Danny Deever in the mornin'.

"What's that so black agin the sun?" said Files-on-Parade.
"It's Danny fightin' 'ard for life," the Colour-Sergeant said.
"What's that that whimpers over'ead?" said Files-on-Parade.
"It's Danny's soul that's passin' now," the Colour-Sergeant said.
 For they're done with Danny Deever, you can 'ear the quickstep play,
  The regiment's in column, an' they're marchin' us away;   30
  Ho! the young recruits are shakin', an' they'll want their beer to-day,
  After hangin' Danny Deever in the mornin'! 1890

Miniver Cheevy

EDWIN ARLINGTON ROBINSON (1869–1935)

Miniver Cheevy, child of scorn,
  Grew lean while he assailed the seasons;
He wept that he was ever born,
  And he had reasons.

Miniver loved the days of old
  When swords were bright and steeds were prancing;
The vision of a warrior bold
  Would set him dancing.

Miniver sighed for what was not,
  And dreamed, and rested from his labors;   10
He dreamed of Thebes and Camelot,
  And Priam's neighbors.

Miniver mourned the ripe renown
  That made so many a name so fragrant;
He mourned Romance, now on the town,
  And Art, a vagrant.

Miniver loved the Medici,
  Albeit he had never seen one;
He would have sinned incessantly
  Could he have been one.   20

Miniver cursed the commonplace
  And eyed a khaki suit with loathing;
He missed the mediæval grace
  Of iron clothing.

Miniver scorned the gold he sought,
  But sore annoyed was he without it;
Miniver thought, and thought, and thought,
  And thought about it.

Miniver Cheevy, born too late,
  Scratched his head and kept on thinking;   30
Miniver coughed, and called it fate,
  And kept on drinking.   1910

At Tea

THOMAS HARDY (1840–1928)

From SATIRES OF CIRCUMSTANCE

The kettle descants in a cozy drone,
And the young wife looks in her husband's face,
And then at her guest's, and shows in her own
Her sense that she fills an envied place;
And the visiting lady is all abloom,
And says there was never so sweet a room.

And the happy young housewife does not know
That the woman beside her was first his choice,
Till the fates ordained it could not be so . . .
Betraying nothing in look or voice
The guest sits smiling and sips her tea,
And he throws her a stray glance yearningly.　1911

By Her Aunt's Grave

THOMAS HARDY (1840–1928)

From SATIRES OF CIRCUMSTANCE

"Sixpence a week," says the girl to her lover,
"Aunt used to bring me, for she could confide
In me alone, she vowed. 'Twas to cover
The cost of her headstone when she died.
And that was a year ago last June;
I've not yet fixed it. But I must soon."

"And where is the money now, my dear?"
"Oh, snug in my purse . . . Aunt was so slow
In saving it—eighty weeks, or near." . . .
"Let's spend it," he hints. "For she won't know.
There's a dance tonight at the Load of Hay."
She passively nods. And they go that way.　1911

In Church

THOMAS HARDY (1840–1928)

From SATIRES OF CIRCUMSTANCE

"And now to God the Father," he ends,
And his voice thrills up to the topmost tiles:
Each listener chokes as he bows and bends,
And emotion pervades the crowded aisles.
Then the preacher glides to the vestry-door,
And shuts it, and thinks he is seen no more.

The door swings softly ajar meanwhile,
And a pupil of his in the Bible class,
Who adores him as one without gloss or guile,
Sees her idol stand with a satisfied smile
And reënact at the vestry-glass
Each pulpit gesture in deft dumb-show
That had moved the congregation so.   1911

At the Draper's

THOMAS HARDY (1840–1928)

From SATIRES OF CIRCUMSTANCE

"I stood at the back of the shop, my dear,
    But you did not perceive me.
Well, when they deliver what you were shown
    I shall know nothing of it, believe me!"

And he coughed and coughed as she paled and said,
    "O, I didn't see you come in there—
Why couldn't you speak?"—"Well, I didn't. I left
    That you should not notice I'd been there.

"You were viewing some lovely things. '*Soon required
    For a widow, of latest fashion*';
And I knew 'twould upset you to meet the man
    Who had to be cold and ashen

"And screwed in a box before they could dress you
    '*In the last new note in mourning*,'
As they defined it. So, not to distress you,
    I left you to your adorning."   1911

The River-Merchant's Wife: a Letter

(*After Rihaku*)

EZRA POUND (1885–)

While my hair was still cut straight across my forehead
I played about the front gate, pulling flowers.
You came by on bamboo stilts, playing horse,
You walked about my seat, playing with blue plums.
And we went on living in the village of Chokan:
Two small people, without dislike or suspicion.

At fourteen I married My Lord you.
I never laughed, being bashful.
Lowering my head, I looked at the wall.
Called to, a thousand times, I never looked back.   10

At fifteen I stopped scowling,
I desired my dust to be mingled with yours
Forever and forever and forever.
Why should I climb the look out?

At sixteen you departed,
You went into far Ku-to-yen, by the river of swirling eddies,
And you have been gone five months.
The monkeys make sorrowful noise overhead.

You dragged your feet when you went out.
By the gate now, the moss is grown, the different mosses,   20
Too deep to clear them away!
The leaves fall early this autumn, in wind.
The paired butterflies are already yellow with August
Over the grass in the West garden;
They hurt me. I grow older.
If you are coming down through the narrows of the river Kiang,
Please let me know beforehand,
And I will come out to meet you
          As far as Cho-fu-Sa.   1915

All in Green Went My Love Riding

E. E. CUMMINGS (1894–1963)

All in green went my love riding
on a great horse of gold
into the silver dawn.

four lean hounds crouched low and smiling
the merry deer ran before.

Fleeter be they than dappled dreams
the swift sweet deer
the red rare deer.

Four red roebuck at a white water
the cruel bugle sang before.   10

Horn at hip went my love riding
riding the echo down
into the silver dawn.

four lean hounds crouched low and smiling
the level meadows ran before.

Softer be they than slippered sleep
the lean lithe deer
the fleet flown deer.

Four fleet does at a gold valley
the famished arrow sang before.   20

Bow at belt went my love riding
riding the mountain down
into the silver dawn.

four lean hounds crouched low and smiling
the sheer peaks ran before.

Paler be they than daunting death
the sleek slim deer
the tall tense deer.

Four tall stags at a green mountain
the lucky hunter sang before.   30

All in green went my love riding
on a great horse of gold
into the silver dawn.

four lean hounds crouched low and smiling
my heart fell dead before.   1923

Bells for John Whiteside's Daughter

JOHN CROWE RANSOM (1888–   )

There was such speed in her little body,
And such lightness in her footfall,
It is no wonder her brown study
Astonishes us all.

Her wars were bruited in our high window.
We looked among orchard trees and beyond,
Where she took arms against her shadow,
Or harried unto the pond

The lazy geese, like a snow cloud
Dripping their snow on the green grass,   10
Tricking and stopping, sleepy and proud,
Who cried in goose, Alas,

For the tireless heart within the little
Lady with rod that made them rise
From their noon apple-dreams, and scuttle
Goose-fashion under the skies!

But now go the bells, and we are ready;
In one house we are sternly stopped
To say we are vexed at her brown study,
Lying so primly propped.   1924   20

CHAPTER 4

Theme, Mood, Tone, and Intention

They Flee From Me

SIR THOMAS WYATT (1503–1542)

They flee from me, that sometime did me seek
With naked foot, stalking within my chamber.
Once have I seen them gentle, tame, and meek,
That now are wild, and do not once remember
That sometime they have put themselves in danger
To take bread at my hand; and now they range,
Busily seeking in a continual change.

Thanked be fortune it hath been otherwise,
Twenty times better; but once especial,
In thin array, after a pleasant guise,
When her loose gown did from her shoulders fall,
And she me caught in her arms long and small,
And therewithal sweetly did me kiss
And softly said, "Dear heart, how like you this?"

It was no dream, for I lay broad awaking.
But all is turned now, through my gentleness,
Into a bitter fashion of forsaking;
And I have leave to go, of her goodness,
And she also to use newfangleness.
But since that I unkindly so am served,
How like you this? What hath she now deserved?   1557

Prothalamion

EDMUND SPENSER (1552?–1599)

A Spousall verse made . . . in honour of the double marriage of the two Honorable
& vertuous Ladies, the Ladie Elizabeth and the Ladie Katherine Somerset,
Daughters to the Right Honorable the Earle of Worcester and espoused to the
two worthie Gentlemen M. Henry Gilford, *and M.* William Peter *Esquyers.*

1

Calme was the day, and through the trembling ayre,
Sweete breathing *Zephyrus* did softly play
A gentle spirit, that lightly did delay
Hot *Titans* beames, which then did glyster fayre:
When I whom sullein care,
Through discontent of my long fruitlesse stay
In Princes Court, and expectation vayne
Of idle hopes, which still doe fly away,
Like empty shaddowes, did aflict my brayne,
Walkt forth to ease my payne   10
Along the shoare of silver streaming *Themmes*,
Whose rutty Bancke, the which his River hemmes,
Was paynted all with variable flowers,
And all the meades adorn'd with daintie gemmes,
Fit to decke maydens bowres,
And crowne their Paramours,
Against the Brydale day, which is not long:
   Sweete *Themmes* runne softly, till I end my Song.

2

There, in a Meadow, by the Rivers side,
A flocke of *Nymphes* I chaunced to espy,   20
All lovely Daughters of the Flood thereby,
With goodly greenish locks all loose untyde,
As each had bene a Bryde,
And each one had a little wicker basket,
Made of fine twigs entraylèd curiously,
In which they gathered flowers to fill their flasket:
And with fine Fingers, crop full feateously
The tender stalkes on hye.
Of every sort, which in that Meadow grew,
They gathered some; the Violet pallid blew,   30

The little Dazie, that at evening closes,
The virgin Lillie, and the Primrose trew
With store of vermeil Roses,
To decke their Bridegromes posies,
Against the Brydale day, which was not long:
    Sweete *Themmes* runne softly, till I end my song.

3

With that, I saw two Swannes of goodly hewe,
Come softly swimming downe along the Lee;
Two fairer Birds I yet did never see:
The snow which doth the top of *Pindus* strew,   **40**
Did never whiter shew,
Nor *Jove* himselfe when he a Swan would be
For love of *Leda*, whiter did appeare:
Yet *Leda* was they say as white as he,
Yet not so white as these, nor nothing neare;
So purely white they were,
That even the gentle streame, the which them bare,
Seem'd foule to them, and bad his billowes spare
To wet their silken feathers, least they might
Soyle their fayre plumes with water not so fayre,   **50**
And marre their beauties bright,
That shone as heavens light,
Against their Brydale day, which was not long:
    Sweete *Themmes* runne softly, till I end my Song.

4

Eftsoones the *Nymphes*, which now had Flowers their fill,
Ran all in haste, to see that silver brood,
As they came floating on the Christal Flood.
Whom when they sawe, they stood amazed still,
Their wondring eyes to fill,
Them seem'd they never saw a sight so fayre,   **60**
Of Fowles so lovely, that they sure did deeme
Them heavenly borne, or to be that same payre
Which through the Skie draw *Venus* silver Teeme,
For sure they did not seeme
To be begot of any earthly Seede,
But rather Angels or of Angels breede:
Yet were they bred of *Somers-heat* they say,

    37. *two Swannes:* Elizabeth and Katherine Somerset (see headnote).

In sweetest Season, when each Flower and weede
The earth did fresh aray,
So fresh they seem'd as day,   70
Even as their Brydale day, which was not long:
    Sweete *Themmes* runne softly, till I end my Song.

5

Then forth they all out of their baskets drew,
Great store of Flowers, the honour of the field,
That to the sense did fragrant odours yield,
All which upon those goodly Birds they threw,
And all the Waves did strew,
That like old *Peneus* Waters they did seeme,
When downe along by pleasant *Tempes* shore
Scattred with Flowers through *Thessaly* they streeme,   80
That they appeare through Lillies plenteous store,
Like a Brydes Chamber flore:
Two of those *Nymphes*, meane while, two Garlands bound,
Of freshest Flowres which in that Mead they found,
The which presenting all in trim Array,
Their snowie Foreheads therewithall they crownd,
Whil'st one did sing this Lay,
Prepar'd against that Day,
Against their Brydale day, which was not long:
    Sweete *Themmes* runne softly, till I end my Song.   90

6

Ye gentle Birdes, the worlds faire ornament,
And heavens glorie, whom this happie hower
Doth leade unto your lovers blissfull bower,
Joy may you have and gentle hearts content
Of your loves couplement:
And let faire *Venus*, that is Queene of love,
With her heart-quelling Sonne upon you smile,
Whose smile they say, hath vertue to remove
All Loves dislike, and friendships faultie guile
For ever to assoile.   100
Let endlesse Peace your steadfast hearts accord,
And blessed Plentie wait upon your bord,
And let your bed with pleasures chast abound,
That fruitfull issue may to you afford,
Which may your foes confound,
And make your joyes redound,
Upon your Brydale day, which is not long:
    Sweet *Themmes* run softlie, till I end my Song.

7

So ended she; and all the rest around
To her redoubled that her undersong,   110
Which said, their bridale daye should not be long.
And gentle Eccho from the neighbour ground,
Their accents did resound.
So forth those joyous Birdes did passe along,
Adowne the Lee, that to them murmurde low,
As he would speake, but that he lackt a tong
Yeat did by signes his glad affection show,
Making his streame run slow.
And all the foule which in his flood did dwell
Gan flock about these twaine, that did excell   120
The rest, so far, as *Cynthia* doth shend
The lesser starres. So they enrangèd well,
Did on those two attend,
And their best service lend,
Against their wedding day, which was not long:
    Sweete *Themmes* run softly, till I end my Song.

8

At length they all to mery *London* came,
To mery London, my most kyndly Nurse,
That to me gave this Lifes first native sourse:
Though from another place I take my name,   130
An house of auncient fame.
There when they came, whereas those bricky towres,
The which on *Themmes* brode agèd backe doe ryde,
Where now the studious Lawyers have their bowers
There whylome wont the Templer Knights to byde,
Till they decayd through pride:
Next whereunto there standes a stately place,
Where oft I gaynèd giftes and goodly grace
Of that great Lord, which therein wont to dwell,
Whose want too well now feeles my freendles case: 140
But Ah here fits not well
Olde woes but joyes to tell
Against the bridale daye, which is not long:
    Sweet *Themmes* runne softly, till I end my Song.

130–1. *Though . . . fame:* a reference to the Spencers of Althorpe.
137. *a stately place:* Leicester House, house of the Earl of Leicester, Spenser's patron; called Essex House when the Earl of Essex lived there in 1596. Hence, *noble Peer* in line 145 refers to Essex.

9

Yet therein now doth lodge a noble Peer,
Great *Englands* glory and the Worlds wide wonder,
Whose dreadfull name, late through all *Spaine* did thunder,
And *Hercules* two pillors standing neere,
Did make to quake and feare:
Faire branch of Honor, flower of Chevalrie,   150
That fillest *England* with thy triumphs fame,
Joy have thou of thy noble victorie,
And endlesse happinesse of thine owne name
That promiseth the same:
That through thy prowesse and victorious armes,
Thy country may be freed from forraine harmes:
And great *Elisaes* glorious name may ring
Through al the world, fil'd with thy wide Alarmes,
Which some brave muse may sing
To ages following,   160
Upon the Brydale day, which is not long:
   Sweete *Themmes* runne softly, till I end my Song.

10

From those high Towers, this noble Lord issuing,
Like Radiant *Hesper* when his golden hayre
In th'*Ocean* billowes he hath Bathed fayre,
Descended to the Rivers open vewing,
With a great traine ensuing.
Above the rest were goodly to bee seene
Two gentle Knights of lovely face and feature
Beseeming well the bower of anie Queene,   170
With gifts of wit and ornaments of nature,
Fit for so goodly stature:
That like the twins of *Jove* they seem'd in sight,
Which decke the Bauldricke of the Heavens bright.
They two forth pacing to the Rivers side,
Received those two faire Brides, their Loves delight,
Which at th'appointed tyde,
Each one did make his Bryde,
Against their Brydale day, which is not long:
   Sweete *Themmes* runne softly, till I end my Song.   1596   180

169. *gentle Knights:* Gilford and Peter (see headnote).

Thou Blind Man's Mark

SIR PHILIP SIDNEY (1554–1586)

Thou blind man's mark, thou fool's self-chosen snare,
Fond fancy's scum, and dregs of scattered thought;
Band of all evils, cradle of causeless care;
Thou web of will, whose end is never wrought;
Desire, desire! I have too dearly bought,
With price of mangled mind, thy worthless ware;
Too long, too long, asleep thou hast me brought,
Who should my mind to higher things prepare.
But yet in vain thou hast my ruin sought;
In vain thou madest me to vain things aspire;
In vain thou kindlest all thy smoky fire;
For virtue hath this better lesson taught,—
   Within myself to seek my only hire,
   Desiring nought but how to kill desire.   1598

Feste's Song

WILLIAM SHAKESPEARE (1564–1616)

From TWELFTH NIGHT

Come away, come away, death,
   And in sad cypress let me be laid.
Fly away, fly away, breath;
   I am slain by a fair cruel maid.
My shroud of white, stuck all with yew,
     Oh, prepare it!
My part of death, no one so true
     Did share it!

Not a flower, not a flower sweet,
   On my black coffin let there be strown;
Not a friend, not a friend greet
   My poor corpse, where my bones shall be thrown.
A thousand thousand sighs to save,
     Lay me, oh, where
Sad true lover never find my grave,
     To weep there!   1600; 1623

Follow Your Saint

THOMAS CAMPION (1567–1620)

Follow your saint, follow with accents sweet;
Haste you, sad notes, fall at her flying feet.
There, wrapped in cloud of sorrow, pity move,
And tell the ravisher of my soul I perish for her love.
But if she scorns my never-ceasing pain,
Then burst with sighing in her sight and ne'er return again.

All that I sung still to her praise did tend,
Still she was first, still she my songs did end.
Yet she my love and music both doth fly,
The music that her echo is and beauty's sympathy.
Then let my notes pursue her scornful flight:
It shall suffice that they were breathed and died for her delight.

1601

When Thou Must Home

THOMAS CAMPION (1567–1620)

When thou must home to shades of underground,
    And there arrived, a new admirèd guest,
The beauteous spirits do engirt thee round,
    White Iope, blithe Helen, and the rest,
To hear the stories of thy finished love
From that smooth tongue whose music hell can move,

Then wilt thou speak of banqueting delights,
    Of masks and revels which sweet youth did make,
Of tourneys and great challenges of knights,
    And all these triumphs for thy beauty's sake;
When thou hast told these honors done to thee,
Then tell, O tell, how thou didst murder me.   1601

Clerimont's Song

BEN JONSON (1572–1637)

From EPICOENE, *or* THE SILENT WOMAN

Still to be neat, still to be dressed
As you were going to a feast;
Still to be powdered, still perfumed:

138

> Lady, it is to be presumed,
> Though art's hid causes are not found,
> All is not sweet, all is not sound.
>
> Give me a look, give me a face
> That makes simplicity a grace;
> Robes loosely flowing, hair as free:
> Such sweet neglect more taketh me
> Than all th' adulteries of art;
> They strike mine eyes, but not my heart.   1608; 1616

Song

WILLIAM SHAKESPEARE (1564–1616)

From CYMBELINE, and sung by Guiderius and Arviragus

GUI: Fear no more the heat o' the sun,
       Nor the furious winter's rages;
    Thou thy worldly task hast done,
       Home art gone, and ta'en thy wages;
    Golden lads and girls all must,
    As chimney-sweepers, come to dust.

ARV: Fear no more the frown o' the great;
       Thou art past the tyrant's stroke.
    Care no more to clothe and eat;
       To thee the reed is as the oak.   10
    The sceptre, learning, physic, must
    All follow this and come to dust.

GUI: Fear no more the lightning-flash,
ARV: Nor the all-dreaded thunder-stone;
GUI: Fear not slander, censure rash;
ARV: Thou has fin'sh'd joy and moan.
BOTH: All lovers young, all lovers must
    Consign to thee and come to dust.

GUI: No exorciser harm thee!
ARV: Nor no witchcraft charm thee!   20
GUI: Ghost unlaid forbear thee!
ARV: Nothing ill come near thee!
BOTH: Quiet consummation have,
    And renowned be thy grave!   1609; 1623

The Canonization

JOHN DONNE (1572–1631)

For God's sake hold your tongue and let me love!
  Or chide my palsy or my gout,
My five grey hairs or ruin'd fortune flout;
With wealth your state, your mind with arts improve,
    Take you a course, get you a place,
    Observe his Honor or his Grace,
Or the king's real or his stampèd face
  Contemplate, what you will approve,
    So you will let me love.

Alas, alas, who's injur'd by my love?   10
  What merchant's ships have my sighs drown'd?
Who says my tears have overflow'd his ground?
When did my colds a forward spring remove?
    When did the heats which my veins fill
    Add one man to the plaguy bill?
Soldiers find wars, and lawyers find out still
  Litigious men which quarrels move,
    Though she and I do love.

Call us what you will, we are made such by love.
  Call her one, me another fly,   20
We're tapers too, and at our own cost die;
And we in us find th' eagle and the dove.
    The phoenix riddle hath more wit
    By us; we two being one, are it.
So to one neutral thing both sexes fit,
  We die and rise the same, and prove
    Mysterious by this love.

We can die by it, if not live by love;
  And if unfit for tombs and hearse
Our legend be, it will be fit for verse;   30
And if no piece of chronicle we prove,
    We'll build in sonnets pretty rooms
    (As well a well-wrought urn becomes
The greatest ashes, as half-acre tombs),
  And by these hymns all shall approve
    Us canoniz'd for love,

15. *plaguy bill:* a list of those killed by the plague.

And thus invoke us: "You whom reverent love
   Made one another's hermitage,
You to whom love was peace, that now is rage,
Who did the whole world's soul extract, and drove   40
   Into the glasses of your eyes
   (So made such mirrors and such spies
That they did all to you epitomize)
   Countries, towns, courts; beg from above
     A pattern of your love!"   1633

The Sun Rising

JOHN DONNE (1572–1631)

Busy old fool, unruly sun,
   Why dost thou thus
Through windows and through curtains call on us?
Must to thy motions lovers' seasons run?
   Saucy, pedantic wretch, go chide
   Late schoolboys and sour prentices,
  Go tell court huntsmen that the king will ride,
  Call country ants to harvest offices.
Love, all alike, no season knows nor clime,
Nor hours, days, months, which are the rags of time.   10

   Thy beams, so reverend and strong
    Why shouldst thou think?
I could eclipse and cloud them with a wink,
But that I would not lose her sight so long.
   If her eyes have not blinded thine,
   Look, and tomorrow late tell me
  Whether both th' Indias of spice and mine
  Be where thou left'st them, or lie here with me;
Ask for those kings whom thou saw'st yesterday,
And thou shalt hear: All here in one bed lay.   20

   She's all states, and all princes I;
    Nothing else is.
Princes do but play us; compar'd to this,
All honor's mimic, all wealth alchemy.
   Thou, sun, art half as happy's we,
   In that the world's contracted thus;
  Thine age asks ease, and since thy duties be
  To warm the world, that's done in warming us.
Shine here to us, and thou art everywhere;
This bed thy center is, these walls thy sphere.   1633   30

Lycidas

JOHN MILTON (1608–1674)

In this Monody the Author bewails a learned Friend, unfortunately drowned in his passage from Chester on the Irish Seas, 1637; and by occasion, foretells the ruin of our corrupted Clergy, then in their height.

Yet once more, O ye laurels, and once more,
Ye myrtles brown, with ivy never sere,
I come to pluck your berries harsh and crude,
And with forced fingers rude
Shatter your leaves before the mellowing year.
Bitter constraint and sad occasion dear
Compels me to disturb your season due;
For Lycidas is dead, dead ere his prime,
Young Lycidas, and hath not left his peer.
Who would not sing for Lycidas? he knew   10
Himself to sing, and build the lofty rhyme.
He must not float upon his watery bier
Unwept, and welter to the parching wind,
Without the meed of some melodious tear.
   Begin, then, Sisters of the sacred well
That from beneath the seat of Jove doth spring;
Begin, and somewhat loudly sweep the string.
Hence with denial vain and coy excuse:
So may some gentle Muse
With lucky words favour my destined urn,   20
And as he passes turn,
And bid fair peace be to my sable shroud!
   For we were nursed upon the self-same hill,
Fed the same flock, by fountain, shade, and rill;
Together both, ere the high lawns appeared
Under the opening eyelids of the Morn,
We drove a-field, and both together heard
What time the grey-fly winds her sultry horn,
Battening our flocks with the fresh dews of night,
Oft till the star that rose at evening bright   30
Toward heaven's descent had sloped his westering wheel.
Meanwhile the rural ditties were not mute,
Tempered to th' oaten flute;

Headnote. *learned Friend:* Edward King, an alumnus of Christ's College, Cambridge, was drowned in the Irish Sea on August 10, 1637.

Rough Satyrs danced, and Fauns with cloven heel
From the glad sound would not be absent long;
And old Damaetas loved to hear our song.
   But, oh! the heavy change, now thou art gone,
Now thou art gone and never must return!
Thee, Shepherd, thee the woods and desert caves,
With wild thyme and the gadding vine o'ergrown,   40
And all their echoes, mourn.
The willows, and the hazel copses green,
Shall now no more be seen
Fanning their joyous leaves to thy soft lays.
As killing as the canker to the rose,
Or taint-worm to the weanling herds that graze,
Or frost to flowers, that their gay wardrobe wear,
When first the white-thorn blows;
Such, Lycidas, thy loss to shepherd's ear.
   Where were ye, Nymphs, when the remorseless deep   50
Closed o'er the head of your loved Lycidas?
For neither were ye playing on the steep
Where your old bards, the famous Druids, lie,
Nor on the shaggy top of Mona high,
Nor yet where Deva spreads her wizard stream.
Ay me! I fondly dream
"Had ye been there"—for what could that have done?
What could the Muse herself that Orpheus bore,
The Muse herself, for her enchanting son,
Whom universal nature did lament,   60
When, by the rout that made the hideous roar,
His gory visage down the stream was sent,
Down the swift Hebrus to the Lesbian shore?
   Alas! what boots it with uncessant care
To tend the homely, slighted, shepherd's trade,
And strictly meditate the thankless Muse?
Were it not better done, as others use,
To sport with Amaryllis in the shade,
Or with the tangles of Neaera's hair?
Fame is the spur that the clear spirit doth raise   70
(That last infirmity of noble mind)
To scorn delights and live laborious days;
But the fair guerdon when we hope to find,
And think to burst out into sudden blaze,
Comes the blind Fury with th' abhorrèd shears,
And slits the thin-spun life. "But not the praise,"

54. *Mona:* the Isle of Anglesey off the coast of Wales.
55. *Deva:* the river Dee in northern Wales which flows into the Irish Sea.

Phoebus replied, and touched my trembling ears:
"Fame is no plant that grows on mortal soil,
Nor in the glistering foil
Set off to the world, nor in broad rumour lies,   80
But lives and spreads aloft by those pure eyes
And perfect witness of all-judging Jove;
As he pronounces lastly on each deed,
Of so much fame in Heaven expect thy meed."
    O fountain Arethuse, and thou honoured flood,
Smooth-sliding Mincius, crowned with vocal reeds,
That strain I heard was of a higher mood.
But now my oat proceeds,
And listens to the Herald of the Sea,
That came in Neptune's plea.   90
He asked the waves, and asked the felon winds,
What hard mishap hath doomed this gentle swain?
And questioned every gust of rugged wings
That blows from off each beakèd promontory.
They knew not of his story;
And sage Hippotades their answer brings,
That not a blast was from his dungeon strayed;
The air was calm, and on the level brine
Sleek Panopè with all her sisters played.
It was that fatal and perfidious bark,   100
Built in th' eclipse, and rigged with curses dark,
That sunk so low that sacred head of thine.
    Next, Camus, reverend sire, went footing slow,
His mantle hairy, and his bonnet sedge,
Inwrought with figures dim, and on the edge
Like to that sanguine flower inscribed with woe.
"Ah! who hath reft," quoth he, "my dearest pledge?"
Last came, and last did go,
The Pilot of the Galilean Lake;
Two massy keys he bore of metals twain   110
(The golden opes, the iron shuts amain).
He shook his mitred locks, and stern bespake:
"How well could I have spared for thee, young swain,
Enow of such as, for their bellies' sake,
Creep, and intrude, and climb into the fold!
Of other care they little reckoning make
Than how to scramble at the shearers' feast,
And shove away the worthy bidden guest.
Blind mouths! that scarce themselves know how to hold

103. *Camus:* the river Cam, which flows through Cambridge.

A sheep-hook, or have learnt aught else the least   120
That to the faithful herdman's art belongs!
What recks it them? What need they? They are sped;
And, when they list, their lean and flashy songs
Grate on their scrannel pipes of wretched straw;
The hungry sheep look up, and are not fed,
But, swoln with wind and the rank mist they draw,
Rot inwardly, and foul contagion spread;
Besides what the grim wolf with privy paw
Daily devours apace, and nothing said.
But that two-handed engine at the door   130
Stands ready to smite once, and smite no more."
  Return, Alpheus, the dread voice is past
That shrunk thy streams; return, Sicilian Muse,
And call the vales, and bid them hither cast
Their bells and flowerets of a thousand hues.
Ye valleys low, where the mild whispers use
Of shades, and wanton winds, and gushing brooks,
On whose fresh lap the swart star sparely looks,
Throw hither all your quaint enamelled eyes,
That on the green turf suck the honeyed showers,   140
And purple all the ground with vernal flowers.
Bring the rathe primrose that forsaken dies,
The tufted crow-toe, and pale jessamine,
The white pink, and the pansy freaked with jet,
The glowing violet,
The musk-rose, and the well-attired woodbine,
With cowslips wan that hang the pensive head,
And every flower that sad embroidery wears;
Bid amaranthus all his beauty shed,
And daffadillies fill their cups with tears,   150
To strew the laureate hearse where Lycid lies.
For so, to interpose a little ease,
Let our frail thoughts dally with false surmise.
Ay me! whilst thee the shores and sounding seas
Wash far away, where'er thy bones are hurled,
Whether beyond the stormy Hebrides,
Where thou perhaps under the whelming tide
Visit'st the bottom of the monstrous world;
Or whether thou, to our moist vows denied,
Sleep'st by the fable of Bellerus old,   160
Where the great Vision of the guarded mount
Looks toward Namancos and Bayona's hold.
Look homeward, Angel, now, and melt with ruth;
And, O ye dolphins, waft the hapless youth

Weep no more, woeful shepherds, weep no more,
For Lycidas, your sorrow, is not dead,
Sunk though he be beneath the watery floor;
So sinks the day-star in the ocean bed,
And yet anon repairs his drooping head,
And tricks his beams, and with new-spangled ore   170
Flames in the forehead of the morning sky.
So Lycidas sunk low, but mounted high,
Through the dear might of Him that walked the waves,
Where, other groves and other streams along,
With nectar pure his oozy locks he laves,
And hears the unexpressive nuptial song,
In the blest kingdoms meek of joy and love.
There entertain him all the Saints above,
In solemn troops, and sweet societies,
That sing, and singing in their glory move,   180
And wipe the tears for ever from his eyes.
Now, Lycidas, the shepherds weep no more;
Henceforth thou art the Genius of the shore,
In thy large recompense, and shalt be good
To all that wander in that perilous flood.

Thus sang the uncouth swain to th' oaks and rills,
While the still morn went out with sandals grey;
He touched the tender stops of various quills,
With eager thought warbling his Doric lay;
And now the sun had stretched out all the hills,   190
And now was dropped into the western bay;
At last he rose, and twitched his mantle blue;
To-morrow to fresh woods, and pastures new.   1638

The Garden

ANDREW MARVELL (1621–1678)

How vainly men themselves amaze
To win the palm, the oak, or bays,
And their uncessant labors see
Crowned from some single herb or tree,
Whose short and narrow vergèd shade
Does prudently their toils upbraid;
While all flowers and all trees do close
To weave the garlands of repose.

Fair quiet, have I found thee here,
And innocence, thy sister dear!   10
Mistaken long, I sought you then
In busy companies of men;
Your sacred plants, if here below,
Only among the plants will grow.
Society is all but rude,
To this delicious solitude.

No white nor red was ever seen
So am'rous as this lovely green.
Fond lovers, cruel as their flame,
Cut in these trees their mistress' name;   20
Little, alas, they know or heed
How far these beauties hers exceed!
Fair trees! wheres' e'er your barks I wound,
No name shall but your own be found.

When we have run our passion's heat,
Love hither makes his best retreat.
The gods that mortal beauty chase,
Still in a tree did end their race:
Apollo hunted Daphne so,
Only that she might laurel grow;   30
And Pan did after Syrinx speed,
Not as a nymph, but for a reed.

What wond'rous life is this I lead!
Ripe apples drop about my head;
The luscious clusters of the vine
Upon my mouth do crush their wine;
The nectarine and curious peach
Into my hands themselves do reach;
Stumbling on melons as I pass,
Ensnared with flowers, I fall on grass.   40

Meanwhile the mind from pleasure less
Withdraws into its happiness;
The mind, that ocean where each kind
Does straight its own resemblance find,
Yet it creates, transcending these,
Far other worlds and other seas,
Annihilating all that's made
To a green thought in a green shade.

Here at the fountain's sliding foot,
Or at some fruit tree's mossy root,   50
Casting the body's vest aside,
My soul into the boughs does glide;
There like a bird it sits and sings,
Then whets, then combs its silver wings;
And till prepared for longer flight,
Waves in its plumes the various light.

Such was that happy garden-state,
While man there walked without a mate;
After a place so pure and sweet,
What other help could yet be meet!   60
But 'twas beyond a mortal's share
To wander solitary there;
Two paradises 'twere, in one,
To live in paradise alone.

How well the skillful gard'ner drew
Of flowers and herbs this dial new,
Where, from above, the milder sun
Does through a fragrant zodiac run;
And as it works, th' industrious bee
Computes its time as well as we.   70
How could such sweet and wholesome hours
Be reckoned but with herbs and flowers?   1681

To His Coy Mistress

ANDREW MARVELL (1621–1678)

Had we but world enough, and time,
This coyness, lady, were no crime.
We would sit down, and think which way
To walk, and pass our long love's day.
Thou by the Indian Ganges' side
Should'st rubies find: I by the tide
Of Humber would complain. I would
Love you ten years before the Flood,
And you should, if you please, refuse
Till the conversion of the Jews.   10
My vegetable love should grow
Vaster than empires, and more slow.

An hundred years should go to praise
Thine eyes, and on thy forehead gaze:
Two hundred to adore each breast:
But thirty thousand to the rest;
An age at least to every part,
And the last age should show your heart.
Nor, lady, you deserve this state,
Nor would I love at lower rate.   20
　　But at my back I always hear
Time's wingèd chariot hurrying near;
And yonder all before us lie
Deserts of vast eternity.
Thy beauty shall no more be found,
Nor in thy marble vault shall sound
My echoing song; then worms shall try
That long preserved virginity,
And your quaint honor turn to dust,
And into ashes all my lust.   30
The grave's a fine and private place,
But none, I think, do there embrace.
　　Now therefore, while the youthful hue
Sits on thy skin like morning dew,
And while thy willing soul transpires
At every pore with instant fires,
Now let us sport us while we may;
And now, like am'rous birds of prey,
Rather at once our time devour,
Than languish in his slow-chapped power.   40
Let us roll all our strength, and all
Our sweetness, up into one ball;
And tear our pleasures with rough strife
Thorough the iron gates of life.
Thus, though we cannot make our sun
Stand still, yet we will make him run.   1681

To the Memory of Mr. Oldham

JOHN DRYDEN (1631–1700)

John Oldham: a satirist and wit who was born in 1653 and died in 1683. Dryden met Oldham shortly before the latter died. Dryden's just criticism of Oldham's poetic ability in this poem was regarded by some as evidence of malignity but was later defended by Sir Walter Scott.

Farewell, too little, and too lately known,
Whom I began to think and call my own:
For sure our souls were near allied, and thine
Cast in the same poetic mold with mine.
One common note on either lyre did strike,
And knaves and fools we both abhorr'd alike.
To the same goal did both our studies drive;
The last set out the soonest did arrive.
Thus Nisus fell upon the slippery place,
While his young friend perform'd and won the race.   10
O early ripe! to thy abundant store
What could advancing age have added more?
It might (what nature never gives the young)
Have taught the numbers of thy native tongue.
But satire needs not those, and wit will shine
Thro' the harsh cadence of a rugged line:
A noble error, and but seldom made,
When poets are by too much force betray'd.
Thy generous fruits, tho' gather'd ere their prime,
Still show'd a quickness; and maturing time   20
But mellows what we write to the dull sweets of rhyme.
Once more, hail and farewell, farewell, thou young,
But ah too short, Marcellus of our tongue;
Thy brows with ivy, and with laurels bound;
But fate and gloomy night encompass thee around.   1684

Ode

JOSEPH ADDISON (1672–1719)

This Ode appeared for the first time on Saturday, August 23, 1712, in the famous essay serial, The Spectator, *No. 465. According to Addison, "The Supreme Being has made the best arguments for his own existence, in the formation of the heavens and the earth, and these are arguments which a man of sense cannot forbear attending to, who is out of the noise and hurry of human affairs. Aristotle says, 'that should a man live under ground, and there converse with the works of art and mechanism, and should afterwards be brought up into the open day, and see the several glories of the heaven and earth, he would immediately pronounce them the works of such a being as we define God to be.' The psalmist has very beautiful strokes of poetry to this purpose, in that exalted strain, 'The heavens declare the glory of God: and the firmament sheweth his handy-work. One day telleth another: and one night certifieth another. There is neither speech nor language: but their voices are heard among them. Their sound is gone into all lands: and their words into the ends of the world.' As such a bold and sublime manner of thinking furnishes very noble matter for an ode, the reader may see it wrought into the following one."*

The spacious firmament on high,
With all the blue ethereal sky,
And spangled heav'ns, a shining frame,
Their great original proclaim:
Th' unwearied sun, from day to day,
Does his Creator's pow'r display,
And publishes to ev'ry land
The work of an Almighty Hand.

Soon as the ev'ning shades prevail,
The moon takes up the wondrous tale,   10
And nightly to the list'ning earth
Repeats the story of her birth:
Whilst all the stars that round her burn,
And all the planets, in their turn,
Confirm the tidings as they roll,
And spread the truth from pole to pole.

What though, in solemn silence, all
Move round the dark terrestrial ball?
What though no real voice nor sound
Amid their radiant orbs be found?   20
In Reason's ear, they all rejoice,
And utter forth a glorious voice,
Forever singing, as they shine,
"The hand that made us is divine."   1712

The Universal Prayer

ALEXANDER POPE (1688–1744)

Father of All! In ev'ry age,
  In ev'ry clime ador'd,
By saint, by savage, and by sage,
  Jehovah, Jove, or Lord!

Thou Great First Cause, least understood:
  Who all my sense confin'd
To know but this, that thou art good,
  And that myself am blind;

Yet gave me, in this dark estate,
  To see the good from ill;   10
And binding Nature fast in Fate,
  Left free the human Will.

What conscience dictates to be done,
  Or warns me not to do,
This, teach me more than Hell to shun,
  That, more than Heav'n pursue.

What blessings thy free bounty gives,
  Let me not cast away;
For God is paid when man receives,
  T' enjoy is to obey.   20

Yet not to earth's contracted span,
  Thy goodness let me bound,
Or think thee Lord alone of man,
  When thousand worlds are round.

Let not this weak, unknowing hand
  Presume thy bolts to throw,
And deal damnation round the land,
  On each I judge thy foe.

If I am right, thy grace impart,
  Still in the right to stay;   30
If I am wrong, oh teach my heart
  To find that better way.

Save me alike from foolish pride,
  Or impious discontent,
At aught thy wisdom has denied,
  Or aught thy goodness lent.

Teach me to feel another's woe,
  To hide the fault I see;
That mercy I to others show,
  That mercy show to me. 40

Mean though I am, not wholly so
  Since quicken'd by thy breath;
Oh, lead me wheresoe'er I go,
  Through this day's life or death.

This day, be bread and peace my lot:
  All else beneath the sun,
Thou know'st if best bestowed or not,
  And let thy will be done.

To thee, whose temple is all space,
  Whose altar, earth, sea, skies! 50
One chorus let all being raise,
  All Nature's incense rise! 1738

Ode on the Death of a Favourite Cat

Drowned in a Tub of Goldfishes

THOMAS GRAY (1716–1771)

'Twas on a lofty vase's side,
Where China's gayest art had dy'd
  The azure flow'rs that blow;
Demurest of the tabby kind,
The pensive Selima, reclin'd,
  Gaz'd on the lake below.

Her conscious tail her joy declar'd;
The fair round face, the snowy beard,
  The velvet of her paws,
Her coat, that with the tortoise vies, 10
Her ears of jet, and emerald eyes,
  She saw; and purr'd applause.

Still had she gaz'd: but 'midst the tide
Two angel forms were seen to glide,
  The genii of the stream:
Their scaly armour's Tyrian hue
Through richest purple to the view
  Betray'd a golden gleam.

The hapless nymph with wonder saw:
A whisker first and then a claw,   20
   With many an ardent wish,
She stretched in vain to reach the prize.
What female heart can gold despise?
   What cat's averse to fish?

Presumptuous maid! with looks intent
Again she stretch'd, again she bent,
   Nor knew the gulf between.
(Malignant Fate sat by, and smil'd)
The slipp'ry verge her feet beguil'd,
   She tumbled headlong in.   30

Eight times emerging from the flood,
She mewed to ev'ry wat'ry god,
   Some speedy aid to send.
No dolphin came, no Nereid stirr'd;
Nor cruel Tom, nor Susan heard.
   A fav'rite has no friend!

From hence, ye beauties, undeceiv'd,
Know, one false step is ne'er retriev'd,
   And be with caution bold.
Not all that tempts your wand'ring eyes   40
And heedless hearts, is lawful prize;
   Nor all that glisters, gold.   1748

The Vanity of Human Wishes
The Tenth Satire of Juvenal, Imitated
SAMUEL JOHNSON (1709–1784)

Let observation with extensive view,
Survey mankind, from China to Peru;
Remark each anxious toil, each eager strife,
And watch the busy scenes of crowded life;
Then say how hope and fear, desire and hate,
O'erspread with snares the clouded maze of fate,
Where wav'ring man, betray'd by vent'rous pride,
To tread the dreary paths without a guide,
As treach'rous phantoms in the mist delude,
Shuns fancied ills, or chases airy good;   10
How rarely reason guides the stubborn choice,
Rules the bold hand, or prompts the suppliant voice;
How nations sink, by darling schemes oppress'd,

When vengeance listens to the fool's request.
Fate wings with ev'ry wish th' afflictive dart,
Each gift of nature, and each grace of art,
With fatal heat impetuous courage glows,
With fatal sweetness elocution flows,
Impeachment stops the speaker's pow'rful breath,
And restless fire precipitates on death.   20
    But scarce observ'd, the knowing and the bold
Fall in the gen'ral massacre of gold;
Wide-wasting pest! that rages unconfin'd,
And crowds with crimes the records of mankind;
For gold his sword the hireling ruffian draws,
For gold the hireling judge distorts the laws;
Wealth heap'd on wealth, nor truth nor safety buys,
The dangers gather as the treasures rise.
    Let hist'ry tell where rival kings command,
And dubious title shakes the madded land,   30
When statutes glean the refuse of the sword,
How much more safe the vassal than the lord;
Low skulks the hind beneath the rage of pow'r,
And leaves the wealthy traitor in the Tow'r,
Untouch'd his cottage, and his slumbers sound,
Though confiscation's vultures hover round.
    The needy traveller, serene and gay,
Walks the wild heath, and sings his toil away.
Does envy seize thee? crush th' upbraiding joy,
Increase his riches and his peace destroy;   40
Now fears in dire vicissitude invade,
The rustling brake alarms, and quiv'ring shade,
Nor light nor darkness bring his pain relief;
One shows the plunder, and one hides the thief.
    Yet still one gen'ral cry the skies assails,
And gain and grandeur load the tainted gales;
Few know the toiling statesman's fear or care,
Th' insidious rival and the gaping heir.
    Once more, Democritus, arise on earth,
With cheerful wisdom and instructive mirth,   50
See motley life in modern trappings dress'd,
And feed with varied fools th' eternal jest:
Thou who couldst laugh where want enchain'd caprice,
Toil crush'd conceit, and man was of a piece;
Where wealth unlov'd without a mourner died,
And scarce a sycophant was fed by pride;
Where ne'er was known the form of mock debate,

49. *Democritus:* "the laughing philosopher," fifth century B.C.

Or seen a new-made mayor's unwieldy state;
Where change of fav'rites made no change of laws,
And senates heard before they judg'd a cause;   60
How wouldst thou shake at Britain's modish tribe,
Dart the quick taunt, and edge the piercing gibe?
Attentive truth and nature to descry,
And pierce each scene with philosophic eye.
To thee were solemn toys or empty show
The robes of pleasure and the veils of woe:
All aid the farce, and all thy mirth maintain,
Whose joys are causeless, or whose griefs are vain.
    Such was the scorn that fill'd the sage's mind,
Renew'd at ev'ry glance on humankind;   70
How just that scorn ere yet thy voice declare,
Search every state, and canvass ev'ry pray'r.
    Unnumber'd suppliants crowd Preferment's gate,
Athirst for wealth, and burning to be great;
Delusive Fortune hears th' incessant call,
They mount, they shine, evaporate, and fall.
On ev'ry stage the foes of peace attend,
Hate dogs their flight, and insult mocks their end.
Love ends with hope, the sinking statesman's door
Pours in the morning worshiper no more;   80
For growing names the weekly scribbler lies,
To growing wealth the dedicator flies,
From every room descends the painted face,
That hung the bright Palladium of the place,
And smok'd in kitchens, or in auctions sold,
To better features yields the frame of gold;
For now no more we trace in ev'ry line
Heroic worth, benevolence divine:
The form distorted justifies the fall,
And detestation rids th' indignant wall.   90
    But will not Britain hear the last appeal,
Sign her foe's doom, or guard her fav'rite's zeal?
Through Freedom's sons no more remonstrance rings,
Degrading nobles and controlling kings;
Our supple tribes repress their patriot throats,
And ask no questions but the price of votes;
With weekly libels and septennial ale,
Their wish is full to riot and to rail.
    In full-blown dignity, see Wolsey stand,

97. *septennial ale:* candidates for Parliament distributed ale to voters prior
to elections, held every seven years.

99. *Wolsey:* Cardinal Wolsey (1475?–1530), powerful Lord Chancellor
under Henry VIII; but removed from office.

Law in his voice, and fortune in his hand: 100
To him the church, the realm, their pow'rs consign,
Thro' him the rays of regal bounty shine,
Turn'd by his nod the stream of honour flows,
His smile alone security bestows:
Still to new heights his restless wishes tow'r,
Claim leads to claim, and pow'r advances pow'r;
Till conquest unresisted ceas'd to please,
And rights submitted, left him none to seize.
At length his sov'reign frowns—the train of state
Mark the keen glance, and watch the sign to hate.   110
Where'er he turns, he meets a stranger's eye,
His suppliants scorn him, and his followers fly;
At once is lost the pride of aweful state,
The golden canopy, the glitt'ring plate,
The regal palace, the luxurious board,
The liv'ried army, and the menial lord.
With age, with cares, with maladies oppress'd,
He seeks the refuge of monastic rest.
Grief aids disease, remember'd folly stings,
And his last sighs reproach the faith of kings.   120
   Speak thou, whose thoughts at humble peace repine,
Shall Wolsey's wealth, with Wolsey's end be thine?
Or liv'st thou now, with safer pride content,
The wisest justice on the banks of Trent?
For why did Wolsey, near the steeps of fate,
On weak foundations raise th' enormous weight?
Why but to sink beneath misfortune's blow,
With louder ruin to the gulfs below?
   What gave great Villiers to th' assassin's knife,
And fixed disease on Harley's closing life?   130
What murder'd Wentworth, and what exil'd Hyde,
By kings protected, and to kings allied?
What but their wish indulg'd in courts to shine,
And pow'r too great to keep, or to resign?
   When first the college rolls receive his name,
The young enthusiast quits his ease for fame;
Through all his veins the fever of renown
Spreads from the strong contagion of the gown;
O'er Bodley's dome his future labours spread,
And Bacon's mansion trembles o'er his head.   140

139. *Bodley's dome:* The Bodleian Library.
140. *Bacon's mansion:* according to Johnson, "There is a tradition that the
study of Friar Bacon, built on an arch over the bridge, will fall, when a
man greater than Bacon shall pass under it."

Are these thy views? proceed, illustrious youth,
And virtue guard thee to the throne of Truth!
Yet should thy soul indulge the gen'rous heat,
Till captive Science yields her last retreat;
Should Reason guide thee with her brightest ray,
And pour on misty Doubt resistless day;
Should no false Kindness lure to loose delight,
Nor Praise relax, nor Difficulty fright;
Should tempting Novelty thy cell refrain,
And Sloth effuse her opiate fumes in vain;   150
Should Beauty blunt on fops her fatal dart,
Nor claim the triumph of a letter'd heart;
Should no Disease thy torpid veins invade,
Nor Melancholy's phantoms haunt thy shade;
Yet hope not life from grief or danger free,
Nor think the doom of man revers'd for thee:
Deign on the passing world to turn thine eyes,
And pause a while from letters, to be wise;
There mark what ills the scholar's life assail,
Toil, envy, want, the patron, and the jail.   160
See nations slowly wise, and meanly just,
To buried merit raise the tardy bust.
If dreams yet flatter, once again attend,
Hear Lydiat's life, and Galileo's end.
    Nor deem, when Learning her last prize bestows,
The glitt'ring eminence exempt from foes;
See when the vulgar 'scape, despis'd or aw'd,
Rebellion's vengeful talons seize on Laud.
From meaner minds, tho' smaller fines content,
The plunder'd palace or sequester'd rent;   170
Mark'd out by dangerous parts he meets the shock,
And fatal Learning leads him to the block:
Around his tomb let Art and Genius weep,
But hear his death, ye blockheads, hear and sleep.
    The festal blazes, the triumphal show,
The ravish'd standard, and the captive foe,
The senate's thanks, the gazette's pompous tale,
With force resistless o'er the brave prevail.
Such bribes the rapid Greek o'er Asia whirl'd,
For such the steady Romans shook the world;   180
For such in distant lands the Britons shine,
And stain with blood the Danube or the Rhine;

164. *Lydiat:* Thomas Lydiat (1572–1646) was a distinguished mathe-
matician and Oxford don who lived and died a poor man.
179. *rapid Greek:* Alexander the Great.

This pow'r has praise, that virtue scarce can warm,
Till fame supplies the universal charm.
Yet Reason frowns on War's unequal game,
Where wasted nations raise a single name,
And mortgag'd states their grandsires wreaths regret,
From age to age in everlasting debt;
Wreaths which at last the dear-bought right convey
To rust on medals, or on stones decay.   190
   On what foundation stands the warrior's pride,
How just his hopes, let Swedish Charles decide;
A frame of adamant, a soul of fire,
No dangers fright him, and no labours tire;
O'er love, o'er fear, extends his wide domain,
Unconquer'd lord of pleasure and of pain;
No joys to him pacific sceptres yield,
War sounds the trump, he rushes to the field;
Behold surrounding kings their pow'r combine,
And one capitulate, and one resign;   200
Peace courts his hand, but spreads her charms in vain;
"Think nothing gain'd," he cries, "till nought remain,
On Moscow's walls till Gothic standards fly,
And all be mine beneath the polar sky."
The march begins in military state,
And nations on his eye suspended wait;
Stern Famine guards the solitary coast,
And Winter barricades the realms of Frost;
He comes, not want and cold his course delay;—
Hide, blushing Glory, hide Pultowa's day: 210
The vanquish'd hero leaves his broken bands,
And shows his miseries in distant lands;
Condemn'd a needy supplicant to wait,
While ladies interpose, and slaves debate.
But did not Chance at length her error mend?
Did no subverted empire mark his end?
Did rival monarchs give the fatal wound?
Or hostile millions press him to the ground?
His fall was destin'd to a barren strand,
A petty fortress, and a dubious hand;   220
He left the name, at which the world grew pale,
To point a moral, or adorn a tale.
   All times their scenes of pompous woes afford,
From Persia's tyrant to Bavaria's lord.
In gay hostility, and barb'rous pride,

192. *Swedish Charles:* Charles XII, King of Sweden, who died in 1718.
210. *Pultowa's day:* a victory over Charles XII by Peter the Great in 1709

With half mankind embattled at his side,
Great Xerxes comes to seize the certain prey,
And starves exhausted regions in his way;
Attendant Flatt'ry counts his myriads o'er,
Till counted myriads soothe his pride no more;   230
Fresh praise is tried till madness fires his mind,
The waves he lashes, and enchains the wind;
New pow'rs are claim'd, new pow'rs are still bestow'd,
Till rude resistance lops the spreading god;
The daring Greeks deride the martial show,
And heap their valleys with the gaudy foe;
Th' insulted sea with humbler thoughts he gains,
A single skiff to speed his flight remains;
Th' incumber'd oar scarce leaves the dreaded coast
Through purple billows and a floating host.   240
    The bold Bavarian, in a luckless hour,
Tries the dread summits of Caesarean pow'r,
With unexpected legions bursts away,
And sees defenceless realms receive his sway;
Short sway! fair Austria spreads her mournful charms,
The queen, the beauty, sets the world in arms;
From hill to hill the beacon's rousing blaze
Spreads wide the hope of plunder and of praise;
The fierce Croatian, and the wild Hussar,
And all the sons of ravage crowd the war;   250
The baffled prince, in honour's flatt'ring bloom,
Of hasty greatness finds the fatal doom,
His foes' derision, and his subjects' blame,
And steals to death from anguish and from shame.
    Enlarge my life with multitude of days,
In health, in sickness, thus the suppliant prays:
Hides from himself his state, and shuns to know,
That life protracted is protracted woe.
Time hovers o'er, impatient to destroy,
And shuts up all the passages of joy: 260
In vain their gifts the bounteous seasons pour,
The fruit autumnal, and the vernal flow'r;
With listless eyes the dotard views the store,
He views, and wonders that they please no more;
Now pall the tasteless meats, and joyless wines,
And Luxury with sighs her slave resigns.
Approach, ye minstrels, try the soothing strain,

241. *The bold Bavarian:* Charles Albert, elector of Bavaria, crowned emperor in 1742; died ignominiously in 1745.
245. *fair Austria:* Maria Theresa.

Diffuse the tuneful lenitives of pain:
No sounds alas would touch th' impervious ear,
Though dancing mountains witness'd Orpheus near;   270
Nor lute nor lyre his feeble pow'rs attend,
Nor sweeter music of a virtuous friend,
But everlasting dictates crowd his tongue,
Perversely grave, or positively wrong.
The still returning tale, and ling'ring jest,
Perplex the fawning niece and pamper'd guest,
While growing hopes scarce awe the gath'ring sneer,
And scarce a legacy can bribe to hear;
The watchful guests still hint the last offence,
The daughter's petulance, the son's expence,   280
Improve his heady rage with treach'rous skill,
And mould his passions till they make his will.
    Unnumber'd maladies his joints invade,
Lay siege to life and press the dire blockade;
But unextinguish'd Av'rice still remains,
And dreaded losses aggravate his pains;
He turns, with anxious heart and crippled hands,
His bonds of debt, and mortgages of lands;
Or views his coffers with suspicious eyes,
Unlocks his gold, and counts it till he dies.   290
    But grant, the virtues of a temp'rate prime
Bless with an age exempt from scorn or crime;
An age that melts with unperceiv'd decay,
And glides in modest Innocence away;
Whose peaceful day Benevolence endears,
Whose night congratulating Conscience cheers;
The gen'ral fav'rite as the gen'ral friend:
Such age there is, and who shall wish its end?
    Yet ev'n on this her load Misfortune flings,
To press the weary minutes' flagging wings: 300
New sorrow rises as the day returns,
A sister sickens, or a daughter mourns.
Now kindred Merit fills the sable bier,
Now lacerated Friendship claims a tear.
Year chases year, decay pursues decay,
Still drops some joy from with'ring life away;
New forms arise, and diff'rent views engage,
Superfluous lags the vet'ran on the stage,
Till pitying Nature signs the last release,
And bids afflicted worth retire to peace.   310
    But few there are whom hours like these await,
Who set unclouded in the gulfs of fate.

From Lydia's monarch should the search descend,
By Solon caution'd to regard his end,
In life's last scene what prodigies surprise,
Fears of the brave, and follies of the wise?
From Marlb'rough's eyes the streams of dotage flow,
And Swift expires a driv'ler and a show.
 The teeming mother, anxious for her race,
Begs for each birth the fortune of a face: 320
Yet Vane could tell what ills from beauty spring;
And Sedley curs'd the form that pleas'd a king.
Ye nymphs of rosy lips and radiant eyes,
Whom Pleasure keeps too busy to be wise,
Whom Joys with soft varieties invite,
By day the frolic, and the dance by night;
Who frown with vanity, who smile with art,
And ask the latest fashion of the heart,
What care, what rules your heedless charms shall save,
Each nymph your rival, and each youth your slave? 330
Against your fame with fondness hate combines,
The rival batters, and the lover mines.
With distant voice neglected Virtue calls,
Less heard and less, the faint remonstrance falls;
Tir'd with contempt, she quits the slipp'ry reign,
And Pride and Prudence take her seat in vain.
In crowd at once, where none the pass defend,
The harmless Freedom, and the private Friend.
The guardians yield, by force superior plied:
By Int'rest, Prudence; and by Flatt'ry, Pride.   340
Now Beauty falls betray'd, despis'd, distress'd,
And hissing Infamy proclaims the rest.
 Where then shall Hope and Fear their objects find?
Must dull Suspence corrupt the stagnant mind?
Must helpless man, in ignorance sedate,
Roll darkling down the torrent of his fate?
Must no dislike alarm, no wishes rise,
No cries invoke the mercies of the skies?
Enquirer, cease, petitions yet remain,
Which heav'n may hear, nor deem religion vain. 350
Still raise for good the supplicating voice,
But leave to heav'n the measure and the choice,
Safe in his pow'r, whose eyes discern afar

 321. *Vane:* Anne Vane was mistress of Frederick, Prince of Wales. She died in 1736 at the age of thirty-one.
 322. *Sedley:* Catherine Sedley was mistress of James, Duke of York. He made her Countess of Dorchester in 1686.

The secret ambush of a specious pray'r.
Implore his aid, in his decisions rest,
Secure, whate'er he gives, he gives the best.
Yet when the sense of sacred presence fires,
And strong devotion to the skies aspires,
Pour forth thy fervours for a healthful mind,
Obedient passions, and a will resign'd;   360
For love, which scarce collective man can fill;
For patience sov'reign o'er transmuted ill;
For faith, that panting for a happier seat,
Counts death kind Nature's signal of retreat:
These goods for man the laws of heav'n ordain,
These goods he grants, who grants the pow'r to gain;
With these celestial wisdom calms the mind,
And makes the happiness she does not find.   1749

On Taking a Bachelor's Degree

CHRISTOPHER SMART (1722–1771)

'Tis done:—I tow'r to that degree,
   And catch such heav'nly fire,
That Horace ne'er could rant like me,
   Nor is King's chapel higher.—
My name in sure recording page
   Shall time itself o'erpow'r,
If no rude mice with envious rage
   The buttery books devour.
A title too with added grace,
   My name shall now attend,   10
Till to the church with silent pace
   A nymph and priest ascend.
Ev'n in the schools I now rejoice,
   Where late I shook with fear,
Nor heed the Moderator's voice
   Loud thundering in my ear.
Then with Aeolian flute I blow
   A soft Italian lay,

3. Smart drew his epigraph from Horace, *Ode* III.30: *Exegi monumentum aere perennius, &c.*

4. *King's chapel:* the chapel of King's College, Cambridge University. The chapel with its many spires was begun in 1446, five years after the founding of the College. Christopher Smart became a student at Cambridge in 1739; upon graduation he remained there for a time as a tutor.

Or where Cam's scanty waters flow,
    Releas'd from lectures, stray.   20
Meanwhile, friend Banks, my merits claim
    Their just reward from you,
For Horace bids us challenge fame,
    When once that fame's our due,
Invest me with a graduate's gown,
    Midst shouts of all beholders,
My head with ample square-cap crown,
    And deck with hood my shoulders.   1750

21. *Banks:* a celebrated tailor.

Light Shining Out of Darkness

WILLIAM COWPER (1731–1800)

From OLNEY HYMNS

God moves in a mysterious way,
    His wonders to perform;
He plants his footsteps in the sea,
    And rides upon the storm.

Deep in unfathomable mines
    Of never failing skill,
He treasures up his bright designs,
    And works his sovereign will.

Ye fearful saints fresh courage take,
    The clouds ye so much dread   10
Are big with mercy, and shall break
    In blessings on your head.

Judge not the Lord by feeble sense,
    But trust him for his grace;
Behind a frowning providence,
    He hides a smiling face.

His purposes will ripen fast,
    Unfolding every hour;
The bud may have a bitter taste,
    But sweet will be the flower.   20

Blind unbelief is sure to err,
    And scan his work in vain;
God is his own interpreter,
    And he will make it plain.   1779

Walking with God

WILLIAM COWPER (1731–1800)

From OLNEY HYMNS

Genesis 5:24

Oh! for a closer walk with God,
  A calm and heav'nly frame;
A light to shine upon the road
  That leads me to the Lamb!

Where is the blessedness I knew
  When first I saw the Lord?
Where is the soul-refreshing view
  Of Jesus and his word?

What peaceful hours I once enjoy'd!
  How sweet their mem'ry still!   10
But they have left an aching void,
  The world can never fill.

Return, O holy Dove, return,
  Sweet messenger of rest;
I hate the sins that made thee mourn,
  And drove thee from my breast.

The dearest idol I have known,
  Whate'er that idol be;
Help me to tear it from thy throne,
  And worship only thee.   20

So shall my walk be close with God,
  Calm and serene my frame;
So purer light shall mark the road
  That leads me to the Lamb.   1779

On the Death of Dr. Robert Levet

SAMUEL JOHNSON (1709–1784)

Robert Levet: (1705–1782). *Spending some time in Paris as a young man, Levet became a waiter in a Parisian coffee house patronized by French surgeons who provided him with instruction in pharmacy and anatomy. When he later settled in London, he acquired some practice as a surgeon. He probably met Johnson about 1746; by 1763 Levet had become a permanent guest in Johnson's house. Levet was notorious for overindulging in drink, but this trait, Johnson observed, was merely the result of extreme prudence on Levet's part. "He reflected that if he refused the gin or brandy offered him by some of his patients he could have been no gainer by their cure, as they might have had nothing else to bestow on him. He would swallow what he did not like, nay, what he knew would injure him, rather than go home with an idea that his skill had been exerted without recompense." After Levet died, Johnson wrote: "How much soever I valued him, I now wish I had valued him more."*

Condemn'd to hope's delusive mine,
　　As on we toil from day to day,
By sudden blasts, or slow decline,
　　Our social comforts drop away.

Well tried through many a varying year,
　　See LEVET to the grave descend;
Officious, innocent, sincere,
　　Of every friendless name the friend.

Yet still he fills affection's eye,
　　Obscurely wise, and coarsely kind;　　　　　　　10
Nor, letter'd arrogance, deny
　　Thy praise to merit unrefin'd.

When fainting nature call'd for aid,
　　And hov'ring death prepar'd the blow,
His vig'rous remedy display'd
　　The power of art without the show.

In misery's darkest caverns known,
　　His useful care was ever nigh,
Where hopeless anguish pour'd his groan,
　　And lonely want retir'd to die.　　　　　　　　20

No summons mock'd by chill delay,
  No petty gain disdain'd by pride,
The modest wants of ev'ry day
  · The toil of ev'ry day supplied.

His virtues walk'd their narrow round,
  Nor made a pause, nor left a void;
And sure th' Eternal Master found
  The single talent well employ'd.

The busy day, the peaceful night,
  Unfelt, uncounted, glided by;   30
His frame was firm, his powers were bright,
  Tho' now his eightieth year was nigh.

Then with no throbbing fiery pain,
  No cold gradations of decay,
Death broke at once the vital chain,
  And freed his soul the nearest way.   1782; 1783

Composed upon Westminster Bridge

WILLIAM WORDSWORTH (1770–1850)

Earth has not anything to show more fair:
Dull would he be of soul who could pass by
A sight so touching in its majesty:
This city now doth like a garment wear
The beauty of the morning; silent, bare,
Ships, towers, domes, theaters, and temples lie
Open unto the fields, and to the sky;
All bright and glittering in the smokeless air.
Never did sun more beautifully steep
In his first splendor, valley, rock, or hill;
Ne'er saw I, never felt, a calm so deep!
The river glideth at his own sweet will:
Dear God! the very houses seem asleep;
And all that mighty heart is lying still!   1802;1807

Ode

On Intimations of Immortality from Recollections of Early Childhood

WILLIAM WORDSWORTH (1770–1850)

"The Child is father of the man;
And I could wish my days to be
Bound each to each by natural piety."

I

There was a time when meadow, grove, and stream,
 The earth, and every common sight,
  To me did seem
  Appareled in celestial light,
The glory and the freshness of a dream.
It is not now as it hath been of yore;—
  Turn whereso'er I may,
   By night or day,
The things which I have seen I now can see no more.

2

 The Rainbow comes and goes,   10
 And lovely is the Rose;
 The Moon doth with delight
Look round her when the heavens are bare;
 Waters on a starry night
 Are beautiful and fair;
 The sunshine is a glorious birth;
 But yet I know, where'er I go,
That there hath passed away a glory from the earth.

3

Now, while the birds thus sing a joyous song,
 And while the young lambs bound   20
  As to the tabor's sound,
To me alone there came a thought of grief:
A timely utterance gave that thought relief,
  And I again am strong:
The cataracts blow their trumpets from the steep;
No more shall grief of mine the season wrong;
I hear the Echoes through the mountains throng,
The Winds come to me from the fields of sleep,

168

And all the earth is gay;
Land and sea   30
Give themselves up to jollity,
And with the heart of May
Doth every Beast keep holiday;—
Thou Child of Joy,
Shout round me, let me hear thy shouts, thou happy
Shepherd-boy!

4

Ye blessèd Creatures, I have heard the call
Ye to each other make; I see
The heavens laugh with you in your jubilee;
My heart is at your festival,
My head hath its coronal,   40
The fulness of your bliss, I feel—I feel it all.
Oh, evil day! if I were sullen
While Earth herself is adorning,
This sweet May-morning,
And the Children are culling
On every side,
In a thousand valleys far and wide,
Fresh flowers; while the sun shines warm,
And the Babe leaps up on his Mother's arm—
I hear, I hear, with joy I hear!   50
—But there's a Tree, of many, one,
A single Field which I have looked upon,
Both of them speak of something that is gone:
The Pansy at my feet
Doth the same tale repeat:
Whither is fled the visionary gleam?
Where is it now, the glory and the dream?

5

Our birth is but a sleep and a forgetting:
The Soul that rises with us, our life's Star,
Hath had elsewhere its setting,   60
And cometh from afar:
Not in entire forgetfulness,
And not in utter nakedness,
But trailing clouds of glory do we come
From God, who is our home:
Heaven lies about us in our infancy!
Shades of the prison-house begin to close

Upon the growing Boy,
But he beholds the light, and whence it flows
    He sees it in his joy;   70
The Youth, who daily farther from the east
    Must travel, still is Nature's priest,
    And by the vision splendid
    Is on his way attended;
At length the Man perceives it die away,
And fade into the light of common day.

6

Earth fills her lap with pleasures of her own;
Yearnings she hath in her own natural kind,
And even with something of a Mother's mind,
    And no unworthy aim,   80
    The homely Nurse doth all she can
To make her Foster-child, her Inmate Man,
    Forget the glories he hath known,
And that imperial palace whence he came.

7

Behold the Child among his new-born blisses,
A six years' Darling of a pigmy size!
See, where 'mid work of his own hand he lies,
Fretted by sallies of his mother's kisses,
With light upon him from his father's eyes!
See, at his feet, some little plan or chart,   90
Some fragment from his dream of human life,
Shaped by himself with newly-learnéd art;
    A wedding or a festival,
    A mourning or a funeral,
      And this hath now his heart,
    And unto this he frames his song:
      Then will he fit his tongue
To dialogues of business, love, or strife;
    But it will not be long
    Ere this be thrown aside,   100
    And with new joy and pride
The little Actor cons another part;
Filling from time to time his "humorous stage"
With all the Persons, down to palsied Age,
That Life brings with her in her equipage;
    As if his whole vocation
    Were endless imitation.

8

Thou, whose exterior semblance doth belie
    Thy Soul's immensity;
Thou best Philosopher, who yet dost keep   110
Thy heritage, thou Eye among the blind,
That, deaf and silent, read'st the eternal deep,
Haunted forever by the eternal mind—
    Mighty Prophet! Seer blest!
    On whom those truths do rest,
Which we are toiling all our lives to find,
In darkness lost, the darkness of the grave;
Thou, over whom thy Immortality
Broods like the Day, a Master o'er a Slave,
A Presence which is not to be put by;   120
Thou little Child, yet glorious in the might
Of heaven-born freedom on thy being's height,
Why with such earnest pains dost thou provoke
The years to bring the inevitable yoke,
Thus blindly with thy blessedness at strife?
Full soon thy Soul shall have her earthly freight,
And custom lie upon thee with a weight,
Heavy as frost, and deep almost as life!

9

    Oh, joy! that in our embers
    Is something that doth live,   130
    That nature yet remembers
    What was so fugitive!
The thought of our past years in me doth breed
Perpetual benediction: not indeed
For that which is most worthy to be blest;
Delight and liberty, the simple creed
Of Childhood, whether busy or at rest,
With new-fledged hope still fluttering in his breast—
    Not for these I raise
    The song of thanks and praise;   140
    But for those obstinate questionings
    Of sense and outward things,
    Falling from us, vanishings;
    Blank misgivings of a Creature
Moving about in worlds not realized,
High instincts before which our mortal nature
Did tremble like a guilty thing surprised:

But for those first affections,
Those shadowy recollections,
Which, be they what they may,   150
Are yet the fountain light of all our day,
Are yet a master light of all our seeing;
   Uphold us, cherish, and have power to make
Our noisy years seem moments in the being
Of the eternal Silence: truths that wake,
      To perish never;
Which neither listlessness, nor mad endeavor,
      Nor Man nor Boy,
Nor all that is at enmity with joy,
Can utterly abolish or destroy!   160
      Hence in a season of calm weather
      Though inland far we be,
Our Souls have sight of that immortal sea
      Which brought us hither,
      Can in a moment travel thither,
And see the Children sport upon the shore,
And hear the mighty waters rolling evermore.

                        10

Then sing, ye Birds, sing, sing a joyous song!
      And let the young Lambs bound
      As to the tabor's sound!   170
We in thought will join your throng,
      Ye that pipe and ye that play,
      Ye that through your hearts today
      Feel the gladness of the May!
What though the radiance which was once so bright
Be now forever taken from my sight,
   Though nothing can bring back the hour
Of splendor in the grass, of glory in the flower;
      We will grieve not, rather find
      Strength in what remains behind;   180
      In the primal sympathy
      Which having been must ever be;
      In the soothing thoughts that spring
      Out of human suffering;
      In the faith that looks through death,
In years that bring the philosophic mind.

11

And O, ye Fountains, Meadows, Hills, and Groves,
Forebode not any severing of our loves!
Yet in my heart of hearts I feel your might;
I only have relinquished one delight   190
To live beneath your more habitual sway.
I love the Brooks which down their channels fret,
Even more than when I tripped lightly as they;
The innocent brightness of a new-born Day
      Is lovely yet;
The Clouds that gather round the setting sun
Do take a sober coloring from an eye
That hath kept watch o'er man's mortality.
Another race hath been, and other palms are won.
Thanks to the human heart by which we live,   200
Thanks to its tenderness, its joys, and fears,
To me the meanest flower that blows can give
Thoughts that do often lie too deep for tears.   1807

For Though the Caves Were Rabbited

HENRY DAVID THOREAU (1817–1862)

For though the caves were rabbited,
   And the well sweeps were slanted,
Each house seemed not inhabited
   But haunted.

The pensive traveller held his way,
   Silent and melancholy,
For every man an idiot was,
   And every house a folly.   *Undated*

I'm Thankful That My Life Doth Not Deceive

HENRY DAVID THOREAU (1817–1862)

I'm thankful that my life doth not deceive
Itself with a low loftiness, half height,
And think it soars when still it dips its way
Beneath the clouds on noiseless pinion
Like the crow or owl, but it doth know
The full extent of all its trivialness,
Compared with the splendid heights above.
　See how it waits to watch the mail come in
While 'hind its back the sun goes out perchance.
And yet their lumbering cart brings me no word,　　　10
Not one scrawled leaf such as my neighbors get
To cheer them with the slight events forsooth,
Faint ups and downs of their far distant friends—
And now 'tis passed. What next? See the long train
Of teams wreathed in dust, their atmosphere;
Shall I attend until the last is passed?
Else why these ears that hear the leader's bells
Or eyes that link me in procession?
But hark! the drowsy day has done its task,
Far in yon hazy field where stands a barn,　　　20
Unanxious hens improve the sultry hour
And with contented voice now brag their deed—
A new laid egg—Now let the day decline—
They'll lay another by tomorrow's sun.　　　*Undated*

To Marguerite—Continued

MATTHEW ARNOLD (1822–1888)

Yes! in the sea of life enisled,
With echoing straits between us thrown,
Dotting the shoreless watery wild,
We mortal millions live *alone*.
The islands feel the enclasping flow,
And then their endless bounds they know.

But when the moon their hollows lights,
And they are swept by balms of spring,
And in their glens, on starry nights,
The nightingales divinely sing;   10
And lovely notes, from shore to shore,
Across the sounds and channels pour—

Oh! then a longing like despair
Is to their farthest caverns sent;
For surely once, they feel, we were
Parts of a single continent!
Now round us spreads the watery plain—
Oh might our marges meet again!

Who order'd, that their longing's fire
Should be, as soon as kindled, cool'd?   20
Who renders vain their deep desire?—
A God, a God their severance ruled!
And bade betwixt their shores to be
The unplumb'd, salt, estranging sea.   1852

The Latest Decalogue

ARTHUR HUGH CLOUGH (1819–1861)

Thou shalt have one God only; who
Would be at the expense of two?
No graven images may be
Worshipped, except the currency.
Swear not at all; for, for thy curse
Thine enemy is none the worse.
At church on Sunday to attend
Will serve to keep the world thy friend.
Honor thy parents; that is, all
From whom advancement may befall. 10
Thou shalt not kill; but need'st not strive
Officiously to keep alive.
Do not adultery commit;
Advantage rarely comes of it.
Thou shalt not steal; an empty feat,
When it's so lucrative to cheat.
Bear not false witness; let the lie
Have time on its own wings to fly.
Thou shalt not covet, but tradition
Approves all forms of competition. 1862 20

When I Heard the Learn'd Astronomer

WALT WHITMAN (1819–1892)

When I heard the learn'd astronomer;
When the proofs, the figures, were ranged in columns before me;
When I was shown the charts and the diagrams, to add, divide, and
measure them;
When I, sitting, heard the astronomer, where he lectured with much
applause in the lecture-room,
How soon, unaccountable, I became tired and sick;
Till rising and gliding out, I wander'd off by myself,
In the mystical moist night-air, and from time to time,
Look'd up in perfect silence at the stars. 1865; 1867

To an Athlete Dying Young

A. E. HOUSMAN (1859–1936)

The time you won your town the race
We chaired you through the market-place;
Man and boy stood cheering by,
And home we brought you shoulder-high.

Today, the road all runners come,
Shoulder-high we bring you home,
And set you at your threshold down,
Townsman of a stiller town.

Smart lad, to slip betimes away
From fields where glory does not stay,   10
And early though the laurel grows
It withers quicker than the rose.

Eyes the shady night has shut
Cannot see the record cut,
And silence sounds no worse than cheers
After earth has stopped the ears:

Now you will not swell the rout
Of lads that wore their honors out,
Runners whom renown outran
And the name died before the man.   20

So set, before its echoes fade,
The fleet foot on the sill of shade,
And hold to the low lintel up
The still-defended challenge-cup.

And round that early-laureled head
Will flock to gaze the strengthless dead,
And find unwithered on its curls
The garland briefer than a girl's.   1896

For a Dead Lady

EDWIN ARLINGTON ROBINSON (1869–1935)

No more with overflowing light
Shall fill the eyes that now are faded,
Nor shall another's fringe with night
Their woman-hidden world as they did.
No more shall quiver down the days
The flowing wonder of her ways,
Whereof no language may requite
The shifting and the many-shaded.

The grace, divine, definitive,
Clings only as a faint forestalling;   10
The laugh that love could not forgive
Is hushed, and answers to no calling;
The forehead and the little ears
Have gone where Saturn keeps the years;
The breast where roses could not live
Has done with rising and with falling.

The beauty, shattered by the laws
That have creation in their keeping,
No longer trembles at applause,
Or over children that are sleeping;   20
And we who delve in beauty's lore
Know all that we have known before
Of what inexorable cause
Makes Time so vicious in his reaping.   1910

The Oven Bird

ROBERT FROST (1874–1963)

There is a singer everyone has heard,
Loud, a mid-summer and a mid-wood bird,
Who makes the solid tree trunks sound again.
He says that leaves are old and that for flowers
Mid-summer is to spring as one to ten.
He says the early petal-fall is past
When pear and cherry bloom went down in showers
On sunny days a moment overcast;
And comes that other fall we name the fall.
He says the highway dust is over all.
The bird would cease and be as other birds
But that he knows in singing not to sing.
The question that he frames in all but words
Is what to make of a diminished thing.   1916

Carrion Comfort

GERARD MANLEY HOPKINS (1844–1889)

Not, I'll not, carrion comfort, Despair, not feast on thee;
Not untwist—slack they may be—these last strands of man
In me ór, most weary, cry *I can no more.* I can;
Can something, hope, wish day come, not choose not to be.
But ah, but O thou terrible, why wouldst thou rude on me
Thy wring-world right foot rock? lay a lionlimb against me? scan
With darksome devouring eyes my bruisèd bones? and fan,
O in turns of tempest, me heaped there; me frantic to avoid thee and flee?

Why? That my chaff might fly; my grain lie, sheer and clear.
Nay in all that toil, that coil, since (seems) I kissed the rod,
Hand rather, my heart lo! lapped strength, stole joy, would laugh, chéer.
Cheer whom though? the hero whose heaven-handling flung me, fóot tród
Me? or me that fought him? O which one? is it each one? That night,
    that year
Of now done darkness I wretch lay wrestling with (my God!) my God.

1918

Thou Art Indeed Just, Lord

GERARD MANLEY HOPKINS (1844–1889)

*Justus quidem tu es, Domine, si disputem tecum: verumta-
men justa loquar ad te: Quare via impiorum prosperatur? etc.*

Thou art indeed just, Lord, if I contend
With thee; but, sir, so what I plead is just.
Why do sinners' ways prosper? and why must
Disappointment all I endeavour end?
    Wert thou my enemy, O thou my friend,
How wouldst thou worse, I wonder, than thou dost
Defeat, thwart me? Oh, the sots and thralls of lust
Do in spare hours more thrive than I that spend,
Sir, life upon thy cause. See, banks and brakes
Now, leavèd how thick! lacèd they are again
With fretty chervil, look, and fresh wind shakes
Them; birds build—but not I build; no, but strain,
Time's eunuch, and not breed one work that wakes.
Mine, O thou lord of life, send my roots rain.   1918

Title. The Latin quotation, from Jeremiah's complaint in the Old Testament, is translated in the first two sentences of the poem. The rest is Hopkins' own development of the theme.

A Prayer for My Daughter

WILLIAM BUTLER YEATS (1865–1939)

Once more the storm is howling, and half hid
Under this cradle-hood and coverlid
My child sleeps on. There is no obstacle
But Gregory's wood and one bare hill
Whereby the haystack- and roof-levelling wind,
Bred on the Atlantic, can be stayed;
And for an hour I have walked and prayed
Because of the great gloom that is in my mind.

I have walked and prayed for this young child an hour
And heard the sea-wind scream upon the tower,   10
And under the arches of the bridge, and scream
In the elms above the flooded stream;
Imagining in excited reverie
That the future years had come,
Dancing to a frenzied drum,
Out of the murderous innocence of the sea.

May she be granted beauty and yet not
Beauty to make a stranger's eye distraught,
Or hers before a looking-glass, for such,
Being made beautiful overmuch,   20
Consider beauty a sufficient end,
Lose natural kindness and maybe
The heart-revealing intimacy
That chooses right, and never find a friend.

Helen being chosen found life flat and dull
And later had much trouble from a fool,
While the great Queen, that rose out of the spray,
Being fatherless could have her way
Yet chose a bandy-leggèd smith for man.
It's certain that fine women eat   30
A crazy salad with their meat
Whereby the Horn of Plenty is undone.

In courtesy I'd have her chiefly learned;
Hearts are not had as a gift but hearts are earned
By those that are not entirely beautiful;
Yet many, that have played the fool

For beauty's very self, has charm made wise,
And many a poor man that has roved,
Loved and thought himself beloved,
From a glad kindness cannot take his eyes.   40

May she become a flourishing hidden tree
That all her thoughts may like the linnet be,
And have no business but dispensing round
Their magnanimities of sound,
Nor but in merriment begin a chase,
Nor but in merriment a quarrel.
O may she live like some green laurel
Rooted in one dear perpetual place.

My mind, because the minds that I have loved,
The sort of beauty that I have approved,   50
Prosper but little, has dried up of late,
Yet knows that to be choked with hate
May well be of all evil chances chief.
If there's no hatred in a mind
Assault and battery of the wind
Can never tear the linnet from the leaf.

An intellectual hatred is the worst,
So let her think opinions are accursed.
Have I not seen the loveliest woman born
Out of the mouth of Plenty's horn,   60
Because of her opinionated mind
Barter that horn and every good
By quiet natures understood
For an old bellows full of angry wind?

Considering that, all hatred driven hence,
The soul recovers radical innocence
And learns at last that it is self-delighting,
Self-appeasing, self-affrighting,
And that its own sweet will is Heaven's will;
She can, though every face should scowl   70
And every windy quarter howl
Or every bellows burst, be happy still.

59–64. The reference is to Maud Gonne, a woman of remarkable beauty
to whom Yeats paid court in vain for many years, and whose participation
in violent political quarrels he deplored.

And may her bridegroom bring her to a house
Where all's accustomed, ceremonious;
For arrogance and hatred are the wares
Peddled in the thoroughfares.
How but in custom and in ceremony
Are innocence and beauty born?
Ceremony's a name for the rich horn,
And custom for the spreading laurel tree.   1921   80

To the Stone-Cutters

ROBINSON JEFFERS (1887–1962)

Stone-cutters fighting time with marble, you foredefeated
Challengers of oblivion,
Eat cynical earnings, knowing rock splits, records fall down,
The square-limbed Roman letters
Scale in the thaws, wear in the rain. The poet as well
Builds his monument mockingly;
For man will be blotted out, the blithe earth die, the brave sun
Die blind, his heart blackening:
Yet stones have stood for a thousand years, and pained thoughts found
The honey peace in old poems.   1922

Anecdote of the Jar

WALLACE STEVENS (1879–1955)

I placed a jar in Tennessee,
And round it was, upon a hill.
It made the slovenly wilderness
Surround that hill.

The wilderness rose up to it,
And sprawled around, no longer wild.
The jar was round upon the ground
And tall and of a port in air.

It took dominion everywhere.
The jar was gray and bare.
It did not give of bird or bush,
Like nothing else in Tennessee.   1923

Here Lies a Lady

JOHN CROWE RANSOM (1888-   )

Here lies a lady of beauty and high degree.
Of chills and fever she died, of fever and chills,
The delight of her husband, her aunts, an infant of three,
And of medicos marveling sweetly on her ills.

For either she burned, and her confident eyes would blaze,
And her fingers fly in a manner to puzzle their heads—
What was she making? Why, nothing; she sat in a maze
Of old scraps of laces, snipped into curious shreds—

Or this would pass, and the light of her fire decline
Till she lay discouraged and cold as a thin stalk white and blown,
And would not open her eyes, to kisses, to wine;
The sixth of these states was her last; the cold settled down.

Sweet ladies, long may ye bloom, and toughly I hope ye may thole,
But was she not lucky? In flowers and lace and mourning,
In love and great honor we bade God rest her soul
After six little spaces of chill, and six of burning.   1924

Piano

D. H. LAWRENCE (1885–1930)

Softly, in the dusk, a woman is singing to me;
Taking me back down the vista of years, till I see
A child sitting under the piano, in the boom of the tingling strings
And pressing the small, poised feet of a mother who smiles as she sings.

In spite of myself, the insidious mastery of song
Betrays me back, till the heart of me weeps to belong
To the old Sunday evenings at home, with winter outside
And hymns in the cozy parlor, the tinkling piano our guide.

So now it is vain for the singer to burst into clamor
With the great black piano appassionato. The glamour
Of childish days is upon me, my manhood is cast
Down in the flood of remembrance, I weep like a child for the past.
                                                    1918; 1928

You, Andrew Marvell

ARCHIBALD MAC LEISH (1892–   )

And here face down beneath the sun
And here upon earth's noonward height
To feel the always coming on
The always rising of the night

To feel creep up the curving east
The earthly chill of dusk and slow
Upon those under lands the vast
And ever-climbing shadow grow

And strange at Ecbatan the trees
Take leaf by leaf the evening strange   10
The flooding dark about their knees
The mountains over Persia change

And now at Kermanshah the gate
Dark empty and the withered grass
And through the twilight now the late
Few travelers in the westward pass

And Baghdad darken and the bridge
Across the silent river gone
And through Arabia the edge
Of evening widen and steal on   20

And deepen on Palmyra's street
The wheel rut in the ruined stone
And Lebanon fade out and Crete
High through the clouds and overblown

And over Sicily the air
Still flashing with the landward gulls
And loom and slowly disappear
The sails above the shadowy hulls

And Spain go under and the shore
Of Africa the gilded sand   30
And evening vanish and no more
The low pale light across that land

Title. MacLeish refers here to Andrew Marvell's poem *To His Coy Mistress*, in which quite different use is made of imagery relating places and the passage of time.

Nor now the long light on the sea

And here face downward in the sun
To feel how swift how secretly
The shadow of the night comes on . . .   1928

Poem 28

CONRAD AIKEN (1889–   )

From TIME IN THE ROCK

And this digester, this digester of food,
this killer and eater and digester of food,
the one with teeth and tongue, insatiable belly,
him of the gut and appetite and murder,
the one with claws, the one with a quick eye,
whose footstep—ah—is soft as treason—
this foul embodied greed, this blind intestine—
this human, you or me—

                look sharply at him
and measure him, digesters! hear his speech,
woven deceit, colossal dream, so shaped   10
of food and search for food—oh believe him
whose hunger shapes itself as gods and rainbows

is he not perfect, walks he not divinely
with a light step among the stars his fathers
with a quick thought among the seeds his sons
is he not graceful, is he not gentle,
this foul receiver and expeller of food,
this channel of corruption,

              is he not
the harbinger, the angel, the bright prophet
who knows the right from wrong, whose thought is pure,   20
dissects the angles, numbers pains and pleasures,
dreams like an algebra among waste worlds—
can we not trust him, sees he not the sure,
disposes time and space, condemns the evil-doer—
is his digestion not an ample measure?

Come, rooted ones, come radicals, come trees,
whose powerful tentacles suck earth, and join
the murderous angels; and let us dance together
the dance of joyful cruelty, whence thrives
this world of qualities which filth ordained.   1936   30

The Mediterranean

ALLEN TATE (1899–   )

Quem das finem, rex magne, dolorum?

Where we went in the boat was a long bay
A sling-shot wide, walled in by towering stone—
Peaked margin of antiquity's delay,
And we went there out of time's monotone:

Where we went in the black hull no light moved
But a gull white-winged along the feckless wave;
The breeze unseen but fierce as a body loved,
That boat drove onward like a willing slave:

Where we went in the small ship the seaweed
Parted and gave to us the murmuring shore   10
And we made feast and in our secret need
Devoured the very plates Aeneas bore:

Where derelict you see through the low twilight
The green coast that you, thunder-tossed, would win,
Drop sail, and hastening to drink all night
Eat dish and bowl—to take that sweet land in!

Where we feasted and caroused on the sandless
Pebbles, affecting our day of piracy,
What prophecy of eaten plates could landless
Wanderers fulfill by the ancient sea?   20

We for that time might taste the famous age
Eternal here yet hidden from our eyes
When lust of power undid its stuffless rage;
They, in a wineskin, bore earth's paradise.

Title. The Latin given by Tate can be translated: "What end can you
grant, great king, to our sorrows?" The line appears to be a variant of
line 241 in Book I of Virgil's Roman epic *The Aeneid*, from the speech of
Venus to Jupiter. In Virgil, the last word of the line is *laborum* (hardships)
rather than *dolorum* (sorrows). Perhaps Tate's alteration is meant to suggest
a change of address from a pagan to a Christian God. At any rate, the
poem abounds with learned allusions to classical poetry which deals with
the question of evil and with man's tragic fate.

Let us lie down once more by the breathing side
Of Ocean, where our live forefathers sleep
As if the Known Sea still were a month wide—
Atlantis howls but is no longer steep!

What country shall we conquer, what fair land
Unman our conquest and locate our blood? 30
We've cracked the hemispheres with careless hand!
Now, from the Gates of Hercules we flood

Westward, westward till the barbarous brine
Whelms us to the tired land where tasseling corn,
Fat beans, grapes sweeter than muscadine
Rot on the vine: in that land were we born. 1936

Lay Your Sleeping Head, My Love

W. H. AUDEN (1907–)

Lay your sleeping head, my love,
Human on my faithless arm;
Time and fevers burn away
Individual beauty from
Thoughtful children, and the grave
Proves the child ephemeral:
But in my arms till break of day
Let the living creature lie,
Mortal, guilty, but to me
The entirely beautiful. 10

Soul and body have no bounds:
To lovers as they lie upon
Her tolerant enchanted slope
In their ordinary swoon,
Grave the vision Venus sends
Of supernatural sympathy,
Universal love and hope;
While an abstract insight wakes
Among the glaciers and the rocks
The hermit's sensual ecstasy. 20

Certainty, fidelity
On the stroke of midnight pass
Like vibrations of a bell,
And fashionable madmen raise

Their pedantic boring cry:
Every farthing of the cost,
All the dreaded cards foretell,
Shall be paid, but from this night
Not a whisper, not a thought,
Not a kiss nor look be lost.   30

Beauty, midnight, vision dies:
Let the winds of dawn that blow
Softly round your dreaming head
Such a day of sweetness show
Eye and knocking heart may bless,
Find the mortal world enough;
Noons of dryness see you fed
By the involuntary powers,
Nights of insult let you pass
Watched by every human love.   1940   40

My Father Moved Through Dooms of Love

E. E. CUMMINGS (1894–1963)

my father moved through dooms of love
through sames of am through haves of give,
singing each morning out of each night
my father moved through depths of height

this motionless forgetful where
turned at his glance to shining here;
that if(so timid air is firm)
under his eyes would stir and squirm

newly as from unburied which
floats the first who, his april touch   10
drove sleeping selves to swarm their fates
woke dreamers to their ghostly roots

and should some why completely weep
my father's fingers brought her sleep:
vainly no smallest voice might cry
for he could feel the mountains grow.

Lifting the valleys of the sea
my father moved through griefs of joy;
praising a forehead called the moon
singing desire into begin   20

joy was his song and joy so pure
a heart of star by him could steer
and pure so now and now so yes
the wrists of twilight would rejoice

keen as midsummer's keen beyond
conceiving mind of sun will stand,
so strictly(over utmost him
so hugely)stood my father's dream

his flesh was flesh his blood was blood:
no hungry man but wished him food;   30
no cripple wouldn't creep one mile
uphill to only see him smile.

Scorning the pomp of must and shall
my father moved through dooms of feel;
his anger was as right as rain
his pity was as green as grain

septembering arms of year extend
less humbly wealth to foe and friend
than he to foolish and to wise
offered immeasurable is   40

proudly and(by octobering flame
beckoned)as earth will downward climb,
so naked for immortal work
his shoulders marched against the dark

his sorrow was as true as bread:
no liar looked him in the head;
if every friend became his foe
he'd laugh and build a world with snow.

My father moved through theys of we,
singing each new leaf out of each tree   50
(and every child was sure that spring
danced when she heard my father sing)

then let men kill which cannot share,
let blood and flesh be mud and mire,
scheming imagine, passion willed,
freedom a drug that's bought and sold

giving to steal and cruel kind,
a heart to fear, to doubt a mind,

to differ a disease of same,
conform the pinnacle of am   60

though dull were all we taste as bright,
bitter all utterly things sweet,
maggoty minus and dumb death
all we inherit, all bequeath

and nothing quite so least as truth
—i say though hate were why men breathe—
because my father lived his soul
love is the whole and more than all   1940

The Bloody Sire

ROBINSON JEFFERS (1887–1962)

It is not bad. Let them play.
Let the guns bark and the bombing-plane
Speak his prodigious blasphemies.
It is not bad, it is high time,
Stark violence is still the sire of all the world's values.

What but the wolf's tooth chiseled so fine
The fleet limbs of the antelope?
What but fear winged the birds and hunger
Gemmed with such eyes the great goshawk's head?
Violence has been the sire of all the world's values.

Who would remember Helen's face
Lacking the terrible halo of spears?
Who formed Christ but Herod and Caesar,
The cruel and bloody victories of Caesar?
Violence has been the sire of all the world's values.

Never weep, let them play,
Old violence is not too old to beget new values.   1941

Sonnet to My Mother

GEORGE BARKER (1913–)

Most near, most dear, most loved and most far,
Under the window where I often found her
Sitting as huge as Asia, seismic with laughter,
Gin and chicken helpless in her Irish hand,
Irresistible as Rabelais but most tender for
The lame dogs and hurt birds that surround her,—
She is a procession no one can follow after
But be like a little dog following a brass band.

She will not glance up at the bomber or condescend
To drop her gin and scuttle to a cellar,
But lean on the mahogany table like a mountain
Whom only faith can move, and so I send
O all my faith and all my love to tell her
That she will move from mourning into morning.   1941

Bearded Oaks

ROBERT PENN WARREN (1905–)

The oaks, how subtle and marine,
Bearded, and all the layered light
Above them swims; and thus the scene,
Recessed, awaits the positive night.

So, waiting, we in the grass now lie
Beneath the languorous tread of light:
The grasses, kelp-like, satisfy
The nameless motions of the air.

Upon the floor of light, and time,
Unmurmuring, of polyp made,   10
We rest; we are, as light withdraws,
Twin atolls on a shelf of shade.

Ages to our construction went,
Dim architecture, hour by hour:
And violence, forgot now, lent
The present stillness all its power.

The storm of noon above us rolled,
Of light the fury, furious gold,

191

The long drag troubling us, the depth:
Dark is unrocking, unrippling, still.   20

Passion and slaughter, ruth, decay
Descend, minutely whispering down,
Silted through swaying streams, to lay
Foundation for our voicelessness.

All our debate is voiceless here,
As all our rage, the rage of stone;
If hope is hopeless, then fearless fear,
And history is thus undone.

Our feet once wrought the hollow street
With echo when the lamps were dead   30
At windows; once our headlight glare
Disturbed the doe that, leaping, fled.

I do not love you less that now
The caged heart makes iron stroke,
Or less that all that light once gave
The graduate dark should now revoke.

We live in time so little time
And we learn all so painfully,
That we may spare this hour's term
To practice for eternity.   1943   40

Cassandra

ROBINSON JEFFERS (1887–1962)

The mad girl with the staring eyes and long white fingers
Hooked in the stones of the wall,
The storm-wrack hair and the screeching mouth: does it matter,
    Cassandra,
Whether the people believe
Your bitter fountain? Truly men hate the truth, they'd liefer
Meet a tiger on the road.
Therefore the poets honey their truth with lying; but religion-
Venders and political men
Pour from the barrel, new lies on the old, and are praised for kindly
Wisdom. Poor bitch be wise.
No: you'll still mumble in a corner a crust of truth, to men
And gods disgusting.—you and I, Cassandra.   1944

Autumnal Equinox on Mediterranean Beach

ROBERT PENN WARREN (1905–)

Sail-bellyer, exciter of boys, come bang
To smithereens doors, and see if I give a hang,

For I am sick of summer and the insane glitter
Of sea sun-bit, and the wavelets that bicker and titter,

And the fat girls that hang out brown breasts like fruit overripe,
And the thin ones flung pale in rock-shadow, goose-pimpled as tripe,

And the young men who pose on the headlands like ads for Jantzen,
And the old who would do so much better to keep proper pants on,

And all Latin faeces one finds, like jewels, in the sand,
And the gaze of the small, sweet octopus fondling your hand.   10

Come howl like a prophet the season's righteous anger,
And knock down our idols with crash, bang, or clangor.

Blow the cat's fur furry sideways, make dogs bark,
Blow the hen's tail feathers forward past the pink mark,

Snatch the laundry off the line, like youth away,
Blow plastered hair off the bald spot, lift toupee.

Come blow old women's skirts, bring Truth to light,
Though at such age morn's all the same as night.

Come swirl old picnic papers to very sky-height,
And make gulls gabble in fury at such breach of their air-right.   20

Kick up the bay now, make a mess of it,
Fling spume in our sinful faces, like God's spit,

For now all our pleasures, like peaches, get rotten, not riper,
And summer is over, and time to pay the piper,

And be glad to do it, for man's not made for much pleasure,
Or even for joy, unless cut down to his measure.

Yes, kick the garbage pail, and scatter garbage,
That the cat flee forth with fish-head, the housewife rage,

For pain and pleasure balance in God's year—
Though *whose* is *which* is not your problem here,   30

And perhaps not even God's. So bang, wind, batter,
While human hearts do the bookkeeping in this matter.   1960

Fall in Corrales

RICHARD WILBUR (1921–   )

Winter will be feasts and fires in the shut houses,
Lovers with hot mouths in their blanched bed,
Prayers and poems made, and all recourses
Against the world huge and dead:

Charms, all charms, as in stillness of plumb summer
The shut head lies down in bottomless grasses,
Willing that its thought be all heat and hum,
That it not dream the time passes.

Now as these light buildings of summer begin
To crumble, the air husky with blown tile,   10
It is as when in bald April the wind
Unhoused the spirit for a while:

Then there was no need by tales or drowsing
To make the thing that we were mothered by;
It was ourselves who melted in the mountains,
And the sun dove into every eye.

Our desires dwelt in the weather as fine as bomb-dust;
It was our sex that made the fountains yield;
Our flesh fought in the roots, and at last rested
Whole among cows in the risen field.   20

Now in its empty bed the truant river
Leaves but the perfect rumples of its flow;
The cottonwoods are spending gold like water;
Weeds in their light detachments go;

In a dry world more huge than rhyme or dreaming
We hear the sentences of straws and stones,
Stand in the wind and, bowing to this time,
Practise the candor of our bones.   1961

CHAPTER 5

Versification

The Cherry-Tree Carol

ANONYMOUS

Joseph was an old man,
  and an old man was he,
When he wedded Mary,
  in the land of Galilee.

Joseph and Mary walked
  through an orchard good,
Where was cherries and berries,
  so red as any blood.

Joseph and Mary walked
  through an orchard green,   10
Where was berries and cherries,
  as thick as might be seen.

O then bespoke Mary,
  so meek and so mild:
'Pluck me one cherry, Joseph,
  for I am with child.'

O then bespoke Joseph,
  with words most unkind:
'Let him pluck thee a cherry
  that brought thee with child.'   20

O then bespoke the babe,
  within his mother's womb:
'Bow down then the tallest tree,
  for my mother to have some.'

Then bowed down the highest tree
  unto his mother's hand;

Then she cried, 'See, Joseph,
 I have cherries at command.'

O then bespake Joseph:
 'I have done Mary wrong;   **30**
But cheer up, my dearest,
 and be not cast down.'

Then Mary plucked a cherry,
 as red as the blood,
Then Mary went home
 with her heavy load.

Then Mary took her babe,
 and sat him on her knee,
Saying, 'My dear son, tell me
 what this world will be.'   **40**

'O I shall be as dead, mother,
 as the stones in the wall;
O the stones in the streets, mother,
 shall mourn for me all.

'Upon Easter-day, mother,
 my uprising shall be;
O the sun and the moon, mother,
 shall both rise with me.' *Before* 1600

The Frailty and Hurtfulness of Beauty

HENRY HOWARD, EARL OF SURREY (1517?–1547)

Brittle beauty that nature made so frail,
Whereof the gift is small, and short the season,
Flow'ring to-day, to-morrow apt to fail,
Tickle treasure, abhorred of reason,
Dangerous to deal with, vain, of none avail,
Costly in keeping, passed not worth two peason,
Slipper in sliding as is an eelë's tail,
Hard to attain, once gotten not geason,
Jewel of jeopardy that peril doth assail,
False and untrue, enticëd oft to treason,
En'my to youth (that most may I bewail!),
Ah, bitter sweet! infecting as the poison,
Thou farest as fruit that with the frost is taken:
To-day ready ripe, to-morrow all to-shaken. 1557

Feste's Final Song

WILLIAM SHAKESPEARE (1564–1616)

From TWELFTH NIGHT

When that I was and a little tiny boy,
    With hey, ho, the wind and the rain,
A foolish thing was but a toy,
    For the rain it raineth every day.

But when I came to man's estate,
    With hey, ho, the wind and the rain,
'Gainst knaves and thieves men shut their gate,
    For the rain it raineth every day.

But when I came, alas! to wive,
    With hey, ho, the wind and the rain,
By swaggering could I never thrive,
    For the rain it raineth every day.

But when I came unto my beds,
    With hey, ho, the wind and the rain,
With tosspots still had drunken heads,
    For the rain it raineth every day.

A great while ago the world begun,
    With hey, ho, the wind and the rain,
But that's all one, our play is done,
    And we'll strive to please you every day.   1600; 1623

An Epitaph on S[alathiel] P[avy], a Child of Q[ueen] El[izabeth's] Chapel

BEN JONSON (1572–1637)

Weep with me, all you that read
    This little story;
And know, for whom a tear you shed
    Death's self is sorry.
'Twas a child that so did thrive
    In grace and feature,
As heaven and nature seemed to strive
    Which owned the creature.
Years he numbered scarce thirteen
    When fates turned cruel,   10

197

Yet three filled zodiacs had he been
  The stage's jewel;
And did act, what now we moan,
  Old men so duly,
As, sooth, the Parcæ thought him one,
  He played so truly.
So by error, to his fate
  They all consented;
But viewing him since, alas too late,
  They have repented,   20
And have sought, to give new birth,
  In baths to steep him;
But being so much too good for earth,
  Heaven vows to keep him.   1603; 1616

Easter Wings

GEORGE HERBERT (1593–1633)

Lord, who createdst man in wealth and store,
  Though foolishly he lost the same,
    Decaying more and more
      Till he became
        Most poor;
        With thee
      Oh, let me rise
    As larks, harmoniously,
  And sing this day thy victories;
Then shall the fall further the flight in me.   10

My tender age in sorrow did begin;
  And still with sicknesses and shame
    Thou didst so punish sin,
      That I became
        Most thin.
        With thee
      Let me combine,
    And feel this day thy victory;
  For if I imp my wing on thine,
Affliction shall advance the flight in me.   1633   20

The Altar

GEORGE HERBERT (1593–1633)

A broken ALTAR, Lord, Thy servant rears,
Made of a HEART, and cemented with tears;
   Whose parts are as Thy hand did frame;
   No workman's tool hath touched the same.
        A HEART alone
        Is such a stone
        As nothing but
        Thy power doth cut.
        Wherefore each part
        Of my hard HEART
        Meets in this frame,
        To praise Thy name:
   That, if I chance to hold my peace,
   These stones to praise Thee may not cease.
O, let Thy blessed SACRIFICE be mine,
And sanctify this ALTAR to be Thine!   1633

Insatiableness

THOMAS TRAHERNE (1636–1674)

  This busy, vast, inquiring soul
      Brooks no control,
     No limits will endure,
  Nor any rest; it will all see,
Not time alone, but ev'n eternity.
    What is it? Endless, sure.

  'Tis mean ambition to desire
      A single world;
     To many I aspire,
  Though one upon another hurled;   10
Nor will they all, if they be all confined,
     Delight my mind.

  This busy, vast, inquiring soul
      Brooks no control;
     'Tis very curious too.
  Each one of all those worlds must be
Enriched with infinite variety
     And worth, or 'twill not do.

'Tis nor delight nor perfect pleasure
        To have a purse   20
That hath a bottom in its treasure,
Since I must thence endless expense disburse.
Sure there's a God, for else there's no delight,
        One infinite.   1665?   1903

A Night-Piece

Or, Modern Philosophy

CHRISTOPHER SMART (1722–1771)

'Twas when bright Cynthia with her silver car,
        Soft stealing from Endymion's bed,
Had call'd forth ev'ry glitt'ring star,
And up the ascent of heav'n her brilliant host had led.

        Night with all her negro train,
        Took possession of the plain;
        In an hearse she rode reclin'd,
        Drawn by screech-owls slow and blind:
        Close to her, with printless feet,
        Crept Stillness in a winding sheet.   10
        Next to her deaf Silence was seen,
        Treading on tip-toes over the green;
        Softly, lightly, gently she trips,
        Still holding her fingers seal'd to her lips.
        Then came Sleep serene and bland,
        Bearing a death watch in his hand;
        In fluid air around him swims
        A tribe grotesque of mimic dreams.

        You could not see a sight,
            You could not hear a sound,   20
        But what confess'd the night,
            And horrour deepen'd round.

        Beneath a plantain's melancholy shade,
        Sophron the wise was laid:
And to the answ'ring wood these sounds convey'd:
        "While others toil within the town,
        And to Fortune smile or frown,
        Fond of trifles, fond of toys,
        And married to that woman, Noise;

Sacred Wisdom be my care,   30
   And fairest Virtue, Wisdom's heir."

His speculations thus the sage begun,
   When, lo! the neighbouring bell
In solemn sound struck one:—
   He starts—and rsecollect—he was engag'd to Nell.
Then up he sprang nimble and light,
   And rapp'd at fair Elenor's door;
He laid aside Virtue that night,
   And next morn por'd in Plato for more.   1750

Song

OLIVER GOLDSMITH (1730–1774)

From THE VICAR OF WAKEFIELD

When lovely woman stoops to folly,
   And finds too late that men betray,
What charm can soothe her melancholy,
   What art can wash her guilt away?

The only art her guilt to cover,
   To hide her shame from ev'ry eye,
To give repentance to her lover,
   And wring his bosom—is, to die.   1766

She Walks in Beauty

GEORGE NOEL GORDON, LORD BYRON (1788–1824)

From HEBREW MELODIES

I

She walks in beauty, like the night
   Of cloudless climes and starry skies;
And all that's best of dark and bright
   Meet in her aspect and her eyes:
Thus mellow'd to that tender light
   Which heaven to gaudy day denies.

II

One shade the more, one ray the less,
   Had half impair'd the nameless grace

Which waves in every raven tress,
　Or softly lightens o'er her face;
Where thoughts serenely sweet express
　How pure, how dear their dwelling-place.

III

And on that cheek, and o'er that brow,
　So soft, so calm, yet eloquent,
The smiles that win, the tints that glow,
　But tell of days in goodness spent,
A mind at peace with all below,
　A heart whose love is innocent!   1815

Ode on Melancholy

JOHN KEATS (1795–1821)

No, no! go not to Lethe, neither twist
　Wolf's-bane, tight-rooted, for its poisonous wine;
Nor suffer thy pale forehead to be kiss'd
　By nightshade, ruby grape of Proserpine;
Make not your rosary of yew-berries,
　Nor let the beetle, nor the death-moth be
　　Your mournful Psyche, nor the downy owl
A partner in your sorrow's mysteries;
　For shade to shade will come too drowsily,
　　And drown the wakeful anguish of the soul.   10

But when the melancholy fit shall fall
　Sudden from heaven like a weeping cloud,
That fosters the droop-headed flowers all,
　And hides the green hill in an April shroud;
Then glut thy sorrow on a morning rose,
　Or on the rainbow of the salt sand-wave,
　　Or on the wealth of globèd peonies;
Or if thy mistress some rich anger shows,
　Emprison her soft hand, and let her rave,
　　And feed deep, deep upon her peerless eyes.   20

She dwells with Beauty—Beauty that must die;
　And Joy, whose hand is ever at his lips
Bidding adieu, and aching Pleasure nigh,
　Turning to poison while the bee-mouth sips:
Ay, in the very temple of Delight
　Veil'd Melancholy has her sovran shrine,

Though seen of none save him whose strenuous tongue
Can burst Joy's grape against his palate fine;
His soul shall taste the sadness of her might,
And be among her cloudy trophies hung.   1820   30

Mariana

ALFRED, LORD TENNYSON (1809–1892)

"Mariana in the moated grange."

MEASURE FOR MEASURE

With blackest moss the flower-plots
    Were thickly crusted, one and all;
The rusted nails fell from the knots
    That held the pear to the gable-wall.
The broken sheds look'd sad and strange:
    Unlifted was the clinking latch;
    Weeded and worn the ancient thatch
Upon the lonely moated grange.
        She only said, "My life is dreary,
            He cometh not," she said;   10
        She said, "I am aweary, aweary,
            I would that I were dead!"

Her tears fell with the dews at even;
    Her tears fell ere the dews were dried;
She could not look on the sweet heaven,
    Either at morn or eventide.
After the flitting of the bats,
    When thickest dark did trance the sky,
    She drew her casement-curtain by,
And glanced athwart the glooming flats.   20
        She only said, "The night is dreary,
            He cometh not," she said;
        She said, "I am aweary, aweary,
            I would that I were dead!"

Upon the middle of the night,
    Waking she heard the night-fowl crow;
The cock sung out an hour ere light;
    From the dark fen the oxen's low
Came to her: without hope of change,
    In sleep she seem'd to walk forlorn,   30
    Till cold winds woke the gray-eyed morn

About the lonely moated grange.
    She only said, "The day is dreary,
      He cometh not," she said;
    She said, "I am aweary, aweary,
      I would that I were dead!"

About a stone-cast from the wall
    A sluice with blacken'd waters slept,
And o'er it many, round and small,
    The cluster'd marish-mosses crept.   40
Hard by a poplar shook alway,
    All silver-green with gnarled bark:
For leagues no other tree did mark
The level waste, the rounding gray.
    She only said, "My life is dreary,
      He cometh not," she said;
    She said, "I am aweary, aweary,
      I would that I were dead!"

And ever when the moon was low,
    And the shrill winds were up and away,   50
In the white curtain, to and fro,
    She saw the gusty shadow sway.
But when the moon was very low,
    And wild winds bound within their cell,
    The shadow of the poplar fell
Upon her bed, across her brow.
    She only said, "The night is dreary,
      He cometh not," she said;
    She said, "I am aweary, aweary,
      I would that I were dead!"   60

All day within the dreamy house,
    The doors upon their hinges creak'd;
The blue fly sung in the pane; the mouse
    Behind the mouldering wainscot shriek'd,
Or from the crevice peer'd about.
    Old faces glimmer'd thro' the doors,
    Old footsteps trod the upper floors,
Old voices called her from without.
    She only said, "My life is dreary,
      He cometh not," she said;   70
    She said, "I am aweary, aweary,
      I would that I were dead!"

The sparrow's chirrup on the roof,
    The slow clock ticking, and the sound

Which to the wooing wind aloof
  The poplar made, did all confound
Her sense; but most she loathed the hour
  When the thick-moted sunbeam lay
  Athwart the chambers, and the day
Was sloping toward his western bower.   80
    Then said she, "I am very dreary,
      He will not come," she said;
    She wept, "I am aweary, aweary,
      O God, that I were dead!"   1830

To Helen

EDGAR ALLAN POE (1809–1849)

Helen, thy beauty is to me
  Like those Nicèan barks of yore,
That gently, o'er a perfumed sea,
  The weary, way-worn wanderer bore
To his own native shore.

On desperate seas long wont to roam,
  Thy hyacinth hair, thy classic face,
Thy Naiad airs have brought me home
  To the glory that was Greece
And the grandeur that was Rome.

Lo! in yon brilliant window-niche
  How statue-like I see thee stand,
  The agate lamp within thy hand!
Ah, Psyche, from the regions which
  Are Holy Land!   1831

A Forsaken Garden

ALGERNON CHARLES SWINBURNE (1837–1909)

In a coign of the cliff between lowland and highland,
  At the sea-down's edge between windward and lee,
Walled round with rocks as an inland island,
  The ghost of a garden fronts the sea.
A girdle of brushwood and thorn encloses
  The steep square slope of the blossomless bed
Where the weeds that grew green from the graves of its roses
  Now lie dead.

The fields fall southward, abrupt and broken,
   To the low last edge of the long lone land.   10
If a step should sound or a word be spoken,
   Would a ghost not rise at the strange guest's hand?
So long have the gray bare walks lain guestless,
   Through branches and briers if a man make way,
He shall find no life but the sea-wind's, restless
    Night and day.

The dense hard passage is blind and stifled
   That crawls by a track none turn to climb
To the strait waste place that the years have rifled
   Of all but the thorns that are touched not of time.   20
The thorns he spares when the rose is taken;
   The rocks are left when he wastes the plain;
The wind that wanders, the weeds wind-shaken,
    These remain.

Not a flower to be pressed of the foot that falls not;
   As the heart of a dead man the seed-plots are dry;
From the thicket of thorns whence the nightingale calls not,
   Could she call, there were never a rose to reply.
Over the meadows that blossom and wither,
   Rings but the note of a sea-bird's song;   30
Only the sun and the rain come hither
    All year long.

The sun burns sear, and the rain dishevels
   One gaunt bleak blossom of scentless breath.
Only the wind here hovers and revels,
   In a round where life seems barren as death.
Here there was laughing of old, there was weeping,
   Haply, of lovers none ever will know,
Whose eyes went seaward a hundred sleeping
    Years ago.   40

Heart handfast in heart as they stood, "Look thither,"
   Did he whisper? "Look forth from the flowers to the sea;
For the foamflowers endure when the rose-blossoms wither,
   And men that love lightly may die—but we?"
And the same wind sang, and the same waves whitened,
   And or ever the garden's last petals were shed,
In the lips that had whispered, the eyes that had lightened,
    Love was dead.

Or they loved their life through, and then went whither?
    And were one to the end—but what end who knows?   50
Love deep as the sea as a rose must wither,
    As the rose-red seaweed that mocks the rose.
Shall the dead take thought for the dead to love them?
    What love was ever as deep as a grave?
They are loveless now as the grass above them
      Or the wave.

All are at one now, roses and lovers,
    Not known of the cliffs and the fields and the sea.
Not a breath of the time that has been hovers
    In the air now soft with a summer to be.   60
Not a breath shall there sweeten the seasons hereafter
    Of the flowers or the lovers that laugh now or weep,
When as they that are free now of weeping and laughter
      We shall sleep.

Here death may deal not again forever;
    Here change may come not till all change end.
From the graves they have made they shall rise up never,
    Who have left naught living to ravage and rend.
Earth, stones, and thorns of the wild ground growing,
    While the sun and the rain live, these shall be;   70
Till a last wind's breath, upon all these blowing,
      Roll the sea.

Till the slow sea rise, and the sheer cliff crumble,
    Till terrace and meadow the deep gulfs drink,
Till the strength of the waves of the high tides humble
    The fields that lessen, the rocks that shrink,
Here now in his triumph where all things falter,
    Stretched out on the spoils that his own hand spread,
As a god self-slain on his own strange altar,
      Death lies dead.   1876   80

Bunthorne's Song

WILLIAM SCHWENCK GILBERT (1836–1911)

From PATIENCE

If you're anxious for to shine in the high æsthetic line as a man of
    culture rare,
You must get up all the germs of the transcendental terms, and plant
    them everywhere.
You must lie upon the daisies and discourse in novel phrases of your
    complicated state of mind,
The meaning doesn't matter if it's only idle chatter of a transcendental
    kind.
        And every one will say,
        As you walk your mystic way,
"If this young man expresses himself in terms too deep for *me*,
Why, what a very singularly deep young man this deep young man
    must be!"

Be eloquent in praise of the very dull old days which have long since
    passed away,
And convince 'em, if you can, that the reign of good Queen Anne was
    Culture's palmiest day.   10
Of course you will pooh-pooh whatever's fresh and new, and declare
    it's crude and mean,
For Art stopped short in the cultivated court of the Empress Josephine.
        And every one will say,
        As you walk your mystic way,
"If that's not good enough for him which is good enough for *me*,
Why, what a very cultivated kind of youth this kind of youth must be!"

Then a sentimental passion of a vegetable fashion must excite your
    languid spleen,
An attachment *à la* Plato for a bashful young potato, or a not-too-
    French French bean!
Though the Philistines may jostle, you will rank as an apostle in the
    high æsthetic band,
If you walk down Piccadilly with a poppy or a lily in your mediæval
    hand.   20
        And every one will say,
        As you walk your flowery way,
"If he's content with a vegetable love which would certainly not suit *me*,
Why, what a most particularly pure young man this pure young man
    must be!"   1881

The Windhover

To Christ Our Lord

GERARD MANLEY HOPKINS (1844–1889)

I caught this morning morning's minion, king-
  dom of daylight's dauphin, dapple-dawn-drawn
    Falcon, in his riding
Of the rolling level underneath him steady air, and striding
High there, how he rung upon the rein of a wimpling wing
In his ecstasy! then off, off forth on swing,
  As a skate's heel sweeps smooth on a bow-bend: the hurl and gliding
  Rebuffed the big wind. My heart in hiding
Stirred for a bird,—the achieve of, the mastery of the thing!

Brute beauty and valour and act, oh, air, pride, plume, here
  Buckle! AND the fire that breaks from thee then, a billion
Times told lovelier, more dangerous, O my chevalier!

  No wonder of it: shéer plód makes plough down sillion
Shine, and blue-bleak embers, ah my dear,
  Fall, gall themselves, and gash gold-vermilion.   1918

"O Where Are You Going?"

W. H. AUDEN (1907–   )

"O where are you going?" said reader to rider,
"That valley is fatal when furnaces burn,
Yonder's the midden whose odours will madden,
That gap is the grave where the tall return."

"O do you imagine," said fearer to farer,
"That dusk will delay on your path to the pass,
Your diligent looking discover the lacking
Your footsteps feel from granite to grass?"

"O what was that bird," said horror to hearer,
"Did you see that shape in the twisted trees?
Behind you swiftly the figure comes softly,
The spot on your skin is a shocking disease?"

"Out of this house"—said rider to reader,
"Yours never will"—said farer to fearer,
"They're looking for you"—said hearer to horror,
As he left them there, as he left them there.   1932

The Express

STEPHEN SPENDER (1909–)

After the first powerful plain manifesto
The black statement of pistons, without more fuss
But gliding like a queen, she leaves the station.
Without bowing and with restrained unconcern
She passes the houses which humbly crowd outside,
The gasworks and at last the heavy page
Of death, printed by gravestones in the cemetery.
Beyond the town, there lies the open country
Where, gathering speed, she acquires mystery,
The luminous self-possession of ships on ocean.   10
It is now she begins to sing—at first quite low
Then loud, and at last with a jazzy madness—
The song of her whistle screaming at curves,
Of deafening tunnels, brakes, innumerable bolts.
And always light, aerial, underneath
Retreats the elate meter of her wheels.
Steaming through metal landscape on her lines
She plunges new eras of white happiness
Where speed throws up strange shapes, broad curves
And parallels clean like trajectories from guns.   20
At last, further than Edinburgh or Rome,
Beyond the crest of the world, she reaches night
Where only a low stream-line brightness
Of phosphorus on the tossing hills is light.
Ah, like a comet through flame, she moves entranced
Wrapt in her music no bird song, no, nor bough
Breaking with honey buds, shall ever equal.   1933; 1955

The Sunlight on the Garden

LOUIS MAC NEICE (1907–1963)

The sunlight on the garden
Hardens and grows cold,
We cannot cage the minute
Within its nets of gold;
When all is told
We cannot beg for pardon.

Our freedom as free lances
Advances towards its end;

210

The earth compels, upon it
Sonnets and birds descend;   10
And soon, my friend,
We shall have no time for dances.

The sky was good for flying
Defying the church bells
And every evil iron
Siren and what it tells:
The earth compels,
We are dying, Egypt, dying

And not expecting pardon,
Hardened in heart anew,   20
But glad to have sat under
Thunder and rain with you,
And grateful too
For sunlight on the garden.   1938

18. Near the end of Act IV of Shakespeare's *Antony and Cleopatra*, Antony says to the Queen of Egypt: "I am dying, Egypt, dying; only / I here importune death awhile, until / Of many thousand kisses the poor last / I lay upon thy lips." Cleopatra replies: "I dare not, dear,— / Dear, my lord, pardon, . . ."

Over Sir John's Hill

DYLAN THOMAS (1914–1953)

Over Sir John's hill,
The hawk on fire hangs still;
In a hoisted cloud, at drop of dusk, he pulls to his claws
And gallows, up the rays of his eyes the small birds of the bay
And the shrill child's-play
Wars
Of the sparrows and such who swansing, dusk, in wrangling hedges.
And blithely they squawk
To fiery tyburn over the wrestle of elms until
The flash the noosed hawk   10
Crashes, and slowly the fishing holy stalking heron
In the river Towy below bows his tilted headstone.

Flash, and the plumes crack,
And a black cap of jack—
Daws Sir John's just hill dons, and again the gulled birds hare
To the hawk on fire, the halter height, over Towy's fins,
In a whack of wind.

There
Where the elegiac fisherbird stabs and paddles
In the pebbly dab-filled   20
Shallow and sedge, and 'dilly dilly' calls the loft hawk,
'Come and be killed',
I open the leaves of the water at a passage
Of psalms and shadows among the pincered sandcrabs prancing

And read, in a shell,
Death clear as a buoy's bell;
All praise of the hawk on fire in hawk-eyed dusk be sung,
When his viperish fuse hangs looped with flames under the brand
Wing, and blest shall
Young   30
Green chickens of the bay and bushes cluck 'dilly dilly,
Come let us die'.
We grieve as the blithe birds, never again, leave shingle and elm,
The heron and I,
I young Aesop fabling to the near night by the dingle
Of eels, saint heron hymning in the shell-hung distant

Crystal harbour vale
Where the sea cobbles sail,
And wharves of water where the walls dance and the white cranes stilt.
It is the heron and I, under judging Sir John's elmed   40
Hill, tell-tale the knelled
Guilt
Of the led-astray birds whom God, for their breast of whistles,
Have mercy on,
God in his whirlwind silence save, who marks the sparrows hail,
For their souls' song.
Now the heron grieves in the weeded verge. Through windows
Of dusk and water I see the tilting whispering

Heron, mirrored, go,
As the snapt feathers snow,   50
Fishing in the tear of the Towy. Only a hoot owl
Hollows, a grassblade blown in cupped hands, in the looted elms,
And no green cocks or hens
Shout
Now on Sir John's hill. The heron, ankling the scaly
Lowlands of the waves,
Makes all the music; and I who hear the tune of the slow,
Wear-willow river, grave,
Before the lunge of the night, the notes on this time-shaken
Stone for the sake of the souls of the slain birds sailing.   1950   60

The Death of a Toad

RICHARD WILBUR (1921–   )

A toad the power mower caught,
Chewed and clipped of a leg, with a hobbling hop has got
   To the garden verge, and sanctuaried him
   Under the cineraria leaves, in the shade
     Of the ashen heartshaped leaves, in a dim,
       Low, and a final glade.

The rare original heartsblood goes,
Spends on the earthen hide, in the folds and wizenings, flows
   In the gutters of the banked and staring eyes. He lies
   As still as if he would return to stone,
     And soundlessly attending, dies
       Toward some deep monotone,

Toward misted and ebullient seas
And cooling shores, toward lost Amphibia's emperies.
   Day dwindles, drowning, and at length is gone
   In the wide and antique eyes, which still appear
     To watch, across the castrate lawn,
       The haggard daylight steer.   1950

The Private Dining Room

OGDEN NASH (1902–)

Miss Rafferty wore taffeta,
Miss Cavendish wore lavender.
We ate pickerel and mackerel
And other lavish provender.
Miss Cavendish was Lalage,
Miss Rafferty was Barbara.
We gobbled pickled mackerel
And broke the candelabara,
Miss Cavendish in lavender,
In taffeta, Miss Rafferty,   10
The girls in taffeta lavender,
And we, of course, in mufti.

Miss Rafferty wore taffeta,
The taffeta was lavender,
Was lavend, lavender, lavenderest,
As the wine improved the provender.
Miss Cavendish wore lavender,
The lavender was taffeta.
We boggled mackled pickerel,
And bumpers did we quaffeta.   20
And Lalage wore lavender,
And lavender wore Barbara,
Rafferta taffeta Cavender lavender
Barbara abracadabra.

Miss Rafferty in taffeta
Grew definitely raffisher.
Miss Cavendish in lavender
Grew less and less stand-offisher.
With Lalage and Barbara
We grew a little pickereled,   30
We ordered Mumm and Roederer
Because the bubbles tickereled.
But lavender and taffeta
Were gone when we were soberer.
I haven't thought for thirty years
Of Lalage and Barbara.   1951

Index of First Lines

Index of Authors